The future isn't what it used to be. . . .

"Not a Traveler!" Patrick screamed, backing away from Courtney, stepping closer to the edge of panic.

"Pendragon, you can't bring a non-Traveler here! What are you thinking? Things are all wrong!"

I gently put my hand on his arm to try and calm him.

"Relax, okay?" I said. "We're here to help figure things out."

I felt him relax. A little. His eyes darted around as if unseen ghosts were closing in on us. He was coming back to Earth. Or Third Earth.

"I'm going out of my mind, Pendragon," he said, gulping air.

Yeah, no kidding.

"You're used to jumping around between territories and dealing with this insanity. I'm just a teacher. I never thought something like this could happen here."

I glanced around to see if there was a place we could talk that was more private. We were still outside of the kiosk leading to the subway and lots of people were passing by. "Let's drive somewhere, okay," I suggested.

Patrick focused on my injured arm. "You're hurt.

"Quigs," I answered. "Down at the gate."

Patrick's eyes suddenly went wide. "Quigs!" he shouted, ramping up again. So much for calming down. "You know what that means? Saint Dane is here! Here! It's starting, isn't it?"

Read what critics and fans have to

"The nonstop plot developments keep the many pages turning and readers wanting more."
—*School Library Journal*, on *The Lost City of Faar*

"A talented world builder, MacHale creates endlessly fascinating landscapes and unique alien characters. . . . The series is shaping up to be a solid addition to the fantasy genre and will keep readers not only busy but also content until the next Harry Potter appears."
—*Voice of Youth Advocates*, on *The Lost City of Faar*

"A fast pace, suspenseful plotting, and cliff-hanger chapter endings . . . Nonstop action, snappy dialogue, pop-culture references, and lots of historical trivia."
—*School Library Journal*, on *The Never War*

"MacHale's inventiveness makes this book the best entry in the series so far. . . . Remarkable insight."
—*Voice of Youth Advocates*, on *The Never War*

"Pendragon rules!" —Java

"PLEASE KEEP THEM COMING!!!! And if you need somebody to pre-read your books like I believe you said your nephew and wife do, I'd be right there to do it. THEY ARE THAT GOOD!!!" —Joshua

say about the Pendragon series:

"I am insanely in love with the Pendragon books. I think that they are even better than the Harry Potter books." —Monique

"I absolutely LOVE your Pendragon books. My two best friends also love them, and whenever I get the next one they fight over who gets to read it first!" —Elisabeth

"Forget the Wands and Rings!! Pendragon all the way!!"
—A Fan

"I'm pretty sure that I no longer have nails, as I was constantly biting them as I read the fourth Pendragon adventure." —Dan

"Pendragon is the best book series of all time." —Dark

"Nothing compares. I can't read another book without thinking 'Pendragon is better than this.' " —Kelly

"The Pendragon books will blow you away like no other books you have ever read." —Karen

"This series just pulls you into a world filled with suspense, treachery, and danger. Five stars easily; it deserves ten!!!"
—Greg

"Man, I gotta tell ya—these books are fantastic!" —Adam

◆ ◆ ◆

PENDRAGON

JOURNAL OF AN ADVENTURE THROUGH TIME AND SPACE

PENDRAGON

JOURNAL OF AN ADVENTURE THROUGH TIME AND SPACE

Book Eight:

The Pilgrims of Rayne

D. J. MacHale

Aladdin Paperbacks

New York   London   Toronto   Sydney

❦

ALADDIN PAPERBACKS
An imprint of Simon & Schuster Children's Publishing Division
1230 Avenue of the Americas, New York, NY 10020
Copyright © 2007 by D. J. MacHale
All rights reserved, including the right of reproduction
in whole or in part in any form.
ALADDIN PAPERBACKS and related logo are registered
trademarks of Simon & Schuster, Inc.
Also available in a SIMON & SCHUSTER BOOKS FOR YOUNG READERS
hardcover edition.
Designed by Debra Sfetsios
The text of this book was set in Apollo MT.
Manufactured in the United States of America
First Aladdin Paperbacks edition November 2008
2 4 6 8 10 9 7 5 3 1
The Library of Congress has cataloged the hardcover edition as follows:
MacHale, D. J.
The pilgrims of Rayne / D.J. MacHale. —1st ed.
p.   cm.—(Pendragon; bk. 8)
"Journal of an adventure through time and space."
Summary: With Saint Dane seemingly on the verge of toppling all of the
territories, Pendragon and Courtney set out to rescue Mark and
find themselves traveling—and battling—their way through
different worlds as they try to save all of Halla.
[1. Adventures and adventurers—Fiction. 2. Space and time—Fiction.
3. Diaries—Fiction. 4. Fantasy.] I. Title.
PZ7.M177535Pil 2007
[Fic]—dc22
2006038131
ISBN-13: 978-1-4169-1416-7 (hc.)
ISBN-10: 1-4169-1416-1 (hc.)
ISBN-13: 978-1-4169-1417-4 (pbk.)
ISBN-10: 1-4169-1417-X (pbk.)

For my brother, TG

PREFACE

Hello everyone.

It's that time again. Time to find a gate, leap into the flume, and travel through the next chapter in the saga of Bobby Pendragon. For those of you who have been following the adventure, you know that Saint Dane's plan for the ultimate conquest of Halla is beginning to take shape. For those of you who are new, well, umm, Saint Dane's plan for the ultimate conquest of Halla is beginning to take shape. Duh. Of course since you're new, you have no idea what that means so I'd strongly recommend that you get with the program and start reading from the beginning! C'mon! I'll wait. (Taps toes, whistles, plays solitaire)

Sorry, can't wait. Gotta go.

As always, before we jump into the flume I want to take a little time to thank some of the many people who help me bring Bobby's story to you. For many years now, the great folks at Simon & Schuster have been incredible supporters of the Pendragon books. Julia Richardson's guidance has once again proved invaluable. Rick Richter, Rubin Pfeffer, Ellen Krieger, Elizabeth Law, Paul Crichton, the folks in design and promotion and marketing and sales and and and . . . the list would add another chapter to this book. I'd like them all to know how grateful I am for their support, talent, and wisdom.

I'd also like to thank the many editors and publishers of all the foreign language editions who have helped turn Pendragon into an international presence. The number of non-English publishers is ever growing. I'm thrilled and grateful for that.

Heidi Hellmich has once again done a masterful job of copyediting. I'm beginning to think she knows more about Bobby than I do. Strange. Thanks, Heidi.

My personal team of acolytes always has my undying gratitude. Without Richard Curtis, Danny Baror and Peter Nelson I might still be writing these words, but I'm not sure how many people would be reading them. Thanks guys.

Though there are many Pendragon readers around the world, I sometimes feel as if I'm writing for an audience of one. My wife, Evangeline. She is always the first to learn of each new danger and dilemma facing the Travelers. Her opinion means the world to me. As long as she's happy, I'm happy. And I'm thinking you will be too. It's worked so far!

I look forward to the day when my daughter, Keaton, will be able to read my stories. I think. I often wonder how she'll react when she figures out that the guy who gives her a bath, gets her dressed, plays hide and seek and reads books to her is actually some nutjob who is able to concoct stories about the potential destruction of all that exists. Until that day, I'll just have to thank her for not running into my office too often to disturb my plotting of inter-dimensional strife.

While traveling (the nonflume kind) to talk about the books, I've had the good fortune to meet many terrific booksellers, teachers and librarians from all over who have played a huge role in bringing Bobby's story to you. Parents fall into that category, too. I owe them all a great debt of gratitude.

Finally, without readers like you, there would be no Pendragon. As many of you know, I love getting letters and e-mails hearing of your experiences and thoughts while reading my books. It's a wonderful feeling to know that my words can mean so much to you. I'm honored. Thank you.

I think that covers most everybody. Now let's get to the good stuff. The last time we were all together, Bobby returned home to discover that Second Earth had changed. New and impossible technology had suddenly appeared, not the least of which was a talking, mechanical cat that was manufactured by the Dimond Alpha Digital Corporation. Yeah, Dimond. *That* Dimond. Mark was gone. He no longer wanted to be an acolyte and jumped into the flume. But to go where? He left Courtney with the responsibility of the ring and the mystery of what he was planning to do. Bobby's task was clear. He had to find Mark and figure out what he might do that would put Halla square into the sights of Saint Dane.

If you haven't been reading these books, aren't you a little bit interested in what the heck I'm talking about? C'mon, admit it. Go on back. Pick up *The Merchant of Death*. Get up to speed and then come here to find out how Bobby and the Travelers are about to go to the wall in a desperate attempt to stop the destruction of all that ever was, or will be.

For everybody else . . . hobey ho, let's go.
D. J. MacHale

FIRST EARTH

The future isn't what it used to be.

I know that makes no sense. What else is new? There isn't a whole lot that has made sense since I left home three years ago to try and stop a shape-shifting demon who is bent on destroying all humanity. At least I think it was three years ago. It's hard to tell when you're out of your mind. And space. And time. My name is Bobby Pendragon. I'm a Traveler. The lead Traveler, in fact. The Travelers' job is to stop this guy named Saint Dane from changing the natural destiny of the ten territories of Halla and plunging them into chaos.

Do I have your attention yet? Stick around. It gets worse.

The Travelers' mission is to protect Halla. Halla is everything. The normal and the exceptional, the common and the impossible. Halla is all that ever was and all that will be. I know, sounds like a bad sci-fi movie. I'd think so too if I weren't living it. Every day. When I left home I was an ordinary fourteen-year-old guy whose biggest worry was whether or not Courtney Chetwynde liked me . . . and if she'd notice the zit that erupted in the middle of my forehead like some third freakin' eye. Now I'm seventeen and the leader of a group that must protect the well-being of eternity. The future is in my hands. The past is in my hands. There's nobody else who can stop Saint Dane.

Kind of makes the whole zit-on-the-forehead thing seem kind of lame, doesn't it?

Why Saint Dane calls himself "Saint" is a mystery to me. He is anything but. He isn't even human. At first I thought he was pure evil, just for evil's sake. But the more I learn about him, the more I realize there's something else that drives him. It's hard to explain because I don't understand it myself, but I've come to think that for some twisted reason, Saint Dane believes what he's doing is right. I know, how can a guy who is pushing societies toward cataclysmic disaster possibly believe what he's doing could be *justified*? When I find that answer, I'll unravel the entire mystery of what has happened to me. Why was I chosen to be a Traveler? What happened to my family? Where did Saint Dane come from? Why does he have these incredible shape-shifting powers? What did he mean when he said all the Travelers were illusions? (I've lost sleep over that one.) What is this all leading to?

Saint Dane talks about something called the "Convergence." I have no idea what it is, and I'm not entirely sure I want to. But I have to. Is it something Saint Dane is creating or was it destined to happen anyway? No clue. The only thing I know is that it's up to the Travelers to make sure whatever the Convergence is, it won't come out the way Saint Dane wants it to. It's the only way to be sure that Halla will continue to exist the way we know it. The way it was supposed to be.

I write these journals for two reasons. One is to document what has happened to me for the ages. You know, history and all that. A thousand—no, a million years from now I believe it will be important for people to know what happened. The other reason is to let my best friends from back home know what's going on with me. Mark Dimond and Courtney Chetwynde are the only people from Second Earth who know the truth.

But things have changed. Mark is missing. Worse, I'm afraid he started a chain reaction that caused serious damage throughout Halla. The cultures of the territories are not supposed to be mixed. I've learned that the hard way more than once. Okay, a lot more than once. Territories have their own distinct destinies that must be played out. Mixing the territories creates havoc. Saint Dane likes havoc. He's mixed the territories at every opportunity, and I believe he has gotten Mark to unwittingly help him do it again. At least I hope it's been unwitting. The alternative is unthinkable. I wish I had never gotten my friend involved in all this by sending him my journals.

As for Courtney Chetwynde, she's with me now. Together we've got to find Mark and try to undo the damage. Courtney and I have come a long way since we were childhood rivals. She is my acolyte and she is one of my best friends. Same as with Mark, I wish she weren't involved in any of this. She's been through hell. But we can't look back. We've got to keep moving ahead, which in some ways means looking back. Don't worry, that will make sense as you keep reading. I think.

With Mark missing and Courtney with me, I have no one to send these journals to. But I have to keep writing. For history's sake, as well as my own. Yes, there's a third reason why I write them. They help keep me sane. They allow me to look back and try to make sense of it all. The whole "making sense" part hasn't worked so well, but the keeping me sane part is a good thing.

I don't know who you are, reader, or how my journal

ended up in your hands. I hope that you've already seen my earlier journals, because I'm not going to repeat everything that has happened. Those early journals, starting with #1 (duh), contain the whole story. If you haven't seen them, go to the National Bank of Stony Brook in Stony Brook, Connecticut. Second Earth. My hometown. There's a safe-deposit box there registered to Bobby Pendragon. That's where my journals are kept. Find a way to get them and guard them with your life. They contain a story that, when complete, will tell of the events leading up to the destruction or the salvation of all that exists. Of Halla. It's a real page-turner, if I do say so myself.

As I write this, Courtney and I have traveled to Third Earth. Our home world in the year 5010. That's three thousand years in the future from the time when we were born. This is where we hope to find answers. This is where we hope to find Mark. After being here for only a short time, we've quickly discovered a scary fact.

The future isn't what it used to be.

This is where the next chapter in my adventure begins.

And so we go.

FIRST EARTH

I hope I haven't made a huge mistake by leaving Second Earth with Courtney Chetwynde.

She isn't a Traveler. Only Travelers are supposed to use the flumes—the highways between territories. I learned that lesson when Mark and Courtney traveled to Eelong on their own. The flume there collapsed, trapping the Travelers Spader and Gunny and killing the Traveler Kasha. Since then I learned that as long as someone uses the flume with a Traveler, nothing bad will happen. At least, nothing bad to the flume. What happens to the future of a territory once a non-Traveler gets there is a whole nother issue. Like I wrote, territories are not supposed to be mixed.

Which is exactly why Saint Dane has been doing it.

He's deliberately brought people and technology and even animals from one territory to another. I don't know if that has been his plan all along, but he's definitely going for it now, and things are getting whacked. When he won Quillan, I'm afraid he tipped the balance of the war for Halla. He's winning. I feel it. It's not that I'm getting desperate, but it's time to level the playing field. Maybe I've waited too long already. Why do the good guys always have to play by the rules while the bad guy does whatever he wants? Where is that written? It's not like I want to start messing with the territories randomly. No way. But if I can gain an advantage over Saint Dane by bringing an element from one territory to another, I'm going to do it.

Right now, that element is Courtney Chetwynde.

Things have gone strange on Second Earth. History has changed. Technology has changed. Whatever caused it has something to do with Saint Dane's plan for our home territory. Courtney is the one person who can help unravel the mystery of what happened. Together we're going to learn the truth and try to make things right. The future of Halla is at stake. The future of Second Earth is at stake.

The future of Mark Dimond is at stake.

Am I making a mistake by bringing her? I don't know. Uncle Press always warned me about mixing the territories, but he isn't here anymore. Is it the right choice? I won't know until the ultimate battle is over and the Travelers have won.

Or lost.

During the journey, Courtney and I floated next to each other on the magical cushion of air that sped us through the flume. We both wore jeans, low hikers, and T-shirts. You know, your basic Second Earth uniform. I had to admit, Courtney never looked better. She'd grown up since I saw her last. I guess we all have. Her incredibly long brown hair was tied back in a practical braid. Her big gray eyes sparkled, reflecting the light from the stars beyond the crystal walls of the flume. I remembered the very first time I saw her. It was at recess the first day of kindergarten. I decided to pick up the dodgeball she had been playing with. She decided to punch me in the head.

"Don't touch my stuff," she scolded, and grabbed the ball back.

I should have been ticked, but something about her playful smile told me she wasn't your typical playground bully. I held back my tears, smiled, and said, "Don't start a fight you can't win." I grabbed the ball and ran away. She took off after me and chased me through the busy playground for the next ten minutes. By the time we stopped, exhausted, we were laughing. That began a love-hate relationship that has lasted to this day. We were always friendly rivals, trying to outdo each other in sports. Sometimes she'd win, other times it would be me. Neither of us really felt superior, but that didn't stop us from trying. The strange thing was that over those years our rivalry turned into serious affection. The night I left home with Uncle Press to become a Traveler, Courtney and I kissed for the first time.

So much had happened since that night. We were different people. As we floated through the flume, I saw it in her eyes—she was older. But "older" didn't really cover it. We'd both seen things that no kid should have to. No adult, either. The fourteen-year-old kids who kissed that night were long gone. We were the keepers of Halla now.

Courtney explained to me what happened when she followed Mark's instructions and went to the flume in the basement of the Sherwood house. Mark had left his Traveler ring for her. When she saw it, she realized the frightening truth. Mark had jumped into the flume. But where had he gone? And why? Mark no longer wanted to be an acolyte, that much was clear, because he left his ring. The flume wasn't damaged, which meant he'd left with a Traveler. But who? Could it have been Saint Dane? Not knowing what else to do, Courtney put on the ring. The flume sprang to life. Seconds later Saint Dane himself blasted out of the tunnel between territories and added yet another twist to the mystery by revealing a disturbing truth.

He had been with us on Second Earth our entire lives.

"It's so strange," Courtney said as we flew along. "Can you believe Saint Dane was Andy Mitchell from the beginning?"

"Yes," I replied flatly.

"Well, it surprised the hell out of me. He's been watching us our whole lives, Bobby. How creepy is that? He's been setting us up."

"No," I corrected. "He's been setting Mark up."

The cruel truth of what Saint Dane had been doing on Second Earth was finally revealed. Sort of. He became a person named Andy Mitchell, a low-life bully who harassed Mark for years. After I left home to become a Traveler, Andy Mitchell showed Mark another side of his personality. He turned out to be smart. Incredibly smart. He joined Mark's science club, which at first freaked Mark out. Courtney told me how it seemed impossible that a nimrod like Andy could suddenly become brilliant. But Mark believed. Soon the victim was drawn to the tormentor.

"That's how he works," I reminded Courtney. "He pretends to be a friend and lures you into doing things you think are right, but lead to disaster. He takes pride in that. He says that whatever happens isn't his doing. He believes the people of the territories make their own decisions."

"That's so bogus," Courtney snapped. "How can people make their own decisions when he's pushing them the wrong way?"

"Exactly. On Second Earth, he pushed Mark."

Andy Mitchell and Mark worked on a science project they named "Forge." It was a small, plastic ball with a computer-driven skeleton that would change shapes when given verbal commands. They were about to fly to Florida to enter a national science contest when Andy asked Mark to stay behind to help him clean out his uncle's florist shop that had been wrecked in a flood. Mark's parents flew to Florida without them.

Mr. and Mrs. Dimond never made it. Their plane disappeared over the Atlantic. Everyone on board was lost. Saint Dane had a hand in that tragedy. No doubt. He killed Mark's parents.

Courtney continued, "Saving First Earth didn't change things, Bobby. Saint Dane is coming after Second Earth. And Third Earth."

"I figured that."

"Whatever he's planning has to do with Mark," Courtney added. "He said their relationship had entered a whole new phase. What was that supposed to mean?"

"I don't know," I answered honestly. "But I think there's a pretty good clue in what happened next."

Second Earth changed. That's the simple way of putting it. It changed. Saint Dane jumped into the flume and Courtney got pulled in after him. Rather than being swept to another territory, Courtney was dumped right back in the cellar of the Sherwood house, where she'd started. But it wasn't the same place she had left only moments before. Second Earth had changed. Courtney quickly recognized strange differences, mostly to do with technology. She returned home to find a computer that was way more elaborate than anything she'd ever seen, and a robotic talking cat that nearly sent her off the deep end. Kinda freaked me out when I saw it too. We discovered it was manufactured by a company called the Dimond Alpha Digital Organization. DADO. It may have been a coincidence, but the robots on Quillan were called dados. That, along with the fact that the company that made the mechanical cat shared the same name as Mark, meant the coincidences were piling up a little too high to be coincidences anymore.

"I think when you did a boomerang through the flume, the history of Second Earth was changed," I concluded. "And since you were in the flume, you weren't changed along with it. You still remembered what the old Second Earth was like."

"Probably because Saint Dane wanted me to remember."

"Probably," I agreed. "I think Saint Dane used Mark to help create a new technology that is somehow going to lead to the turning point of Second Earth. Killing the Dimonds made Mark emotionally vulnerable. Who knows what Saint Dane told him to get him to leave Second Earth?"

"Still," Courtney countered. "I can't believe Mark would leave Second Earth with that monster, no matter how badly he felt about his parents."

"I know," I said softly.

"We've got to find him," Courtney concluded soberly.

The jumble of sweet musical notes that always accompanied a trip through the flume grew louder and more frequent. We were nearing our destination—Third Earth. It was where we would start our investigation. Patrick, the Traveler there, would be able to research the incredible computer databases of Earth in the year 5010 to trace how the Dimond Alpha Digital Organization came to be, and what may have happened to Mark. We were about to step into the future to try and piece together the past. But when we hit Third Earth . . .

Third Earth hit back.

No sooner had my feet touched ground when I got slammed and knocked backward. The next few seconds tumbled together wildly. At first I had no idea what was happening. That is until I felt the hot breath on my face and a searing pain tear through my left forearm. I was being attacked. It only took a few seconds to realize why. It was a quig-dog. The yellow-eyed beastie was on my chest. Its razor teeth gnashed to get at my neck, while its slobber dripped into my eyes.

"Kick it! Kick it!" I shouted, hoping that Courtney wasn't dealing with her own quig.

The beast was strong and had the benefit of surprise. I saw from the corner of my eye that it had slashed open my arm. I wasn't strong enough to stop it. In seconds its teeth would tear into my neck.

Fummm! I heard a familiar, sharp sound. The quig yelped and lurched away. I quickly jumped to my feet, braced for another attack. It didn't come. The vicious devil lay unconscious at the mouth of the flume. I quickly looked around to see Courtney holding a small silver cylinder about the size of a roll of quarters. She held it up like a weapon because, well, it was a weapon. When she had gone to the Sherwood house to meet Mark, she'd brought two canisters of pepper spray with her in case she ran into any quigs. After her roundtrip through the flume, they had transformed into silver canisters that shot out an energy burst like the weapons of Quillan. It was another example of how Second Earth technology had been changed.

"Nice shot," I gasped.

Her eyes were wide. "Was that bad?" she asked with a shaky voice. "Should I have left these stun guns back on Second Earth?"

"Bad?" I exclaimed, gulping air. "If you had, I wouldn't have a neck right now."

"Right," she gasped. "Did I kill it?"

"I wish," I said, nudging it with my toe. The monster didn't budge. "This is good news."

"How's that?" she asked, incredulous.

"If there are quigs here, it means Saint Dane is here. We're in the right place. This territory is hot."

"Should I be happy or scared?"

"Both," I answered.

Courtney looked at my arm and winced. She gently took my hand to get a closer look at the wound. There was a four-inch gash that ran across the top of my forearm. It wasn't deep, but it was bleeding. It hurt, too.

"I'll tie my T-shirt around it until Patrick can get me to a doctor," I said.

Courtney helped me pull off my T-shirt, which wasn't easy since I couldn't use my left arm. She ripped off a strip and tied it around my wound. Satisfied that the bleeding was stopped, she looked at me with a sly smile. "Dude, working out much?"

I was suddenly embarrassed that I didn't have a shirt on.

"Hey," I said, trying to sound flip. "You go through training like Loor put me through and you'd look like this too."

"Uhh, not exactly," Courtney said with a playful wink.

I was feeling all sorts of awkward so I ducked the subject. "Let's get changed."

The first task when arriving on a territory was to change into the proper clothing. There was a pile of clothes at the side of the flume, waiting for us. One of the great things about Third Earth was that the clothes weren't much different from Second Earth. Except for the shoes. I picked out a pair of straight, dark green pants and a white, long sleeved T-shirt that could have come right from Old Navy. Courtney chose a white pair of pants and a navy blue shirt. We turned our backs for modesty and got changed.

I kept on my boxers, as usual.

My clothes fit perfectly. Courtney's didn't. The shirt was a size too big and the pants were too short. I have no idea why the clothes at the flumes always fit me. Maybe because I am a Traveler. I'm not sure what difference that should make, but I can't think of any other explanation.

"I look like a dweeb," Courtney announced with a frown.

She did, but I wasn't going to agree with her. No way. "You look great!" I meant it too. It didn't matter that her clothes looked like they belonged to somebody else, Courtney was stunning. A stunning dweeb.

The shoes looked like big doughnuts. I picked out a black pair and stuck them on my feet. Instantly they formed themselves around each foot into a perfect, comfortable, sneakerlike fit. Courtney did the same with a white pair.

"Okay, freaky," she said, though she wasn't complaining, because unlike her clothes, her shoes fit.

I went back to the pile of clothes, dug through and quickly found what I was looking for. It was a small, silver panel about the size of a baseball card.

"It's a communicator," I explained to Courtney. "It's how Gunny alerted Patrick the first time I came here."

The one Gunny used had a button on it. This didn't. It looked much sleeker, with a silver touch pad. I wondered if it was another example of how things had changed on the Earth territories. Either way, I hoped it did what it was supposed to. I touched the button. It gave off a quick hum.

"Is that it?" Courtney asked.

"I don't know," I answered truthfully. "I hope so. Let's get out of here."

The route was familiar to me. I led Courtney to the far wall and a wooden door that might have been three thousand years old. I knew this ancient piece of woodwork gave no hint to the modern wonders that lay beyond. I pulled the door open and bright light filled the cavern. With a quick "after you" gesture to Courtney, we stepped outside into the gleaming white subway tunnel of Third Earth. The door closed behind us with a soft click. The only sign that it was there was the star symbol that marked it as a gate to the flume. The subway tunnel was exactly as I remembered it. It was incredibly clean, with shiny white tile walls and two silver monorail tracks about ten feet apart. So far, nothing was different about Third Earth except for the slight change in the communicator. And the quig that nearly ate my Adam's apple.

"This way, before a train comes," I said, and jogged toward the subway station. "This is the exact same station that was abandoned on Second Earth. But with a few changes."

"I remember what you wrote," Courtney assured me.

We quickly found ourselves at the modern subway station of Third Earth. Courtney climbed up to the platform first and then helped me because of my injured arm. It was all pretty much the same as I remembered it. The station was busy with people, but not crowded. We were able to sneak onto the platform without drawing attention. Courtney immediately ran across the platform. I knew exactly what she wanted to see.

On the far side, opposite the tracks, was a railing. Below that railing was a vast, multitiered underground mall that stretched fifty stories beneath us. Some levels were full of shops and offices. Other levels had apartments. All were busy with people, either hurrying about or riding two-wheeled vehicles that sped them silently on their way. Far down below was an indoor lake where people paddled boats and swam. It was a city built entirely underground. This is what Earth had become. Overcrowding and overpopulation had forced cities to expand underground. It was actually a good thing. The surface of the planet was allowed to heal. Pollution was a thing of the past. People learned to respect our natural resources, while utilizing the planet as best they could.

Courtney looked down at this impossible city of the future. I watched her silently as she saw the words in my journal come to life.

"It's just awesome," she gasped.

I scanned the station, trying to collect my thoughts. It looked as if everything had progressed the way it was supposed to. Things didn't look any different from when I had been there before. It was a total relief. . . .

Until something odd caught my eye. It wasn't obvious at first, but after taking it all in for a few minutes, I noticed something that at first seemed impossible. I looked more closely, thinking I had to be wrong. What I saw made no sense. Besides the various passengers in the station, there were dozens of people who worked there. A guy sold newspapers. Another guy sold snacks. There was a subway conductor waiting for the next train and a transit cop walking his beat. A quick look down to the first few levels of the mall below showed me people working in stores, cleaning floors, and polishing shiny railings. There were mail carriers, ticket takers, window cleaners, and a hundred other people doing the various jobs it took to run a subway station and all the retail stores of the elaborate complex.

"What's the matter?" Courtney asked, sensing my tension.

"Look at the workers."

Courtney scanned the subway platform. At first it didn't click for her. Then I saw her react. She gave me a quick, nervous glance, and frowned.

"Am I crazy?" I asked.

"If you are, I am too," she answered. "Everybody looks exactly alike. I mean *exactly*! Was it like that when you were here before?"

"No, which means I know how it can be. You do too."

Courtney nodded and said the word I didn't want to say myself. "Dados."

"Yeah," I replied. "Third Earth has dados now. Lots' of 'em."

"Which means the future isn't what it used to be," Courtney said softly.

"Let's find Patrick." I gently took Courtney's arm and led her to the up escalator. We needed to see the rest of Third Earth.

The *new* Third Earth.

FIRST EARTH

The last time I was on Third Earth I was a few years younger and way more naive. I still remember the excitement I felt while riding the escalator up and out of that subway city to get my first glimpse of the future. I was pretty excited this time too. Or maybe excited isn't the right word. It was more like a burning knot of fear was twisting in my gut. Yeah, that's a better description. The future had been changed. The robot dados in the subway were proof of that. Question was, would the new future be better, or worse? My aching stomach feared the worst.

Courtney was just plain excited. She had read my journals describing Third Earth, but reading about something and seeing it for yourself are two different animals. The last thing she said to me before the flume took us from Second Earth was, "I want to see the future." She was about to.

When we arrived at the top and stepped out from under the green kiosk that marked the entrance to the subway, Courtney did a slow three-sixty, her eyes wide with wonder.

"Don't forget to breathe," I cautioned.

"Unbelievable," she gasped.

I'm relieved to say that Third Earth looked pretty much the same as I remembered. Gone was the crowded city of cement that was the Bronx of Second Earth. In its place was a vast parklike meadow. The air smelled sweet, with the faint hint of pine. I saw several green kiosks scattered about, marking other entrances to the underground city. Not too far away were the low, boxy buildings where some people still lived aboveground. The winding roads were there, with quiet electric cars gently moving along their way. People still rode bicycles.

Courtney took a few steps away from me to soak it all in. I followed, in awe of what Earth had become, yet nervous about how the dados might have changed the equation.

"People finally got it right," she exclaimed. "No pollution. Respect for the environment. No overcrowding. No wars—"

"And a bunch of robots to do the grunt work," I added.

"Yeah, that."

In the distance I could make out the few remaining buildings of Manhattan, including the Empire State Building, which now had a shiny steel coat of silver. It seemed like nothing was different about Third Earth.

Except for the dados.

They were everywhere. Some repaired a section of roadway. Others were mowing the acres of beautifully kept grass. I saw a team of dados putting a fresh coat of blue paint on a footbridge that spanned one of the winding streams. A silent delivery truck cruised by with a dado at the wheel. One of the squat apartment buildings had several dados clambering on the outside walls, washing windows. None of the activity was strange, except that all the workers looked the exact same. Most wore deep red coveralls, but some had uniforms that designated a particular job, like the crossing guard who stood in the road to halt traffic, allowing a group of giggling kids to run across. That guy wore a white sash, like the safety-patrol kids in my grammar school. The dado driving the delivery truck also wore a uniform that looked like the UPS guys wear. After all those years, the UPS guys still wore brown uniforms.

All the dados seemed to be men, though with a robot there's no such thing as sex. At least I don't think there is. Let's not go there. They all had the exact same perfect haircut: short and dark, parted in the middle. They were exactly the same size, too. I'm guessing about six feet tall with medium builds. The odd part was they all had the same face. I mean, exactly the same face. It wasn't the same face as the dados on Quillan, but they were definitely all the same.

"Why would they make them all look alike?" Courtney asked.

"I'm thinking if they didn't, you'd never be able to tell them apart from real humans."

Courtney did a quick look around at the dados and nodded. "Really. Put a mustache on one of those dudes and he'd disappear into a crowd. How creepy is that?"

"Creepy" was the word. I didn't get it right away, but there was something about these dados that gave me the heebies. I mean, beyond the fact that they were even there. There was something about them that felt a little off. I kept staring, trying to focus on what it might be. It was right there, but I couldn't grab on to it. They looked way more like real people than the robots of Quillan. When you watched those robots closely, you could tell their movements were stiff and almost too perfect. That was the difference. The dados of Quillan moved too perfectly. Real people don't move perfectly. The dados of Third Earth didn't move perfectly either. They seemed every bit as human as Courtney and I. If I had seen only one, I never would have guessed it was a dado. But seeing hundreds of exact replicas, well, that pretty much screamed robot to me. Was that it? Was I bugged because these dados looked so much like real people?

Nope.

Courtney realized it first. "Look at them, they're all the same," she gasped.

"Yeah, I get that."

"No!" She swallowed hard and looked at me, pained. "Look closer." Her voice cracked as she said, "They all look like . . . Mark."

I snapped a look to the nearest dado. They were taller, their hair was short, and there wasn't a zit in sight, but there was no mistake—these robots looked exactly like Mark Dimond. Every last one of them. We were seeing hundreds of clones of my best friend.

"I want to cry," Courtney whimpered.

"It's okay," I assured her, though I didn't feel even close to okay. "It just means we're on the right track."

"Mark really did have something to do with this," Courtney said, shaking her head.

We were interrupted by a quick *beep* from a car horn. We both jumped and turned to see a small, silver car speed up and stop next to us. It was easy to see the driver since there was no roof.

"Pendragon!" Patrick yelled.

Patrick was the Traveler from Third Earth. I'm guessing he was in his twenties. He was about my size with longish brown hair. He wore the same type of clothes as the last time I'd been there, jeans and a short-sleeved shirt. He looked more like a preppy from Second Earth than a teacher and librarian from the year 5010. Then again, I'm not really sure what a teacher and librarian from the year 5010 should look like. The thing I remembered most about Patrick was that he had a calm, confident way about him.

Not anymore. That was another thing that had changed about Third Earth.

Patrick drove up and slammed on the brakes, looking anything but calm. Frantic, scared, nervous . . . those were all better words to describe him. I'd only met him once, but he seemed to be a guy who was in perfect control. He was an intellectual. A guy who lived to study and teach. Now he looked like a crazed guy who lived to rant and drool. He leaped out of the car without opening the door, ran to me, and grabbed both my arms. His eyes were wild. His hair was tangled. He hadn't shaved. He was a mess.

"What happened?" he demanded. "What's going on?"

I looked to Courtney. She shrugged.

"Uh, not following you, Patrick," I said.

Patrick looked as if his head was about to explode. He looked at Courtney. "Who's that?" He ran to her and grabbed her arms. "What territory are you the Traveler from? Do you know what happened?"

Courtney froze. "N-No. I'm not a Traveler—I—"

"Not a Traveler!" Patrick screamed, backing away from her, stepping closer to the edge of panic. "Pendragon, you can't bring a non-Traveler here! What are you thinking? Things are all wrong!"

I gently put my hand on his arm to try and calm him.

"Relax, okay?" I said. "We're here to help figure things out."

I felt him relax. A little. His eyes darted around as if unseen ghosts were closing in on us. He was coming back to Earth. Or Third Earth.

"I'm going out of my mind, Pendragon," he said, gulping air.

Yeah, no kidding.

"You're used to jumping around between territories and dealing with this insanity. I'm just a teacher. I never thought something like this could happen here."

I glanced around to see if there was a place we could talk that was more private. We were still outside the kiosk leading to the subway, and lots of people were passing by. Lots of Mark-looking robots, too. The creepy factor was still very high.

"Let's drive somewhere, okay?" I suggested.

Patrick focused on my injured arm. "You're hurt."

"Quigs," I answered. "Down at the gate."

Patrick's eyes suddenly went wide. "Quigs!" he shouted, ramping up again. So much for calming down. "You know what that means? Saint Dane is here! Here! It's starting, isn't it? That's why you came, right?"

It was Courtney's turn to try and calm him down. She put her arm around his shoulder and started out softly, saying, "It's okay. We're here to help." Her calm, reassuring voice quickly amped up into a tirade. "But we can't do anything unless you get a grip! All right! Now calm down!"

Good old Courtney. Patience wasn't her strength.

"Nice," I said sarcastically, pulling Patrick away from her. "Let's take a breath and go someplace quiet."

"I'll take you to a doctor," Patrick said. "You need to get that treated."

"Fine, whatever. Let's just go." My first thought wasn't about the slash on my arm, but if letting Patrick focus on getting me help would put him back under control, I wasn't going to stop him. He jumped behind the wheel of the tiny car.

"You sure you can drive?" Courtney asked. She wasn't thrilled about riding in a car being driven by a maniac. To be honest, neither was I.

"I'm okay," Patrick said, taking a deep breath. He was definitely calming down.

We all got in, with Courtney in the back and me next to Patrick. I could feel Courtney's tension radiate from the back-seat.

"My doctor is in Manhattan," Patrick explained. "He'll take care of you."

"Good," I said. "No hurry."

"Yeah, no hurry," Courtney echoed. "Safe and boring. That's the ticket. Let's get there in one piece."

Patrick looked at her, then at me. "She's not a Traveler?" he said, as if I had just brought a martian into his life.

"It's cool. She's as much a part of this as we are."

"But she's not a Traveler," Patrick argued.

"That's the least of our problems," Courtney said sharply.

I hoped she was right.

Patrick gave me a worried look, then turned over the ignition. The engine made no sound. Moments later we were rolling along the peaceful road, headed toward Manhattan. The trip was exactly as I remembered it, except for the dados. I didn't say anything to Patrick about them at first. I wanted to make sure he was completely calm. I also wanted to make sure his mind was on his driving. Crashing into a tree wouldn't have helped matters. I noticed that his eyes were darting everywhere. It seemed like every time we rounded another bend, he'd see something so shocking that the sight actually made him tense up and give out a little gasp—as if he were seeing ghosts or something. The guy was a raw nerve. It finally clicked that it happened whenever he saw another group of dados.

I couldn't take it anymore and said, "Okay, tell me why you're so freaked."

Patrick answered, "I was hoping you could tell me."

"Uhh," I answered dumbly. "We just got here. You're the one acting all mental."

Patrick thought a second. "You'd be a little crazy too if you woke up to find your territory wasn't the same as when you'd gone to sleep."

I shot a look back to Courtney. She raised an interested eyebrow.

"Explain that," I demanded.

Patrick took a shaky breath. "When I went to bed last night, everything was normal. Do you know how I woke up this morning?"

"No," I said patiently.

"A stranger was shaking me, saying it was time to get up to go to work."

"Who was it?" Courtney asked.

Patrick laughed, but it wasn't because he thought it was funny.

"Not 'who,' *what!*" he shouted. "It was a mechanical man! I jumped up screaming and demanded to know who he was, but he just gave me this confused look and said he'd been my domestic da . . . da . . ."

"Dado?" I asked.

"Yes, dado! He said he'd been working for me for five years and didn't understand what game I was playing. I thought somebody was playing a practical joke. I ran out of the house to get away, but there were mechanical men everywhere! Pendragon, they weren't here when I went to sleep. Now there are more robots than people and nobody seems surprised but me! Am I crazy?"

"Unfortunately, no," I answered.

Patrick continued, "I drove around in a daze, not believing what I was seeing. That's when my communicator activated, saying you were at the gate. I knew it couldn't be a coincidence." He pulled the silver card out of his pocket. "But this isn't my communicator! It's changed! How can that be?"

The communicator looked exactly like the one at the flume.

Patrick added, "You can explain all this, right?"

I looked at Courtney. She shrugged and said, "Go for it."

"I only have theories. We're here to find the real answers."

"But I don't have any!" Patrick cried.

"History might," I shot back quickly. "The same thing happened on Second Earth. One minute all was normal, the next minute technology changed. It's your computer archives that we're hoping will tell us why."

"You're saying this all happened in the past?"

"I think so," I answered. "I think the reason nobody is reacting to the change is because it happened long before they were born. These robots are now a normal part of Third Earth."

"But if something happened in the past, I shouldn't have noticed a change," Patrick argued. "I mean, this should all seem normal to me, too, right?"

"Except you're a Traveler," I said. "This gets into a whole nother thing, but from what I'm learning, Travelers aren't like normal people. According to Saint Dane, we're illusions."

Patrick gave me a blank look. The car started to drift off the road.

"Hey!" Courtney barked. "Eyes on the road, Professor!"

Patrick quickly snapped the car back onto the road. "You're not making things better, Pendragon."

"I know," I said with sympathy. "Let's get me patched up, then go to the library. The answers we're looking for are going to be found in the past, and you're the only one I know who can find them."

Patrick smiled. "That's the first thing I've heard all day that makes sense."

"You're the man, Patrick. If anybody can solve this, it's you."

"And I will," he said with confidence. "I will."

Patrick was back in control. I knew he'd find the answers. What worried me now was what those answers might be.

FIRST EARTH

Our first stop was at Patrick's doctor. Though we Travelers seem to heal incredibly fast (for some reason I haven't yet figured out), I didn't need to be slowed down by an injury, even for a little while. We rolled over a bridge to Manhattan and Courtney's first look at the future of New York City. The island of Manhattan was much more citylike than the Bronx, but there was still more green grass than cement. Tall buildings were few and far between, though the roads now straightened out into a grid pattern. Shortly after crossing the river, Patrick parked next to a green kiosk where we stepped onto an escalator that brought us down to another vast, underground part of the city. After descending a few levels, we ended up on a floor that was ringed by silver doors. Each was marked with a five-digit number. Patrick led us to one, and we entered an office that wasn't much different from my doctor's office on Second Earth.

Except the receptionist was a dado.

Patrick stiffened and approached the desk cautiously. "Where's the receptionist?" he asked suspiciously.

The dado looked exactly like all the other robots, except that he wore a white medical jacket. I now knew what Mark would look like if he were a medical professional. And a robot. The dado smiled pleasantly and said in a calm, soothing voice, "I *am* the regular receptionist, Mr. Mac."

Mr. Mac. I'd never heard Patrick's last name before. I'd also never heard a robot speak in Mark's voice. Yes, the dado even *sounded* like Mark. I wondered if they'd programmed in the little stutter Mark had when he got nervous. Probably not. I didn't think robots got nervous.

"You know me?" Patrick asked, his voice shaking.

The dado smiled kindly. "Of course," answered the Mark robot. "You've been a patient of Dr. Shaw's for nine years and four months. Your last examination was over two years ago. You are overdue."

Whoa. This robot had the ability to instantly recall information based solely on a visual of Patrick. These dados were definitely more advanced than those goons on Quillan.

Patrick swallowed hard. "My friend is hurt. Is Dr. Shaw available to treat him?"

The dado looked at his computer screen, input something and looked back to Patrick. "Step right inside," he answered cheerily.

Whoa. Again. That was easy. Every time I'd gotten banged up and had to go to the emergency room at home, we had to wait hours before a doctor could see us. This was another example of how things were better in Earth's future. Mark-looking robots or not.

I looked at Courtney. "Maybe you should wait here."

"Alone? With RoboNurse? No way. I'm coming too."

"It's okay," Patrick said.

The dado called out, "I hope you feel better."

I looked back at the Mark-like mechanical man. It was a twisted, creepy feeling. I was talking to Mark, but not.

Patrick led us through an inside door, down a corridor, and up to another door that opened into a clean, modern exam room. Waiting for us was another dado wearing medical whites. When we opened the door, he stood facing the wall, not moving. A second after we entered, he came to life, turned to us, and smiled. It seemed like by entering the room, we activated it. I guess if robots have nothing to do, they stand around staring at walls.

Courtney said, "Okay, that was odd."

Patrick said to the dado, "We need to see Dr. Shaw."

The dado approached me and gently took my arm. I pulled back at first, not sure I wanted to be handled by a robot whether he looked like Mark or not. The robot looked at me with kind eyes, as if to say, "Relax, I know what I'm doing." I let him check me out. He first removed the strip of T-shirt we'd used to stop the bleeding.

"Ick" was Courtney's comment.

The fabric was covered with crusty dry blood. It didn't bother me. I was much more creeped out by the fact that the robot's touch was cold. He looked and acted totally human, but he wasn't. I guess mechanical men don't need to have human-body temperatures.

"Shouldn't you get Dr. Shaw?" Patrick asked.

"No need," the dado said kindly. "This is a simple procedure." He walked to a wall that was covered with silver drawers.

I looked at Patrick and asked, "Should I be nervous about this?"

Patrick shrugged. He didn't know. Swell. The dado pulled out a device that looked like a thick, white pipe. It was about ten inches long and five inches in diameter. He reached inside and peeled back a clear piece of soft plastic wrap that was covering the entire inside surface of the tube, kind of like you'd pull off the backing of a Band-Aid.

Courtney stepped forward, standing between me and the dado protectively. "Why don't you get the doctor now, Tin Man," she said firmly.

"It's okay," Patrick assured her. "That's the same treatment the doctor would use."

The dado gave her a kind smile. Courtney wasn't sure what to do. She stepped away, but reluctantly.

"Have I mentioned how creepy this whole Mark-robot thing is?" she muttered.

The dado held out his hand, gesturing for my injured arm. I held my breath and raised my arm. The dado gently slipped the white tube over my hand and positioned it over the wound. He gently grasped the tube and squeezed it. I felt the tube tighten and heat up. Just as I was about to complain, the tube released and the dado slipped it off. The wound on my arm had been sealed. What was in that tube? Antibiotic? Bactine? Super Glue? Whatever it was, it created a thin, clear seal that completely closed the wound. It didn't hurt anymore either.

"That's it?" I asked the dado.

"You are as good as healed," he answered. "Tomorrow it will be completely gone."

"Is this a new thing?" I asked Patrick.

"No," he answered. "Medical science has come a long way since your day. I'm just not used to seeing robots administer it."

We left the doctor's office without ever seeing the doctor. I guess that's not a bad thing, considering my wound was miraculously healed, and we didn't even have to pay for it.

Patrick explained that medical care on Third Earth was paid for by the community as a whole. Nobody needed insurance or got hit with monster bills. Not bad.

The three of us got back into Patrick's vehicle and drove downtown to our final destination on Third Earth: the public library. Getting to this library was the main reason Courtney and I had come to Third Earth. I learned when I was there the first time with Gunny that the database in the library held most every bit of information concerning the history of Earth from the beginning of recorded time. If you've read my Journal #11, you'll know what I'm talking about. The computers didn't just contain the usual information you could get from newspapers or books. Not even close. Data was collected from billions of sources throughout time to make a repository that was pretty much the complete history of Earth. Sound incredible? It is. I knew the best way to begin piecing together what might have happened on Second Earth was to go to the future in order to see the past.

"I don't believe it!" Courtney exclaimed as we pulled up to the cement steps leading to the library. "It's exactly the same as Second Earth!"

She was almost right. The steps were the same steps that led to the New York Public Library on Fifth Avenue, complete with the oversize stone lions guarding the door. Though the actual building was much smaller and more modern than the imposing library from Second Earth. In 5010 the people of Earth no longer used paper books that took up space. Sad, but true.

As a teacher and a librarian, Patrick had full access to the library computers. He knew how to dig deep. This was Patrick's world. He now had a mission and looked much more confident. He led us up the wide cement steps into the large, marble-floored lobby of the library. It was exactly as I remembered it, with several rows of chairs where people read from computer screens. A corridor led deeper into the building and the computer rooms. There was only one difference from the last time I was there—a small one, but disturbing.

Courtney was the first to notice. "Where is it?"

"Where's what?" I asked.

"The book. The display. You wrote that it was here in the lobby."

She was right. There had been a single, old-fashioned book on display in the lobby. It was an important relic of the past, encased in glass for all to view. That book was *Green Eggs and Ham* by Dr. Seuss. It wasn't there. I stood on the spot where it had been and glanced around.

"Did they move the display?" I asked Patrick.

Patrick looked grim. "No," he said. "It was here yesterday."

"Yeah," Courtney added. "Before things changed."

"It might not mean anything," I offered hopefully.

Courtney added, "Or it might mean that not all the changes are for the better."

The three of us stood for a moment, trying not to think about how different the world might actually be once we started digging below the surface.

"Let's continue," Patrick said, and strode quickly down the corridor.

We followed right behind him. Most of the doors were closed, which meant other teachers were using the computers. The final room was open. That was good. I was too anxious to have to wait any longer. The room was much like the one I had been in on my last trip. Six black chairs were spaced around a raised silver platform that was about eight feet across.

"How do you want to start?" Patrick asked.

"Let's go with what we already know," I suggested. "Let's see what history has to say about Mark Dimond."

Patrick nodded and sat down in one of the black chairs. Courtney and I each took a seat. On the armrest of Patrick's chair was a white glowing button. Patrick pressed it and said clearly, "Computer, new search."

A voice from the computer answered him. It wasn't the pleasant woman's voice I remembered from the last time. It was a man's voice. It was Mark's voice. I saw Patrick start in surprise.

The voice said, "Identify, please."

Patrick frowned. "It never asked for my code before." He shook off his concern and said clearly, "Patrick Mac. Access code three-seventeen-ninety."

"Welcome, Patrick," the voice said. "How can I help you?"

Courtney leaned over to me and whispered, "This is awesome!"

Patrick cleared his throat and said clearly, "Dimond, Mark." He looked to me and asked, "Where was he born?"

Courtney answered, "Stony Brook, Connecticut."

Patrick pushed the button again and said, "Born in Stony Brook, Connecticut." "Near the turn of the twenty-first century."

An image blinked to life on the platform in front of us. I knew it was only a hologram, but it still took me by surprise.

"Mark!" Courtney shouted.

I thought she was going to cry. I almost did too. We were looking at a life-size three-dimensional image of Mark. My best bud Mark. He looked to be about ten years old and had on the cap and gown we all wore when we graduated from the Glenville School. It hurt to see my friend standing there, even if it was just an image. It made me realize how much I missed him, and my old life.

"Computer," Patrick said, "last significant entry for Dimond, Mark."

Two more people appeared behind Mark in the hologram. Courtney gasped. They were Mark's parents.

The computer said, "History of Mark Dimond ends in his eighteenth year of life. Final entry occurs when both his parents were killed in the loss of a commercial airline flight."

"Did he die?" Patrick asked.

"Unknown," the computer answered.

"Speculation?" Patrick asked while pressing the button.

"Suicide," the computer answered.

The word jolted me. The thought of Mark committing suicide never entered my head. I looked at Courtney.

"No way," she declared. "Not a chance. Stupid computer. Ask it something else."

Patrick said, "Additional speculation?"

The computer answered, "Potential runaway with peer."

"What?" Courtney shouted with surprise. "What peer?"

"Name that peer," Patrick ordered.

I already knew the answer. The holograms of the Dimonds disappeared and were replaced by the image of a girl. She wore the field-hockey uniform of Davis Gregory High School. She stood looking all sorts of cocky, leaning on her field-hockey stick.

"Oh," Courtney gasped.

The computer announced, "Chetwynde, Courtney. Last seen by her parents on the same day Mark Dimond was last seen."

Patrick and I didn't know what to say. Courtney stared at her own image as if looking at a ghost of herself.

"It's the day we left to come here," Courtney croaked. "It was only a few hours ago."

Patrick corrected, "It was three thousand years ago."

"You okay?" I asked.

Courtney swallowed, but didn't take her eyes off her image. "Better than okay," she declared. "Look at me! I look great!"

She was putting on a brave front, but her voice cracked. She was shaken. I'm guessing the reality of what she had done by leaving home hadn't hit her until that moment. Only a few hours before she had been sitting at her kitchen table writing a good-bye note to her parents. That was by our own clocks. On Third Earth she had been missing for three thousand years. That's enough to make anybody's voice crack. Even Courtney's.

"Keep going," Courtney ordered.

Patrick hit the button and said, "Computer, clear and new search."

The image of Courtney disappeared. The image of Mark returned.

"Computer, clear!" Patrick said impatiently.

"Discrepancy," the computer responded.

I looked at Patrick. He shrugged.

"Explain," he demanded.

"Searching," the computer responded.

"What does that mean?" Courtney asked Patrick.

"I've never seen this before. It seems to be cross-referencing several different entries."

"Is it gonna crash?" I asked.

"Crash? What does that mean?"

I didn't press. I figured computers on Third Earth were too advanced to crash, the way ours did on primitive old Stone Age Second Earth.

"Discrepancy in search for disappearance of Dimond,

Mark," the computer finally announced. "Multiple, conflicting entries."

"What the heck does that mean?" Courtney asked.

"Explain," Patrick demanded.

Another image appeared next to Mark. The original hologram was a ten-year-old Mark in his cap and gown. The second image was also of Mark, but he looked older. He was more like the Mark of today, or yesterday, or whatever. He looked about seventeen and much taller. He was dressed strangely in long pants, a stiff white shirt, and a bow tie. His hair was cut short and parted in the middle, like I'd never seen it before. He wore round, wire-rimmed glasses. This image of Mark looked like the dados on Third Earth. It chilled me.

"Details," Patrick requested.

"Person of note," the computer responded. "Dimond, Mark. Father of Forge technology."

"Forge!" Courtney screamed. "That's the thing Mark invented!"

The hologram of Mark came to life. He reached into his pocket, took out a small, rubbery object, and held it in his open hand. The hologram of Mark spoke. "Cube."

"Whoa," Courtney muttered, sitting back in her chair.

The little object writhed and changed from a round blob into a perfect cube.

"Is that how it worked?" I asked. "Is that Forge?"

"Yup," Courtney answered, dumbfounded. "Man, I so want one of these computers."

"Details of Forge and Mark Dimond," Patrick pressed.

"Forge technology. United States Patent Number 2,066,313. Issued to Dimond, Mark. President of the Dimond Alpha Digital Organization."

"Dado!" Courtney yelled.

The computer continued, "The Dimond Alpha Digital Organization, along with its parent company, KEM Limited, developed Forge technology. It became the basis for an innovative robotics system. It changed the course of manufacturing and created the field of computer science. Mark Dimond is considered to be the genius visionary who began the computer age."

"Once again, whoa," Courtney gasped.

"When?" I blurted out. "When did this happen?"

"Computer," Patrick announced, "What was the Forge patent application date?"

The cap and gown image of young Mark disappeared, leaving the older Mark, holding his invention. Andy's invention. Saint Dane's invention. The computer answered, "United States Patent Number 2,066,313 was filed on October sixth, 1937."

"First Earth," I whispered.

"That's it," Courtney exclaimed. "He went to First Earth and brought Forge with him. He changed the course of history by introducing his simple computer years before it was supposed to be invented. No, forget simple. That thing was advanced, even by Second Earth standards. He jumped the natural evolution of computer science by, like, sixty years. That's why Second Earth changed. That's why Third Earth changed. That's why freaking robots are everywhere. Mark changed the future by bringing Forge to the past."

I wanted to say I was surprised, but it was exactly what I feared. By bringing his invention to the past, Mark had mixed the territories and changed the natural destiny of Halla. I didn't say anything. My mind was working over the possibilities.

"What the matter?" Courtney asked impatiently. "This is

exactly the kind of thing we thought happened."

"Yeah," I said. "But it doesn't answer the bigger question."

"What's that?" Patrick asked.

"It doesn't tell us why. Why did Mark do it? He knew how wrong it was. How did Saint Dane get to him?"

The three of us sat there, looking at our feet. None of us had that answer, and I doubted the computer would either, but I had to try. I stood up, strode to Patrick's seat and hit the white button myself. "Computer!" I demanded. "What is the discrepancy?"

The computer answered, "There is no history of Dimond, Mark prior to the patent filing for his Forge technology in October of 1937."

"Makes sense," Courtney said. "He dropped in from the future."

The computer continued, "There is no history of Dimond, Mark beyond the announcement of the Dimond Alpha Digital Organization partnering with KEM Limited in November of 1937."

"What does that mean?" Patrick demanded to know. "Mark Dimond disappeared twice?"

Mark's image vanished. We waited. Nothing happened. We stood silently, letting the reality sink in.

"So what happened to him on First Earth?" Patrick asked nobody in particular.

"We got what we came for," I declared. "Patrick, keep searching."

"For what?" he asked.

"For anything that will give us a clue as to what happened to Mark on First Earth."

"And what're you going to do?"

I looked at Courtney. "We're going after him."

Courtney walked up next to me, looked me in the eye, and asked, "Are we on the wrong territory?"

"Yeah, we're on the wrong territory."

FIRST EARTH

Patrick drove us quickly back to the subway city in the Bronx. On the way we grabbed a quick bite to eat. If there was one thing I learned while bouncing through time and space, it was to eat when you could. You never knew when you'd get another chance . . . or find yourself on a territory where food tasted like shoes. We got the food at a drive-through. Or maybe it was more of a drive-*under*, since we had to go underground to get it. We ate cheeseburgers, fries, and sodas. Some things never change, no matter what century you're in. We ate while Patrick drove. I took the time to fill him in on what had happened to me since I'd seen him last. The wins and the losses. The territories that were set straight, and those that were in trouble. I told him how Gunny and Spader were trapped on Eelong, how many Travelers had been killed, and how Nevva Winter, the Traveler from Quillan, had joined Saint Dane. I also told him about the mysterious Convergence that Saint Dane said was near. I told him quickly and succinctly, only hitting the highlights. Saying it all at once like that made the whole story seem so, I don't know, impossible.

It also made me lose my appetite. So much for the cheeseburgers.

"KEM Limited," I said. "That's important. Mark wouldn't have been able to spring his invention on the world by himself. He would have needed somebody to help him."

Courtney asked, "So if we find this KEM company, we'll find Mark."

My mind ripped through the possibilities.

"Bobby?" Courtney pressed. "What are you thinking?"

"The turning point of First Earth has passed," I said. "Saint Dane tried to get me to save the *Hindenburg*. I didn't and history continued the way it was supposed to."

"Old news. So what?"

"So when we step into that flume and call out First Earth, where is it going to send us? No, *when* is it going to send us? What if it sends us back too late to stop Mark? Or way too early? We might be totally spinning our wheels."

Patrick gave me a dark look. Courtney thought for a moment and said, "You've written in your journals a thousand times how the flumes send the Travelers where they need to be, when they need to be there. It's pretty clear we need to be on First Earth in time to do something about Mark."

"Yeah," I said, frowning. "That scares me even more."

"Why?" she asked impatiently.

"If the flume sends us back in time to do something about Mark, does that mean First Earth has another turning point? Does that mean it's possible for *all* the territories to have more than one turning point? Did the Travelers before us chase Saint Dane from territory to territory, constantly monkeying with turning points? What about after us? Is this battle going to go on forever?"

Courtney had an answer for everything. Not this time. All

she could do was stare at me. Patrick didn't even do that. He kept his eyes on the road. I knew what they were thinking. I could sum it up with one simple question: "What's the point?"

"Stop," Courtney snapped. "The point is to save Mark. Over and out. We can go nuts thinking about all the cosmic implications of what's been happening, but that's only going to make us *more* nuts. Worrying about anything else is a waste of time."

"Or is this all just a waste of time?" I asked. "Are we killing ourselves to prolong the inevitable? If Saint Dane can't be destroyed, and he can go back and tinker with territories we've already saved, there'll be no end to this. Until he's won."

Courtney grabbed my shoulder and yanked me around until we were nose to nose. "I don't believe that," she said with passion. "Neither do you. You're just feeling sorry for yourself. We've come too far and gone through too much to give up now."

She was right, of course. We had no choice. The battle would continue. But I was discouraged. Was this going to be a never-ending struggle, with Saint Dane jumping through time, turning events on a whim, twisting the territories, and creating new turning points until Halla finally cracked?

"Are you with me, Bobby?" Courtney asked.

"You know I am." I didn't have the heart to tell her about the serious doubts I was having.

Patrick dropped us off at the green kiosk in the Bronx that led down to the subway city and the flume. He said to Courtney, "I've only known you a short while, but I can see why Pendragon wants you with him."

"I should have been with him from the start," she said. Classic Courtney. "We're going to make things right, don't worry."

Patrick told me, "If I find out anything more about Mark Dimond, I'll send a note to your acolyte."

Courtney wiggled her finger bearing her Traveler ring. "That would be me."

There was an awkward moment. Nobody knew how to say good-bye. It was Patrick who put the situation into perspective.

"It's started," he said. "Whatever the Convergence is, it feels like Saint Dane is pulling the pieces together by orchestrating events here on Earth."

"Pulling the pieces together?" Courtney asked. "Or ripping them apart?"

I added, "Saint Dane told me a long time ago that all he had to do was tip over one territory and the rest would fall like dominos. He said the first was Denduron. It wasn't. With the territories being mixed and history changing, I'm beginning to feel as if those dominos are finally lining up."

We exchanged dark looks. Courtney broke the tension by declaring, "This isn't over."

We said our good-byes and made our way to the flume. After making sure we weren't being watched, we quickly slipped down onto the tracks and ran for the star that marked the gate. Our timing was just right, for when we reached it, the light of an oncoming monorail train appeared in the distance. I pushed on the star and the door instantly opened. Courtney and I ducked inside and closed the door with plenty of time to spare before the train sped by. We stood together and gazed into the mouth of the flume.

"Should we put our Second Earth clothes back on?" she asked.

"Nah, we'll only have to change again on the other side."

Courtney nodded. "Hey, the quig is gone," she exclaimed.

Sure enough, the vicious dog she had blasted into dreamland was nowhere to be seen. I drew no conclusions, but was thankful we didn't have to deal with that snarling monster.

Courtney pulled the silver weapon from her pocket. "I should leave this here. It doesn't belong on First Earth."

I looked at the silver cylinder. It didn't belong on Second or Third Earth either. Not really. It was a weapon that was developed on Quillan.

"Bring it," I said with finality. "I'm tired of playing by the rules."

"You sure?" Courtney asked cautiously.

"No, but if First Earth is back in play, there might be quigs there. If you see one, nail it."

Courtney nodded and slipped the cylinder back into her pocket. She reached out and took my hand. "I don't know if we're doing the right thing, but it's the only thing."

Together we stepped into the mouth of the flume.

"First Earth!" I shouted. The flume sprang to life. The giant rock tube began to writhe. Far in the distance a light appeared that quickly grew brighter as it came to carry us away. The dark walls melted into crystal, revealing the sparkling stars beyond them. The jumble of sweet musical notes grew louder. I felt the slight tug of energy pulling us into the void . . . and we were off.

We didn't talk much on our journey back through time. I think we both made up our minds that we were going to stop guessing at what we might find, and wait until we actually found it. That didn't stop me from thinking, though. And worrying about Mark. How did Saint Dane convince him to change the course of history? What had happened? The computer said he was last seen in November of 1937. What happened to him after that? Did he go to another territory? My only hope was that we would arrive with enough time to track him down and stop him from introducing his Forge technology to the world. No, that's not true. That wasn't my only hope. I also hoped we wouldn't be faced with another turning point on First Earth.

I couldn't bring myself to look out at the star field. I knew what was there. Beyond the crystal walls of the flume were images from all the territories, floating together in the giant celestial sea. With each trip through the flume, more random images were appearing. It was getting crowded. I didn't know if the images were real, or spirits, or some kind of symbols, but their presence was all too clear. The walls between territories were breaking down. I was failing.

The journey lasted only a few minutes. The musical notes grew louder and more frantic. Soon we were on our feet, back in the rocky cavern room. It looked exactly like the same rocky cavern from Second and Third Earths because, well, it was. The difference lay beyond the wooden door.

I'm happy to say we weren't pounced on by any snarling quigs.

"There!" I said, pointing to a pile of clothes stacked neatly near the mouth of the flume. I found the same clothes from my last trip to First Earth all neatly cleaned and folded. There was the starched white shirt, light gray pants with the darker gray jacket, and leather shoes. There were even those long-legged white grandpa boxers I learned to get used to.

"No way!" Courtney said, disgusted. "I'm not wearing this." She picked up a pretty dress with a pattern of tiny blue flowers. She also held up a pair of big white underpants that looked like the waist would come up to her armpits. "And what the hell is this?" she added, holding up a white bra that looked like twin, white waffle cones with a wide white strap holding them together. "You gotta be kidding!"

"Keep your own underwear," I said, laughing. "I don't think we have to worry about anybody seeing your sports bra."

"How do you know I wear a sports bra?" she said, squinting suspiciously.

"Just a guess," I said quickly. "But you gotta wear the dress."

I took my clothes to the other side of the cavern to get out of the embarrassing situation, and for modesty. Because I had grown a few inches and packed on several more pounds of muscle, I worried that the clothes wouldn't fit me anymore. But they did. Strange. They seemed to be the same clothes that I had worn a few years earlier, but they weren't the same size anymore. I figured I should stop stressing over the details and just go with it.

"I hate dresses," Courtney complained from across the cavern.

Courtney may have hated dresses, but dresses didn't hate Courtney. She looked awesome. Unlike the clothes on Third Earth, this dress was perfect. It was fitted on top, with a loose skirt that moved when she did. It came down to just below her knees. The blue flowers were bright, like spring. The sleeves were short, and she kept the top few buttons open. She even put on a pair of low, leather shoes that looked practical, if not very comfortable.

"People actually dressed like this?" she said with disgust. "It's just . . . queer."

"C'mon!" I cajoled. "You look really good. Like a girl and everything."

"Give me a break," she snarled. "How come you get to be

comfortable and I have to look like some dorky schoolmarm?"

"I don't think they use the word 'dork' in 1937," I kidded.

"Well they should because that's exactly what I look like!"

"I mean it, Courtney, you look good. But if you seriously hate it, we can find something else when we—" A creaking sound stopped me short. I knew that sound. The flume was coming back to life.

Courtney and I both snapped a look into the tunnel. Somebody was coming in. The two of us stepped closer to each other.

"Any guess?" Courtney asked.

"No idea."

The light grew brighter, lighting up the rocky cavern.

"Maybe we should take off," she suggested nervously.

"What if it's a friend? Or Mark?" I asked.

"What if it isn't?" Courtney countered.

Music filled the room. It wasn't a tune, just the clear, sweet notes that always accompany the Travelers through the flume. Courtney slowly bent down to pick up her Third Earth pants. I thought she was going to put them back on, but she dug into the pocket to retrieve the silver Quillan weapon.

The light got so bright that we had to shield our eyes. Squinting through the light, I saw a dark shadow appear at the mouth of the flume. Because the light was so bright, it was hard to make out who it was. The shadow took a step forward. The light didn't diminish.

"This is bad," Courtney said. "When the light doesn't go away, it's always been—"

"Gee, what a shock!" came a familiar, sarcastic voice. "Seeing you two here!"

"Oh man," I gasped.

It was Andy Mitchell. It was Saint Dane.

The guy stood at the mouth of the flume, facing us with his hands on his hips. He snorted and spit, still playing the part of the creep from Second Earth.

"So sweet seeing you two together again," Mitchell said. "And Chetwynde! In a dress! There's something you don't see every day."

"Where's Mark, Saint Dane?" I demanded.

"Living the life is my guess" Mitchell said. "He's a big shot now, Pendragon. A real fantasy come true for a geek like that. Everybody thinks he's a genius. But, oh man, such a thing he started. Such a thing!"

Mitchell laughed. It made my skin crawl. I wanted to strangle him. I took a step toward him. Mitchell took a step back and the light from the tunnel enveloped him. He didn't leave, though. He transformed. I stopped as he stepped back out of the light in his familiar form. He wore the black suit I knew so well. His bald head was crossed with the red scars that looked like lightning bolts. He grew back to his full height of well over six feet. None of that struck me as much as his eyes. It was always about the eyes. They burned brighter than the light that danced around him, staring me down with their blue-white madness. When he spoke, it was no longer in the voice of Andy Mitchell. It was the low growl of the demon Saint Dane.

"Everything that has happened, all that you see has been planned from the beginning. What is it that your kind is so fond of saying? Ah, yes: 'That is the way it was meant to be.' Well, my friends, this is truly the way it was meant to be. The Convergence is nearly here."

Courtney stepped up behind me and shouted, "Where is Mark?"

"Does it matter?" Saint Dane responded. "You can't undo

what he's done. Though I will enjoy watching you try."

He took a step back into the flume. I didn't want to let him get away. We needed some kind of clue as to how to find Mark.

"Wait!" I shouted. "We have to talk. About the things you told me on Quillan."

"I'm done reasoning with you, Pendragon." He sneered. "It is time for the journey to end. The last piece of the puzzle awaits me, on Ibara." He took another step back into the tunnel. The light grew around him.

"No! Wait!" I shouted.

"You might think about leaving now," he added. "Before it's too late."

The light flashed and quickly grew smaller as it swept Saint Dane off. In seconds the event was over. The tunnel was dark and eerily silent.

"What did he mean by that?" Courtney asked.

"Who knows? He always talks in riddles."

"That was no riddle," Courtney countered. "He said we should get out of here before it's too late. That sounded pretty clear to me."

A sound came from deep within the tunnel. Not a flume sound. A real-world sound.

"Someone's in the tunnel," Courtney gasped.

She grabbed my arm. The footsteps grew louder. It sounded like more than one person.

"Hello?" I called out.

No answer. The footsteps were regular and rhythmic, like marching. The sound of hard leather on stone was unmistakable. Someone was marching out of the flume. More than one someone.

"This is wrong," Courtney said, backing away toward the door. "Let's get out of here."

"No," I said, holding my ground. "We have to know."

The marching grew louder. Who was in there? Did someone from First Earth discover the flume and go spelunking? I often wondered what would happen if regular people entered the flume and walked deep inside. Did it go on endlessly? I began to make out human forms in the inky darkness. There were definitely people in there, but I couldn't tell how many. Three? Six? They marched close together, moving relentlessly from deep inside the tunnel toward the mouth of the flume, and us.

"Bobby?" Courtney called nervously. "Not liking this."

Neither did I, but we had to stay and see. The marchers were twenty yards from reaching the mouth of the flume. I finally saw that it was a group of men. Tall men, with square angular features. I knew those guys. I hated those guys.

"Dados!" I gasped. "From Quillan."

We backed away from the mouth of the flume as the dados marched slowly, incessantly forward.

Toward us.

FIRST EARTH

They were security dados from Quillan. No mistake. I knew them too well. They had that square Frankenstein look that made them seem human but . . . not. They each had a golden stun pistol in a holster belted at the waist. The odd thing was that they weren't wearing the green security uniforms. Their clothes were raggy and torn, as if they had been through a war. I definitely got a *Night of the Living Dead* zombie vibe, which chilled me. Bottom line? These weren't friends.

"Get outta here!" I shouted to Courtney.

She took a step toward the door and stopped when she realized I wasn't following.

"C'mon!"

"I'll catch up. Watch out for trains!"

"Bobby!" she pleaded. "I'm not leaving you."

"One of us has to find Mark!" I shouted. "Go!"

Courtney hesitated. I knew she didn't want to leave, but one of us had to be sure to get out of that tunnel or Mark would be lost. She knew that, so she ran for the door. She opened it quickly, glanced back at me, and was gone.

I didn't know what these goons were after, but it couldn't be good. Their presence alone on First Earth wasn't good. I couldn't let them get beyond this cavern. Problem was, there were lots of them and not-lots of me. I had one chance and I had to take it.

"*Quillan!*" I shouted.

The flume sprang to life. My idea was to send them back to where they came from. The dados stopped and looked back into the tunnel curiously. They looked like confused dogs who didn't know what to make of a strange sound. Their curiosity cost them. Light blasted from the tunnel and enveloped them. I didn't know how many of them were in the flume, but they got sucked back in and sent on their way home to Quillan. My idea worked. I let out a relieved breath. . . .

A little too soon. One of them realized what was happening. Before the pull of the flume could grab him, he sprang forward, leaping out of the tunnel and into the cavern. I was ready. I braced myself, expecting him to jump me. He didn't. Instead he ran right past me, headed for the door to the subway. Whatever their mission was, it wasn't to mess with me. In that brief instant I had the sick feeling that they weren't there because of Courtney and me—I feared they were coming to invade First Earth.

I had to attack. That wasn't something I was used to doing or even knew how to do. Loor had taught me to defend myself, not be the aggressor. Most of her training was about letting the other guy make the mistakes. If I had done that, the dado would have left me alone standing there at the gate, crouched down, ready to defend myself. Looking stupid.

Bright light from the flume filled the cavern as I spun and tackled the robot from behind, wrapping my arms around his legs. He sprawled forward, hitting the rock wall next to the wooden door with his shoulder. Hard. The impact was strong enough to knock a chunk of rock out of the wall. The robot didn't even grunt. Not good. Dados didn't feel pain, which meant they had no fear. I didn't know what to do, so I held his legs in a bear hug. His clothing crumbled in my grip, as if the fabric were rotten. Weird. But I didn't let go. I could feel the strength of his robot legs. He was a machine. I wasn't. My only hope was to somehow wrestle the dado back into the flume and send us both out of there. There was no way I could beat the mechanical thug in a fight without a weapon.

A weapon! I quickly reached up to grab his pistol from its holster. Bad idea. The dado's leg was free. He kneed me in the head. I fell back, reeling. I saw stars, and not the kind you see through the flume. I had to shake it off fast or this thing would be loose on First Earth. I scrambled back to my feet to see I had given the dado an idea. He was reaching for his pistol. Oops. I looked around desperately. The light was already receding into the flume. I had missed the bus. Could I activate it again quickly? Nope. Not before this thing would take a shot at me. The only thing I could do was attack.

I leaped forward, launching myself parallel to the ground. I hit the robot as it fired and . . . *Fum!* The dado fell backward as the charge from its weapon smashed the wall, blasting out a spray of rocks. The dado landed on its back. I landed on the dado. For a brief instant I was eye to eye with the robot, staring into its mechanical, lifeless doll eyes. Yikes.

The moment didn't last long. The robot threw me off like I was made of straw. I was running out of ideas, not that I had that many in the first place. I hit the ground and rolled toward the mouth of the flume.

"Quillan!" I shouted again. The flume sprang back to life. It was the only thing I could think of doing, though I had no

idea how I was going to wrestle the dado into the tunnel. As the light from the flume began to fill the cavern, I stood with my back to the entrance. The dado stood with its back to the door of the cavern. It was a standoff. No, I take that back. The dado was in complete control. The only thing I could do was step back into the flume and get out of there. The dado raised its pistol, aiming at me. I instinctively took a step back, then stopped. I couldn't leave. I had to let it shoot me. At least when I came to, I'd still be on First Earth and could figure out a way to chase it down. Leaving wasn't an option. I braced myself, ready to get nailed.

The dado didn't fire. It held the gun on me, keeping me back as it took a step toward the door. It didn't care about me. I was nothing more than a nuisance. It wanted to get to First Earth. There was nothing I could do. The dado knew it. While keeping its doll eyes on me, it reached back for the door that was the gate to the flume. With one quick movement, it holstered its pistol, pulled the door open, and sprang out into the tunnel. . . .

As a subway train came barreling by.

The dado hit the train. Or the train hit the dado. I guess the specifics didn't matter. What *did* matter was that the robot was thrown under the wheels of the speeding locomotive. The engineer hit the brakes. It must have been a shock for him to see a man suddenly jump in front of his train from out of nowhere. A horrible screeching sound filled the tunnel. It was so shrill I felt as if it were cutting into my brain. It was followed quickly by a rumble and the sound of twisting, wrenching metal. I ran to the doorway to see the train was jumping the tracks! If it was full of passengers, it would be a disaster.

Through the tortured sound of metal being twisted, the big train bucked and rocked, moments from flipping over.

There was nothing I could do but watch through the open doorway. I flashed back to the disaster of the *Hindenburg*. Would this go down in history as a tragedy on that level? Was this my fault? Was my presence on First Earth going to be the cause of a new epic disaster?

I saw the wheels near me lift off the track as they flew by. I held my breath. The brakes shrieked. But then the wheels came crashing back down onto the track. It wasn't going over. Its forward movement was slowing. People weren't going to die. The train groaned to a stop. This was going to be a massive bottleneck that would mess up the subway system for who knew how long, but it wasn't going to be a disaster.

I had to get my head back together, fast. What should I do? Hide? Flume out of there? Run after Courtney? I took a deep breath to calm myself. The dado. I had to get rid of the dado, or what was left of it. The smell of hot oil and brake fluid filled the tunnel. I felt safe enough to poke my head out to survey the carnage. Looking both ways, I saw that the train had only three cars. Several yards to my right, the wheels of the engine were off the track. The other cars had somehow managed to stay gripped to the steel, but this train wasn't going anywhere. I figured the dado had gotten caught under the engine's wheels, causing the derailing. Soon there would be all sorts of emergency people flooding the tunnel. They'd find a wreck, and a mysterious robot that would seem as if it had dropped in from another planet. There was nothing I could do about the wreck, but I had to hide the evidence of what had caused it.

Smoke filled the tunnel, burning my eyes. Nobody had left the train cars yet. They must have all been in shock. Or too afraid to move. I figured I'd have a short window of opportunity. I moved as quickly as I could without tripping or bashing myself into something. I made my way toward the engine, while scanning the ground for any signs of the dado. I didn't see anything at first and had the fleeting thought that the robot had survived. I had no idea how strong the dado was. It was definitely solid enough to derail a train. Would it be strong enough to walk away after getting slammed like that?

I had only gotten a few feet when I saw, well, a few feet. Lying next to the track were the legs of the dado. It wasn't moving. It was done. I didn't appreciate just how done it was until I grabbed the feet and started to pull it back toward the gate. The dado was a lot lighter than I expected. That's because I was only pulling half a dado. Yeah, gross. The robot had been cut in two at the waist. I dropped the legs, feeling all sorts of disgusted. I had to force myself to get a grip. This wasn't a person. It was a machine. It wasn't any more human than a toaster oven.

I looked under the engine to see the upper half. Okay, so maybe it was a lot more gruesome than seeing a toaster oven cut in half. But still. I couldn't let the fact that I wanted to puke stop me. I was already hearing the shouts of people coming from the subway station, calling to the passengers to see if they were okay. I had to move quickly. I grabbed the legs again and dragged them to the gate. As I pulled the legs along, I noticed again that the clothing was flimsy and rotted. The security dados on Quillan wore crisp, green uniforms. This clothing was so threadbare, it crumbled in my hands. I didn't have the time to try and guess what it might mean. There was no telling how much time I had to ditch my half friend.

I got the legs to the gate, shoved them inside, and ran back for the rest. Moving the upper half wasn't as easy. Not that it was heavier, but it felt more like moving a real body. I grabbed the hands and pulled, dragging it along. I couldn't take my eyes off the head as it bounced along the gravelly track bed. I don't mean to be gruesome about it, but it was kind of gruesome. I had to keep telling myself it was a machine. Just a machine. Just a machine. A toaster oven. A lawn mower. A weed whacker.

Then the machine grabbed my leg.

I screamed like a little girl. The thing was still alive! Or whatever the robot equivalent of "alive" is. It yanked my leg, trying to pull me off my feet. I grabbed a fistful of rotten clothing and struggled to drag it the rest of the way into the flume cavern. I now had two body halves to deal with. The legs were dead. The upper torso wasn't. I kicked at it, trying to get the grisly thing to let go. It was the single creepiest thing I had ever experienced in my life. Finally I gave the arm a sharp kick with my free leg and knocked it away. Without hesitation I ran for the flume and shouted, *"Quillan!"*

The flume came to life. I spun to face the upper half. It lay next to its lower half, facedown. Unmoving. I wondered if it had grabbed me in some kind of involuntary reaction, or if it could still think. I didn't want to take any chances. I walked cautiously back to the legs, keeping my eyes on the upper half, ready for it to grab at me again. I bent down, grabbed the legs, and quickly dragged them toward the mouth of the tunnel. The thing still had its holster on with the pistol. I thought of grabbing the gun but remembered the blast of energy had no effect on dados. With a grunt I heaved the legs up and used the weight of its butt to fling the whole mess into the flume. It was time to get the upper half.

Unfortunately, the upper half decided it was time to get me. When I turned, I saw the dado up on its hands, bracing its body in a macabre handstand. Worse, it was running toward me. It was like some twisted horror movie. I moved one way, the torso mirrored me. I moved the other way, the torso did too. I faked back, then quickly circled behind it. Now the torso of the robot was between me and the flume. It may have been relentless, but it didn't have much agility. It turned around to face me. Yes, face me. The head was upside down, but the eyes fixed on me. Its prey. It wasn't going to give up.

Neither was I. The explosion of light and music blasted from the flume. I ran forward, swept up the torso, spun, and heaved it into the light. Even as it sailed away from me, its hands grasped at the air, trying to grab me. That's a nightmare I won't soon forget. The thing disappeared into the light, headed back to Quillan. Along with its legs. Good riddance.

I felt the tug of the flume as it tried to suck me along with it. The idea of sailing through the flume along with those gruesome body parts gave me the burst of adrenaline I needed to dig my heels in and back away from the tunnel. I didn't need to be grappling with half a robot in the flume. I needed to be on First Earth, with Courtney.

Courtney. Right. Where was she? I wasn't done yet. I had to get out of the gate and past the subway wreck without anyone realizing the crash was sort of my fault. We hadn't been on First Earth for more than ten minutes and I was already longing to be somewhere else.

FIRST EARTH

I had to get gone. The last thing I needed was for some panicky victim of the train wreck to stumble onto the gate, throw it open, and see me standing there out of breath, looking like an idiot. I cautiously opened the wooden door and peeked out. The last of the three subway cars was right there. Luckily the door to the car was already past the gate. People were starting to climb out, helping one another slip down the few feet to the track bed. Choking smoke was everywhere. That was okay by me. It was good cover. I slipped out of the gate, closed it behind me, and walked quickly to join the others. I hoped nobody would notice one more victim.

"Keep moving!" shouted a firefighter with a flashlight. "Everything's okay! The platform's not far. Keep moving!"

I put my head down and got in line behind an older guy who was having trouble making his way over the uneven surface. I took his arm to steady him and helped him the rest of the way. The guy needed a strong arm. I needed cover. Perfect. There wasn't any panic. I think everyone was too dazed for that. I helped the older guy all the way to the cement stairs that led up to the station platform.

"Thank you, son," he said gratefully. "I can take it from here."

He was a little shaky, but okay. He climbed the stairs and disappeared into the mass of people on the platform.

"Let's go! Let's go!" a policeman yelled. They were trying to herd people toward the exits. "It's over! Nothing to see here!"

Actually, there was a lot to see, but I guess that was their standard line. I stood next to a white-tiled pillar to get away from the crowd of people who were moving toward the exit. Now that I was just another face in the crowd, my head was already on to the next challenge. Find Courtney. The station looked the same as I remembered it. This was 1937. People were dressed up. The men had on suits and hats. The women wore dresses. No jeans or sneakers anywhere. On the far side of the platform I saw a newsstand.

A newsstand! With newspapers. With dates! The big question was still out there—what was today's date? The success or failure of our trip to find Mark would ride on when the flume had deposited us on First Earth. I pushed my way through the crowd, which wasn't easy because nobody was going the same way I was. There wasn't a whole lot of interest in buying newspapers just then. Finally I stepped up to the newsstand and grabbed a copy of the *New York Times*.

The date? November 1, 1937.

Was this good or bad? My mind flashed back to the library on Third Earth. History showed that the patent for Mark's Forge thingy was filed in October. We were too late to stop that. But the computer also said that some kind of announcement was made between that KEM company and the Dimond Alpha Digital Organization in November. Mark disappeared right after that. According to the paper, today was November 1. Whatever happened to Mark probably hadn't happened yet. We might have arrived in time to find out what exactly had happened. Or what was going to happen. Or . . . you get the idea. I wasn't sure how to feel about the news. Yes, we had a shot at intervening in Mark's history. Did that mean First Earth was about to have another turning point?

"Hey! You gonna buy that paper or what?" came a gruff voice.

I looked to see the exact same newsguy sitting behind the counter who chewed me out for the exact same thing the last time I was there. He was a porky little gnome wearing a red plaid shirt. He still chomped on the little stub of a cigar and still needed a shave.

But he wasn't talking to me.

I heard a girl's voice bark, "Oh, relax, Yoda. People are too busy running for their lives to buy your stupid newspapers!"

It was Courtney. She was standing a few yards away doing the same thing I was—checking the newspapers for today's date.

"Yoda?" I called out with a smile.

Courtney lit up with a big, relieved smile. She ran over and gave me a hug like she thought she'd never see me again.

"Bobby! I never thought I'd see you again!"

See.

"What happened?" she asked frantically. "Are you all right? What happened with the dados? Did they cause the wreck of the—"

"O-kay!" I shouted, cutting her off. "Let's talk outside."

"Yeah," the newsguy grumped. "Take it outside and stop getting fingerprints all over the goods."

"It's old news anyway," Courtney sniffed. "In case you

missed it, there was a train wreck." She always had to get in the last shot.

We joined the crowd to get out of the subway station. The people were all pretty calm considering what they'd just been through. As we moved with the flow, I began to form a plan. I didn't want to spring it on Courtney until I had the chance to think it through and set things up, but the more I thought about it, the more I realized it was the best thing for us to do. Maybe the only thing.

No matter how tough it was going to be.

We climbed the stairs into the bright, November sun. Luckily it was a warm day because Courtney didn't have a sweater or anything. I'm not so sure she would have cared. She was too busy gawking at the new sights. Or should I say the *old* sights. The Bronx of 1937 was once again busy. Ancient black cars rolled bumper to bumper through the busy intersection. The sidewalks were packed with people. Strangely, the buildings didn't seem all that alien since tall, cement-faced buildings like this still existed in our time. They just looked a little newer in 1937. The odd thing was what we *didn't* see. There wasn't a single modern-looking steel or glass structure anywhere.

The chemical smell was overwhelming, especially after being on Third Earth, where the air was so clean. I'm guessing it was a mixture of gas, dust, oil, manufacturing exhaust, and BO. Pretty much the normal smells of a crowded city. Giant billboards loomed overhead that advertised everything from soap to liniment. I didn't even know what liniment was, but the advertisement made it look like I really needed it to "REDUCE PAIN AND CURE ILLS." I had plenty of ills that needed curing—if I thought a bottle of some bizarre medicine could actually do that, I'd have bought a case. People moved quickly along the sidewalks, headed to wherever it was they were headed. Making the street that much more crowded were the fire trucks that were lined up near the subway entrance. Wailing sirens said there were more on the way. It was a busy day in the Bronx. Thanks to us.

I didn't say anything to Courtney at first. I wanted her to soak it all up. I knew what it was like to arrive in a new territory. Part of the wonder was seeing a place that was so completely alien. The real brain freeze comes from realizing that you're standing in the middle of it. There's no way to get used to that, no matter how often you jump through time and space.

After doing a few slow turns, Courtney focused on me and summed it all up with one simple statement. "Hell of a day."

I laughed. In the span of a few hours we had gone from Courtney's house on Second Earth to three thousand years into the future, only to jump back fifty years before we were born. It was definitely a hell of a day. It wasn't over.

I grabbed her hand and pulled her away from all the excitement. We crossed a few blocks to a wide avenue where traffic was moving faster than a crawl.

"Where are we going?" she asked.

"Someplace familiar," I answered.

I hailed a yellow taxi that was headed downtown. Courtney was about to duck into the backseat when she popped back out and asked, "Do we have money for this?"

"Stop worrying," I said, and gently pushed her into the car.

The cabbie was a jovial-looking guy with a checkered cap. "Where to?" he asked.

"The Manhattan Tower Hotel."

The guy whistled in appreciation and said, "Well! Ain't we the fancy ones!"

He stepped on the gas and we were on our way home. At least to my home on First Earth.

"So?" Courtney asked. "What's the plan?"

I didn't want to reveal that just yet. I had to make sure it was possible.

"I still have friends at the hotel" was my answer. "They'll take care of us."

"Perfect!" Courtney exclaimed. "Then we track down Mark."

I put my finger to my lips in the "shhh" gesture, and pointed to the cabbie. "One step at a time."

Courtney huffed and fell silent. The rest of the trip she spent looking out the window at another era. She didn't say much. She was too busy marveling at the past. It wasn't until we were almost at the hotel that she finally said, "It's like watching an old movie, but it's real, isn't it?"

I didn't answer. I didn't have to.

"Fifty-ninth and Park!" the cabbie announced as he pulled the cab up to the curb. Instantly a bellhop ran up and opened the car door for us.

"Welcome to the Manhattan Tower!" he exclaimed with a big smile. "Checking in today, sir?"

I got out of the cab and looked at him. "Pay the cabbie for me, would you, Dodger?"

Dodger, the bellhop, looked at me blankly, as if I had just spoken Latvian. I looked at the confused guy, and smiled. I knew it would take a few seconds for him to catch up. A moment later his confused look turned to one of wonder.

"Pendragon?" he asked in awe. "Wha—"

"You know I'm good for it," I said.

"Uh, yeah. Sure, sure," Dodger said, scrambling to get his wits back. He reached into his pocket and pulled out a fistful of coins. Tip money.

While he paid the cabbie, I leaned back into the car and smiled at Courtney. "Come on out and tell me if my description did this place justice."

Courtney leaped out of the car and looked up at the imposing, pink building. By modern standards it wasn't monstrous. It stood only thirty-two floors high. But in 1937 it was pretty impressive, complete with the three-foot-high letters near the roof that spelled out its name: THE MANHATTAN TOWER. At night those letters glowed a brilliant neon green and could be seen all over the city. The hotel took up a whole block, resting in a perfectly manicured garden that was like an oasis in the middle of the city. Being November, the leaves on the trees had turned brilliant colors of red, yellow, and orange. There were pumpkins placed everywhere, probably as Halloween decorations from the night before.

Courtney didn't comment on how impressive it all was. Or on the beauty of the grounds. Or even on how well I had described it in my journals. Her comment was much more Courtney than that.

"Where did it happen?" she asked.

"Where did what happen?"

"Where did that gangster land that Saint Dane threw out the window?"

I gave her a sour look. That particular gruesome event was one I'd managed to forget about. Until then, thank you very much Courtney.

Dodger came running back to us, looking all wide-eyed. I'm guessing he was around nineteen years old, with slicked-back black hair. He was a feisty little guy who couldn't have been more than five foot three. What he lacked in size he made up for in energy. He was constantly in motion, with eyes that were always looking around for what needed to be done next. On Second Earth you'd call him "hyper."

"Hey, old pal! I thought you was gone for good!"

When Dodger wasn't being a professional and speaking with hotel guests, he had a fast way of speaking that he called Brooklynese. To me he sounded like Bugs Bunny. He spoke quickly, changing subjects in midsentence, barely waiting for answers. If you weren't up to his speed, he'd leave you in the dust. "Is Spader comin' back too? Did you know Gunny disappeared? Nobody's seen him since last spring." He focused on Courtney, leaned in to me, and whispered, "Hey, who's the skirt?"

"Skirt?" Courtney shouted.

Apparently Dodger's whisper wasn't quite low enough. He froze in surprise.

"That's the sexist stereotype you reduce girls to? Skirts?" Courtney growled.

"Hey, no offense, doll—"

Uh-oh.

"Doll?" Courtney screamed even louder. "Oh, that's much better."

She stepped toward Dodger, ready to do battle. The little guy backed away in fear. I didn't think he was used to a skirt, uh, a girl being so aggressive.

"What kind of name is Dodger, anyway? That's a dog name."

"It's a nickname is all," he stammered. "I like baseball."

"Baseball? I'll bet you've never even been to Los Angeles!"

"Los Angeles?" Dodger said, confused. "Who said anything about—"

I quickly stepped between them and glared at Courtney. "Dodger's real name is Douglas. He calls himself Dodger because he likes the Dodgers. The *Brooklyn* Dodgers."

That stopped Courtney. She had forgotten about the whole time-travel thing. The Brooklyn Dodgers wouldn't move to Los Angeles for another twenty years. I looked to Dodger and said, "This is my sister, Dodge. Her name's Courtney. We're going to stay in Gunny's apartment for a while. Okay?"

I figured it would be better to tell everybody Courtney was my sister so nobody would get freaked out about us being together.

"Hey, fine with me," Dodger said. "You're lucky Caplesmith didn't clean the place out. He thinks Gunny's coming back. Is he?"

I didn't know how to answer that. Of course I couldn't tell him that Gunny and Spader were trapped on a territory called Eelong that was full of talking cats and carnivorous dinosaurs. I was just happy to hear that the hotel manager, Mr. Caplesmith, had kept the apartment. Gunny was the bell captain at the hotel. He'd worked there most of his life and pretty much ran the place. I'd bet that Mr. Caplesmith would hold his apartment forever on the remote chance that Gunny would be back. That's how great a guy Gunny was. It was lucky for us. It meant we had a place to stay.

"I don't know," I answered truthfully. "I hope he's coming back."

Man, I missed Gunny. Spader too. But I couldn't let myself go there. Self-pity didn't help things.

"No luggage?" Dodger asked. He kept stealing nervous looks at Courtney, as if waiting for her to tee off on him again. Courtney just glared.

"We're traveling light," I said.

"Is that a problem?" Courtney asked aggressively.

"Not for me," Dodger said. "If you don't need a change of undies, that's your business, sister."

"I'm not your sister," Courtney shot back, then looked at me and smiled. "I guess I'm *his* sister."

"Let's just go inside," I suggested, trying to diffuse the situation.

Dodger went ahead of us, leading us up the wide front stairs into the hotel.

"Be cool," I said softly to Courtney. "Dodger's okay."

"He's overcompensating because he's short," Courtney sniffed.

"Whatever. We need him."

"Okay, I'll be good . . . little bro." She smiled as she said this. It was weird pretending that we were brother and sister.

The hotel was just as I remembered. It was the height of luxury, 1937-style. The lobby had a high, stained-glass ceiling. There were huge, dark oriental carpets everywhere and lots of soft, leather furniture. It was a place that catered to the highfalutin, so all the guests were dressed impeccably. The bellhops looked neat and crisp in their burgundy uniforms with gold trim. They were the same uniforms that Spader and I had worn when we lived and worked there. I actually had lots of happy memories of the place.

Some lousy ones too.

"You hear the big news?" Dodger asked as he strutted through the lobby.

Courtney said, "Heard it? We were there!"

Dodger frowned. "You were in Hollywood last night?"

Courtney and I shared a look.

"You're not talking about the subway wreck?" I asked.

"Nah, I'm talking about Dewey Todd."

"The elevator operator?" I asked in surprise.

"Yeah," Dodger said. "He went out to Hollywood to work

in his old man's new hotel. Last night there was some kind of strange accident. He was running the elevator and it got hit by lightning."

"Is he okay?" I asked, horrified.

"That's the strange part. Nobody knows. Everybody on the elevator disappeared. Halloween night. Spooky, aye? Poor sap. I liked the little guy."

"Littler than you?" Courtney asked.

Dodger gave her a quick look, but let it go.

Poor Dewey. He was clueless, but a nice guy. I hated to hear that something might have happened to him. It seemed like a real mystery, but I couldn't worry about it. I had enough mysteries of my own to deal with.

Dodger led us to the elevator.

"We'll take the stairs," I told him.

"What'sa matter? Afraid lightning might hit?" he asked, snickering.

Neither of us laughed. Dodger stopped chuckling quickly. "Okay, bad joke. You got a key?"

"I know where Gunny keeps it."

"Okay, if you need anything, you know where to find me." He started to leave, then turned back to me, as if wanting to say something.

"What?" I asked.

"Don't take this wrong, Pendragon. But you look different. I mean, you've been gone for what? Four months?"

It was true. By my clock I had left First Earth a couple of years before. But the flume put us back there not much later than when I had left. It was just another example of how the flumes were guided by some knowing force.

"How come you look so different?" Dodger asked.

"Growth spurt," Courtney said flatly.

"It's been a rough four months" was all I could think of saying.

Dodger looked at me quizzically, then shrugged, and walked off. "If you say so."

"I'll get you the cash for the cab ride," I called after him.

"It's on me," he said. "Consider it an apology for getting off on the wrong foot with your sister."

He looked at Courtney, and gave her a genuine, apologetic smile.

"Thanks, peewee," she said.

Dodger winked at her and took off. We watched him as he strutted back into the lobby.

"He winked at me," Courtney said, disgusted. "What is up with that?"

"He can't help it if he was born in a different era."

"I'll let him get away with the skirt comment, but if he calls me a dame, he's done."

I laughed and said, "Let it go, all right?"

"And I don't care where they play, Dodger is still a dog name."

Gunny had a small apartment on the first basement level of the hotel. It sounds worse than it was. I led Courtney down the stairs and along the corridor, passing the hotel laundry, the vault, and the baggage checkroom. Gunny's apartment was at the very end. I reached up to an exposed, overhead pipe where, sure enough, Gunny's key was waiting.

"Not exactly high-tech security," Courtney scoffed.

"Not needed." I reached for the door and turned the knob. The door was already unlocked. "Half the time Gunny never even locked it."

The apartment was dark, as you might imagine a basement apartment would be. There were a few narrow windows near the ceiling that were just above ground level. They didn't let in much light, but it was enough to make the place a little less claustrophobic. I flicked on a lamp to see that the apartment was exactly as Gunny had left it. There was a small living room with a sofa and two easy chairs positioned around a big-old radio in a wooden cabinet made by some company called Philco. There were no TVs in 1937. The radio was the center of home entertainment. One wall of the living room was actually the kitchen, with a small sink and stove next to a tiny refrigerator. Beyond the living room was Gunny's bedroom. Off that room was his bathroom. That was it. Gunny didn't need much to be comfortable.

There weren't a lot of knickknacks or personal touches, other than one painting that hung on the wall above the radio. It was an oil painting of a U.S. Civil War battle where the union soldiers were all members of the Fifty-fourth Massachusetts Volunteer Infantry Regiment, one of the first black army units in the Civil War. Gunny was really proud of that.

Standing in that room, I expected to see Gunny walk out of his bedroom with a big smile and a greeting of "Hey there, shorty!" That wasn't going to happen. The thin coating of dust on everything was a sad reminder that nobody had lived here in a while.

"Are we ever going to see him again?" Courtney asked somberly, reading my thoughts.

"I think so," I answered optimistically. "When this is all over."

"So let's make that happen," she said, getting down to business. "Can we make this our base while we're looking for Mark?"

"That's the plan," I said. I walked to Gunny's tiny kitchen and opened the oven. Inside was a metal cookie tin that looked like a log cabin.

"Stale cookies?" Courtney said.

"These cookies don't get stale, and they are very sweet." I opened the tin and pulled out a roll of money that was held together by a rubber band.

Courtney whistled in awe. "Yikes! Didn't he ever hear of a bank?"

"He kept this in case of an emergency. I think this qualifies." I tossed the roll of bills to her. "For food and more clothes and anything else that comes up."

Courtney stared at the huge roll of cash nervously. "I think I'd rather have you in charge of this. My palms are already sweating."

It was time to tell Courtney of my plan. From what I'd seen, everything was working out the way it had to. Gunny's apartment was still here and available; money wasn't a problem; and the people at the hotel remembered me. The hunt for Mark could happen from here. That was the easy part. I led Courtney over to the couch. We sat, facing each other while I scrambled to think of the right words.

"This looks serious," she said. "I'd say you're breaking up with me, but since we're not even going out I don't think—"

"I can't stay on First Earth," I said.

Courtney stared at me, not sure how to react. She laughed. Stopped herself. Gave me a curious look. Laughed again and finally shook her head.

"We just got here. We have to find Mark."

"I know. You need to do it alone."

"What?" Courtney jumped up. "No way! Just . . . no way!"

"I'm sorry," I said.

"Don't be sorry," she shot back. "Be serious."

I took a breath to try and keep my voice calm. It was

killing me to do this but I couldn't see any other way.

"I am being serious. I can't stay here because Saint Dane went to Ibara. That's where I need to be."

Courtney paced. I couldn't tell if she was angry or frightened. Probably both.

"He wants to beat me, Courtney. He *has* to beat me. I think that's just as important to him as taking control of Halla."

"Then don't let him!" Courtney screamed. "He's luring you there, Bobby, don't you see that? He wants you to follow him so he can beat you."

"You're right. That's exactly why I have to go. I don't think he can control Halla until he beats me, once and for all. But it works both way. If we want to stop him, I mean really stop him, forever, I'm going to have to beat him straight up. That's the only way this can all end."

"That's pretty arrogant, don't you think?" she sniffed. "I mean, thinking that the future of all existence is only about the two of you."

"It's not," I countered. "It's about how we influence events, and the people of the territories and the choices they make."

Courtney shook her head. "I don't understand."

"This has been torturing me from the beginning," I answered. "On every territory, with every conflict, Saint Dane has challenged me. You've read about it all. He always gets me to follow him to his next target. The Travelers have ruined his plans more often than not. The guy is a lot of things, but he's not an idiot. He could have won every single territory if the Travelers hadn't stopped him, but we never would have gotten the chance if we didn't always know where he was going. But he always tells me. Don't you wonder about that?"

Courtney plopped down in one of the cushy easy chairs,

shooting out a small cloud of dust. "Yeah," she said, resigned. "I have. Are you saying he really wants to be beaten?"

"No!" I said quickly. "He wants to win, all right, but winning for him isn't just about toppling a territory. It's about beating the Travelers. Beating me. I think the battle here is more complicated than we even realize. It isn't just about wars or destruction or us trying to make sure the people of a territory have a peaceful way of life. I think it's more about the *way* it happens. The decisions people make. The paths they choose."

"You're getting a little cosmic on me," Courtney said.

"I know, I'm on shaky ground here, but the more I learn about Saint Dane and the way he thinks, the more I realize he's trying to prove some kind of point. He talks about the people of the territories being greedy and arrogant and shortsighted. He thinks that whatever horror happens to the territories, the people deserve it."

"Because he's a monster," Courtney added.

"Yeah, but he doesn't see it that way. He thinks he's giving the people what they want."

"Death and destruction and misery?" Courtney asked.

"I know, it doesn't really follow. But the point is, he thinks he's serving a grander purpose. I don't think it's as simple as him being some kind of megalomaniac James Bond–type villain who wants to rule the universe, muhahahahaha! In some twisted way, he thinks he's doing the right thing."

"But that's just it," Courtney pleaded. "He thinks the right thing is to steer the people of the territories into disaster. How can that possibly be right?"

"I'm not saying it is. I'm saying that's how he thinks."

Courtney looked around the room, letting my confused logic sink in. "So if Saint Dane is on a quest to prove that his way of running the territories is the right way, and the only way he feels he can do that is by beating the Travelers, then by his way of thinking, the Travelers are the bad guys."

Those words hit me hard. I hadn't thought of it that way, but if my theory was true, then Courtney was right. If Saint Dane thinks he's trying to save the territories, in his mind the bad guys who must be defeated are the Travelers.

"That's not all, Bobby," Courtney added. "If Saint Dane is trying to prove something, who exactly is he trying to prove it to?"

I sat forward and rubbed my eyes. I was feeling very tired. "That's the biggest question of all," I said softly.

"It's coming to an end, Bobby," Courtney said. "Whatever the Convergence is, it sounds like it's what this has all been leading up to. I think what Saint Dane did as Andy Mitchell, what he got Mark to do, has broken down the walls between the territories for good. There are dados on Second Earth. There are dados on Third Earth and Quillan."

"Dados tried to get onto First Earth," I reminded her. "For all I know, more are showing up right now."

"The destinies of four territories have been altered. It's sounding like those dominos are being lined up."

"I agree," I said. "That's why I've got to go to Ibara. I hate to say this, but I'm afraid it's too late to undo what Mark has done. Too many events have been set in motion. A Traveler has joined Saint Dane, remember? Nevva Winter is on his side. She told me on Quillan that she was thinking of taking the place of the Traveler from Ibara. All signs point to Ibara being that first domino that's going to be tipped."

Courtney looked at the floor.

I continued, "I don't think we can change the future by trying to re-alter the past. We're too far down the road for that. I've got to look forward."

"So you want to give up on Mark?" she asked.

"No!" I shouted. "It may be too late to undo the damage he's done, but we still don't know why he did it. That's not about Halla. Or dados. It's about our friend. According to Patrick's computer, Mark Dimond disappeared sometime in November 1937. Disappearing is bad. Mark is an innocent victim in all this. If something bad is about to happen to him, we've got to try and stop it."

Courtney walked over to the couch and sat down next to me. She held my hand and said, "No, *I've* got to try and stop it. You've got to go to Ibara."

I'm finishing this journal while Courtney is sleeping in Gunny's bed. I'm lying on his couch, writing. I can't sleep. My mind is going in too many directions. My plan is to finish this journal and leave it with Courtney. She'll find a safe place to keep it. From now on, I'll send my journals to her through the rings.

Courtney is going to stay on First Earth to track down Mark. If anybody can do it, she can. She's as much a part of this now as I am. She's been together with Mark from the beginning. They are a team. Or, they *were* a team. Though I'm worried about both my friends, this feels right. I've made loads of sacrifices since becoming a Traveler in the name of saving Halla from Saint Dane. Now I'm abandoning my two best friends. It's a hollow, dark feeling. But what else can I do? I honestly believe that there's nothing we can do about the dados. The real concern here is Mark. Where is he? What happened that he knowingly changed the course of history? Is he okay? I believe that Courtney's mission here on First Earth is not to try and realign Halla. It's to save Mark's life. Knowing that I won't be here to help is killing me, but it's a sacrifice I have to make. While Courtney tries to save Mark, I've got to try and save Halla. I've got to face Saint Dane on Ibara. It's about him and me. It's about proving the Travelers aren't the bad guys.

I've got the same queasy feeling I always have when I'm about to go to a new territory. What will I find? What kind of culture will they have? Will it be modern? Ancient? Civilized? Primitive? Or will I land square in the middle of a society run by robots?

Anything is possible. There's only one thing I know for sure.

Saint Dane is there waiting for me.

END OF JOURNAL #28

◉ FIRST EARTH ◉

Courtney was alone.

More alone than she had ever been in her life. At least that's what it felt like to her. Even when she was lying in the hospital after having nearly been killed by Saint Dane, there were people watching out for her. But that was on Second Earth. On First Earth she had no one. Nobody knew she even existed, because technically, she didn't. She was out of place, out of time, and feeling a little bit out of her mind. She wanted to cry. She wanted to go home in the worst way, but that was impossible because to use the flumes without a Traveler would mean disaster. No, she was stuck. She wanted to lie in Gunny's bed, pull the covers over her head, and pretend she was at home with her mom and dad.

Instead she focused on her mission. She didn't resent Bobby for leaving. She agreed that he had to go to Ibara. But it didn't stop her from wishing that he was still around. What kept her going was the hope that she would soon find Mark. History said he disappeared and she knew that couldn't be a good thing. She needed to find him before whatever was going to happen, happened. She even held out hope that in spite of what

Bobby thought, finding Mark and learning why he'd done what he did might somehow re-alter the course of history and put Halla back on track. But there was another reason she had to find Mark. She needed him. She needed her friend. She needed to hold on to him and cry and hear his dumb stutter and be back together with the only person in Halla who had traveled the same road she had. Mark had become her best friend, her support, her confidant. He saved her life. She needed to return the favor. She needed to get Mark back.

Her first order of business was to get new clothes. She hated the flowery dress from the flume. It didn't matter what the current cultural standards dictated, girly dresses and Courtney Chetwynde did not go together. After a quick meal in the hotel restaurant of bacon, eggs, potatoes, and orange juice (that cost a whopping thirty-two cents) she went looking for Dodger, the bellhop. She found him at his same post, standing outside the hotel, greeting guests. When Dodger spotted her, his eyes lit up. Courtney wasn't sure if he was happy to see her, or terrified that she'd start yelling at him again.

"G'mornin'," he said cautiously. "Everything okeydokey?"

"It's all good," Courtney answered. "But I need a favor."

"Name it."

"I need to buy some clothes. Are there any shops nearby?"

"You kiddin'?" Dodger chuckled. "We got the greatest shops in the world just steps away. Pendragon knows that."

Uh-oh. Courtney hadn't thought of a plausible story about why Bobby was gone.

"Right, she said, trying to buy time to think. "He went home to Stony Brook. A family thing."

Dodger nodded. "Everything okay?"

"Everything's fine. Could you tell me where the shops are?"

"I'll do better than that. I'll take you there myself. I got a break comin' up."

"That's okay. Just tell me where to go."

"Tut-tut," Dodger said, trying to be gallant. "Pendragon and I go way back. I gotta give the red carpet treatment to his sister."

"Sister?" Courtney asked a little too quickly. "How do you know Shannon—" Oops, she stopped herself. She'd forgotten about the setup. "Right! Sister. I'm his sister. For a second I thought you meant his *other* sister, Shannon. Who of course is my sister too. We're all sisters. And brothers. Bobby is our brother. Right?" She giggled nervously.

Dodger gave her a strange look. Courtney smiled innocently. A few minutes later they were walking along Fifty-seventh Street headed for the shops on Madison Avenue.

"Here's a swell place," Dodger suggested as they walked by a small boutique with posed mannequins wearing flowered dresses like the one Courtney was wearing.

Courtney kept walking.

They came upon another storefront that displayed lacy clothes and large, straw hats with oversize flowers on them.

"Lots of gals like this place and—"

Courtney kept walking. Dodger shrugged and followed. They passed by several other stores that catered to women and girls. Courtney didn't want anything to do with them.

"What exactly are you looking for?" Dodger finally asked.

"I don't know," Courtney admitted. "Something less . . . Barbie."

Dodger frowned. "I got no idea what that means, but maybe you should go someplace that's got a little bit of everything."

"Is there a place like that?" Courtney asked.

Fifteen minutes and a short subway ride later, Courtney stepped up to the entrance of "the World's Largest Department Store" on Thirty-fourth Street. Macy's. The same Macy's she knew from home, that had all sorts of everything, including a parade on Thanksgiving. Dodger didn't make the trip because his break was over. That was fine by Courtney. He asked too many questions. She felt that he meant well, in an old-fashioned, "I'm a smart guy who knows best how to take care of a helpless little gal" sort of way, but she didn't need that. Her plan was to avoid Dodger like the plague.

Walking through Macy's was an alien experience. It looked nothing like the Macy's of Second Earth. The clothes were heavy and dark. There was no music. The lighting was dim. The floors were made of wood. Even the escalators had wooden steps. But it was still Macy's, and Courtney knew she'd find what she needed.

She walked past the ladies' and girls' departments and headed straight to menswear. There, as a perplexed salesman wearing a neat suit with a white carnation in the lapel watched in wonder, Courtney bought two pairs of men's woolen pants and a few white, cotton shirts. She also bought socks, a pair of brown leather shoes that were much more comfortable than the ones from the flume, and a pair of green striped suspenders to hold the pants up. She found a gray woolen cap with a short, soft brim that was big enough to tuck all of her long brown hair under. Courtney put her hands in her pockets and admired herself in the mirror.

The salesman scowled. "Halloween was two days ago, young lady."

Courtney smiled. "I think I look pretty good."

She did. Courtney may have been wearing men's clothes, but there was no hiding the fact that she was a girl. The final piece was an oversize, dark green turtleneck sweater that she knew she'd need once the weather got cold. Satisfied, she paid the salesman and headed out.

"What do I do with this?" the salesman called to her. He was holding up the flowered dress that Courtney had worn into the store.

"I don't need it anymore," she said brightly. "Halloween was two days ago."

The salesman gave her a disapproving frown and Courtney went on her way. She had one more chore before beginning her search for Mark in earnest. She traveled a route she had taken many times before, in another era. From Thirty-fourth Street in Manhattan she took a subway train to Grand Central Terminal. The ride cost a nickel. From there, she got on a New Haven Line train, headed for her hometown of Stony Brook, Connecticut. The hour-long trip was familiar yet alien. The train wasn't anywhere near as comfortable as the sleek, shock-absorbed cars of Second Earth. She felt herself bouncing around as if she were on a freight train. There was an incessant squeak and rattle that didn't seem to bother anybody else but her. The constant bouncing was especially annoying because she was trying to read the newspaper.

If she had been tracking Mark on Second Earth, her first stop would have been the Internet. On First Earth all she had were newspapers and the occasional radio news broadcast. At Grand Central Station she bought five different daily papers: the *New York Advocate*, the *Manhattan Gazette*, the *New York Daily Mirror*, the *New York Post* and the *New York Times.* She quickly searched through every paper, desperate to find a mention of Mark Dimond, Andy Mitchell, the Dimond Alpha Digital Organization, or KEM Limited. Her thinking was that if Mark's presentation of the Forge technology was so important, it would have to hit the news, even if it was a small blurb.

She found nothing. The big news item of the day was the mysterious subway derailment in the Bronx. Courtney read that the engineer swore he saw a man jump in front of the speeding train, but no body was recovered. It would forever remain a mystery.

Finding no news of Mark was frustrating and reassuring at

the same time. With nothing in the papers, Courtney hoped the news about Mark's Forge technology hadn't been released yet. She brightened. Maybe there was still hope of pulling it back before the damage was done.

The train pulled into Stony Brook Station. Courtney stepped onto a wooden platform that had been torn down three decades before she was born. She was tempted to take a tour around Stony Brook to see what her hometown looked like so many years before, but decided she didn't have the time. She was there for a very specific purpose. The quicker she got back to New York, the better. It was a short walk from the train station to the main street of Stony Brook, which years later would come to be known as "the Ave" to all the kids. Courtney actually recognized some of the older buildings that no longer looked that old. There was an ice-cream soda fountain that on Second Earth would become a bicycle shop; a barbershop that in her day would become an art gallery; and a vegetable market that one day would be the Apple store where Courtney's parents would buy her an iPod. It was a fascinating and odd trip through the past.

Her destination was the National Bank of Stony Brook. It was the bank where Bobby set up a safe-deposit box to keep the journals he wrote on First Earth. Sixty-some years later on Second Earth, Mark and Courtney would open up that vault to find them. It became the place where Mark kept all Bobby's journals. Now they were entrusted to her, and she wasn't going to do any less of a job than Mark. She had the key on a chain around her neck and she had memorized the account and box number. With absolute confidence she presented the information to the stuffy bank manager, who led her into the vault and left her alone. Inside the safe-deposit box were Bobby's journals from his earlier adventure on First Earth, waiting for her and Mark to discover them on Second Earth.

She had been carrying around a large cloth purse since she left the hotel. In it was Bobby's Journal #28. Courtney added it to the earlier ones and locked the box back up. For a moment she wondered if she and Mark would find this new journal when they opened up the box for the first time on Second Earth. Was that possible? She decided that worrying about how monkeying with history might change the future made her head hurt. She needed to get out of there and back to New York to find Mark.

A few hours later she was back in Manhattan, walking up Park Avenue toward the Manhattan Tower Hotel. It was midafternoon, but the November shadows were already growing long. It would be dark soon. Courtney's plan was to go back to the hotel, eat something at the restaurant, then hide under the covers in Gunny's bed and try to come up with a brilliant plan to find Mark. She got as far as the entrance to the garden in front of the Manhattan Tower, when she felt an odd sensation. She didn't know what it was at first, so she stopped short. Her every sense was on alert. A second later she realized what it was.

Her ring was activating.

She looked around quickly to make sure nobody was watching. Dumb thought. She was in midtown Manhattan. Everybody was watching. The dark stone in the ring was already melting into crystal. She slapped her other hand over the ring to hide it and ran onto the hotel grounds. Frantically she looked about for a place that would give her some cover. She found it among the perfectly manicured trees and bushes. She leaped off the sidewalk into the dense foliage. The ring was growing. She came upon a small clearing that had a marble bench in front of a pond full of gold fish. Nobody was there, which was good, because whether she liked it or not, the ring was about to open up.

She put it on the ground and watched as the silver circle grew to Frisbee size, revealing a tunnel to the territories. Shafts of sparkling light shot from the dark hole, as did the sweet music. Courtney didn't watch. She kept glancing around to make sure nobody else was witnessing this impossible, magic event. It was over in a matter of seconds and Courtney was finally able to breath. Her fear turned to curiosity as she jumped at the ring, ready to grab Bobby's first journal from Ibara. She knelt down to see . . .

It wasn't a journal. It was a gray envelope. Courtney curiously turned it over in her hands. It looked like a regular, old, everyday letter. Why would Bobby send her a letter? She quickly put the ring back on her finger and anxiously ripped open the mysterious envelope. Inside was a single piece of paper with printing. Courtney read it once. Twice. A third time more slowly, making sure she understood every word.

It wasn't from Bobby. It was from Patrick. It was from Third Earth. It was trouble.

Bobby and Courtney,

I am sending this letter to First Earth in hopes that you are there, and that the flume sent you back to a time where you can still affect what happened. After you left Third Earth, I continued my research into what may have happened to Mark Dimond. When you were here, we learned that he disappeared sometime in November. I now know more and must share it with you.

First, I learned that the company KEM Limited was based in London, England. KEM stood for Keaton Electrical Marvels. Company officials there were the first to have reported Mark Dimond missing. He was due to meet with them in London on November 13, 1937. He didn't attend that meeting and was never seen again. There is no mention as to what may have happened to him. Foul play was suspected, but there was no proof of that.

I also found a small article that ran in a newspaper published in southern New Jersey. On November 20, 1937, a body washed up on shore in Atlantic City. It was a male who was so badly decomposed it was impossible to identify him, though the cause of death was clear. He didn't drown. He was shot. Oddly enough, he was wearing a tuxedo. In his pocket was a silver spoon that was engraved: RMS Queen Mary.

Bobby, Courtney, I found a record that stated Mark Dimond booked passage and left for London aboard the ocean liner Queen Mary on November 7. The implication is frightening. The coincidence is too great. I'm afraid that Mark Dimond never made it to London. I fear he was killed aboard the Queen Mary and his body dumped overboard.

If that's the case, then your goal is clear. You've got to get to Mark before November 7 and stop him from boarding, because somebody on that ship means him harm.

If I learn any more I will send it to you. I hope you've received this. Good luck.

Patrick Mac

"So that's how it works," came a voice.

Courtney jumped and yelped. Somebody had been watching her. She quickly crumpled Patrick's note, shoved it in her pocket and stood up to face . . . Dodger.

"Y-You're spying on me," Courtney said angrily, her voice cracking. Her head was spinning. Too much was happening too fast.

"Sorry," Dodger said. "I saw you walking toward the hotel then suddenly get all snaky and run into the bushes. What can I say? I was concerned."

Courtney froze. How much had he seen? Dodger seemed troubled. He looked at her as if wanting to say something, but couldn't find the right words. She decided the best way to deal with him was to get away.

"Don't spy on me," she said sharply, and started to walk.

"Wait!" Dodger exclaimed.

Courtney stopped, waiting for him to make the next move.

"Gunny's my pal," he said in the voice of a frightened little boy. "He's one of the good guys. There's nothing I wouldn't do for him."

Courtney didn't respond. She didn't know where Dodger was going.

"Before he left for wherever it was he went, he asked me for a favor. He never asked favors of nobody, so I figured it had to be important. He told me there might come a time when he'd need my help. He wasn't specific or nothin', he just said he had an important job to do. Him and Pendragon and Spader. You know what he was talking about?"

Courtney did, of course, but she didn't say.

"Anyhow, he said he was gonna leave for a while, but there might come a time when somebody came here looking for help. He asked me to do what I could for 'em. Of course I said I'd do it. I'd do anything for Gunny. But when I asked what it was all about, he said he hoped I'd never have to know. Now I'm thinking it's time I know."

"Why's that?" Courtney asked.

Dodger lifted his hand. He was wearing a silver band around one finger. He twisted it, showing Courtney that he was wearing it backward. When he spun it around, Courtney gasped.

It was a Traveler ring.

"He asked me to be his acolyte. I got no idea what that means, but I've been wearing this ring ever since. Then all of a sudden Pendragon comes back with you, and you've got one of these rings, and I just saw yours spew out sparks like it was the Fourth of July. I'm thinking it's time I found out what Gunny was talking about."

Courtney's mind raced. What should she do? She definitely needed an ally, but was he telling the truth? She trusted a stranger once before and it nearly killed her. Was Dodger exactly what he said he was? An innocent friend that Gunny chose to be his acolyte? Or was there something sinister going on? Was this another disguise of Saint Dane's?

"I just want to do what Gunny asked," he said sincerely. "I want to help you."

"Are you Saint Dane?" Courtney asked, point blank. "Not that I think you'd tell me if you were, but I figure I have to ask, just to let you know I'm thinking you might be."

Dodger gave her a puzzled look. "Saint Dane? You mean like the dog? Or is that Saint Bernard? Or Great Dane? I'm more confused now than a second ago."

Courtney didn't know what to do. Confide in Dodger? Blow him off? Run away and never look back? She knew she needed to make a decision, but couldn't.

A second later the decision was made for her.

"You're telling me you have no idea what this is all about?" she asked.

"Not a clue," Dodger said.

"Then here's your first," Courtney said, lifting up her hand. It was the hand with her ring. The stone was glowing again.

Dodger's eyes grew wide, "What the—"

Bobby's next journal was about to arrive.

IBARA

I hope you're reading this, Courtney.

And I hope you're doing okay. I guess that's an understatement. It killed me to leave you alone on First Earth. I wish there was another way, but I'm not smart enough to think of one. I'm glad that Dodger is still at the hotel. He comes on a little strong, but you can trust him. Gunny did. If you need anything, don't think twice about asking him.

In spite of feeling bad about leaving you alone to find Mark, it was a good thing I came to Ibara. I still haven't pieced together what Saint Dane is doing here, but there's one thing I'm sure of: The turning point is close. I don't know what it is yet, but some of the things I've seen make me believe that this territory is in for a big change. Maybe a scary one. As I write this journal, I've been here for about a week. With every new bit of information I learn, five more questions pop up. Nothing is as it seems, but I think I've found a way to start putting the pieces of the puzzle together. I'm about to take off on an adventure and do something I never thought possible.

I'm going to become an outlaw.

I know, not exactly good news, but I think it's the best

way to put myself square in the middle of the conflict that will lead to the turning point of Ibara. That's why I'm writing this journal now. I don't know when I'll get another chance, because tomorrow it's all going to hit the fan.

Let me get you up to speed with what's happened since I left the Manhattan Tower Hotel. My trip to Ibara was nothing out of the ordinary.

My arrival was.

I left Gunny's apartment before you woke up. We said our good-byes the night before, and I couldn't go through that agony again. I traveled by cab to the Bronx subway station to find that the city transit workers had already cleared the wreck. Subway service had been returned to normal. I snuck down onto the tracks and made my way back to the gate quickly. I wasn't worried about quigs or dados or anything else that might stop me from getting to Ibara. When Saint Dane wanted me somewhere, I got there. Without so much as stopping for a moment to think about what I might find on the new territory, I opened the wooden door, marched right into the flume and announced *"Ibara!"* I think I was afraid that if I hesitated, I'd change my mind. The door barely had time to close behind me before I was swept up and carried off.

My head was in a strange place . . . along with the rest of me. Since I was once again on my own, I had the chance to think. That's always a dangerous thing. I'm much better reacting to situations. When my mind wanders, my thoughts invariably go to the larger questions. The questions I have no answers for. On top of that list is the fact that Saint Dane told me the Travelers were illusions. Illusions. What the heck did that mean? I sure didn't feel like an illusion, though I'm not exactly sure how an illusion should feel. Was he using the word as a metaphor, like we weren't who we seemed to be? Or did he mean it literally?

He said I wasn't an advanced Traveler. Meaning I couldn't shape-shift into other beings. People, birds, smoke. Yeesh. But Nevva Winter could. He said he taught her. Was it as simple as that? With a couple of lessons and a little homework could I learn how to become somebody else? That would be a handy little tool. But even without the ability to transform myself, there are a few realities about being a Traveler that I have no explanation for. We heal easily. Not instantly, but easily. We can influence people's thoughts, though I have to admit, I was never very good at that. And of course the most disturbing truth of all is that Loor was killed, and through whatever force of will I possessed, I brought her back from the dead.

Knowing those few things makes me wonder if what Saint Dane said about illusions might somehow be true. I mean, I feel totally human. But humans don't come back from the dead. Are we flesh and blood? Or something else? Trouble is, I have no idea what that something else might be. Maybe there are some people who think it would be cool to shape-shift and turn into other beings. I'm not one of them. The concept is way more interesting than the reality. I'm Bobby Pendragon. I was born on Second Earth. I have a great mother and father. I have a little sister. I'm normal. I want to stay normal. I don't want to be an illusion.

I try not to think about it too often. One thing at a time. One challenge at a time. One crisis at a time. Thinking about it all was making me too anxious. I was tired of thinking. I wanted some action.

I heard the musical notes grow louder, signaling I was near the end of my journey. But there was another sound. One I hadn't heard at the end of a flume ride before. It sounded like white noise that grew louder as I got closer to Ibara. I didn't have long to wonder what it might be, because seconds after I heard it, I was underwater.

There was no warning. One second I was sailing along, the next I was wet. The force of my landing shot water up my nose, as if I had jumped off a high dive, feet first, without holding my nose. The pain wasn't my worst problem. I couldn't breathe, because, well, I was underwater. I was about to drown. I actually wondered if the inhabitants of Ibara were fish and changed my mind about not wanting to be able to transform into other beings. Sprouting gills and turning into a flounder would have helped just then. I didn't know which way was up, or how deep I was. I knew if I didn't get my wits back, I'd be done in seconds. I relaxed, and let a little precious air out of my lungs to see which way the bubbles would float. They drifted past my eyes toward a wide circle of light. That had to be the surface. I kicked for it.

I'm happy to say that I was only a few feet down. I quickly broke the surface, gasping for air. I was okay, except for the pounding headache from the nasal enema. I blew the water out of my head and took a quick look around. I was treading water in the middle of a round cauldron made from black rock in an underground cave. The big pool of water was about twenty feet across. I quickly kicked to the side and held on to the rocky edge to catch my breath. I was safe. I had made it. I was on Ibara.

The entire cavern was made out of the same black, volcanic-looking rock as the pool. The ceiling wasn't high like the big gate on Cloral. This was a smallish cave, with a biggish vat of water taking up most of the floor. I had to conclude that this round pool of water was the flume. Yup, the flume was full of water. Was it possible that the inhabitants of Ibara were fish after all?

I hoisted myself out of the pool. The sides were about two feet high, forming a ring of craggy rocks that made the pool seem like a minivolcano. I swung one leg up and over to discover the floor outside the pool was sand. Not dirt, sand. I sat down on the soft surface and took another look around. Light seeped in through long cracks in the cavern walls that were randomly spaced all around me. That meant this cave wasn't far underground. Or underwater. My clothes from First Earth were soaked of course, but I wasn't at all cold. If anything, I was feeling kind of hot and sticky. Glancing around I saw a small pile of colorful clothes not far from where I was sitting. There were a couple of pairs of shorts that looked like board shorts. They were longer than board shorts though. It looked like they would come down below my knees. I wondered if maybe they were actually supposed to be long pants and the people of Ibara were little. If so, I'd be a giant on Ibara. Or at least a really tall guy. That would be cool. I've always been kind of medium. I wouldn't have minded being the tall guy for once. The pants were simple, with no zippers or buttons, just a drawstring. The material was light and cottonlike, with no tags inside. These simple shorts told me that on some level, the people of Ibara were civilized.

There were three pairs, each a different bright solid color: red, orange, and green. After Quillan I never wanted to wear anything red again, so I peeled off my wet First Earth clothing and put on a pair of bright green shorts. They fit perfectly, of course. I debated about wearing my boxer shorts but figured they'd be too obvious. So I went jungle.

There was also a pile of shirts. At least I thought they were shirts. They looked more like vests—no sleeves. I couldn't tell which was the front and which was the back. I figured it didn't matter. I picked out a green one that sort of matched the green color of the shorts and slipped it over my head. It fit loosely, which was good, because it was hot on Ibara. Tropical hot. If I learned anything from the clothing, it was that the people were pretty casual and lived in a warm tropical climate.

Oh, and they weren't fish.

The last touch were shoes, or what looked like shoes. There were a couple pairs of sandals that looked woven out of some natural material. I picked a pair that fit perfectly. They slipped between my toes like flip-flops, but there were also little bands that fit over my heels and kept them from truly being flip-flops. They were comfortable, and more practical than flip-flops. If I had to, I could run in them. I was ready. It was time to get out of there.

I wanted to see Ibara.

Scanning the rocky walls, I saw several wide cracks that ran vertically from the sandy floor. Some looked wide enough to squeeze through. I poked my head into a few, only to find a rocky dead end. I continued to search the perimeter of the cavern, feeling sure that one of these rough openings would be the way out. As I explored, I became more aware of sounds. I heard the same white noise as I had when I was still in the flume. Whatever it was, it came from beyond the walls of this cave. There was also another sound. It was a faint, far-off hum. I could barely hear it, but it was there. Constant. Steady. Mysterious.

I had nearly made my way completely around the perimeter when I found it—the way out. It was an opening that was larger than the others, which was the first giveaway. The second was the sandy floor that stretched inside. This was definitely the route away from the flume. I left the cave and found myself in a twisting, dark tunnel. It was so narrow I had to turn sideways a few times to fit my shoulders through. Every so often the route opened into another small cave before narrowing down again. I passed a few intersections and had to guess which route to take. The winding passageways started feeling like a maze. I made one turn, walked several feet, and hit a dead end. It was a very complicated series of tunnels. That was good because it would prevent people from accidentally discovering the flume. On the other hand it made it tough to get the heck out.

As I walked along, I heard the humming grow louder. I passed through one rock opening and heard the sound more distinctly. A few times I made a turn and the sound dimmed. My curiosity about Ibara continued to grow. The twisting caverns were dark. Every so often a crack of light appeared to help me on my way, but mostly I had to walk slowly, with my hands out in front for fear of introducing nose to rock.

Finally I made a turn and sensed movement. It was fast. So fast I thought I imagined it. It was a quick streak of light that was there for an instant, then gone. I stopped and looked up, but saw nothing. A few steps later I sensed another movement of light. By the time my eyes went to it, it was over. It was like trying to see a shooting star. Unless you were staring right at it the instant it flashed by, you'd miss it.

The white noise grew louder too. It seemed like I was getting closer to the outside. I made a turn and found myself at the mouth of a cavern that was slightly smaller than the cavern with the flume. I instantly noticed the change in sound. The humming was much louder. So loud, in fact, that it drowned out the white noise. Whatever was doing all the humming, I was close to it.

This cavern wasn't as dark as the rest of the labyrinth. It had a warm, inviting glow. The light that bled through the cracks from outside was white, like daylight. But the light that filled this cavern was golden. I figured it had to be some kind of phosphorous. I took a step through the opening and scanned the cavern, looking for the next opening to continue my journey. As soon as my eyes adjusted to the warm glow, I saw it. The vertical crack was directly opposite me on the far side of the cavern. That was the exit.

I can't say why, but as soon as I recognized the way out, I was hit with a feeling of dread. Nothing had happened. Nothing changed. It was just an uneasy feeling. Some sixth sense told me this cavern was a bad place. I wanted to get out, fast, and started for the far side. When I got halfway across, the humming suddenly stopped. Just like that. Silence. All I heard was the white noise. What had stopped it? Better question, what the heck was making it in the first place? I felt as if my sudden movement through the cavern had made the sound end. But how? Was it something mechanical? Had I crossed a trigger that turned the machine off?

The little hairs on the back of my neck stood up. I wasn't sure if I should keep moving or stand still. I decided to wait for something to happen. It wasn't a long wait. The golden glow that painted the room began to grow brighter. The humming returned. It was low at first, but as the light grew, so did the humming. The steady drone became louder as the light grew around me. The warm light.

The yellow light.

Something flashed in front of me. A yellow streak of light that was gone as quickly as it arrived. The same kind of streak I'd sensed farther back in the tunnels. This time I saw it. Another streak streaked by. It shot in front of me, stopped, and flashed back the other way. Fast. Whatever it was, it was under control. Another shot past, close to my face. I heard a sharp buzz. It wasn't phosphorous. It was some kind of bug, like a firefly. Another flew past, then another. The yellow light grew brighter. The humming sound grew louder. I realized it wasn't a humming sound. It was a buzzing sound. The light grew brighter, as if a large overhead lamp were ramping up to illuminate the cavern. Slowly I looked directly overhead to see a wondrous sight.

The entire ceiling of the cavern was sparkling. It was like the rock was decked with thousands of yellow Christmas lights. It was dazzling. The ceiling was coming alive. Was this some strange, natural power source? Was it chemical? Electrical? Was it—

"Ouch!" Something stung my leg. I quickly brushed it off and saw it was one of the fireflies. The little creeps stung like bees!

"Ow!" Another one hit me on the left shoulder, and it hurt! Another buzzed by my face. Two more buzzed my head. A sick reality hit me. The light on the ceiling wasn't chemical or electrical. It wasn't there as a friendly, warm canopy to guide my way. No, the ceiling was covered with thousands of little banshees. They were firing up. They were buzzing louder. They gave off a yellow glow. It all added up to one, horrifying conclusion.

Quigs.

The quigs on Ibara were bees. As if on cue, the ceiling came to life. The quig-bees dove down like a swarm of angry, burning fireflies. They were headed for me! I took off running for the cleft on the far side. The swirling storm of quigs chased me like an angry, glowing cloud. There was no way I could outrun them. My only hope was to make it to the mouth of this cavern, and outside, before they caught me. I hoped daylight would stop them. I hit the cleft, bashing my shoulder into the rock, but I didn't stop. I barely felt it. Fear will do that. Any thought of caution was gone as I desperately danced through the twisting cavern. I could hear the bees grow louder, like a buzz saw at my heels.

Ahead I saw the tunnel was growing brighter. I had to be nearing the end.

A quig stung my back. Then another. Why they didn't all attack at once, I didn't know. I didn't care. It only made me run faster.

The tunnel grew brighter. The entrance was near. I had to get there. I had to get out. I had to get to the light. I had to hope the killer bugs wouldn't follow. It was the only chance I had. Three more stings came quickly. It was like being stabbed with needles. I didn't swat at them. That would have slowed me down.

I rounded a bend and saw it, the bright opening to the cave. The entrance to Ibara. My only hope for safety. I had made it. I was going to get out of the cave and into the light before the quigs did any serious damage.

Good news was, I made it out.

Bad news was, it didn't matter.

I broke out into the open to find myself on a beach. Ahead was a calm, green ocean that looked like a postcard for the Caribbean. I sensed tall palm trees swaying in the breeze, the sweet smell of tropical flowers, and gentle, rolling surf. That was the white noise—the surf. The rocky cave that held the flume was near this ocean. When I ran into the light I was no more than thirty yards from the water's edge. I sprinted through the sand, headed for the shore. My plan was to dive into the surf and get underwater to protect myself from the quig-bees.

I didn't make it. The quigs attacked. All of them. Being in the sunlight didn't stop them. If anything, it made them bolder.

Now that we were outside, they no longer seemed like yellow, glowing fireflies. They now looked like nasty black bees. Swarming bees. Angry bees. I was hit from behind by what felt like a small wave. The stinging pain soon followed. Like hundreds of burning little needles, the quigs jabbed their stingers into me. They swarmed my legs. For a second it actually tickled the hair. A very short second. The pain followed. It was like they all stung at once. It's hard to describe the pain because it was like nothing I had ever experienced. They swarmed my head. There were so many of them that the bright beach seemed to grow dark. It was like being enveloped in a dark cocoon. I tried to bat them away. It was futile. There were too many. Instead I covered up. I didn't want them getting at my eyes.

They stung my arms. Hundreds and hundreds of times. It was like getting hit with drops of burning acid. They stung my cheeks and my nose. I felt sharp stings on my ears and under my arms. I wanted to open my mouth to scream, but feared they would fly inside.

The buzzing was deafening. They had me. I was theirs. The pain was so intense, I stopped feeling it. My brain must have shut down. I went into pain overload. I grew dizzy. Whatever poison their stings were unloading into me was doing its job. I staggered, trying to keep moving toward the water, in hope that I could dive in and shake them. No go. I was too far away. The beach started to spin. The buzzing was everything. I dropped down to one knee, fighting to stay conscious, though I'm not sure why. Conscious meant torture. I had to give in to the poison. It was a relief.

My last thought was that there was no way I could be an illusion. An illusion could never hurt so bad.

And everything went black.

IBARA

I was swimming again.

At least that's what it felt like. I drifted, weightless, not sure of up or down or in between. I could breathe, too. For a second I thought maybe I'd grown those gills after all. In that dreamlike state, nothing seemed strange. I was hanging out somewhere south of nowhere, and not minding it one single bit.

It didn't last. My first clue that I was returning to reality was the weight. My body felt heavy. Impossibly heavy. It was like I was living in somebody else's skin. I didn't like it much. I felt paralyzed. And hot. Very hot. It was like I was wrapped tight in an itchy wool blanket but couldn't lift my arms to scratch. Not that I would have known what to scratch anyway. I was one, massive burning itch. I eventually became aware enough to realize I was lying down and my eyes were closed. It was too much of an effort to crack them open, so I decided not to try. I was afraid of what I might see. My head felt like some guy had his hands on either side and was squeezing. I thought about telling whoever it was to back off, but my lips wouldn't open. They were stuck shut. I swallowed. Ouch. Sandpaper throat.

Reality slowly slipped in. I kind of wish it hadn't. The more aware I became, the more I realized how hurting I was. I finally cracked one eye open. The light was painful. I forced myself to look around. I'm not sure why I bothered—there wasn't much to see. I was on my back staring up at a sea of grass. Yes, grass. I tried to focus, but I was too uncomfortable to think about anything except how uncomfortable I was. Besides the head squeeze, I felt as if I had an Olympic case of poison ivy. No, poison oak. That's worse. If there's anything worse than poison oak, that's what it felt like. But it wasn't poison oak. It was the bees. The quig-bees. I was aware enough to remember those buggers. I looked down at my arm to see it was covered in red, hideous welts. Stings. Ouch. I had been stung more times than I could count. Note to self: Avoid mirrors. That would be ugly. I figured I'd look like that "It's clobberin' time!" guy from the *Fantastic Four.* I'd just as soon pass on that image, thank you very much. As bad as I felt, I realized there was something good in all this. I was alive. I would heal. I was good at that. What I didn't know was where I had landed, and how I got there.

"You're awake," came a soft, feminine voice.

That was nice. Soft and feminine was nice. She didn't sound like a fish, either. I cracked my eye open again and she came into view, looming over me, upside down. She looked into my eyes. Or eye. I first noticed her hair. It was long and dark red. She had it pulled back and tied with a yellow ribbon. Very practical. Her eyes were green. I'd never seen such deep green eyes. They could have been colored contact lenses, that's how stunning they were. She was pretty, I guessed. It was hard to tell, looking at someone upside down and with one eye.

As she looked at me, I saw the worry in those green eyes. Worry was good. I was pretty worried myself. At least we were on the same page.

"How long?" I croaked.

"You've been asleep for three days. We've given you medicine to make you sleep. You have to heal. You were very lucky."

"Really?" I groaned, trying to sound sarcastic.

She smiled. She got it.

"The venom from the bee stings isn't fatal, unless you're allergic. I'm guessing you're not, or you'd be dead."

Good guess.

"You've got to keep still until the poison passes through your system."

Fine. Whatever. The last thing I wanted to do was get up. Or walk. Or talk. Or anything else that involved movement or thought. That pretty much ruled out everything but sleep.

"I've never seen so many stings," she said with concern. "Did you do something to aggravate the bees?"

I wondered how she would have reacted if I'd told her that they were mutant bees sent by a demon from another territory to attack me because I was there to stop him from destroying her world. I decided to keep that to myself.

"No," I croaked.

"Drink this," she said, and held a small cup to my lips. I had to lift my aching head. Ouch. I took a few swallows, though more dribbled down my chin than my throat.

"You're healing remarkably fast. I've never seen anything like it."

I had.

"A little more sleep and you'll be up on your feet so we can begin."

"Begin what?" I asked.

She leaned down and said, "We've got to learn who you are, and why you're on Ibara."

Oh. That.

Whatever she gave me was already making me drowsy. I was swimming again. I liked it. Before I got back into the pool, I forced my eye open one more time and asked, "What's your name?"

"Telleo."

Telleo. Nice name. Nice hair. Nice to know somebody was taking care of me, whoever she was.

"Thank you, Telleo."

She gave me a warm smile. "And what is your name?"

That was an easy one. The tougher questions would come later. I was going to have to come up with some answers. But not just then. I had to go swimming. "It's Pendragon. Good night."

When I woke up, I felt much better. Not good. Better. The nasty, burning itch had settled into a seminasty, burning itch. The hundreds of bee stings had scabbed over. Sometimes it's good to be a Traveler. I wondered how long it would take a non-Traveler to recover from that kind of an attack. Don't get me wrong, I was still a mess. But I could function.

"Can you sit up?" came a familiar voice. Telleo appeared at the foot of my bed.

"I think," I croaked. "How long did I sleep this time?"

"Two days. I stopped giving you the medication this morning. It's time for you to rejoin us."

I was so stiff I could barely move. I wasn't sure if that was because of the bee stings, or because I had been lying there for five days. Probably both.

"Oil can," I murmured through clenched teeth.

"Excuse me?"

"Nothing." I had to stop making Second Earth jokes.

When Telleo helped me sit up, my head went light. "Whoa, not good," I babbled.

She eased me back down. "Let's try that again later."

I lay on my back and stared at the ceiling. It was made of woven, green grass. I hadn't imagined it before. I really was seeing grass. It was a simple cottage with wooden walls. I was lying on a bed that was about a foot off the wooden floor. The mattress was comfortable, but thin. The door was crudely fashioned out of lengths of something that looked like bamboo. The furniture was simple, straight and wooden. There were a few chairs and a table made out of the same bamboo-looking stuff as the door. The table was loaded with earthen jugs of various sizes. I figured these contained the medicine Telleo had been giving me. From what I could see, there weren't any other rooms. This was it. On first glance the place looked like a primitive hut.

On second glance I saw things that didn't fit the rustic profile. There was a tube of light that ran the length of each wall near the ceiling, like a neon bulb. These people didn't rely on fire for light. They had power. Though we were inside, there was a soft breeze. I looked across the room to see a series of fan blades, built into a frame, turning slowly. Again, they were powered. The final weirdness came when Telleo walked to the table of earthen jugs, reached to the far side, and picked up a small, cream-colored device that looked like a bar of soap.

She touched it a few times and spoke into it. "He is awake," she said.

It was a telephone. I watched as she mixed together a concoction in the earthen jugs. She was a small girl, not much taller than five feet. She was light skinned, but tan. She wore a short, yellow dress that seemed to be made from the same material as my clothes. It was kind of the same style, too, with a loose, sleeveless top. She also wore the same kind of sandals. I guessed she was older than I was, but not by much.

As I watched her work, I wondered how big a part she was going to play in my adventure on Ibara. Would she be a friend? An enemy? Or would her role end as soon as I left this place?

"Hungry?" she asked, bringing me a brown mug of something.

"I don't want to go back to sleep."

"You won't. This is broth. You need to get your strength back."

I took the cup gratefully and sipped. It was warm, salty, and good. It tasted like chicken soup. I guess it doesn't matter where or when you are, chicken soup is the universal tonic. As I sipped, Telleo went back to work at her table. She busied herself with whatever she was doing, but kept stealing curious looks at me. She had no idea who I was or where I came from. I, on the other hand, had no idea where I was or how I got there. Between the two of us, we were pretty clueless. I needed to learn about Ibara, but had to choose my questions carefully.

"Thank you for taking care of me," I said.

"You're welcome. It's my job."

"You're a doctor?"

"I assist the doctors."

"So this is a hospital?"

"No, it is a community hut used by the tribunal."

Tribunal. I was beginning to learn. I still had no idea what kind of society this was. From what I'd seen of this small hut, it was a weird mix of the primitive and the modern. The thought hit me that this might actually be some kind of vacation resort.

You know, where people spend loads of bucks to stay in authentic huts and pretend like they're roughing it.

"You were brought to the village by a group of fishermen who saw the attack," she explained. "If they hadn't arrived and sprayed the bees, there's no telling how badly you would have been hurt."

"So I guess I really *was* lucky," I declared.

Telleo looked like she wanted to say something, but wasn't sure if she should.

"What?" I asked.

She looked around, as if making sure we were alone, then quickly knelt down by me. When she spoke, the words came quickly, like she didn't have enough time.

"Where did you come from?" she asked curiously. "I know you aren't from here."

She wasn't being aggressive or anything. She seemed genuinely curious. Trouble was, I had no idea of how to answer. It was time to get vague.

"You're right. I'm not from here."

I figured that was about as generic and truthful an answer as I could risk.She looked at me with wide, innocent eyes. She suddenly seemed much younger than I first thought. It was like talking to a naive little girl.

"But there was no boat," she countered. "At least not where the fishermen found you. They searched the beach."

"There are other ways to travel," I said, again being vague.

She gave me a curious look. "I don't understand. How else could you get here without a boat?"

I didn't mention the flume. My answer was a noncommittal shrug.

"There is so much I don't know," she said, mostly to herself. She looked at me and her eyes grew sharp. "Some thought you should be left on the beach to die. I wouldn't let them. We aren't savages."

"Nice to know. Thank you," I said sincerely.

"Don't thank me," she said. "Tell me the truth. Are you a Flighter?"

Gulp. Flighter? I had no idea. Was it good or bad to be a Flighter? I decided to be vague again. "I didn't come here to cause trouble. That's the absolute truth."

Telleo stared at me for a long moment, as if trying to decide whether she believed me. Finally she gave me a relieved smile. "I didn't think so. You don't seem at all like a Flighter. I'm glad."

Phew. Me too. Note to self: Flighters = Bad.

She stood up, excited again. "So tell me where you're from. I've never been much farther than the border of Rayne. There must be so much to see. I hear stories, but it's not the same as seeing things for yourself."

Rayne. What was that? I wished I could have just asked, but that would raise too many questions in return.

"I'd like to go outside," I said, ducking the question.

Telleo bit her lip nervously. "That's not wise."

I forced myself to sit up, more slowly this time. "Why not? I'm feeling better. I think I can—"

The door burst open. Three men strode in, each wearing the same kind of clothes I had on. They stood together, glaring at me. Glaring was bad. They were all about my size, or bigger, which meant I wasn't going to be the tall guy. Oh well. They all had long hair, nearly to their waists. They wore leather straps around their middles, like belts. Tucked into these were short, wooden clubs. Weapons. One on each hip. This was not a welcoming committee.

Telleo faced them boldly, her legs apart. "He shouldn't be

moved yet." She tried to sound all bad, but she didn't have it in her.

The guy in the center, the biggest of the three, stepped past her and looked down his nose at me like I was a disease.

"You are under arrest," he growled.

Oh. Great. I'd only been awake on Ibara for a few minutes and I was already in trouble. I didn't want to challenge his authority, so I didn't stand up. "Why?" I asked innocently. "I didn't do anything wrong."

"And you won't get the chance," he spat back.

"You can't arrest me for something I *might* do wrong," I complained.

"He's not a Flighter," Telleo argued. "He doesn't mean any harm."

The big guy gave her a steely look. "And how would you know that?"

Telleo said sincerely, "Because he told me, and I believe him."

Yeah, go Telleo!

The guy smirked. I hate smirks. "And that's why you care for the sick, and we handle security."

Telleo wouldn't back down. "He must stay until he gets his strength back."

"Strength is the *last* thing we want him to have," the big guy snarled.

He motioned to his two pals. They strode quickly toward me. Uh-oh. Before I had a chance to react, they each grabbed one of my arms and yanked me to my feet. I didn't fight. I couldn't. My head was too busy spinning.

"Please!" Telleo begged. "He is ill."

"Your duty is complete, Telleo," the big guy barked. "Return to the medical section and forget you ever saw this man."

"Whoa, no!" I shouted. "Don't forget me, Telleo. They can't arrest me if I didn't do anything. That's not how you live here, right? You're not savages, remember? You don't let people die and you don't hurt innocent people."

It was getting scary. This suddenly had all the makings of a mob hit. No questions, no trial, no trail. The scabby guy gets taken away and is never seen again. I wanted to fight back, but didn't have the strength. Heck, I could barely see straight.

"Don't worry," Telleo said as they pulled me toward the door. "The tribunal will understand. If you've done nothing wrong they will just send you away."

I didn't know what "away" meant. Heck, I didn't even know what "here" meant. I didn't know much of anything except I was being dragged away by three thugs who thought I was guilty until proven innocent. But of what?

She gave me a sad, helpless smile. I wondered if I would see her again.

"Thank you," I said.

The big guy kicked the door open, and I was pulled out of the hut to get my first real view of Ibara—the world I was supposed to try and protect from Saint Dane. The world that had already branded me a criminal.

IBARA

"Paradise."

I'm not sure what other word could better describe Ibara. It was paradise. Of course it was a paradise where I was nearly stung to death by a swarm of killer bees and arrested for crimes I didn't commit. Other than that, it was paradise.

I was taken from the hut where Telleo had been caring for me and pulled roughly across flat sand. I didn't resist. There were three of them and one of me. Worse, I was operating at about 20 percent. I went along quietly while trying to take in my surroundings. I wanted to learn as much about Ibara as I could. It wasn't easy. The three guys who arrested me weren't exactly acting like tour guides. I had to see what I could while being dragged through town.

Yes, town. Maybe it would be more accurate to call it a tropical village. There were no tall buildings, only wooden huts with grass roofs, like the one I'd been recovering in. There were hundreds of them in all sizes, lined up in orderly rows that created streets of sand. The huts were set back from these sandy pathways with lots of space between them. Instead of yards, the huts were surrounded by green leafy plants that were dotted with an amazing array of colorful flowers—bright reds, deep blues, brilliant oranges, and many more, all gleaming in the tropical sun. It looked as if each hut were resting in its own colorful nest. It smelled like a flower shop, but not in an overpowering, sweet way. The air just smelled fresh.

There were no vehicles. Everyone was on foot. Some people hung out in front of the huts, reading. Others carried baskets of food or large containers filled with I-don't-know-what. I saw people working to repair huts and weaving fresh grass into the roofs. Others were building new huts. Everyone wore variations of the simple clothing I had found at the flume. Many of the men didn't wear shirts or shoes. Some women wore short dresses. All the clothing was colorful and light. There were lots of kids, too, running around acting like, well, like kids.

The village was built on the shore of a calm, green ocean. A wide beach of powder-white sand separated the huts from the water. I only got a quick glance but saw several boats of all sizes floating just off shore. Some looked like small fishing boats, others were under sail. There were people fishing on shore, too, using long poles. The circular beach curved around, forming a huge bay, the entrance to which looked about a few hundred yards wide. The water inside was as calm as a lake. Beyond the entrance to the bay were the white lines of waves. That meant open sea. Huts were built all along the curve of the beach. It wasn't crowded, though. There was plenty of greenery, with trees and bushes and flowers. Tall palm trees provided much-needed shade from the killer-hot sun.

The village was built in what seemed like a pretty sweet spot. On one side was the vast, protected bay. On the other, looming high over the village, was a majestic green mountain that rose to a sharp peak. High above on the mountain's face I saw multiple waterfalls cutting the lush surface. At its base were more huts built onto its gently rising slope. Sounding like paradise yet?

It wasn't a small village. It was more like a tropical city that was completely protected by water on one side and a spectacular mountain on the other. It seemed like a perfect fishing village. Still, there were enough odd touches that made it seem a little off. I couldn't get a feel for how advanced this civilization was. Were these simple fishermen who spent their lives picking fruit and catching what they needed from the sea? Or was there more? There had to be, based on the technology I was seeing. Besides the telephone that Telleo used and the lights in the hut, there were lights in the trees of the village. That meant they had power. I also saw that some people were tending the flowers around their huts by spraying water from hoses. That meant they had plumbing. I already told you that I saw people reading books, which meant they had the ability to print.

There were other signs that didn't jump out at first, but the more I thought about them, the less sense they made. The people weren't of any particular race. I saw every skin and hair color you could imagine. They had a wide mix of facial features too. This definitely wasn't a single race of people. I'm no anthropologist, but you'd think if this were a secluded village built by a single tribe, everybody would have the same general look. They didn't. These people definitely came from different parts of Ibara. I actually started to think that maybe the idea of this being a resort might not be so far-fetched. It fit all the criteria: beautiful setting, awesome beach, a mix of different people, boats, fishing, killer weather, and all the comforts of home. The only thing missing was a boat pulling some water skiers and some guy playing a steel drum. There was only one problem with this theory.

At resorts people didn't get abducted and falsely arrested. That would seriously ruin a vacation.

Most of what I described here I saw in the few minutes I was being dragged through the village. I tried to take it all in, while the people we passed were looking back at me with just as much interest. And why not? It must have been a sight to see three men dragging a dazed, scab-encrusted guy through the streets. A few bystanders applauded and yelled encouragement to my abductors.

"Nice work!" "Thank you!" "Wonderful!"

What was up with that? What had I done? Was it a crime to get munched by a swarm of bees?

"Where are we going?" I asked as we moved quickly through the sandy streets.

"You'll be brought before the tribunal," the big guy answered gruffly. "They'll decide what to do with you."

Tribunal. That sounded official. I figured I had better start forming a plausible story as to who I was and why I was there. It seemed like the best thing that could happen to me was to be sent away. At least that's what Telleo said. I didn't want to think about what the worst thing might be.

"Help! Thief!" came a woman's cry.

Instantly two young guys ran out from a cross street in front of us. They each carried cloth sacks and were running away like, well, like thieves. They looked to be a little younger than I was. One had long dark curly hair and dark skin, the other's hair was long and blond. Neither wore shirts or sandals. Both were laughing as if they had just gotten away with the crime of the century. They turned in our direction, saw us, stopped short . . . and stopped laughing.

"Uh-oh," the blond guy gasped.

They took off running in the other direction. My captors stood frozen, not sure what to do.

"Maybe you should go after some *real* criminals," I suggested.

"Go!" The big guy barked at the others. "I can handle him."

The other two bolted after the thieves. It was now one-on-one. Me against the big guy. I'm embarrassed to say that he was right. He was definitely able to handle me. He slipped a thin cord around my wrist and pulled it tight. He grabbed my other arm, pulled it behind my back and looped the other end of the cord around it, handcuffing me. He knew what he was doing. He pushed me forward and I stumbled on. We passed the street that the two thieves had run down in time to see the two other security guys tackle the thief with the dark hair. He was done. His blond friend got away though. Seeing this scene made me wonder if this idyllic tropical town was not so idyllic after all. It seemed to have a real crime problem.

"What exactly did I do wrong?" I asked the big guy.

"You're an outsider," he snapped, all business. "Outsiders are taken before the tribunal."

Not good. There was no way I could convince anybody I wasn't an outsider, so if being an outsider was bad, I was in trouble. At least that meant I didn't have to pretend I knew anything about their town.

"What exactly is the tribunal?" I asked.

"It is the government of Rayne," he answered.

"So this town is called Rayne?"

The guy didn't answer.

"What do you have against outsiders?" I asked.

Again, no answer.

"What happens if the tribunal thinks I'm guilty of being an outsider? What's the worst that can happen?"

"You'll be executed," the guy said flatly.

Oh. This definitely wasn't a vacation resort. It was time to start worrying.

We didn't say another word for the rest of our walk (drag) through the village. The farther away we got from shore, the more dense the jungle became. The trees were thicker, creating a protective overhead canopy. We passed open areas of cleared jungle where kids played, large huts that seemed to be community gathering places, and even a section of shops that sold clothing, tools, and food. One large hut looked like a school, with a group of kids sitting in rows, attentively listening to a lesson being given by an older woman. We passed a large, open-air canopy structure where a performance was taking place. About a hundred people sat on the sand listening to a group of musicians play instruments made out of natural materials like bamboo and wood. They sounded pretty good, too. There was a lot of percussion, with a driving rhythm that had many people up and dancing. I wouldn't have minded stopping to listen for a while. It would have been more fun than being dragged off to a possible execution.

The terrain grew steeper, and we soon had to climb up rocky steps. A few minutes later we came upon a sheer rock wall that looked like a dead end. As we walked closer, high above us on the sheer face of the mountain I saw a large opening cut into the rock. That told me we hadn't hit a dead end after all. We were going inside the mountain. Sure enough, the path led to a cave opening that looked big enough to drive a car through. It wasn't scary or anything, unless you considered there were people inside who would decide on whether or not I should be executed. It was a busy place, with people strolling in and out. As we got closer, I saw that it was well lit inside, with tubes of bright light running along the walls. The big guy led me inside and along a long corridor of rock that looked the same as the black rock cave where the flume was. There were open doorways on either side that led into large rooms where people were busily doing things like sewing clothes, preparing food, and doing repair work on small machines. The mountain was honeycombed with rooms and tunnels. There was no way these tunnels could be natural; it was way too complicated. That meant the people of this village cut through rock. Even more impressive was the fact that there was fresh air, even deep inside the mountain. They had ventilation. This living mountain once again pointed to the fact that this was an advanced society. It was a modern, primitive village. Ibara was an enigma.

After walking deep into the mountain, the big guy pushed me toward an opening where rock stairs led upward. I stopped. I was still dizzy from the medication, squirmy from the bee stings, and weak from having slept for five days. The last thing I wanted to do was climb stairs. Too bad for me. The guy gave me a shove. I willed my feet to keep moving, and the two of us climbed for what felt like forever. When we finally got to the top, we were faced with two guards who blocked our way. When they saw the big guy who'd arrested me, they backed off to let us pass.

We had arrived on another level built into the mountain, and a huge cavern. On the far side was the opening I had seen from the ground. Light from outside filled the immense room, making it nearly bright as day. The space was big, but empty. The only sign of life was on the far side, in front of the opening. Three people were there, talking.

The big guy removed the cord from around my wrists and handed it to me. "Don't do anything foolish," he warned. "There are guards everywhere."

I nodded and rubbed my wrists, grateful that the tight

cord was no longer scraping my healing bug wounds.

"Is that the tribunal?" I asked.

His answer was to shove me toward them. The guy was starting to annoy me. In the next few moments my future on Ibara was going to be decided. What was I going to say to this tribunal? If my only crime was being an outsider, I was guilty. Was that enough to have me executed? My mind raced, trying to come up with some kind of plausible story as to why I wasn't an outsider, but I didn't know anything about Ibara. Or this village called Rayne. I looked beyond the group and out past the cave opening. I first saw nothing but sky, then the beach, and finally the huts of the village below. It was an awesome sight. It reminded me of being on that lofty platform for the Tato match on Quillan. That was an incredible view too. I would have enjoyed it a lot more if I hadn't been up there to fight for my life. I hoped I wouldn't have the same problem here on Ibara.

An idea hit me. Remembering the Tato match did it. I wasn't exactly sure how to use it, but it could very well have been my only hope.

There was a long, low desk with three large chairs behind it. The desk was full of papers and one of those small telephones. This is where the tribunal worked. I wondered why they were set up in such a huge place. I'm guessing it had something to do with security. Nobody could get close to them without being seen from far off. If they were paranoid about outsiders, what better place to protect their leaders than in the middle of a space where nobody could get close to them without being seen?

There were two women and a man. The man had gray in his hair, and the two women looked like your basic moms. One had very dark skin, the other was white and freckled, but with almond-shaped eyes. Weird. The guy was white, but really tan. He had a scratchy salt-and-pepper beard that made him look like a grizzled sea captain. They each wore light green clothes, but with long sleeves and long pants. I'm guessing this was their idea of being formal. The three of them were locked in debate, until the dark woman spotted us. She nodded to the others. They straightened up and sat in their chairs. The guy sat in the middle, a woman on either side of him. I was led to a red line in the floor and roughly pulled to a stop.

"Don't cross the line," the big guy commanded.

"Don't worry," I replied.

The tribunal looked me over with no expression. I tried to look innocent, though I wasn't really sure how to do that. I mainly wanted to be respectful and nonthreatening. We stood that way for several seconds. I wasn't sure if they were trying to psyche me out or if I was supposed to say something. I chose to keep quiet. I kept going over in my head what I was going to say when the questions began. I had come up with a plan. It was something I hadn't tried before on any of the territories. This seemed like as good a time as any to give it a shot.

"My name is Genj," the man in the middle finally announced. "I am the chief minister of the Rayne tribunal." He spoke calmly, with authority. He gestured to the women and said, "This is Moman and Drea."

The dark woman was Moman, the freckled woman was Drea.

"And who are you?" he finally asked.

This was it. Do or die. Literally.

"I was hoping you could tell me," I answered.

I saw the surprise on their faces.

"I don't understand," Genj said. "I asked you who you are."

"And I'm saying I don't know. I remember my name, but that's pretty much it."

"What is your name?" Drea asked.

"Pendragon. At least I think it is. My mind is kind of . . . blank. I remember being swarmed by bees, but it's a blur. The next thing I knew I woke up in your village. I have no idea how I got here or who I am."

The three tribunal members looked to one another, not sure how to respond. It was a totally bold move on my part to fake amnesia, but I figured there was no way I was going to convince them I wasn't an outsider. And if being an outsider meant death, I had to hope that putting a little doubt in their minds would spare me.

Moman asked, "You are saying you have no memory of anything before you were attacked by the bees?"

I had one more card to play. If I was lucky, it would confuse them a little more.

"I do have one other memory," I answered. "It's a name, I think."

"What is it?" Genj asked.

I knew exactly one thing about Ibara. I knew the name of the Traveler. He was lured to Quillan by Nevva Winter and killed playing Tato, one of the deadly Quillan games. I hoped he would be able to reach back from the grave to help save my life.

"Remudi," I answered.

The effect on the tribunal was instant. All three sat bolt upright. Even the big guy who arrested me stiffened. I didn't know why it was such a shock, but it definitely had an effect. I continued to pour it on by saying, "I can't get that name out of my head. Remudi. Who knows? Maybe that's my name and I'm not Pendragon. Do you know who I am? Do you know someone named Remudi?"

They looked off balance. That was good. I needed them to be confused and curious enough to want to keep me around to find out more.

Genj looked to the big guy who arrested me and asked, "Is the report we just received correct?"

"I'm afraid so," the big guy answered.

"Bring him to us right away," Genj commanded.

The big guy backed away respectfully and jogged off. I was left standing there with my toes on the red line. What report was he talking about? Who was being brought in? The three members of the tribunal stared at me. I felt like I was standing in my underwear. I'd done what I set out to do: I confused them. I didn't want to say anything else that might mess that up.

"You nearly died," Genj said. "It's possible that amount of venom effected your memory."

Awesome. If they thought a thousand bug bites caused my amnesia, cool.

"Do you have other injuries?" Drea asked.

"I don't think so," I said, keeping the possibility open. Though I knew I was fine. "Telleo told me I was saved by some fishermen. She really helped me, by the way."

"Telleo has a gift," Moman said kindly. "Her calling is to help people. She would even give aid to a Flighter in need."

"I don't know what a Flighter is," I said honestly.

The three of them exchanged looks. Did they believe me? Probably not. I wasn't so sure I believed me either. I had no idea what a Flighter was, so how could I be sure I wasn't one?

"You are not from Rayne," Genj stated. "That much we are sure of. But you may be from another part of Ibara. The fact that you know the name of Remudi makes us believe that is possible. A Flighter would not know that name."

Remudi's name may have saved my life. But Genj said he thought I *may* be from some other part of Ibara. What did that mean? If I didn't come from another part of Ibara, where did he think I came from? Did they know about other territories?

"There is someone you should meet," Genj said. "Perhaps it will bring light to a confusing situation."

I sensed someone walking up behind me. I didn't dare turn around to look. To be honest, I was afraid to. I heard the voice of the big guy who had arrested me. "Don't cross the line," he ordered. I thought he was talking to me, but realized it was intended for the person he was bringing in.

"He stole some clothing and some tools," the big guy announced. "There were two of them. The other thief escaped."

Stepping up beside me was the big security guy. With him was the dark-haired thief, the one I'd seen being tackled earlier. The young guy pulled away from the thug's grip and angrily snarled, "Relax. I'm not going anywhere." He looked at me and said, "What did they get *you* for?"

The young thief wasn't intimidated by the tribunal. Or me.

"This is becoming a habit, Siry," Genj said to the young guy. "A *bad* habit."

"I didn't do anything," the kid named Siry boldly shot back at the man. "Those clothes were ours. We worked for them. That lady was crazy."

The big thug poked Siry in the back. "Show some respect," he ordered.

"Hey!" Siry protested. "I'm not the guilty one. Talk to that lady. She was supposed to pay us."

The kid was cocky. From the scowls on the faces of the tribunal, they didn't believe a word he said. I had the feeling they'd been to this dance before.

"Look at this young man," Genj ordered Siry while pointing to me.

Siry gave me a quick once-over. His eyes were blank. I meant nothing to him.

"Yeah, so?" he asked, annoyed.

Drea asked, "Have you seen him before?"

"Why?" he asked without looking at me again. "Is he blaming me for something too?"

"Answer a simple question for once, Siry," Genj said, growing impatient.

"Don't know him," Siry said dismissively.

Moman added, "He says his name is Pendragon. Have you ever heard that name?"

"I told you," Siry said, still annoyed. "I don't know the guy."

"Yet he knows the name of your father," Genj said.

I snapped a look to Genj. Did I hear right?

"This is Remudi's son?" I blurted out.

"Does that stir memories?" Drea asked.

Oh man, did it ever. Not the kind I wanted to share.

"Maybe there's more than one Remudi," I offered, my mind racing.

"There was only one Remudi from Rayne," Genj answered. "Jen Remudi. This is his son. Look at him. Does he look at all familiar?"

I focused on the guy. He looked bored. He had the attitude of a street-tough kind of guy. I had only seen Remudi on the big screen on Quillan when he fought in the Tato match. The match that killed him. I tried to see a resemblance in Siry, but there was nothing about him that reminded me of Remudi. Then I remembered. Remudi was the Traveler from Ibara. As far as I knew, none of the Travelers knew their biological parents. Did it follow that the Travelers wouldn't have biological children of their own? Siry might have been adopted, which meant there would be no resemblance.

It also meant something else. Something I needed to know. Badly. Siry's arms were folded across his chest in a show of boredom and defiance. I couldn't see his hands. I grasped the handcuff cord I had been holding and tossed it at the thief.

"Catch," I barked.

Surprised, Siry caught the cord, revealing his hands. On his right ring finger was a familiar gray band.

I had found the new Traveler from Ibara.

IBARA

Siry didn't fit the profile. Each and every Traveler was special in some way. Even before they discovered the whole Traveler thing, they each had proved themselves to be smart and competent, and above all else, honorable. I can't really speak about myself that way, seeing as I was pretty young when I left home, but I think I was a pretty good kid. I'm not sure I could say the same about Siry. At least, that's what I thought after knowing him for a total of two minutes.

He looked at the handcuff cord I tossed him as if it were infected. "What was that for?" he barked angrily, and threw it back at me. He took a step toward me, ready to throw a punch. I didn't move. The big security goon grabbed him. Good thing. I'm not so sure I had the strength to defend myself.

"That's enough!" scolded Genj.

"What?" bellowed Siry, complaining. "He threw it at me! You saw it! Are you going to say that was my fault too?"

Genj sighed. I got the feeling that he was tired of dealing with Siry. He stood up and paced, thinking. He had two problems: an obnoxious thief and a semiobnoxious, mystery guy with amnesia and scabs. The two women joined him and they stepped away to discuss the situation. At least, I assumed they were discussing the situation. I didn't think they were deciding on what to have for dinner. The big guy stayed between Siry and me, making sure we behaved.

Siry shifted back and forth, bored. He was smaller than I was and looked around fifteen, though he carried himself with confidence, as if he were older. His hair was kinky curly, but long. It fell to his shoulders in long corkscrews. When he moved, they bounced like springs. His clothes were like everyone else's, but old and worn. His shirt was darker blue, with cutoff sleeves revealing thin, strong arms. His pants were probably long at one time, but were cut off to just below the knees, with raggy ends. I couldn't be sure, but it looked as if his clothes hadn't been washed in a while. I'm not saying he smelled, but where everyone else in the village wore clothes that were bright and new, Siry looked kind of, well, grungy. I guess he was a street kid, tropical style.

He was full of nervous energy. I wondered if he was always like that, or if it was because three people were debating his future. His skin was dark, like Remudi's. I guess on Second Earth we'd call him black. He was thin, but strong looking. "Wiry" is a good word. My guess was he was athletic. His eyes were dark brown, almost black. They were intense. Or angry. Back at home if I saw him walking toward me, I'd get out of his way. Not because he was big and intimidating, but because he seemed like someone who would snap with no warning. He was not the kind of guy you'd want to mess with.

Unfortunately, I was going to have to mess with him.

After a few minutes of concerned debate, the tribunal came back. The women sat in their chairs. Genj stood facing us.

"There may be an opportunity here," the older man said. "Jen Remudi was my friend. He was a friend to all three of us and a trusted member of this tribunal."

Whoa. Remudi was on the Tribunal of Rayne. He was a leader. He was respected. There again was a guy who was special in his own way, on top of being a Traveler. I wondered why his son turned out to be such a slug.

"His disappearance remains a mystery," Genj continued. "Pendragon, if you are telling us the truth, and I'd like to believe you are, we're hoping you might help us learn of what happened to our friend."

Uh-oh. I could tell them *exactly* what happened to him. But I wasn't going to. No way.

Moman said, "We'd like you to remain here in Rayne until you are fully healed. Hopefully, that will include recovering your memory. You can stay in the same common house where Telleo cared for you. You're free to explore our village. Make no mistake, you will be watched. If there is trouble, you will find yourself right back here, where there will be a very different outcome."

"Thank you," I said. "If I can help you, I will." I meant it too. Though not exactly in the way they were hoping. Still, if there was a way I could give them closure on Remudi, short of telling them the whole truth, I'd do it. They seemed like good people. Their village looked like a peaceful and decent place to live. It was the perfect target for Saint Dane. My goal was to figure out what it was about this village that could create a turning point that would affect all of Ibara. Things were looking up.

Genj stepped in front of Siry. The kid smirked, as if daring him to say something he'd actually care about.

"Siry," Genj began, "you are a disappointment to the

~ IBARA ~ 127

tribunal, to your village, and to your father. You are a thief and a liar."

If this bothered Siry, he didn't show it. He'd probably been called worse.

"This is the fifth time you've been brought before us on charges of thievery, mischief, vandalism, and brawling. Out of deference to your father, we've never given you a fitting punishment. That changes today." He stepped back and took his place between the two women.

Drea declared, "Siry, you are assigned to work with our fishing fleet for a year of hard labor. Our hope is that by spending a concentrated time on a constructive, important task, you will learn the value of the individual's place in our society, and return to it a more respectful, useful citizen."

Siry's eyes went wide. "Wha—? No!" he shouted. His cool finally cracked. "I've never done work like that. I don't know how."

"You'll learn," Moman assured him. "Hopefully, you'll learn a lot of things, including respect for yourself."

"I won't go," he shouted defiantly, stabbing his finger at me. "You let an outsider free in the village, but sentence the son of a tribunal member to a year of hard labor? That's not fair!"

The three leaders exchanged knowing looks. I wasn't sure if it was because they were satisfied that they had finally gotten to Siry, or had other plans.

Genj said, "You make a good point. There might be another way."

"Anything!" Siry shouted.

The older man stood back up and walked to us. "Perhaps we shouldn't let Pendragon roam our city so freely."

Uh-oh. Now it was my turn to complain. I held back

though. Genj wasn't finished. He put his hand on my shoulder and said, "Siry, you can serve your sentence in another constructive manner. You can supervise Pendragon."

"What!" Siry exclaimed.

"He would be your responsibility," Genj said. "If there are problems, all you need do is contact security. We hope that won't be necessary. We want Pendragon to recover. If there's a chance to learn what happened to your father, don't you think we should take it?"

Siry stared at his feet, his jaw clenching.

"Of course you do," Genj said, satisfied, as he sat back down. "It's your choice, Siry. Either act as Pendragon's overseer, or set sail with the fishing fleet in the morning."

Siry gave me a sideways look. He may have been debating his options, but I knew what choice he'd make. It was a no-brainer.

A few minutes later I walked out of the mountain cave, free. Better still, I was with the next Traveler from Ibara. It was all good. Well, mostly good. Siry wasn't exactly the kind of guy who seemed willing to put his life on the line to save humanity. My plan was to find out about him and his father. Siry had other ideas. As soon as we left the cave, he stormed away from me without saying a word.

"Hey," I called. "Where you going?"

He stopped and sighed. I annoyed him. He walked back and got in my face, trying to intimidate me. I still felt as weak as wet lettuce. If he had taken a swing, he'd have knocked me out.

"Look," he said with disdain. "I don't care if you're an outsider or a Flighter or a slug from the sea. I'm not going to be your keeper."

"Aren't you afraid they'll put you on a fishing boat?"

Siry scoffed. "They won't get the chance."

I wasn't sure what he meant by that, but I let it slide.

"Don't you want to know what happened to your father?" I asked.

"No," he said flatly.

"I don't believe you."

"I don't care what you believe," Siry shot back. He gave me a little shove and walked off.

"Where did you get that ring?" I called.

Siry stopped short and twisted his Traveler ring.

"It was from your father, wasn't it?" I asked.

He stalked back to me. His eyes were on fire. I wasn't sure if it was with curiosity or anger. Was he going to hit me? I turned my body subtly, in case this turned into a fight.

"Why do you care?" he hissed.

I lifted my hand and showed him mine. Siry flinched.

"What did your father tell you about that ring?" I asked.

Siry backed off, no longer seeming so sure of himself. "No way," he said, shaking his head.

"No way what?" I pressed.

"It was a story. He was always telling stories."

"What was the story, Siry?"

Siry glanced around nervously. I think he was debating whether to answer or take off. Or throw a punch, for all I knew. He chose to answer, I'm happy to say.

"He talked about some place called Halla and . . . and what did he call them? Travelers. But he always made up stupid stories, ever since I was a kid. They weren't real."

"What else did he tell you?"

"I don't know!" Siry snapped. "I wasn't even listening."

"Yes you were. What else did he tell you?"

"He talked about some guy who was making trouble, and

the Travelers had to stop him. That's why he said he was leaving, to deal with the guy."

"Is that all?" I asked.

Siry pulled himself back together. His cocky attitude had returned.

"He told me that one day a guy might show up looking for help." He grabbed my hand with the ring and held it up. "He said I'd know him by his ring. He said if he wasn't around, it was my job to help him. There's only one problem."

"What's that?"

"I don't want the job," he said, and he threw my hand down. I kept my eyes locked on his as he backed away.

"Now my father's missing, and you know what? I don't care. He's off somewhere being a big man and taking charge. That's what he's good at, you know? Taking charge. Wherever he is, he can be a hero and that's fine. It's good not having him around."

He turned and started to walk away.

"He's dead, Siry," I said with no emotion. "Your father's dead. I saw him die."

My words stopped him cold. I hated to tell him that way, but he was tough. I had to be just as tough.

"He died trying to stop Saint Dane," I continued. "That's the name of the guy he told you about. Saint Dane killed him. Now Saint Dane is here on Ibara."

Siry didn't move. I walked around to face him and saw something I didn't expect. Tears.

"I thought you didn't care," I said softly.

"I thought you lost your memory."

"Your father died for something he believed in," I said. "What do *you* believe in?"

Siry sniffed and shot me a look. The wild, angry guy was back with a vengeance.

"You want to know?" he challenged. "You really want to know?"

"Yes."

"Come with me," he snarled.

He pushed past me, knocking my shoulder aside, headed toward the village. I stood there, wondering how this was going to play out. Did this loser really have to be the next Traveler from Ibara? The guy had some baggage. But whatever problems he had were nothing compared to the reality I was about to dump on him. How would he handle it? The sick truth was that I had to trust a kid with major attitude, authority issues, and a history of violent crime. Oh joy. I'd faced impossible situations before, but this was like nothing I'd ever had to deal with. Suddenly, at seventeen, I had to be a responsible adult in charge of a problem kid. How wrong was that?

I did the one and only thing I could do.

I went with him.

IBARA

I followed Siry on a twisted route through the tropical village. He didn't say a word the whole way. The few times I asked him a question, he ignored me. I was exhausted, but there was no way I'd show weakness. We took some turns around huts that made me feel as if we were walking in circles. At first I thought he was testing me, or trying to wear me out so I'd give up. It was neither. He was leading me on a route so impossible to follow, I'd never be able to find my way on my own. It got more complicated when our journey took us away from the populated village and into the jungle. The huts became fewer and farther between. The jungle grew thicker. The path grew narrower.

I was lost.

As we moved deeper into the jungle, the creepy thought hit me that maybe this wasn't so much about my not finding my way here again. It might be about my not finding my way back. Alarm bells started going off in my head, but I didn't know what else to do but continue following. He was the Traveler from Ibara! Never mind that he was some kind of juvi who hated his father's guts and probably hated mine and was leading me into a trap. I had to go. Just another day in my twisted life.

The path narrowed to a single track. Thick brush whipped at my arms. It had gotten long past old.

"How much farther?" I asked.

No answer. I was getting dizzy. My scabs were burning. I didn't want to show weakness, but this was just dumb. The path opened up to a small clearing, and I put on the brakes.

"That's it," I declared. "You gotta tell me where we're going."

Siry turned around. He had a knowing smile on his face. I hated knowing smiles. Almost as much as I hated smirks. I've mentioned that, right?

"Getting tired?" he asked snidely. I didn't care much for snide, either.

"I trusted you," I gasped between breaths. "I followed you to wherever the heck it is we are, and I want to know why."

I got my answer. It wasn't the answer I wanted.

The jungle came alive. Before I could react, I was tackled by three guys. I hit the ground. Hard. Yes, it was a trap. They'd been waiting for me. They quickly tied a blindfold around my eyes and pulled me to my feet. I stood there, dazed, being held by several strong hands. They didn't have to try so hard. I had no strength. Not a word was said. It all happened quickly and efficiently.

"Are you afraid?" Siry whispered in my ear. He was so close I could feel his breath.

"Terrified," I answered, trying to sound bored.

"I could have you killed," he hissed. "Nobody would know. Nobody would miss you. Nobody would care.

"That would be a mistake," I said calmly.

"Why is that?"

"Because you're a target, and I'm the only one who can help you. Without me, you're done."

Siry gave no comeback. I hoped my words hit home, or at least made him think. I sensed him move away. I tensed up. Would he be crazy enough to kill me? I had to be ready. It didn't matter how exhausted and weak I was, I had to defend myself. I couldn't see a thing. For all I knew, death was seconds away. I had had enough. I took a breath and summoned what little strength I had left. I was about to lash out and start kicking some Ibara butt, when Siry barked out an order.

"Bring him," he commanded.

I stopped. They weren't going to hurt me. At least, not right away. The guys who held me started to walk, and I was once again dragged along to an unknown destination. At least it was unknown to me. These guys knew exactly where they were going. We walked quickly through what felt like dense jungle. All I could do was go along and hope they didn't run me face-first into a palm tree. Things were not going well. My one ally on Ibara was a thieving kid who'd just threatened to kill me, and had a bunch of friends to help him. I had to go along with whatever game he was playing. At least for a while.

Our trip ended when I was roughly pushed down into a seat. My arms were rudely pulled behind my back and tied together. These guys weren't pros like the security drones who worked for the tribunal. They may have tied me up, but I felt as if I could break free pretty easily. Their last act was to yank off my blindfold. I squinted, and got my first look at Siry's world.

It looked like a jungle junkyard.

We were in a clearing that had been hacked out of dense

foliage. The surrounding growth was a thick wall of vines and vegetation that looked too tangled to walk through. The trees overhead formed a canopy that blocked out the sun. A quick scan showed only two paths out. Or in. There were bamboo platforms built everywhere. Some were at eye level, others on the ground. Two structures rose high up toward the canopy of trees, with several levels from the ground to the top. There were lots of makeshift ladders and bridges, tying the structure together. The whole thing was lashed together by rope and twine. It was impressive and crude.

The place was outfitted with an odd assortment of junk. Wooden and bamboo furniture was randomly scattered. Tables held dirty bowls and cups, along with the remnants of half-eaten fruit. This wasn't a neat bunch. I saw several large, wooden chests tucked under platforms. Clothes were hanging all around, giving the place the appearance of a messy bedroom. There were books and drums, baskets and tools.

It wasn't all a random mess. I saw a few beautiful sculptures made out of black rock. There was the head of a girl, a hand, a man's torso. Very cool and probably very stolen.

Most everything I saw looked as if it could have come from the village. A few things didn't. There were large chunks of sheet metal being used as roofing over some huts. High up on one of the platforms was a brass telescope on a tripod. There was a picture frame dangling from one platform. It was golden and intricate, with no picture. One thing stood out that I had no explanation for. It was a metal sign hanging between two vertical poles. It was about two feet square and looked as if one side had been eaten away, leaving only the left half. The sign had been white at one time, with faded black letters that now read:

It looked to me like a chunk of an old traffic sign. But there was no such thing as traffic on Ibara. It made the mystery of this territory grow deeper. This clearing looked like it was home to a bunch of castaways who had to make do with bits and pieces left over from their wrecked ship, while using whatever else the jungle provided to make shelter.

The people who hung out in this odd little oasis completed that image.

I counted fifteen people. They all looked to be in their midteens, the same as Siry. There were mostly boys, but a few girls were mixed in. They all had the same grungy look. Their clothes were worn, and nobody seemed to be too concerned about taking a bath. They all looked pretty healthy though. They weren't out here in the jungle starving. Most hung out on the various levels of the bamboo structure, looking down at the new guy. Me. The group that had ambushed me stood on the ground, circling me. I looked into each of their eyes. They all had the same look as Siry. It was an odd mixture of boredom and anger. Not a good combination.

A thin girl with long, stringy, blond hair jumped at me to see if I'd flinch. I didn't. She laughed and got right up close, nearly putting her nose on my cheek. She sniffed, then giggled. "Scared," she said playfully. "I can smell it. Yes I can." She gave me a quick kiss on the cheek and scurried away.

A big guy walked up to me, holding out a cup of liquid. "Thirsty?" he asked.

My answer was to stare at him.

"Me too," he said, and drank it himself. Most of it ended up spilling down his cheeks. He let out a belch and dropped the cup. The others laughed. Another little guy, who had the pointed nose and tiny eyes of a rat, skittered up and pulled the top of my shirt aside to look at my back.

"Bee stings," he snorted. "Lots of 'em. Do they hurt?"

"No," I said.

The little ferret slapped me on the back with his open hand, hard. "How about now!" He cackled out a laugh and scurried away. Creep.

This was a real fun bunch. Siry was beginning to seem like the normal one. I looked beyond the group that was having fun annoying me to see Siry with the blond thief who had escaped from the security goons earlier. They were looking through the sack the blond thief had gotten away with. He pulled out two small saws and a hammer. Siry patted the blond guy on the arm, as if to say, "Nice job."

"Hey!" I shouted to Siry. "I'm hungry."

Siry gave the tools back to blondie and walked slowly toward me. He had a cocky air about him. He was completely in charge and knew it.

"I'm sorry," he said sarcastically. "You expect me to care?"

"No," I said. "I expect you to give me something to eat."

Siry snorted, as if to say, "You're dreaming." But he waved at the girl with stringy hair and said, "Twig, get him something."

"Get it yourself!" the girl named Twig shot back.

Siry gave her a withering look. She backed off and left the group. It was pretty clear that Siry was the boss here. A moment later the girl came back with half a piece of fruit that looked like a pear. She held it out to me. I looked at it, then to the girl.

"Untie me," I said.

The girl hesitated, then made a move for the chair. I think she was actually going to do it until . . .

"Stop," Siry commanded. "Feed him."

The girl shrugged and held the pear up to my mouth. The fruit looked like it had been sitting in the sun too long. I didn't care. I was hungry. I took a big bite. It was mushy and sweet. It was delicious. I needed the energy.

"Thank you, Twig," I said sincerely.

The girl softened. She smiled, then jammed the rest of the fruit into my mouth.

"Feed yourself," she said snottily, and walked off as the others laughed. I closed my teeth, took a big bite, and let the rest fall to the ground.

Siry stood in front of the group, facing me. "You asked me what I believe in. I believe in the Jakills."

The group erupted in spontaneous cheers. "Yeah! The Jakills!" they shouted.

When they calmed down I said sarcastically, "Cute name. What does it mean?"

"It means the tribunal hates us, because we stand for everything they fear."

Several of the others grumbled in agreement, including the Jakills peering down from the platforms above.

"Like what?" I asked.

"Like change," Siry said. "And truth. The leaders of this village won't face the truth. They won't let anyone face the truth."

"What is the truth?" I asked.

Siry looked around. Every last eye was on him. He was their leader, no question.

"The truth is," he said, playing out the drama, "the truth is we're the future of Ibara."

The group cheered. It was the most sincere thing I'd heard from him. Siry was pretty charismatic. He knew how to play to his people.

He went on, "The tribunal fears us because they know we're going to take away their power."

"Yeah?" I laughed. "How? By hanging out in the jungle and eating rotten fruit?"

Everyone fell silent. The kids hanging off the platforms leaned down a little closer. I had challenged Siry and insulted all of them. It might have been a dumb thing to do, but I had to be just as bold and confident as they were. I had to prove that I was a match for Siry.

He stared at me with dead eyes. That was worse than looking angry. Angry is predictable. Siry took a step toward me and said in a low voice, "You told me my father died willingly for something he believed in. Would you?"

"Willingly?" I scoffed. "Nobody dies willingly. Your father didn't. He fought for what was right."

"And what exactly was that?" Siry asked. "Tell me. Tell us all!" He threw his arms out and walked around the group, saying, "We all want to know, Traveler man! You say my father was a hero who battled an evil demon? Who is this demon? What does he want? Bring him here, I want to see him."

Everyone laughed at his cocky posturing.

"He's already here," I said coldly.

That made everybody quiet down real quick. Siry hesitated. A few threw him questioning looks. Siry reloaded and continued the performance. He called out to the jungle, "Hello? Demon? Where are you? I'd like to see the man who killed the great Remudi."

Some of the kids laughed. Others glanced around nervously, as if a demon might actually show up. Siry waited for dramatic effect then stalked back toward me. "If you want to find true evil, you don't have to look any further than the tribunal of Rayne."

"What are they guilty of?" I asked.

"They've committed the worst crime of all," Siry said through gritted teeth. "They've stolen our souls."

Tweeeeee!

A harsh whistle pierced the jungle. Everyone looked up in surprise. Suddenly two more boys blasted into the clearing from the jungle. One was blowing the whistle. They were out of breath and sweating. They looked scared.

"They're coming," one gasped.

"Here?" Siry shot back.

"No," the other boy said. "Rayne. They're moving toward the village. We saw them in the jungle. It's hard to tell how many. More than ever."

The others grumbled nervously. Siry stared into space, calculating. The blond thief ran up to him.

"What do we do?" he asked.

Siry looked around, making quick eye contact with each and every kid. They all looked squarely back at him. I'd seen that look before. Whatever he was going to ask them to do, they were ready.

Siry shot me a look and said, "You think we're criminals, and maybe we are. But it doesn't mean we're wrong."

He grabbed the blond kid by the shirt and commanded, "Let's go."

An excited buzz went through the crowd. That's what they wanted to hear. The blond kid smiled and ran across the clearing with two others. They went right to the wooden chests, threw them open, and pulled out armloads of the same short, wooden weapons I'd seen on the hips of the security force. I heard a steady buzzing sound and looked up to see several kids sliding down zip lines from the higher platforms. They hit the ground running and joined the others. Their excitement was growing. They were getting ready for a fight.

The blond kid and the others returned to the group and handed out weapons.

Siry stood over me. "I want you to see this." He reached behind the chair and untied me. "That is, if you can handle it."

"Depends on what I'm supposed to do," I said, rubbing my wrists.

"Follow and watch. I want you to see what the Jakills are about."

"I'm there," I said, trying to sound stronger than I felt.

Truth be told, I was feeling better. The excitement of the group was getting to me. My heart started racing. So long as I only had to watch, I'd be okay. More than that and I'd probably crash.

The others began disappearing into the jungle.

"What happens now?" I asked Siry.

He grabbed a wooden baton from the blond guy and shoved it in his belt. "We hunt."

"For what?"

"Flighters" was Siry's response as he took off to join his friends.

Before I knew it, I was alone in the bizarre campsite. I was about to become involved in something that sounded dangerous. I wondered if the tribunal would consider this the kind of trouble I wasn't supposed to get into. Before I had a chance to talk myself out of it I ran into the jungle after Siry and the Jakills, ready for . . . I didn't know what.

IBARA

I followed the Jakills through the dense jungle, running to keep up. It wasn't easy. They knew every root and rock. I had to stay focused and drive myself forward without driving my head into the ground. They ran like jungle cats, leaping over fallen trees and ducking under branches without breaking stride. I ran more like a confused turtle, getting slashed by branches and trying not to break my neck. Making it worse, I had to keep looking up to see where they were going. It took all of two minutes before I totally lost them. I was alone in the jungle. Lost. I looked around, ready to run, but to where? I was tired and frantic and felt a little more than helpless.

I gulped air, turned, and came face-to-face with the blond thief. I jumped in surprise. Where had he come from?

"This way," he commanded, and took off again.

I didn't hesitate and ran after him. Soon we were climbing up a vine-tangled rocky ridge. I kept scraping my arms on the sharp walls and getting my ankles caught by vines that seemed to be reaching out to grab me. The blond guy didn't have trouble at all. If anything, he kept slowing down to let me catch up.

Finally we broke out of the jungle cover, onto a rocky ledge on the side of the mountain. Several of the Jakills were already there, including Siry. They were all looking intently below. Nobody acknowledged my arrival.

It was an incredible view. The village was spread out beneath us. Beyond that was the vast green bay and then the ocean. It made me feel as if we were on an island. I sat down to catch my breath and watch Siry. He crouched low, scanning the village like a cat searching for prey. His eyes were narrow and focused. Nobody spoke until . . .

"There," he said, pointing.

We looked to see movement in the jungle far below. There seemed to be a group of people making their way through the dense brush toward the edge of the village. We were too high up and the jungle was too thick to see what they looked like, but by the movement of trees and the brief flashes of bodies I could tell they were spread out and moving cautiously.

"There's more than just them," one of the guys warned who had first run into the clearing to sound the alarm. "Lots more."

"What are they doing?" Twig whispered.

While everyone kept their eyes on the movement below, Siry looked elsewhere. Up until then, Siry's attitude was one of defiance and anger. At that moment I saw he had more going on than that. He was focused. His mind was working. There was definitely more to Siry than I first had thought.

"Look," Twig exclaimed. "Smoke. They're going to burn something."

I saw a thin wisp of black smoke rise above the trees where the group of Flighters were moving. Who were those guys? I figured I'd find out soon enough.

"Let's go," the little guy with the ratty eyes exclaimed. He made a move to climb down, but Siry quickly put an arm out to stop him.

"No." Siry ordered with authority.

"Why not?" the ratty guy whined. "We can stop them."

"Wait," Siry insisted.

A few moments later I saw smoke rising up near the edge of the village. Twig was right. The Flighters had set fire to something.

"They're torching huts!" Twig exclaimed.

Siry didn't react. He kept his eyes on the jungle below. Focused. Scanning. "An alarm will sound," he said as if thinking out loud. "The security force will come running."

Sure enough, a loud horn began to wail. The sharp, droning sound grew loud enough so that every person in the village could hear it.

Siry nodded knowingly. "The entire force will rush to put out the fire and meet the enemy like the heroes they think they are. Idiots."

The ratty guy laughed and said, "Yeah! Idiots!" He quickly frowned and asked, "Why are they idiots?"

Siry kept his eyes on the village. I kept my eyes on Siry. He pointed down to the other side of the village from where the fire was being set.

"The fire is a decoy," he announced. "There are the others."

We all looked to see more movement in the jungle below. A group of Flighters, or whatever they were, was moving in the opposite direction from the fire.

The blond guy declared, "They're headed for the mountain. The tribunal. If the entire security force is on the other side of the village—"

"The tribunal isn't protected," Siry said. He stood up and

looked at the others. "That's where we need to be," he said, and scrambled down the side of the mountain.

The Jakills were right after him. I was right after them. None of this made sense. I thought the Jakills were a bunch of outlaws. There was no question that the tribunal thought Siry was a criminal. They had just sentenced him to a year of hard labor! Yet he was willing to take on invaders to protect the very people he called "evil." There was nothing about Ibara that made sense. All I could do was keep up and hope to find some answers.

I also had to hope I wouldn't trip and crash while running down the rocky, vine-covered slope. The Jakills had grown up in this jungle. They knew it and moved through the uneven terrain as easily as if they were running across artificial turf. They were nearly silent, too. The only sound I heard was my own clumsy crashing and bashing along. Nobody slowed down to help me this time. They had to get down the slope and head off the Flighters before they reached the mountain cave. I'm guessing the ledge we were on was about a half mile up the side of that mountain. When we started after them, the Flighters were only a few hundred yards from the mouth of the cave leading to where the tribunal met. If there was any hope of catching them, we'd have to be fast, and hope the Flighters were slow.

The ground leveled out. I hadn't fallen, yet. The Jakills had gotten pretty far ahead of me, but the jungle was thinning, so I could see them. Or most of them. I wasn't entirely sure where I was going, so I ran straight ahead. I would have kept going if I hadn't been suddenly grabbed by some strong hands and pulled down into the shadows of a leafy bush.

It was the blond guy, again. He looked at me and gave me a silent "shhhh" sign. It's not easy to catch your breath silently, but I tried. Glancing around I saw the Jakills stretched out around me, all looking ahead. All hiding. All alert.

I felt a tap on my shoulder and nearly jumped out of my skin. Spinning, I saw that Siry had slid in next to me. Man, he was quiet.

"They're just ahead of us," he whispered.

"Who are they?" I whispered back.

"Stay here and watch," he ordered.

"What are you going to do?"

Siry gave me a cocky smile and said, "My father thought we were a bunch of misfit kids. Maybe he was right. But never, ever cross us."

"Siry, what are you going to do?" I asked again.

He motioned for the others. The entire line of Jakills, I'm guessing there were around fifteen, crept slowly forward, crouched low, moving silently. I stayed behind them. I was only there as an observer. The line moved forward, creeping through the brush. Nobody said a word. I had the feeling they had done this kind of thing before. We'd been moving for about a minute when I saw something ahead of us. Everyone noticed at the same time and stopped.

We had caught up with the Flighters. I saw movement ahead and to the right. They were traveling in the same direction we were, about thirty yards ahead. They had no idea we were behind them. Now that I was closer, I could make out some details of these mysterious "Flighters." I didn't know what I expected to see, but it definitely wasn't this.

They were mostly men, though I think I saw a few women. They didn't seem like trained guerrillas or anything. Just the opposite. They looked like ordinary people. The only thing that stood out about them was their clothes. If I didn't know better, I'd say they looked as if they wore clothes that came from Second Earth. There was a mix of pants and shirts and jackets of all sorts. The clothes looked old, too, like *really* old. I saw patches and tears and raggy pants. Some had two different kinds of shoes. I saw one guy with a sneaker on one foot and a boot on the other. Some wore hats that looked as if they'd been run through a blender. That's how mashed up they were.

These people were dirty, too. There was a lot of shaggy hair and dark stains. Their skin seemed gray, which was strange considering they lived in a tropical paradise. They definitely didn't come across as a dangerous band of commandos. They looked more like a bunch of raggy homeless people lost in the jungle.

Siry lifted his hand. The Jakills stopped. He made a circular motion and the entire line of Jakills moved to the left. I moved behind them. It looked like Siry wanted them to circle around in front of the Flighters. After moving to our left for several yards, we broke into the clearing. We were back in the village of Rayne. To our right was the mountain that held the cave leading to the tribunal. Villagers were running away from the cave, headed toward the burning huts. It wasn't full-on panic, but there were a lot of people running to see what was happening. They didn't know they were running past a bunch of Flighters who were hidden in the jungle, quietly waiting. It finally made sense how we were able to catch up with the Flighters. They were waiting until everyone left to investigate the fire. When the area cleared, they'd make their move on the tribunal.

The Jakills were in the perfect position to cut them off.

Siry silently motioned for his band to quickly move toward the cave. They ran from hut to hut, moving against the stream of people leaving the mountain, trying to stay hidden from the Flighters. They finally grouped together behind a hut on the far side of the sandy road from the jungle. I knew that somewhere behind that thick curtain of jungle, the Flighters waited. Not far from us was the cave into the mountain, and the tribunal.

Siry motioned for everyone to wait. More people left the cave, running for the fire. The siren continued to wail. Eventually the area cleared. Everyone was gone. The cave lay open. The Jakills pulled out their short weapons. I could feel the tension. Not fear, tension. They were ready to fight.

I saw a head peer out of the dense jungle across the way. Then another, and another. The Flighters were making their move. Like ghosts appearing out of the ether, they crept from the foliage. It was a strange-looking bunch. There didn't seem to be any leader. They randomly drifted out of the thicket and crept toward the cave. I counted ten. Ten Flighters. Fifteen Jakills. I was glad to be with the Jakills.

Siry gave me a cocky smile and said, "Watch."

He lifted his weapon and charged for the Flighters. The rest of the Jakills were right behind him. They ran as a group, headed for the invaders. They didn't scream or let out a war whoop. They wanted every second of surprise they could squeeze out. To be honest, they didn't look much more organized or trained than the Flighters, but I couldn't criticize. Their tactics had worked perfectly. They recognized that the fire was a decoy, they spotted the second group of Flighters, they tracked them silently, they outmaneuvered them, and their counterattack was a complete surprise. Everything they did was perfect. Except for one thing.

They didn't know how to fight.

One of the gray-looking Flighters spotted the oncoming Jakills. The surprise was over. Siry screamed out a chilling war cry. "Yahhhhh!" The other Jakills followed with their own screams. If the Flighters were surprised, they didn't show it. They didn't panic. They didn't show any emotion. They quickly and efficiently formed a group and prepared for the fight. They didn't have any weapons. As it turned out, they didn't need them.

Unlike the Jakills, the Flighters knew how to fight.

The Jakills descended on them, wildly swinging their short clubs as if trying to scare them into scattering. They didn't scatter. The Flighters took them on. When a Jakill would swing his weapon, a Flighter would block it, or duck to make him miss, then knock the Jakill into next week. They ripped the wooden weapons from the young defenders and clubbed them mercilessly. There was no contest. I didn't expect that. Siry and the Jakills had been so confident. I hadn't thought the raggy band of Flighters stood a chance.

Reality was, the Jakills didn't stand a chance.

I stood near the hut where we had been hiding to watch the carnage. Even though the Jakills were taking a beating, I hoped that their presence alone would be enough to scare off the Flighters and send them back to wherever it was they came from. It didn't. The Flighters stayed to fight. The Jakills were getting hammered. But they didn't give up. I'll say that much for them. They had guts. They kept screaming and flailing, but they got spanked. Siry took the worst beating. He spun like an out-of-control top, swinging his short clubs, trying to get a piece of a Flighter. What he got instead was a lot of air, followed by a shot in the head. At first the Flighters backed toward the jungle, but after handling the Jakills so easily, they grew bold and continued toward the mountain cave.

The Jakills' counterattack had failed. I may not have known much about Ibara, or the politics or history of the village of

Rayne, but it was pretty clear that the Flighters weren't friends. Even the Jakills, who hated the tribunal, were willing to fight to stop them. It looked like it was only a matter of time before the Jakills were knocked senseless and the Flighters would be free to enter the cave and attack the tribunal. There was nothing to stop them.

Well, almost nothing.

I've written many times before how amazing adrenaline is. I was exhausted. I was sick. I was starving. I was scabby. But watching that fight made me forget about all that. It was a massacre. That tends to get your blood boiling. Mine was heating up fast. I had to make a decision. Did I get involved? I didn't know who the Jakills were or what they stood for, but Siry was the son of a Traveler. He had the ring. If history meant anything, Siry was now the Traveler from Ibara . . . and I had to help him.

Like it or not, it was time to stop being an observer.

I scooped up a short weapon that had been knocked away from one of the Jakills. I grabbed another from the hand of a Jakill who was out cold. He didn't need it anymore. I wasn't experienced in handling those short weapons, but they were all I had. The clubs were small, but solid. I gripped one in each hand, took a breath, and ran forward to begin my own personal battle to save Ibara.

It didn't take long to get involved. A Flighter took a swing at me. I dodged back, let him follow through, then clocked him on the back of the head with the butt of the club. A second Flighter launched himself at me. I ducked, took his weight on my back, and flipped him over . . . in time to face another Flighter who tackled me head-on. He hit me in the gut, driving me down and onto my back. I hit the ground hard, but let my momentum carry us both. I rolled with my attacker, then, using his own momentum, flipped him over my head.

I was fully into the fight. Any pain or leftover rustiness I had from the quig-bee attack was gone. It was survival time. The battle had changed and the Flighters knew it. A ringer had entered the game. They were more cautious about attacking me, which is exactly what I needed. They may have been better fighters than the Jakills, but they weren't trained.

I was.

My hope was that the Jakills had done enough damage to soften them up a little. Ten-on-one is not a good thing, no matter how good I thought I was. The Flighters kept coming after me, but with enough hesitation that I could exploit their weaknesses. I nailed one in the gut, spun, cracked another on the back of the legs and sent him crumbling. Another Flighter came after me from behind. I didn't see him; I sensed him. Loor's lessons were well learned. He took a swing. I grabbed his arm and flipped him over my shoulder.

I may have felt like I was in this battle alone, but I wasn't. The Jakills kept on fighting. They even had a few surprises of their own to offer. I saw Siry raise a wooden club to his mouth and give it a hard, sharp blow on one end. I didn't get what he was doing until I heard a Flighter yelp and grab at his back. Those weapons weren't just clubs, they were blowguns that shot some kind of projectile. The Flighter fell to one knee. He seemed disoriented. I thought maybe Siry had fired a poisonous dart. The Flighter staggered off, headed for the jungle. His fight was over.

Twig fired her blowgun and hit another Flighter in the leg. He squealed, grabbed at it, and limped off. The whole time I continued to defend myself, while getting in a few shots at the Flighters, who were quickly growing less enthused. They had given up on the cave. They wanted to escape. One guy dragged an unconscious Flighter toward the jungle. I knew he was unconscious because I made him that way. Another Flighter quickly helped him, and the three scampered into the bush.

I looked around, ready for the next attack. It never came. I had only been in the fight for a minute or two, but it was over. The Flighters had disappeared into the jungle, carrying their wounded. I looked around the clearing to see several Jakills looking dazed. Three were out cold. One of those was the little guy with ratty eyes. Most stood around, breathing hard, not wanting anything to do with chasing the Flighters.

Siry stood in the center of it all, surrounded by his fallen friends, breathing hard. It looked like he was barely able to stand. Blood flowed from his nose and a gash on his cheek. It reminded me of my own wound that I got from the quig that attacked me on Third Earth. I looked at my forearm. The wound was completely gone. I didn't know whether to credit my Traveler powers of recuperation, or the incredible medical technology of Third Earth. Either way, I was better. In all sorts of ways. I had shaken the last effects from the bee attack and the medication.

"You can fight," Siry said breathlessly.

I replied with a shrug.

I glanced up the face of the mountain to the cave opening that led to the tribunal cavern. Standing there were the three members of the tribunal. Genj and I made eye contact. I expected them to send help, or to yell a quick "You okay?" or even give us a simple wave that acknowledged what had just happened. But nobody moved. Several kids lay at their feet, bleeding. They didn't seem to care. How messed up was that?

I had no idea who the Flighters were, or why they were after the tribunal, or why the Jakills were playing the game from both sides. There was a very strange dynamic happening on Ibara.

Siry knelt down by the little guy with ratty eyes and gently turned his head over. The kid moaned. A nasty-looking black-and-blue mark was already forming on his cheek, right next to a nastier-looking gash.

"He needs help." Siry was worried. I was glad to see that he cared about his guys.

"What about the tribunal?" I asked.

Siry scoffed.

"I don't get it. You just saved them from the Flighters."

"We're dirt to them, Pendragon," Siry said with venom. "Their reward will be to let us sink back into the jungle and not arrest us."

I shot a look up at the tribunal, to see Genj, Moman, and Drea step away from the cave opening. Siry was right. They didn't care about the wounded Jakills. They didn't care about Siry, the son of a tribunal member. What was going on? The tribunal wasn't evil. At least, I didn't think so. How could they be, if Remudi was one of them? Nothing added up. I couldn't tell the good guys from the bad guys.

The blond thief knelt next to Siry. "Telleo," he suggested.

Siry nodded. "Yes. She'll help."

"We can bring the wounded to the hut where I'm staying," I offered. "There's medicine and——"

Siry shot me a vicious look. "We don't need your help."

"No? You've got a short memory."

The blond thief played peacemaker. "Why not let him come?" he asked Siry. "Without him, more of us would be bleeding."

"He was an ally of my father's," Siry argued.

"And he won the battle for us," the blond guy countered.

Siry gave me a dark look. "What do you want, Pendragon? Why are you here?"

"That's a long story, but you gotta know I'm here as a friend."

Siry was torn. He wanted me gone, but I'd gotten some credibility by helping them turn back the Flighters.

"The things I showed you, it was to make you understand how different I am from my father. Whatever he stood for, I don't want any part of it."

"I understand that."

"Don't be an idiot. You're an outsider. As long as the tribunal thinks they need you, they'll leave you alone. But if they change their minds and think you're a threat . . ." He didn't finish the sentence. He didn't have to.

"I'll risk it," I said.

I heard a sniffing sound as if my dog, Marley, were around and I had bacon in my ear. I turned quickly to find the girl named Twig had her nose by my cheek. "You don't smell scared anymore." She looked at Siry and smiled. "I like him."

"We might need him again," the blond thief added.

Siry gave me another look. He scowled and said to me, "Don't get in my way."

I had been accepted by the Jakills. I hoped that was a good thing.

IBARA

Siry picked out four Jakills to help move the wounded, including his blond friend. The others were told to scatter. The six of us awkwardly carried the unconscious through the village and back to the hut. Along the way we got strange looks from the people of Rayne. We were a bunch of scruffy-looking kids, carrying three bodies. I'd stare too. Many of them quickly turned away and hurried back into their homes, as if we were carrying the plague. When we got back to the hut where I had first woken up after being attacked by the quig-bees, Telleo was sitting outside, reading. She looked so peaceful sitting there. It wouldn't last.

"What happened?" she asked, jumping to her feet. She looked around anxiously, as if worried that others were watching the scene.

"A group of Flighters tried to attack the tribunal," Siry answered.

"Bring them inside quickly," Telleo instructed while glancing around again. She definitely didn't want anybody seeing us. We carried the wounded inside the hut and gently laid them down on beds. Telleo did a quick appraisal of each.

"We have to get a doctor," she concluded.

"No!" Siry barked.

"They need care," Telleo protested.

"Then give it to them," Siry shot back. "I don't want doctors here."

Telleo was on the verge of panic. "But I can't—"

"You can't or you won't?" Siry asked sharply.

This shut Telleo down. She nodded. "I'll do what I can."

Siry pointed to the other Jakills and said, "Go home. There's nothing more to do here."

Three of them left right away. The blond thief came up to me. "My name is Loque. Thank you."

"Pendragon," I responded.

He gave me a friendly hit on the shoulder and left.

"Let her work," Siry said to me, and left the hut.

Telleo and I were the only ones left. Or at least, the only ones conscious. She looked scared.

"Can you help them?" I asked.

"I can try."

"Why doesn't Siry want doctors?"

"Doctors work for the tribunal. He doesn't want anything to do with them."

"What about you?" I asked. "Are you a Jakill?"

Telleo gave me a surprised look and chuckled. "No, I'm not. I don't think the tribunal even knows that name. I'm surprised that you do."

I shrugged. "Yeah, well, I work fast."

"The tribunal would not be happy if they knew I was helping them. I could lose my job."

"Isn't that kind of . . . wrong?"

"It's complicated," she said with a resigned shrug. "I'm glad the tribunal didn't send you away."

"I'm glad they didn't have me executed! They made Siry my babysitter instead. He's supposed to keep me out of trouble. Some joke, huh?"

Telleo's expression turned dark. "Be careful of him," she said softly. "He's not a bad person, but he's playing a dangerous game."

I walked for the door. "I'll be careful. Good luck with these guys."

She nodded. As soon as I left her and stepped out the door, Siry jumped me, grabbed my shirt and got right in my face.

"Did my father send you here?" he demanded. "Did he tell you to stop me?"

I could have dropped the guy in a heartbeat, but that wouldn't do anything to earn his trust. I had to show strength, but not seem like a threat.

"No. To both questions."

"Then why are you here? And don't tell me it's to battle some fantasy demon monster."

He was making it tough. That's exactly why I was there.

"What are you afraid of, Siry? What's happening here?"

He pulled away from me. The guy was a mess of emotions, most of them negative. He was angry, distrustful, and scared. He started to speak, but stopped, as if the words were difficult. He was struggling to keep his emotions in check. The other Jakills were gone. We were alone. I didn't think he'd have let his feelings show like that if the others had been around.

"Is it true?" he finally asked. "About my father?"

I nodded. Siry winced. The guy had a tough shell, but there was a heart in there somewhere.

"I didn't know him," I explained. "But I know a lot about him. Maybe I can help you understand him."

"I know all I want to know," he snapped viciously.

This wasn't going well. I needed an ally on Ibara. I needed a Traveler, but all I had was an angry kid who had issues with his father. It wasn't going to be easy to get him to accept his role as a Traveler and take on a whole bunch more.

"Your father was telling the truth," I said. "I need your help."

"You say that like I should care," Siry shouted. "My father was on the tribunal. He was just as guilty as the rest of them."

"Then help me understand," I pleaded with him. "What is the tribunal guilty of?"

Siry stared at the ground. I felt as if he wanted to trust me, but didn't know how.

"You said I was a target," he said softly.

"We're all targets. All Travelers. You don't want to hear that, but it's true. You're going to find out soon enough. Better to hear it from me than—"

"Than Saint Dane?" he interrupted.

"I'm here to find the truth, Siry," I said again. "Maybe I can help you get what you want too, but you have to trust me. I need to know about the tribunal and the Jakills and the Flighters."

Siry looked at me as if I were from Mars. Or Second Earth.

"You really don't know anything, do you?"

"What can I say? I'm from out of town."

Siry gave me a look that actually chilled me. "If you do anything to hurt the Jakills, I'll kill you."

He meant it too.

Without another word, Siry walked toward the bay. He led me along the sandy path, down to the perfect white-powder beach and along the shore. The water was warm, like Cloral. It felt good to splash in it. Siry didn't speak. I didn't think he was used to opening up to anybody, especially a stranger, and I was about as strange a guy as he'd ever met. He was angry. Angry with the tribunal, with his father, and with life in general. He didn't speak again until we were too far from the village to be overheard.

"We're being lied to" was the first thing he said. "Everybody. Every last person in Rayne. Maybe everyone on Ibara."

"Who's lying? The tribunal?"

"It starts with them," he answered. "They're manipulating us all. They say they're doing what's best for everyone, but it's not the truth."

"What are they lying about?"

"Everything!" he snapped. "It's about getting us to conform to their way of thinking. Their way of life. Living in this village is like being dead."

"Really? Seems pretty sweet to me."

"You don't live here," Siry snarled. "This is it. There's nothing more. People live their boring little lives in their little huts doing little jobs. Every day. Everyone has his place. Nothing varies. When you turn seven, you're evaluated and told what job you'll do for the rest of your life. You have no choice. You know what job they've got for me? Farming. I'm supposed to grow food to feed the people who make the clothes that are worn by the people who catch the fish that are eaten by the people who build the huts for the people who pick up the trash of the people who repair the lights for the people who bring the water to the people who teach other people how to do all the boring jobs in the first place. It never ends. Every single day. That's not living. It's surviving."

"So where does the lying come in?" I asked.

"There's more to this world than that. To life. The tribunal is keeping it from us."

"How?" I asked.

"They control information. There are plenty of books, but none talk about our history, or about anything that happens beyond our little world. Don't even try to ask. You won't get answers. Worse, if you ask too many questions, they put you away. It's a crime to be curious."

"I don't get that."

"People disappear. One day a guy might be heard openly wondering about why we aren't allowed to move to other villages; the next day he's gone. His whole family is gone. Nobody knows where or why. They're just . . . gone, and never seen again."

"So why don't people just leave?" I asked.

"Because nobody is allowed off the island!" Siry shouted.

"This is an island?" I asked, surprised.

"Yes," Siry answered. "Rayne is the largest village, but there are others. I've been to a few with my father, but traveling is discouraged. We're conditioned from birth to live our lives in the little village where we were born and to be happy about it. I'm not. None of the Jakills are. We know there's something more out there. The Jakills are going to find it."

"Wait, go back. This is an island that nobody has ever left?"

"Yes."

"So who are the Flighters? People trying to leave?"

"No, they come from somewhere else. That's why the tribunal is afraid of them. They're worried the Flighters will poison our way of life. The security force usually keeps them away, but sometimes a few make land, like today."

"Where do they come from?"

"That's just it. Nobody knows! If the tribunal knows, they're not saying. The tough thing is, the Flighters are savages. If they were friendly, there might be a way to learn from them, but they aren't. They're scavengers who raid farms and steal whatever they can carry. They've attacked villagers and destroyed huts. They're all about random violence. Now they're going after the tribunal."

"So it looks like the tribunal has more to worry about than whether they'll poison Rayne's way of life."

Siry nodded.

"If you hate the place so much, why did you protect the tribunal from the Flighters?"

Siry chuckled and shook his head, as if I were an idiot. "We don't want to destroy Rayne, Pendragon. If people are happy with their lives, that's their choice. We just want everyone to know the truth and live their lives the way they want. We aren't heartless. The Jakills have families. We want change, not destruction. We want to help the people of Rayne, not hurt them. That's why we fight the Flighters."

Good answer.

"So that's what brought the Jakills together? You want to change your lives?"

"Most of us are the sons and daughters of village leaders," Siry answered. "We all heard things, growing up. Little things our parents let slip. It got each of us thinking on our own. Once we started pooling our information, the questions kept coming. Who are we? Why are we stuck here? Why can't we learn about the rest of our world?"

"What did your father tell you?" I asked.

Siry laughed. "He was the worst of all. He wanted nothing to do with the outside world. I have a hard time believing he was some kind of 'Traveler.' That wasn't him. I'm sorry he's dead. I really am. He was a good guy when I was little. But once I started having opinions of my own, we stopped getting along."

"What about your mother?" I asked.

"I didn't know her. Remudi adopted me when I was a baby."

No surprise there. That's how it worked with Travelers. I was getting a better picture of Ibara. Remudi was a Traveler. I couldn't help but think that if he had a hand in the kind of disinformation policy that Siry was talking about, it might have something to do with the future of Ibara. The turning point. I felt I was on the right track. Not close, but at least on the right track.

"We just want the truth," Siry said. "You saw the Jakill clearing in the jungle. You saw the things we have. None of that came from any village on the island. Over the years things have washed up on shore. What wasn't confiscated and destroyed by the security force has been secretly passed around and hidden. It may all be junk, but it means a lot more to us. Each piece is a clue to what exists beyond the shores of this island. We want to know what it is."

"You might not like it," I cautioned.

"Maybe. We want the chance to find out for ourselves."

I nodded in understanding.

"I've been honest with you. It's your turn. What do you really want here?"

It was a critical moment. Siry didn't trust me, but he'd opened up. It made me think there was hope for an alliance.

"I think you're right," I began. "The tribunal is keeping

secrets. Your father was keeping secrets. I want to know what they are."

"Why?" he pressed. "Why do you care?"

"I know you didn't agree with your father or anything he stood for. I do. He was a Traveler, which means there's more going on here than even the tribunal realizes."

That made Siry perk up. He liked the idea that there might be secrets being kept from the tribunal.

I continued, "I know you don't care about being a Traveler, but I think that what you want, what the Jakills want, is exactly what I want. We may have different reasons, but we're on the same side. We both want the truth. Let me help you find it."

Siry stared deep into my eyes, as if he were trying to read my mind and gauge whether or not I could be trusted. He was a passionate guy. That was good. He was also a thief and a brawler who hated authority. Not so good. But I agreed with his philosophy. People should be in charge of their own destinies. And he was loyal. He cared about his friends and wanted what was right for them. Maybe he had the makings of a Traveler after all.

"All right," he finally said. "But I meant what I said. If you betray us, I'll kill you."

I had been cautious with Siry till then, but I was tired of playing games. I got right into his face and said, "Whether you believe it or not, you are way over your head. I've asked for your help, but pretty soon you're going to need me as much as I need you. Don't threaten me, Siry."

Siry blinked. I called his bluff. He was a lot of things, but he wasn't a killer.

"You want to help us?" he asked. "You really want to help us?"

"Yes," I said.

"Then come with me."

He took off running down the beach. I hoped this wasn't going to be a long trip. The adrenaline from the fight had worn off and I was feeling kind of worked. I wanted a nap, not a tour. But this was Siry's show. If he was going to show me something important, I had to go along. He led me along the shore of the cove, ducking into the dense jungle near the outer limits of Rayne. He seemed to pick a random spot to enter the jungle, but I soon realized we were on a small path. Back in Stony Brook I knew every twist, turn, rock, path, tree, and ditch in the woods behind my house. It was the same for Siry. He knew exactly where he was going. We shot along the narrow, twisting path for several minutes. The foliage was thick, making the jungle seem darker than it was. The path rose gradually and soon became so steep I thought about using my hands to scramble up. We were climbing, high. It was tough going. I knew we were coming to the end of our trip when the path became lighter again. Siry climbed on to a rock outcropping at the edge of the jungle and turned back to me. I could see the excitement in his eyes.

"We're not just a bunch of angry kids," he declared. "We mean what we say, and we're going to do something about it."

He motioned for me to take a look. I climbed up next to him to find we were on a rock ledge, high above the shore. We were facing the ocean that bordered the large protected bay. Looking out, I saw nothing but green sea. Down below was a curious sight. This wasn't a sandy beach. It was a rocky, rugged coastline. Jutting out from the shore were five long, wooden piers. Tied up to either side of each pier was a sailing ship. Ten in all. Each was identical. They looked to me like old-fashioned pirate ships, complete with double wooden masts.

I'm guessing they were about a hundred feet long, with a structure at the stern. They were identical, except for their colors. Each was painted a different bright, tropical color. There were vibrant greens, brilliant blues, and a few deep corals. It was an awesome sight. The ships gleamed in the sun. Their brilliant colors made them look more like amusement park rides than practical ships. I'd seen old-fashioned sailing ships at the Mystic Seaport back home, but I'd never seen so many in one place. It was a small fleet.

"They look new," I observed.

"They are," Siry answered. "They've only been out for short test sails."

"Is this the fishing fleet?" I asked.

"No," Siry answered. "They're way bigger than any fishing boat. Officially, the tribunal says they're to replace the older fishing boats, but people who've been aboard say they aren't outfitted for fishing."

"What do *you* think they're for?" I asked.

Siry looked down at the colorful fleet. He thought for a moment, then said, "I don't know. I don't care. When I look at these ships I only think of one thing."

"What's that?"

Siry looked at me with dead seriousness and said, "Escape."

"What?"

"Many of the Jakills have been on ships since they could walk. They know how to sail. They'll have no trouble handling one of those."

"Whoa, wait," I said. "You're not thinking of—"

"Yeah, we are," Siry said. "We're going to steal one of those ships and leave the island."

"What about the security force? Aren't they guarding the ships?"

"They're more worried about Flighters coming from the sea. They won't expect a threat from Rayne. That's part of the problem, Pendragon. The people here have given up. No, worse, it's like the spirit of adventure has been bred out of them. They go along, living on the beach, catching their fish, picking fruit, and singing songs. There's no life here. No excitement. It's a dead culture. The Jakills are going to change that."

"No offense but I've seen you guys fight," I said vehemently. "If the security force jumps in, you'll never set foot on one of those ships, let alone sail it away."

Siry stepped in front of me, folded his arms, and smiled. "I agree. It was the one thing that kept us from going forward with our plans. I think we've solved that."

He gave me a wide, Cheshire cat grin. It didn't take long to understand what he was thinking.

"You're kidding, right?" I said quickly.

"You said you wanted to help us."

"Yeah but, we're talking about piracy!"

"There was one thing my father said that stuck with me, Pendragon. He said that Ibara was getting close to a turning point. He said the future of our home depended on how that turning point went. I think he was right, and I think the Jakills are that turning point. We want to get out from under this controlling society and explore Ibara. We want to make this a better place. You said you wanted to help? Get us onto one of those ships. I think that's what my father would have wanted you to do."

I stepped past Siry and looked down on the brightly colored sailing fleet. This territory was an enigma. It seemed the people who lived on this island were being sheltered from the bigger world beyond. But why? What was out there? Did the tribunal know? Were they protecting their people? Or keeping them prisoner? There was a big fat truth lying out there, somewhere across the ocean. I had no doubt that whatever it was, it had something to do with the overall destiny of Ibara, which meant it had to do with Saint Dane. I needed to know what was out there, not for the same reasons as Siry and the Jakills, but for the sake of the whole territory.

How could I do that? I could go to the tribunal and try to learn from them. But in spite of my loose connection to Remudi, I was an outsider. If the tribunal totally controlled the lives of everyone in Rayne, what chance did I have of getting them to be truthful with me? Unfortunately, the answer was clear. There was zero chance of that. It was looking as though my best hope of learning the truth about Ibara was in joining up with a renegade band of kids who were hungry for adventure.

"When do we leave?" I asked.

This is where I'm going to end this journal and send it to you, Courtney. Like I said, I'm about to become an outlaw. I've decided to put in with Siry and the Jakills and help them hijack one of the sailing ships. The flumes have always put us where we needed to be, when we needed to be there. I don't think it's a coincidence that I've landed on Ibara when the next Traveler is about to make such a bold move. Something is about to happen on this island. Change is coming. The Jakills are at the leading edge. Their disenchantment with the status quo feels like a revolution. Things are definitely coming to a head. By all accounts the strange Flighters have become more aggressive. Just as strange is the mystery fleet of sailing ships that the tribunal constructed. What are they for? Why are they being so secretive about them?

Strangest of all, I need to know what lies beyond the shores of this island. In some ways I feel as if I haven't even discovered Ibara yet. I've only experienced this one small, secluded island. Is the rest of Ibara like this? Who are the Flighters, and why are they harassing the people of Rayne?

And of course, where is Saint Dane and how is he involved? Each time I meet a new person, my first thought is that he might be Saint Dane. It's tough to live in that constant state of paranoia. I've got to go with my gut, and my gut tells me that to unravel the mystery of Ibara, I've got to become a Jakill.

No, I've got to become a pirate.

END OF JOURNAL #29

◉ FIRST EARTH ◉

Courtney read Bobby's journal, by herself, in Gunny's lonely basement apartment in the Manhattan Tower Hotel. The pages were almond colored and perfectly square. Each measured about twelve inches across. Bobby had written them in black ink and placed them in a flat, watertight pouch that he rolled up and tied with a band. As the story on Ibara unfolded on the pages before her, Courtney realized again how much she missed Mark. Learning of Bobby's problems alone was a lonely, torturous experience. She needed Mark. She needed a friend. She wanted to trust Dodger. But after what happened with Whitney Wilcox on Second Earth, she wasn't going to put her faith in a stranger too quickly. So after the bellhop witnessed Bobby's journal arrive in the garden outside the hotel, Courtney panicked. She swooped it up and hurried into the hotel to get away.

"Hey!" the bellhop yelled, chasing after her. "Where you going?"

"Leave me alone!" Courtney shouted without breaking stride.

"That thing showed up out of nowhere!" he exclaimed, stunned. "How did you do that?"

"Magic. I'm a magician. Pretty good, huh? Show's over. Go away."

She hurried up the steps of the hotel. Dodger was right after her.

"You ain't no magician," he said. "There's something else going on here. You're not some kind of spaceman, are you? Or spacegirl?"

Courtney stopped again. "You're kidding, right? You won't believe it was phony magic, but you'd buy that I'm from Pluto?"

"I'm not buyin' nothing. I just want to know what's going on."

Dodger seemed to Courtney like an okay guy. Bobby trusted him. Gunny trusted him. In the past that would have been enough for Courtney. Not anymore.

"You're right," she exclaimed. "You got me. I'm from outer space. Keep it to yourself or I'll vaporize you."

She tried to walk off again, but Dodger took her shoulder. Courtney pulled away angrily.

"Look," he said, backing off, "Gunny asked me to help anybody who showed up with one of them rings. How can I do that if you don't level with me?"

Courtney wanted to trust the little guy. Badly. "I'm sorry," she said sincerely. "It's not your fault."

She left him standing on the steps of the hotel, dazed. She hurried to Gunny's apartment and spent the next hour pouring over every word of Bobby's journal. Reading about Bobby's adventures wasn't new to Courtney, but this time felt different. Aside from her trip to Black Water, Courtney always felt as if she were nothing more than an observer. The events Bobby wrote about didn't affect her directly.

Those days were over.

The territories were folding in on themselves. Dados had turned up on Quillan and the three Earth territories. They turned up in her home in the form of a mechanical cat. Courtney knew the events Bobby described weren't about Ibara alone. The puzzle was getting more complicated. The battle with Saint Dane was suddenly less about the struggle for individual territories. It was now about Halla.

Sitting in that lonely apartment, Courtney knew that finding Mark wasn't just about saving her friend. It could affect events on all the Earth territories. It could affect Bobby on Ibara. It could affect every being in Halla. Saint Dane was making his final push to bring the territories down. The realization staggered her. She was worried about Bobby and what he'd found on Ibara, but she also knew there was nothing she could do about that. She had to stay focused on her mission on First Earth.

She had to find Mark.

The telephone rang. Courtney jumped. The bell was loud and jangling, not like the soft tone of her kitchen phone on Second Earth. Gunny's phone sounded like a fire alarm. She calmed herself and picked up the heavy, black receiver. "Hello?" she said tentatively.

"Don't hang up," Dodger begged.

Courtney didn't, but she didn't speak, either. She didn't know what to say.

"I think I got it figured," Dodger said. "Are you and Pendragon on the lam from the law?"

Courtney burst out laughing. "On the lam?" she echoed. "What are you, some kind of mob guy?"

"No!" Dodger said quickly. "I got nothin' to do with them guys! Honest!"

Courtney forced herself to refocus. She knew she couldn't look at this world from a Second Earth perspective. This was 1937. It was a different territory with different rules.

"Look, Dodger, I understand that what you just saw freaked you out."

"It did what?" he asked quickly.

"What I mean is, you saw something . . . unusual, and it's making you . . . nervous."

"You can say that again, sister," Dodger agreed.

"And stop calling me 'sister.' Or 'skirt' or 'dame' or 'broad' or whatever clever macho demeaning term you can think of."

"Sorry."

"Look, I wish I could trust you. I can't. I've been burned before. I mean, I've been fooled before."

"Oh, I get it," Dodger said knowingly. "You've been dumped by some chump boyfriend?"

"Yeah," Courtney said. "You could say that." Courtney laughed to herself, thinking that Dodger didn't realize how close to the truth that was.

"Then there's no problem!" Dodger continued. "I don't want to be your boyfriend. I got no time for skirts, uh, girls. Sorry, that slipped out."

Courtney was weakening. Dodger was getting to her, but she knew that was exactly the kind of thing Saint Dane would do. He was offering to give her what she needed most, friendship and help.

"Thanks, Dodger," she said curtly. "But no thanks. Maybe someday I'll get the chance to explain it to you, but not today."

Courtney hung up. She barely had time to gather the journal pages and put them back into the waterproof pouch, when a knock came at the door. She looked around for a place to hide the journals and chose Gunny's favorite hiding place . . . the oven.

"Who is it?" she called while quickly closing the oven door.

"Room service," came a professional man's voice.

"I didn't order room service," she called back.

Another knock. Courtney started to panic. There was no way

out of this room. She ran to the door and put her eye to the peep-hole to see . . .

A smiling Dodger staring back at her through the fish-eye peephole. He had to stand on his toes to get up high enough.

"Compliments of the house!" he announced cheerily.

Courtney couldn't help but smile. The guy was either a sincere goof, or Saint Dane was better than she imagined. She hesitated, then unlocked the door, and threw it open. Dodger stood there behind a dinner cart loaded with plates of food that were covered by silver warming domes. Courtney's stomach rumbled.

"How did you get here so fast?" she asked suspiciously.

"I called you from the house phone in the laundry back there," Dodger said, pointing to a door a few yards down the hall. "I figure you gotta be hungry after rocketing through the universe. Pluto, right?" He gave her an innocent, sincere smile.

"Come on in," she said. "If you're going to give me trouble, it might as well be on a full stomach."

"Oh, no," Dodger said. "It ain't right being in a lady's boudoir."

"Ain't that your, I mean . . . isn't that your job?"

"Yeah, but I ain't here on official business. I'm here on Gunny business."

Courtney gave Dodger a good long look. The delicious smells rising up from the covered plates made her mouth water. "Tell you what," she said. "If you're telling the truth, I guess you'd call it being 'on the level,' I'm sorry for being so mysterious. If you're not telling the truth, you know exactly where I'm coming from, so back off."

"Jeez, you're confusing me," Dodger said. "You gotta under-stand. I owe Gunny a lot. I wasn't the best kid growing up, you know. Gunny took me in and gave me a job. He trusted me. Nobody ever done that before. I think I did all right, too. All because Gunny gave me the chance. So if he asked me to swim over to Germany and give old Adolph a smacker on the lips, I'd be swimmin' and puckerin' up. The way I see it, helping you is easy-peasy."

"All right! I give up! Jeez, you're making me cry here . . . and now I'm starting to sound like you. Unbelievable."

"I grow on people," Dodger said with a sly smile.

"Look, it's got to be on my terms. Don't ask questions. Don't follow me. And only do what I ask. If that's okay with you, I welcome your help."

Dodger let out a big, genuine smile. He tipped his bellhop cap and said, "I am at your service, ma'am. When do we start?"

"Tomorrow morning. Nine o'clock. And don't call me 'ma'am,' either."

"What should I call you?"

"'Courtney.' No title. No colorful slang. Just 'Courtney.'"

"Done. Nine o'clock it is. Meet you in the lobby?"

"Done." She couldn't help but smile. "Thank you, Dodger. And just know that if you're Saint Dane, I'm ready for you."

"And maybe someday I'll know what the heck that means," Dodger said. "Until then, enjoy this delicious meal. I'll see you bright and early!"

He tipped his cap again and left Courtney to pull the cart of food into the room. All thoughts of Dodger and Saint Dane and Ibara evaporated for the few minutes it took her to enjoy the feast. Dodger had brought her a fabulous dinner of sliced turkey with mashed potatoes and gravy, nut stuffing, cranberry sauce, and buttered green beans. Thanksgiving had come a few weeks early. Courtney was all set to chow down when the thought crossed her mind that somehow Saint Dane knew how much she liked Thanksgiving dinner, and this meal was another way to earn her trust. Was he that incredibly devious? She decided she was too hungry to care. She put her fear of manipulation-by-turkey out of her head, and tucked in. It was delicious. She ate too fast and ended up feeling totally bloated, but she didn't care. Dodger had thought of it all, including the pumpkin pie and milk. Courtney decided to hold off on eating the pie until she digested a little. That held her back for a whole five minutes. It was too tempting. She downed the pie and enjoyed every last decadent crumb.

It was late. Courtney didn't finish feasting until nearly ten o'clock. She knew it wasn't smart to go to bed on such a full stomach, but she was dog tired and the tryptophan was working its magic. She could barely keep her eyes open long enough to brush her teeth and pull off her clothes, before she fell into bed and dropped off to sleep. One of her last thoughts before nodding off was that Dodger's thoughtful meal had an added bonus. She was going to get a good night's sleep without all the tossing and turning she usually had to endure while her mind raced and worried. She was on her way out. That was good, because she knew the next day would be busy. She was going to begin her quest to find Mark in this alien world.

The next morning she was woken up by the jangling telephone. She leaped up, ready to grab her clothes and run out of the building to escape from the fire. It took her a second to realize it was only the annoying phone.

"What's with these old-time people?" she asked herself. "Are they all deaf?"

She answered the phone and heard Dodger's friendly voice. "Change your mind?"

Courtney glanced at the bedside clock. It was nine thirty. She had slept nearly twelve hours.

"Yikes, sorry. I'll be right there."

Courtney didn't bother with a shower. She quickly dressed in her woolen pants and white shirt. She threw on socks, tied up the leather shoes, and slipped into the green sweater. The finishing touch was the floppy hat that she tucked her hair into. She had no idea what she'd find on First Earth, but there was one thing she knew for sure. She didn't want anybody treating her like a "skirt." Satisfied, she left the apartment and headed upstairs.

The hotel lobby was bustling with people. Courtney saw Dodger leaning against a big, marble column near the lounge. She watched him for a moment. He looked innocent enough, she thought. He wore plain black pants and a short charcoal gray cloth jacket. Without his bellhop uniform, he looked even younger. Being short added to that impression. He stood watching the hotel guests as they passed by, waving and smiling to those he knew. One elderly woman was having trouble getting the attention of the busy bellhops, so Dodger jumped in and helped her carry her suitcase to the front desk, even though he wasn't on duty. There was nothing about Dodger that made Courtney think he could be Saint Dane, other than the fact that she thought everybody could be Saint Dane. She wasn't going to let her guard down, but she needed help finding Mark. She decided it was worth the risk. She left the doorway, stuck her hands in her pockets, and walked toward him. When Dodger saw her, he brightened up.

"There you are!" he said. "Good afternoon!"

"Yeah, very funny," Courtney said, all business. "Let's go talk."

"Yes, ma'am," Dodger said obediently, then winced. "I mean, yes, Courtney."

Courtney led him into the lobby lounge. It was loaded with people chatting and socializing.

"No good," she said, putting on the brakes. "Is there someplace private?" She thought a second and added, "But with other people around?"

"You want private but with other people?"

"Uh, yeah." She realized how ridiculous that sounded.

"Still don't trust me? Even after the turkey dinner?"

"Especially after the turkey dinner," Courtney said. "But thanks anyway."

"You're welcome. Follow me."

Dodger led Courtney through the opulent lobby. The short guy walked with a cocky strut, like he owned the place. He brought Courtney through the hotel restaurant and into the bustling kitchen.

"Hey, Dodger!" one of the cooks called out. "Ain't this your day off?"

"Nah, I'm always workin'," Dodger shot back quickly.

Another cook whistled and yelled, "Dodger! Whose the Kewpie?"

"That's 'dame' to you, pal!" Courtney shouted back.

The cooks laughed in mock fear. Dodger laughed too. Courtney could see that he was well liked. Would Saint Dane be well liked? She shook off the thought. It was making her nuts.

Dodger brought Courtney to the back of the kitchen, where the dishes were washed. It was hot and steamy, with only a few dishwashers at work.

"How's this?" Dodger asked. "Quiet but not too quiet, nobody to bother us, and a couple of witnesses in case I do something you don't like. All you gotta do is put up with a little steam and some dirty dishes."

"This is fine."

"Now, how can I help you?"

"If you are who you say you are, you won't understand what I'm about to tell you. If you aren't who you say you are, then you already know everything I'm going to say anyway, so it probably doesn't matter if I tell you or not. Get it?"

Dodger gave her a sour look. "I lost you after 'This is fine.'"

"Good. Here's the deal. I'm trying to find somebody. He's a friend of mine. And Bobby's and Gunny's."

"Is he on the lam too?"

"No! None of us are on the lam!" Courtney snapped.

One of the dishwashers turned from his work to see what the shouting was about.

Dodger yelled to him, "Relax, Tony. Everything's peachy."

Tony the dishwasher shrugged and went back to work.

Courtney continued, "It's critically important that we find him. I'm not even going to begin to tell you why, because it's too long of a story and you wouldn't believe me anyway."

"And I wouldn't understand if I am who I am, but if I'm not who I am, then I should already know, but I have no idea what you're talking about so what the heck does that make me?"

"It's starting to make you annoying. This is serious."

"Sorry. Tell me about this pal you're looking for."

"His name is Mark Dimond. He's seventeen with dark curly hair and glasses."

"Oh," Dodger said. "Easy-peasy. Only about a million guys fit that description in New York."

"He stutters when he gets nervous," Courtney added.

"That narrows it down to a half million guys. We're getting there."

"Stop making fun!" Courtney barked.

They both looked at Tony. The dishwasher didn't turn around this time.

"Sorry," Dodger said. "Ain't you got something a little more specific to go on?"

"There's one thing," Courtney admitted. "If I was home, I think I could use it to try and track him down, but I'm not. I don't know how things work around here, and that's why I'm talking to you in the first place."

Courtney was getting worked up. Tony looked around again. Courtney yelled, "Hey! Tony! Mind your own business!"

Dodger led Courtney away from the dishwashers into a storage area that was surrounded by shelves loaded with clean plates.

"It's okay," Dodger said reassuringly. "Tell me about the thing."

Courtney took a breath to calm herself and said, "On October sixth, Mark filed a patent application at the US Patent Office. I have to believe that when you do that, they ask for an address or something, where you can be contacted. I was hoping that if we look up that information, it might give me a lead as to where to find him."

Dodger waited for Courtney to say more. She didn't.

"That's it?" he asked.

"That's it."

"That's all we got to go on?"

"Afraid so."

"You're telling me this mystery guy is some kind of inventor?"

Courtney was about to say no, but that's exactly what Mark was. "Yeah," she said. "He's an inventor. If Gunny were here he'd tell you how important it is that we find him. But he's not. It's just me. Can you help?"

Courtney watched as Dodger frowned, deep in thought. He paced. He scratched his head. He paced some more. None of this looked good to Courtney. Her spirits sagged.

"I know," she admitted, defeated. "It's hopeless. There's no way we can find somebody that way."

"No!" Dodger said. "Finding him is no problem. I got friends who work for the government."

"Are you kidding?" Courtney shouted, her spirits suddenly back up. "Why are you looking all concerned?"

Dodger said, "I can't figure out what's so important about some kid inventor that Gunny would want me to find him so bad."

Courtney grabbed Dodger by the lapels and shouted, "Ask him when you see him. Right now, let's find Mark. Got that Tony?"

Tony the dishwasher shrugged and went back to work.

A few minutes later Courtney stood outside a telephone booth near the lobby while Dodger made a call. The door was closed, so she couldn't hear what he was saying, but she could tell he was doing a lot of laughing and gesturing. Courtney noticed that Dodger did a lot of gesturing with his hands when he spoke, for emphasis. Finally, after what seemed like a lifetime, Dodger hung up and pulled open the glass door of the phone booth. He looked at Courtney without saying a word. He had no expression. There were no hand gestures.

"Well?" Courtney demanded impatiently.

"People think bellhops are just guys who carry around luggage and flag down cabs, you know? But we have power most people don't see. For example, if somebody's big-shot boss was coming to town and the hotel was booked solid, I could make that somebody look really good by getting his boss a room, because I know that some of the real special suites are saved for last-minute VIPs."

Dodger smiled proudly at Courtney. Courtney stared blankly at Dodger.

"And you're telling me this because . . . ?"

"Because a friend of mine needs a favor, and I'm gonna fix his boss up with the best suite in this joint. Now that friend owes me a favor, get it?"

"Not really," Courtney said.

Dodger stood up and combed his already perfectly combed hair. "This friend just so happens to work in Washington and has access to certain files that aren't always open to the public, if you get my drift."

"Just tell me!" Courtney shouted.

"Two forty Waverly Place."

"And that is . . . ?"

"It's an apartment building in the village where your friend Mark Dimond lives," Dodger announced proudly. "Now do you think I am who I am?"

Courtney threw her arms around Dodger and hugged him tight. "I don't know who you are and right now I don't care, because you might have just saved all humanity from total destruction!"

She let go of Dodger and ran for the exit. He stood there for a moment, basking in the glory.

The smile dropped off his face.

"I just did what?" he shouted as he ran after her.

☻ FIRST EARTH ☻

(CONTINUED)

The cab ride from midtown Manhattan to Waverly Place was a short one. It seemed to Courtney that the deeper they got into the neighborhoods of Manhattan, the less it felt like she was in the past. The buildings didn't look all that different from the buildings of Second Earth, especially as they drove through Greenwich Village. Most buildings were three- or four-story brick walk-ups. The ground floors had restaurants and cleaners and clothing shops. The upper stories looked like apartments. It was pretty much the same as on Second Earth. With no Starbucks. The only obvious, in-your-face sign that things weren't like home was the cars. The streets were clogged with big, growling monsters with gleaming chrome grills. They had names like "Studebaker," "Hudson," and "Cord." There wasn't a single Honda, Volkswagen, or Volvo in sight.

The streets of Greenwich Village were narrower than the wide avenues of midtown. They crossed one another at odd angles and had weird names like "Bethune," "Gansevoort," and "Bleecker." Courtney was happy to see that the cabbie knew exactly where he was going. In no time he made the turn from

Bank Street onto Waverly Place and stopped in front of a quaint corner eatery called "Ye Waverly Inn." Dodger wanted to pay the cab fare, but Courtney wouldn't let him. This was her mission, after all. As they got out of the car, Dodger looked around at the narrow street and shook his head in wonder.

"Coming down here feels like taking a trip into the past," he marveled.

"You have no idea," Courtney said with a snicker.

Dodger put on a brown hat that made Courtney chuckle.

"What?" he asked innocently.

"You trying to be Indiana Jones or what?"

Dodger shook his head in frustration. "You know what I'd like? Just once I'd like it if you said something that made sense."

"Don't count on it," Courtney replied.

Next to the restaurant was the entrance to a four-story brick building—#240.

"This is it," Courtney said nervously.

"Now do you trust me?"

"No."

Dodger took a small piece of paper out of his pocket. "My friend said the patent was issued to Mark Dimond at this address. Apartment number four-A." He put the paper back into his pocket and asked, "If you could get the patent number, how come you couldn't get the address?"

"I don't know," Courtney answered as she started toward the door. "Computers aren't infallible I guess."

"There you go again not making sense," Dodger said as he followed her toward the door.

"It's only going to get worse," Courtney said. She stopped at the bottom of the steps that led up to the black front door.

"Now what's the problem?" Dodger asked.

"I'm debating about letting you come in with me."

"Why?" he whined. "I got you this far, didn't I?"

Courtney nodded.

"So why don't you trust me?" Dodger asked.

Courtney looked him over, thinking, then said, "You can come. If you're Saint Dane, I'd rather know where you are."

"Good. I think."

Courtney walked up the stairs and scanned the door.

"What are you looking for?" Dodger asked.

"The panel with the security buttons so we can get buzzed in."

Dodger gave her a strange look and opened the front door. It wasn't locked.

"Oh," Courtney said, and stepped inside. It was yet another subtle sign that she was in a different time.

The building was too small to have an elevator, so they climbed the marble staircase up to the fourth floor. It wasn't a fancy building, but it was clean. The smells of cooking filled the stairwell. Good cooking. Courtney thought it was either spaghetti sauce or some yummy soup. It gave the building a warm, inviting feel. She was glad that Mark had landed in such a comfortable place.

Mark. With each step up, Courtney grew more tense. What would she say to him? More important, what would he say to her? Courtney couldn't imagine any excuse for why he'd brought technology from home to a different territory. He knew how wrong that was. She couldn't come up with a scenario that would explain it. As she grew closer to her reunion with Mark, Courtney wasn't sure how she should feel. Angry? Hurt? Frightened? Sympathetic? All the above? The best thing she could do was take it one step at a time. First find Mark and make sure that he's okay. After that, the way to go would be clear. Or so she hoped.

They arrived on the fourth floor, where they were faced with five doors leading to different apartments. Number 4A was to the far right of the landing.

"What do we do?" Dodger asked.

Courtney's answer was to stride across the landing to Mark's door. Before she could change her mind, she boldly knocked. No answer. She knocked again, louder. Still no answer. They waited a solid minute, knocking a few more times.

"Either nobody's home or they don't want company," Dodger said.

"I'm not leaving until we find out who lives here," Courtney said adamantly.

"That thing you said before? You know, about saving humanity from total destruction? That was a joke, right?"

Courtney gave him a serious look. She didn't confirm it, but she didn't scoff and say, "Nah! Just kidding!" either.

"Right," Dodger said thoughtfully. "Never mind. I don't wanna know."

"I can't begin to tell you how huge it is," Courtney finally answered.

"Right," Dodger said again. "Just making sure." He took a step away from the door, rolled his shoulders, cracked his neck, then suddenly ran for the door of apartment 4A.

"Hey!" Courtney shouted in surprise.

She had to jump out of the way or she would have been bulldozed. Dodger hit the door with his shoulder, hard. With a loud *crack* the door gave way, swinging in and smashing against the inside wall. Dodger tumbled inside, falling to his knees. Courtney ran to him.

"You're crazy!" she exclaimed.

"A little."

Courtney helped him to his feet. "Are you okay?"

Dodger rubbed his shoulder. "Sure," he answered casually. "Wasn't the first time I had to break down a door. Won't be the last. Being a bellhop ain't all glamour."

Courtney quickly closed the door. She didn't want nosy neighbors peeking in to see strangers smashing into the apartment.

"Looks like we're too late," Dodger said.

Courtney saw that the place was empty. It was a small, clean apartment with white walls. The short front hallway led into a small living room. To the right was a door leading to a kitchen. To the left was another short hallway that led to a bedroom and bathroom. There were no pictures on the walls. No plants. No rugs. No clues as to who may have lived there. Courtney walked into the kitchen. There was a small stove and a table. That was it. She left the kitchen, walked through the living room and into the bedroom. She found a small bed with no sheets or blankets. The one piece of furniture was a wooden bureau. Courtney deflated.

Dodger said, "If he was here, he's long gone now."

They were about to leave the room when something caught Courtney's eye. On the floor was a plain white piece of paper. Most of it was underneath a closet door. One corner stuck out, which was the only thing Courtney saw. She knelt down and pulled it out. The paper turned out to be a four-by-five-inch rectangle. Courtney turned it over. When she saw what it was, she started to cry.

"What is it?" Dodger asked.

"It's an accident," she said, wiping her eyes. "No way this was left on purpose."

Courtney handed him the paper. Dodger took a long look and asked softly, "This him?"

Courtney nodded. It was a photo that could have been taken at a local drugstore on Second Earth. It had a cheesy fake background that looked like a Cape Cod beach. Courtney knew it was fake because she didn't think Mark had ever been to Cape Cod and nobody in the picture was dressed for the beach. It was a photo of Mark and his mom and dad . . . the mom and dad who had been killed. It was the sudden, shocking death of his parents that catapulted Mark into the trouble he now faced, and the trouble he was bringing to Halla.

"He looks about fourteen here," Courtney said. "He's older now."

"His parents?" Dodger asked.

Courtney nodded. She took the picture back. She wanted to see it again. She wanted to see the old Mark. The Mark who ate too many carrots and loved Japanese animation. The Mark who was Bobby's best friend and had become her best friend once the doorway to Halla had opened. She wanted to see that Mark again. She wanted to hear him stutter. She wanted to know why the hell he had done what he did.

Courtney wiped her eyes and stood up, tucking the photo into her back pocket. She was in control again.

"So what do we do?" Dodger asked.

"We talk to the neighbors," Courtney announced, all business. "Somebody here must have known him. Maybe they know where he went."

They started on the fourth floor and worked their way down, knocking on doors and asking suspicious neighbors if they knew anything about Mark and where he might have gone. They pretty much got the same answer each time. Many people saw Mark, but nobody spoke with him. Nobody had a clue as to what had happened to him either. After a futile hour Courtney and Dodger found themselves back out in front of the building, not knowing much more than when they had started.

"At least we know he was here," Dodger offered hopefully. "That's something. Maybe I can call the city, or the post office, and see if he left a forwarding address."

Courtney brightened. "That's a good idea!"

"Thank you," Dodger said. "Trust me yet?"

"No. No offense, but no."

"None taken. Let's go back to the hotel."

As if on cue, a taxicab screeched to a stop at the curb next to them.

"See?" Dodger exclaimed. "Things are looking up already!"

The two got in the cab and settled in for the ride uptown.

"Manhattan Tower Hotel," Dodger said to the cabbie. "Don't take the scenic route."

"No, sir!" the cabbie said brightly. "I'll get you right where you need to be."

Courtney froze. She knew that voice. It took her two seconds to process the information and make a decision.

"Get out!" she yelled at Dodger.

"Wha—?" he asked dumbly.

"Get out of the car!" she screamed, and grabbed at the door handle. It was locked. She went for the door lock. It was sawed off. She lurched across Dodger's lap to the door on his side. It was just as locked and just as sawed off.

"What are you doing?" Dodger asked in confusion.

"Yeah," the cabbie said. "What are you doing? Don't want to take a spin with me?"

Courtney didn't have to look at the cabbie to know who it was, but she looked anyway. A glass partition separated the front seat from the back, but she could still see the cabbie as plain as could be. Staring back at them, wearing the floppy hat of a New York cabbie, was Andy Mitchell.

"Saint Dane," Courtney whispered.

"Who?" Dodger asked.

Mitchell snorted, smiled, and exclaimed, "Let's roll!"

The cab lurched forward, throwing Courtney and Dodger back into the seat.

"Hey!" Dodger screamed. "Are you nuts?"

"If I had a nickel for every time somebody asked me that . . . ," Mitchell said with a laugh.

"Who is he?" Dodger asked Courtney.

"He's the bad guy," Courtney answered.

"Pleased to meet you!" Mitchell said, tipping his cap. "Mitchell's the name."

"I thought you said his name was Saint Dane?" Dodger asked Courtney.

The cab screeched around a corner, seemingly up on two wheels. Courtney fell into Dodger. The tires dug into the road. The car flew forward.

"Where's Mark?' Courtney yelled.

"You're too late." Mitchell laughed. "He's a big shot now. He won't be living in dumps like that anymore."

Horns blared as the cab snaked through traffic.

"Hey, Mac! Slow down!" Dodger ordered, banging on the glass.

"What's the matter, bellboy? Ain't you up for a little adventure?"

Dodger yanked on the door. It was a waste of energy.

"How did you do it, Saint Dane?" Courtney snarled. "How did you get Mark to come here?"

Andy Mitchell laughed and gave a humble shrug. "Hey, it's what I do."

He turned the wheel hard, cutting off another car, sending it careening off the road and onto a sidewalk.

"Yeehaaa!" Mitchell shouted with exhilaration.

Dodger yelled just as loud. In terror.

Andy yanked the wheel the other way. They bounced off the sidewalk and screamed across three lanes of traffic. Cars spun out and skidded into one another to avoid the cab from hell. Dodger leaned back in his seat and kicked at the glass partition that kept them away from Saint Dane.

"Stop . . . the . . . car!" he ordered.

"Why are you doing this?" Courtney yelled. "If you wanted to kill me, you could have done it a thousand times over."

"I don't want to kill you, Chetwynde. I just want to have a little fun."

"It's below you to torture me," Courtney said, trying to keep her voice in control. She was scared to death, but she didn't want to let Saint Dane know that.

"Then consider this a favor," he said.

"Favor?" Dodger shouted. He kicked at the glass. It was too thick to break.

Mitchell skidded into a turn. Courtney saw the Hudson River directly in front of them. The demon spun the wheel again and they were on the West Side Highway, headed south, parallel to the wide river.

"Why is this a favor, Saint Dane?" Courtney asked, trying to stay focused and keep the fear back.

"Your job is done, Chetwynde," Andy Mitchell said. "You did exactly what I needed you to do. Now it's time for you to toddle on home."

"I can't break the glass," Dodger screamed.

Courtney barely knew Dodger was even there. She was focused on Andy. On Saint Dane.

"What did I do?" she asked.

"Isn't that obvious?" Mitchell laughed. "Sorry you nearly died in Vermont but, hey, if that's what it took, so be it. Nice to see you're not crippled anymore."

Mitchell laughed and jammed past two drivers who were going too slowly for him. They blasted their horns. Mitchell giggled and waved at them.

"What are you talking about?" Courtney demanded.

"Are you stupid or do you just look it?" Mitchell asked. "We came to your rescue. Dimond and me. It was a real bonding experience. After I helped save your life, I looked like a real hero to him. After that, he trusted me, and it was all thanks to you."

Mitchell bashed into the traffic divider, blowing out the right front wheel. The car lurched to the right, but Mitchell kept in control and charged on.

"That's why you ran me off the road in Massachusetts?" Courtney asked. "So you and Mark could come to my rescue?"

Mitchell turned all the way around, taking his eyes off the road. He looked right at Courtney and grinned. "Face it, Chetwynde. You delivered Mark Dimond. Now that I've got him, I've got Halla."

"No!" Courtney lost it. She screamed and banged on the glass. Her fists were only inches from Andy Mitchell. From Saint Dane. She wanted to hurt him. She wanted to bash his smug face. She wanted him to die.

"Look out!" Dodger shouted.

The cab flew down an exit ramp and off the elevated highway. Andy Mitchell casually looked forward and took the wheel, steering clear of a cement barrier.

"Whoa, that would have hurt," he said calmly.

The flat tire was shredded but the car charged on. Sparks flew from the metal rim that was now the fourth wheel. They were at the bottom of Manhattan, where the river widened out to become a harbor. Long piers jutted out into the water. Traffic picked up, but Andy Mitchell didn't slow down.

"Where is he?" Courtney screamed, banging on the glass. "Tell me where he is!"

Mitchell turned the wheel one last time. He flew off the road, cut off a car, and bounced over the sidewalk. They were headed for one of the piers that stretched into the river. People strolled along casually, enjoying the day and admiring the view. Not for long. At the sound of the oncoming cab, they dove out of the way to avoid being mashed. The cab charged forward, blasting onto the wide pier.

"Hey! Dead end!" Dodger shouted.

"Is it?" Mitchell asked innocently. "Oops."

Courtney didn't care. She was beyond caring.

"Go home, Chetwynde," Mitchell said calmly. "See your parents. Cuddle up with your mechanical cat. You have a couple of older brothers, don't you? Spend some time with them. The battle is over. There's nothing left for anybody to do but sit back and watch me fly."

Courtney became calm. It didn't matter that they were hurtling toward the end of the pier. She sat back in the seat and folded her arms.

"You're wrong," she said calmly. "It's not close to being over. Bobby won't let that happen, and neither will I."

Andy Mitchell whipped around to look into the backseat. Only he wasn't Andy Mitchell anymore. His face had transformed into that of Saint Dane. His blue-white eyes flashed. The bloodred veins in his bald head flared.

"Then you'll just have to die!" he hissed.

Dodger screamed.

The car crashed through a wooden barrier at the end of the pier and sailed into the air. Saint Dane melted into black smoke and blew out the window. Courtney and Dodger were alone as the cab sailed down and hit the water with a bone-jarring shudder.

● FIRST EARTH ●
(CONTINUED)

Cars didn't come equipped with seat belts in 1937.
When the cab hit the water, Courtney and Dodger were thrown forward. They hit the glass partition separating the seats and bounced back like rag dolls being tumbled in a clothes dryer. Courtney hit her head, hard. She was knocked senseless.

"Courtney!" Dodger yelled. "Courtney, you all right?"

Courtney didn't hear him. She was barely conscious.

"We're going down!" Dodger yelled.

The car floated on its belly for only a few seconds. The nose tipped down quickly. That's where the weight was. The engine acted like an anchor, pulling the vehicle under. Water poured in the open front windows. The heavier the front became, the steeper the angle became. Soon the car was floating near vertical, with the tail up in the air.

"Courtney!" Dodger yelled. He shook her. Courtney was totally disoriented.

"What happened?" she asked dreamily.

"We're gonna drown!" Dodger screamed.

The back of the front seat was now the floor. Courtney and

Dodger sat on the glass partition as water rose up around them.

"Where's Saint Dane?" Courtney asked.

"Gone!" Dodger shouted. "He turned into smoke and flew out the window! I swear!"

"I believe you," Courtney said, dazed.

The water was up to their waists and bubbling higher. In seconds the car would be submerged and on its way to the bottom.

"Move!" Dodger ordered Courtney.

He pushed her out of the way and slid toward one of the back doors. He pushed up off his bottom with his hands and kicked at the window, desperate to smash it out. The higher the water got, the tougher it was to get enough leverage to put force into his kicks.

"Help me!" he shouted at Courtney.

Courtney rolled over. Her head went underwater. She sputtered, coughed, and sat back up. The cold shock cleared her head.

"What's going on?" she shouted.

"We're sinking," Dodger shouted. "We've got to kick out the window or we're done."

He gave another kick, and another, but it was tough getting power because of the rising water. Courtney scrambled next to Dodger, put her arms down and started to kick the window on her own. The window didn't budge.

"Together!" Dodger commanded.

They sat next to each other, up on their arms, their bellies pointed to the sky. The water was nearly at their shoulders.

"Ready?" Dodger called out. "One, two, three, kick!"

They both kicked the window with their heels, but not at the exact same time.

"Again!" Dodger ordered. "One, two, three, kick!"

They both pounded the window again, hitting it together this time. It didn't budge.

"We can't get enough force!" Dodger yelled.

"Don't stop!" Courtney ordered.

She shifted position, moving her hands so she was closer to the window, when something slipped, making her lose balance.

"Whoa!" Courtney exclaimed as her face slid under the water.

Dodger quickly pulled her back up.

"What happened?" he asked.

"Something moved down there," Courtney exclaimed. "I had my weight on my hands and it made something slide."

Dodger looked down into the water, then ducked below the surface. A second later he came up, sputtering.

"The glass partition!" he exclaimed. "It's not locked anymore. I can slide it open!"

As he spoke, Dodger pushed with his feet to slide open the glass partition that separated the backseat from the front seat. The water was now tickling their chins.

Courtney gasped, "Is the opening big enough to go through?"

"I think."

"If we can get down there, maybe the front doors are unlocked."

"What if they're not?" Dodger asked.

"Dumb question."

"Yeah, dumb question," Dodger echoed.

The water was rising faster. Soon their heads would be bobbing against the rear window.

"It's good the doors are underwater," Courtney added hopefully. "It means the water pressure is equal, and the doors should open."

"If they're unlocked."

"Yeah, if they're unlocked."

They looked at each other. Neither budged. Courtney saw the fear in Dodger's eyes. "If we're going, we gotta go now," she said. "The car is sinking like a brick."

"I'll go," Dodger said. "Give me time to get the door open."

"Dodger?"

"Yeah?"

"I trust you now."

Dodger smiled. "I guess I better not mess up." He took a deep breath and ducked below the surface. Courtney watched as he went straight down through the opening in the partition, feet first. He pushed himself all the way down until his head was below the glass, then turned toward the front passenger door. He reached for the handle, twisted it, and pushed against the door. It didn't move. He put his foot against the steering wheel and leaned into the door. It wouldn't budge.

"Come back up!" Courtney shouted down through the water.

He didn't. He pushed away from the passenger door and went to the driver's door. He grasped the handle with one hand and the steering wheel with the other.

Courtney took a breath to say something, and got a mouthful of water. Her head bumped the glass of the rear window. She was underwater. The car was nearly full and beginning its final plummet to the bottom. She had no choice but to follow Dodger down into the front seat. She found the opening in the partition with her feet, hooked her toes under the glass, bent her knees, and pulled herself down. She grabbed the opening with her hands and pulled herself down the rest of the way. The water was dark and green . . . and getting darker. They were headed for the bottom. Still, she could see the blur of Dodger. With her back to the passenger door, she watched the small bellhop make one last attempt to save them. He twisted the door handle and put his shoulder against the door. Courtney leaned into Dodger, adding whatever force she had. She anchored her feet against the passenger door for leverage and pushed.

The door moved. Dodger forced it open just enough that he could slide out of the car into open water. Quickly he turned back for Courtney. She was already after him. She pushed off the passenger door and swam, head first, out of the driver's door. They were free, but not safe. Neither knew how deep they had been pulled by the car. Courtney gave a quick glance down to see the blurry yellow cab sinking quickly beneath them. She stared at the ghostly image, mesmerized as it slid into the murky green depths. The idea that they might have been in that car froze her.

She felt a strong hand grab her arm. It brought her back to reality. They had to get to the surface. Courtney was already feeling the strain of having held her breath for too long. They were out of the death car, but if they couldn't hold their breath long enough to get to the surface, it wouldn't matter. They'd be just as dead. Dodger tugged, pulling her up. Courtney kicked, and the two rocketed for the surface. With nothing around them for perspective there was no way to know how deep they were. All Courtney could do was focus on the light above and hope they'd hit it before running out of air. She kicked and kicked. Her lungs ached. She wanted to exhale, but feared losing the last remaining bit of air in her lungs.

Dodger kicked just as furiously. They didn't look at each other. There was no need. They knew where they had to go. Up. Up was air. Down was death. Courtney wanted to scream. She wanted to breathe. She felt she could last a little longer, if only she knew how many more seconds she'd have to hold out for. Two? Five? Twenty? She knew if it were twenty, she'd be dead.

It wasn't. They both broke the surface, gasping for air. Courtney looked for Dodger. He bobbed next to her, looking just as scared as he had when they were trapped in the sinking car.

The two laughed. They couldn't help themselves. It seemed like the thing to do. Total relief will do that.

"Can you make it to the pier?" Dodger asked.

Courtney nodded. Now that she could breathe, she was fine. She didn't even feel the bump on her head. They weren't far from the pier. It only took a minute to swim to the base of the huge wooden pilings and a metal ladder that reached into the water. Courtney got there first. She grabbed the ladder and held tight. Dodger joined her a second later. The two of them clung to the ladder to catch their breath.

"Saint Dane," Dodger gasped.

"What about him?"

"You said you thought I might be Saint Dane."

"I don't think that anymore. He can do a lot of things, but he can't be two people at once."

"So now that we're square, maybe you could tell me what's really goin' on?"

Courtney chuckled. "Yeah, you earned it. But you're not going to like what you hear."

"I don't see how it can get any worse than this," Dodger said.

"This?" Courtney scoffed. "This was nothing."

Dodger looked sick.

Courtney pulled herself up on the ladder and made the climb to the top of the pier. Dodger followed close behind. It was low tide, so the climb was a long one. Neither looked down as they made their way up to safety.

When Courtney got to the top, she saw that a group of people had already gathered to see what was going on. More came running along the pier from the street. They peppered her with questions. "Are you okay?" "What happened?" "Do you need an ambulance?" "Did everyone get out?"

Courtney ignored them. It's not that she was being rude.

Something else had gotten her attention. The people on the pier might as well have been invisible, because the sight before Courtney was too incredible, too breathtaking for her to focus on anything else. Rising high above her, on the far side of the pier, was a vast black wall. The sheer size was enough to make her knees buckle. It stretched nearly the entire length of the pier and reached high into the blue New York sky. At first she didn't register what it could be. A building? Buildings weren't black. She gazed up at the monstrous sight, feeling like an ant next to a house.

Reality intruded when Dodger stepped up next to her. "She's something, ain't she? Fast, too."

Along the top of this impossible black wall was a wide, white band. Courtney's eyes followed this band the length of the wall until she saw two words. Two simple black words against white. The letters had to be three feet high, big enough to be seen clearly from the buildings of Manhattan. Seeing the words made Courtney gasp. Those two words hit her harder than the breathtaking image of the black wall itself. It was like seeing history come to life. It was like seeing the future come to life. Seeing those words told her exactly what she needed to do. They told her the wall wasn't a wall. It was the hull of a ship. A huge ship. An impossibly huge ship. The words were near its bow, proudly displaying her name for the world to see.

"*Queen Mary,*" Dodger said in awe. "This is the closest I'll ever get to sailing on her."

"Don't be so sure about that," Courtney said.

Dodger gave her a confused look. Courtney's response was to grab his hand and run for shore. The two quickly escaped from the pier before the police showed up and started asking questions they wouldn't have answers for. Or answers they wanted to give. They headed back to the hotel. On the subway. Neither had the stomach for getting into another cab. They traveled silently, both lost in thought. Courtney thought long and hard about what she was going to tell Dodger. She no longer thought he was Saint Dane. If there was anything good that came out of their cab ride from hell, it was that she now knew for sure that he wasn't Saint Dane. She couldn't ask him to ignore reality any longer. That wouldn't be fair. No, she figured, Dodger was going to want the truth. The question was, how much of it should she reveal? She didn't want to scare him off, but he needed to know what he had gotten himself into. His allegiance to Gunny aside, he nearly died in that cab. He deserved to know why.

By the time they got back to the hotel, their clothes were dry. Aside from a few scratches and a nasty bruise on Courtney's forehead, they weren't much the worse for wear. Both had lost their hats, but hats were replaceable. The two were walking through the garden toward the front door of the hotel when Courtney stopped Dodger.

"Thank you," she said.

"For what?"

"For helping me even though you didn't have to."

"But Gunny asked—"

"Yeah, I know," Courtney interrupted. "But thanks just the same."

"You're welcome," Dodger said sincerely.

"I've decided to tell you the truth. All of it."

"You don't have to," Dodger said quickly.

"But I want to," Courtney countered. "You deserve that."

"Yeah, maybe, but still, you don't have to."

"I don't get it," Courtney said with a frown. "Before you were all about wanting to know what was going on. Now you don't care? Why's that? Are you giving up on me?"

"Who said anything about giving up? All I said was you didn't have to tell me."

"Uh . . . confused."

"I'll show you something, " Dodger said with a sly smile.

He led Courtney into the hotel and down the stairs toward Gunny's apartment. But they didn't go to Gunny's. Dodger brought her to the hotel vault, where a gray-haired guy in a bell-hop suit sat behind a desk, reading the newspaper.

"Hey, Mike, working hard?" Dodger asked.

"Hardly working," Mike answered grumpily without taking his eye off the paper.

"I need that strongbox you're holding for me," Dodger said.

Mike looked up at him, over his half-glasses. "You got some identification?"

"Yeah," Dodger said. He held up his right hand with his fingers spread. "I got five friends to vouch for me. One, two, three, four, five." With each number he curled a finger, until he ended up with a fist . . . and gave Mike a sharp but friendly punch in the arm.

"Ow!" the old guy winced. "Good enough." Mike pulled himself off the high stool and shuffled into the large vault.

"What's this about?" Courtney asked.

"Patience," Dodger said. "It's my turn to be mysterious."

Courtney shrugged and waited. A few minutes later Mike shuffled out, carrying a gray, metal strongbox that looked about twenty-four inches square. He put it on the desk and slid it over to Dodger.

"I should make you sign for this," Mike grumped.

"But you won't," Dodger replied.

"What you got in there?' Mike asked. "The family jewels?" The old guy cackled a laugh.

"That's exactly what I got," Dodger answered as he slid the box off the desk. "Thanks, Mike. You're a prince."

"So they say," Mike replied. "So they say." He was already

back to reading his paper before Dodger and Courtney left the vault room.

"Let's take this to Gunny's apartment," Dodger said. "It's private."

Courtney walked the rest of the way to Gunny's door and used the key that was hidden overhead. Before going in, she said teasingly, "I thought it was wrong to go inside a lady's boudoir unless it's official business."

Dodger answered without a trace of humor, "This *is* official business."

Courtney's smile dropped. She had never seen Dodger so serious. Courtney closed and locked the door behind them, while Dodger put the strongbox on Gunny's kitchen table.

"So?" Courtney asked curiously.

"You said you wanted to tell me the truth. I figured I'd save you some breath." He reached under his shirt and pulled out a chain. Hanging from it was a silver key that he used to open the strongbox. "Thing is, I already know the truth."

Dodger opened the box and took out a handful of papers. Some were rolled up and wrapped with twine. Others were typed sheets bound into leather volumes. Courtney stared, not sure what she was seeing.

"I know it all, Courtney," Dodger said. "Or at least, as much as Gunny does. These are the journals of the Traveler from First Earth. I told you, I'm Gunny's acolyte."

Courtney was stunned. "Gunny's been sending these to you through the ring?"

Dodger nodded. "I know it all. Pendragon, Third Earth, the *Hindenburg.* I gotta keep that one pretty quiet. It wouldn't do no good for the cops to find out Gunny was responsible for bringing it down. I know about Eelong and Spader and the poison from Cloral and Black Water, and even about how Kasha died. It's all here."

Courtney was reeling. "Why didn't you tell me?"

Dodger chuckled. "Hey, I had to be careful. You weren't sure if I was Saint Dane? I wasn't sure if *you* were."

Courtney punched him in the arm.

"Ow! What's that for? It works both ways, you know!"

"I guess," Courtney said insincerely. She didn't like the idea that anybody could think she was Saint Dane.

Dodger pulled a single sheet of folded parchment out of the box. "Now that I know you're legit, I can deliver this."

Dodger held out the sheet to Courtney.

"For me?" Courtney asked, numb.

"Straight from Eelong, from Gunny and Spader . . . to you."

Dear Mark and Courtney,

I'm sending this note to my acolyte, Dodger, on First Earth in hopes that he can deliver it to you. You can trust Dodger. He's a good man. If you're reading this, you already know that. I think it's important you learn some of the things that have happened since you left Eelong.

First off, Spader and I are doing just fine. We're living in Black Water. It's not First Earth, and I sure do miss the food and the friends back home, but it's good enough. So if anybody out there is worried about us, don't be. Until we find a way off this territory, we'll be fine.

As I'm writing this, I'm guessing that Spader and I have been here about two years. You might say the changes we've seen are pretty spectacular. The movement to repeal Edict Forty-six was defeated. The klees will not be hunting gars anymore. But that was just the beginning. There is a spirit of cooperation between the two races (or is it species?) that has turned this territory completely around. Black Water has become a center of technology and education. Their radio invention is now used throughout Eelong, and they've even started figuring out how to send out pictures. That's more advanced than that television thing they're talking about on First Earth. Isn't that just amazing? Now there are regular gig flights between Leeandra and Black Water.

They're about to finish a permanent railway line that will connect the two cities. In return, the klees provide security for the gars, which mostly means keeping the tang population down.

Farms are secure now that the tangs are under control, so food is no longer a problem. That's mostly thanks to the klees. The two groups have formed a joint government. The Circle of Klee was renamed as simply the Circle. There are now two viceroys sitting on the Circle—one from Leeandra and one from Black Water. A klee and a gar. The gars are given full voting rights. It certainly is a sight to see.

I won't kid you, there is still prejudice. Old habits die hard. Many klee still consider the gars to be an inferior race. But that's only because the gars have only recently been given the opportunity to thrive. I believe that will change in time. Gars are now routinely sent to Black Water for education. Gars who leave Leeandra as slaves or family pets, return as vital citizens. For some klees that's hard to accept, but more walls are breaking down each day. It's truly miraculous.

I'm telling you all this for two reasons. One is to let you know that Spader and I are fine. We're both teachers now! I can't begin to describe the feeling of meeting a gar who can barely speak and eats his food from the ground, and working with him to bring out the intelligent person within. It isn't a rare occurrence. We are personally helping to change the lives of hundreds of gars. As much as we both want to be back with Pendragon and our mission to stop Saint

Dane, until that day comes, we feel that we are doing a lot of good here on Eelong. Who knows? Maybe that is the way it was meant to be.

The second reason is I want to say something about what happened at the flume when you two left with Bobby. It was a tragedy that Kasha was killed. No question. But her death was an accident. Nobody is to blame. After what we all went through on Eelong, it's a miracle that any of us are still alive. I hope you two believe that. Her death was not your fault.

Though it's unfortunate Spader and I are trapped here on Eelong, that too was an accident. I won't lie to you. As much as things are working out here, we'd both rather be with Bobby. But our being here is a small price to pay for the good you two did by coming to Eelong. I know you weren't supposed to travel. The territories are not supposed to be mingled. But if you hadn't come, I can't imagine the state that Eelong would be in right now. If you could see the wonderful advances that have been made, you'd agree with me. By your coming to Eelong, the turning point of this territory most definitely went the right way.

Nobody can replace Kasha. She was a wonderful klee and Traveler. If she were alive to see the Eelong of today, she would be thrilled. We're all thrilled. As for Spader and myself, we're proud of you two for making the tough decision and saving Eelong. Things don't always turn out exactly the way we'd like them to, but in this case, I believe it was worth the price.

I'll finish by saying I hope to see you again someday. With any luck, it will be at a time when Saint Dane is finally done causing mischief. That's a time we all look forward to. Until then, be well, remember us, and always follow your instincts.

With all best wishes,
Gunny

P.S. This is from Spader, mates. Tell Pendragon that I've thought long and hard about the things he's said to me. I guess you might say I've done a little growing up here in the jungles of Eelong. Tell him I'm ready. I'm with him. And when the time comes, I'll follow him to the ends of Halla.

After that, the last one to Grolo's buys the sniggers.

Hobey-ho,
Your mate, Spader

☯ FIRST EARTH ☯
(CONTINUED)

Courtney read the letter once, then twice. When she got through it a third time, she put it down and closed her eyes. She wasn't sure if she should cry, or laugh. She had been beating herself up over what happened on Eelong for a long time. For years. After reading Gunny's letter, she didn't feel any better about Kasha having died, but she felt a little more secure in knowing the decisions they'd made were smart ones. Eelong was a very big victory and that helped to ease the pain a little. Maybe more than a little.

Once again it made her miss Mark.

According to Gunny's letter, he felt that mixing the territories in some cases was okay. Eelong was proof of that. But he hadn't seen the negative results of what could happen when the territories were mixed. The destinies of four territories had been altered, with the threat of more to come. She was happy for Eelong, but it didn't take away her fear of what might be in store for Halla. As Bobby said many times, it wasn't about winning battles, it was about winning the war. Eelong was a battle that was won. The war was far from over.

After leaving Courtney alone with her thoughts, Dodger cleared his throat. "Like I said, I know what's going on."

Courtney folded the note and gave it to him. He placed it back in the strongbox.

"You know a lot," Courtney said. "Not everything."

Courtney filled Dodger in on all she knew, starting with their lives on Second Earth before Bobby left home to become a Traveler. From there she filled in all the gaps of the story he wouldn't know about, because Gunny didn't know. She told Dodger about Denduron and Cloral, Lifelight on Veelox, the battle for Zadaa, the games of Quillan, and most important, the way Saint Dane had been a part of their lives as Andy Mitchell since they were little kids. She told him all about the Sci-Clops science club, and the Stansfield school where Saint Dane had turned himself into a boy that Courtney developed a crush on. It was a crush that nearly killed her. She finished by talking about the death of Mark's parents, and about Forge technology that led to the creation of dados, the lifelike robots that had changed the course of history on Earth and on Quillan. Finally, Dodger read the letter from Patrick telling of Mark's voyage on the *Queen Mary*, and his disappearance.

It was a lot easier to explain it all than Courtney thought it would be. Dodger had already accepted the concept of Halla and territories and the Travelers and, of course, Saint Dane. All she did was add to the story and bring it to where they now stood.

Dodger took it all in, then said, "So you want to find Mark and stop him from bringing this future gizmo into our time."

"That," Courtney said. "And save him from the danger he's in. I believe Saint Dane's plan for Second Earth started when we met Andy Mitchell back in kindergarten. It was all a devious plan to steer Mark into creating Forge, gain his trust, and get him to spring it on the other territories. Once that happens, I think Mark won't be needed anymore and—"

Courtney didn't finish the sentence. Dodger whistled in awe. "Does Saint Dane think that far ahead?"

"Time means nothing to him. He bounces back and forth between territories like we walk across the street. Saint Dane keeps talking about this thing called the Convergence. Bobby thinks that whatever it is, it's the mother of all turning points. The turning point for Halla. By mixing the territories, Saint Dane is making sure it goes the way he wants it to. It's not about individual territories anymore. Maybe it never was. He's lining up the dominos. We've got to knock some of them out of line."

Dodger stared at Courtney, wide eyed. "I liked it better when I thought you were from Pluto."

Courtney grabbed a newspaper from the bed. She'd bought it when they got back to the hotel because of the big picture on the front page. It was a shot of a large ship docked in lower Manhattan.

"RMS *Queen Mary*," Courtney said, staring at the picture. "Big ship."

"The biggest," Dodger added. "The hotel's always lousy with passengers after they make a crossing. They say it's the cat's meow."

"The what?"

"It's a nice ship. Like a fancy, floating hotel."

Courtney stared at the picture. "According to the database on Third Earth, Mark Dimond was on board when she sailed for England on November seventh. He never showed up in England."

"And you think his body washed up in Jersey a few weeks later?"

"That's what Patrick thinks. It makes sense." She dropped

the paper and paced, thinking out loud. "Mark filed his Forge technology application with the US Patent Office in October. He had a meeting scheduled with a company called 'KEM Limited' in London on November thirteenth and booked passage on the *Queen Mary*. He boarded the ship but never showed up at that meeting, and was never seen again. A few weeks later the body of a passenger in a tuxedo washed ashore in New Jersey with a spoon from the *Queen Mary* in his pocket. He was killed by a bullet. The body was never identified."

"And nobody filed a missing-person report," Dodger added.

"Because nobody knew Mark here. I think it all fits."

"Except for one thing," Dodger cautioned. "You're saying all this like it's history." He picked up the paper and pointed to the headline. "It's November second. The *Queen Mary* doesn't sail for five days. None of that happened yet."

"Exactly!" Courtney exclaimed. "On November seventh Mark is going to board that ship."

"Unless we stop him."

"Unless we stop him," Courtney echoed.

● FIRST EARTH ●
(CONTINUED)

The next few days were busy ones. While Dodger worked his shifts at the hotel, Courtney did all she could to track down Mark. She made dozens of phone calls to different city offices, trying to find the former tenant of 240 Waverly Place, apartment #4A. She tried the housing authority, moving companies, the police department, the fire department, banks, the phone company, and even the US Patent Office again. The answer was always the same. "We can't help you." It was frustrating because she had to do so much legwork just to get to a place where somebody would tell her to "forget it." There was no Internet. She couldn't leave messages on anyone's answering machine because those wouldn't be invented for another fifty years. She went back to scouring newspapers for information about Mark Dimond or the Dimond Alpha Digital Organization or even KEM Limited.

Two days before the *Queen Mary* was scheduled to sail, she found something. It was a small item in the *New York Times* about a British company called "Keaton Electrical Marvels, Ltd." They announced plans to manufacture a new, portable phonograph machine. Courtney wasn't even sure what that was. She had to go back to Macy's to learn it was a device that played records. The only records Courtney had ever seen were vintage albums that her parents never played anymore. But in 1937, phonographs were popular. The design made by KEM Limited was touted as being incredibly innovative, with the ability to store energy in batteries that would allow the phonograph to be played for short periods without being plugged in. The article made it sound as if this were an amazing scientific breakthrough. Of course to Courtney, it seemed about as amazing as a flashlight, but knowing that KEM Limited was involved in electronic technology made sense. She realized a company like that might be able to take Mark's invention and actually do something with it.

The pieces of the puzzle were coming together.

However, on November 6, the day before the *Queen Mary* would leave, Courtney was no closer to finding Mark than she had been on November 2. It was looking more and more like the only way they would be able to stop him would be to intercept him at the ship itself. She took the train back to Stony Brook, where she put Bobby's latest journal in the safe-deposit box. She had no idea what to expect the next day, but she knew that one way or another, things would happen. She wanted the journals to be safe. Her last stop of the day was at Macy's, where she replaced her floppy cap that she'd lost in the sinking taxicab. She also bought Dodger a new brown fedora. She liked that it made him look like Indiana Jones. A short Indiana Jones, but still. She hoped he'd have the same luck as the fictional character.

She barely slept that night. She knew her mission on First Earth would end the next day. Either she would prevent Mark from getting on that ship, or she would fail, and history would play out the way the computers of Third Earth said it would. She vowed not to let that happen.

The next morning was sunny and warm for November. The *Queen Mary* was scheduled to leave the pier at 1:00 p.m. The plan was for Dodger and Courtney to be on the pier early, to intercept Mark before he could set foot on the gangway. The two arrived at the pier by 9 a.m., long before any passengers were likely to show up. They positioned themselves at the entrance to the pier, ready to inspect each and every person headed for the ship. Dodger was armed with the family photo of the Dimonds, though Courtney didn't think Mark looked much like that picture anymore. She couldn't rely on Dodger to recognize him. It would be up to her. She positioned herself square in the middle of the mouth of the pier. They had anticipated everything . . .

Except for the size of the crowd. By 11 a.m. the place was packed with people. It was a carnival-like atmosphere as throngs arrived by car, by bus, by limousine, and even by horse-drawn carriage. With each passing minute the pier grew more crowded. A band played near the ramps leading to the gangways, adding to the party. People were hugging and crying and generally thrilled by the prospect of sailing on the greatest ocean liner of their time. Porters hurried along with carts loaded down with suitcases and steamer trunks. Horses and cars were put into the hold. Huge crates were hoisted up by a crane and lowered into the cargo areas.

There was far too much going on for Courtney or Dodger to recognize anyone. Making matters worse was the fact that most men wore hats, so they couldn't get a good look at their faces. To Courtney *everybody* looked like Indiana Jones. She stood on a cement barricade, desperately scanning the crowd, but fearing Mark could walk right past without her knowing.

Half an hour before the ship was scheduled to sail, Dodger ran to her and exclaimed, "This ain't workin'."

Courtney was near panic. "He could easily have gotten past us. He could already be on board!"

"I've got a better idea," Dodger announced.

He took her by the hand and pulled her through the crowd. Courtney didn't argue. She figured anything would give them a better chance of weeding out Mark than what they were doing. The two ended up bumping into more people than they avoided, but they didn't stop until they got to the bottom of a long gangway that led up and onto the ship.

"We've got to get to the purser," Dodger announced.

"The who?"

"The guy in charge of the passengers. He can tell us what cabin Mark is in. Once we know that, we'll go there, grab him, and get him off the ship with time to spare."

"Wait, you want us to board the ship?" Courtney exclaimed, horrified.

"It's okay. Families and friends are let on during boarding to get the lowdown on the ship. They get bounced before shove-off. Trust me."

Dodger dragged her to an official in uniform who looked to Courtney like a naval officer. He stood at the bottom of the gangway with a clipboard, checking off names. Dodger ran up to him and spoke with a British accent. " 'Ello, guvna! Got here just in time to see me brother off, we did!"

Courtney thought it was the worst British accent she had ever heard.

The officer gave Dodger a sour look. He didn't think much of the accent either. But he was polite and helpful. "And what would your brother's name be, lad?"

"It would be Dimond," Dodger answered, his accent getting worse. "Mark Dimond. He's an inventor, he is! Going back to Merry Old to make his fortune!"

The officer scanned his clipboard. Courtney bit her lip nervously. She wished Dodger had just spoken normally. Was the lie going to work? Was Mark even on the passenger list? Dodger gave her a sideways look. He may have been putting on a confident air, but he was just as nervous as she was.

"Right!" the officer finally announced. "Mark Dimond."

"Has he boarded yet?" Courtney asked excitedly, with no British accent.

"Yes, he has. You've just enough time to wish him well."

"What's his cabin, guvna?" Dodger asked.

"Afraid I don't have that information, lad. You might want to check with the purser's office on board."

"That we will! Thank ya, guvna!" Dodger tipped his cap and pulled Courtney on to the gangway. The two ran quickly up the incline.

The officer yelled after them, "Be quick about it! We sail in twenty!"

"Will do, guvna!" Dodger yelled back.

"What is this 'guvna'?" Courtney asked sarcastically.

"Hey, no complainin'. It got us on, didn't it?"

The two boarded the ship and found themselves on a deck called "Promenade." It was even busier than the pier. Between the excited passengers, the porters, the crew, the band, the family members and friends wishing a bon voyage, it was a jammed madhouse.

Dodger grabbed one of the ship's officers by the arm and asked, "We're looking for our brother to say good-bye. How do we find his cabin?" Courtney was relieved that he had dropped the lousy accent.

"Try the purser's office," the officer said. "Forward on this deck to the Regent Street shops. From there take the lift down one level and you'll find it."

The two bolted without taking time to thank him. They needed every possible second. It was like trying to fight their way through a 1930s version of a rave. People were dressed elegantly, as if attending a grand ball, not an ocean cruise. Everyone had excited smiles and spoke a bit too loud. They found the place called "Regent Street," which was lined with elegant shops and was already teeming with people. The shops sold jewelry and crystal and knickknacks of all sorts. Courtney had never been aboard a luxury ship of any kind and couldn't believe these stores actually existed on a ship.

Chimes sounded.

"What's that?" Courtney asked.

"Don't know, don't care," Dodger declared. He was on a mission, but getting through the mass of people was nearly impossible. They ran into an elderly woman who was coming out of a jewelry shop. She had a small white poodle on a leash who looked every bit as anxious as Courtney and Dodger.

"Oh!" the old woman screamed as if they had just knocked her down and beaten her.

Instantly her little dog started barking. And barking. And barking.

"Sorry, sorry!" Courtney apologized.

The woman looked at them as though they were prison escapees.

"This is not an area for hooligans!" the woman bellowed. "Officer!"

She raised her hand, summoning one of the ship's officers as if he were her personal servant.

"What's the problem, mum?" he asked, tipping his uniform cap.

"These ruffians should be escorted to . . . to . . . somewhere else," she bellowed haughtily.

Courtney froze. She squeezed Dodger's hand.

"We've got to get out of here," she said under her breath.

"Not yet," Dodger said. He turned to the officer and said with his most polite voice, "Sorry for the disturbance, sir, but we're looking for our brother, who's sailing with you today. Perhaps we don't belong on this deck, but we're sure that our brother does and *OWWW!*"

Courtney squeezed Dodger's hand again. "Now!" she hissed under her breath.

"Too late to see him off now, I'm afraid," the officer said. "All ashore that's going ashore. Please make your way back to the gangway."

"Yes," the elderly woman added. "Sooner rather than later."

"No problem!" Courtney said, and pulled Dodger away. She didn't pull him toward the gangway. She brought him deeper into the ship.

"What are you doin'?" he complained. "We gotta get off the ship."

"We can't!" Courtney squealed.

"Why not?" Dodger asked.

Courtney lifted her hand. Her ring was glowing. In seconds it would be shooting out light and music for the hundreds of people around them to see.

Dodger didn't hesitate. He grabbed her hand and the two quickly made their way through the mass of excited people, making no friends as they slammed into most every person they passed. Dodger kept glancing around, looking for a place to go. Any place to go.

"There!" Courtney shouted.

They were in a lounge area. Near them was an open door leading to somewhere. It didn't matter where. They had to get away from the crowd. They blasted through the door to find themselves in a pantry where white-smocked waiters hurried through with drinks for the passengers.

Courtney clamped her hand over the ring to try and keep the light from leaking out. They ran to the end of the pantry and into a small kitchen. The crew was too busy to notice them or care. Courtney knew that in a few seconds they'd see a show that would make them notice and care a whole lot. Dodger pulled Courtney to a door on the far end of the kitchen that had a heavy, metal handle.

"Cold storage, just like at the hotel," Dodger said. "We might get lucky."

They did. He pulled the door open. Nobody was inside. Courtney jumped in and yanked on an overhead chain. A single bulb burned to life. Dodger closed the door behind them. A quick look around showed they were in a vegetable locker. There were hundreds of heads of lettuce, piles of carrots, and bags of onions—enough to prepare thousands of meals for the passengers and crew of the floating hotel. While Dodger stood at the door, ready to throw out anybody who came in looking for a potato, Courtney took off the ring and placed it on the deck. It had already grown to three times its size and was shooting out light that flooded the small space. The music grew louder. Courtney hoped the refrigerator door was soundproof. Lightproof, too. They covered their eyes as the ring performed its familiar task. Moments later it was over. Dodger and Courtney looked at the deck to see the ring had returned to normal. Another watertight pouch lay next to it. Bobby's next journal from Ibara had arrived.

"Get it!" Dodger said as he went for the door. "Let's go!"

"No," Courtney said calmly.

"Wadda you mean no? The ships gonna shove off!"

"We haven't found Mark yet."

"I know, but—" He stopped himself. "You're not thinking . . . ?"

"Yeah, I am," Courtney answered. She calmly bent down and picked up Bobby's journal, along with her ring. "I'm going on a cruise. I'd understand if you took off, but I can't."

"We'd be stowaways!" Dodger complained. "They'll arrest us and . . . and . . . I don't know what they'll do, but I'd lose my job at the hotel for sure."

"Probably," Courtney said. "But if this ship sails without me, it means Mark will die, history will be changed, and the dados will infest the territories. I don't want you to lose your job, but if Saint Dane has his way and the Earth territories are changed, I can't guarantee you'd find yourself in a world where the Manhattan Tower Hotel even exists."

Dodger had to think about that one. He frowned. "I gotta tell ya, when Gunny asked me to help the guy who showed up with that ring, I wasn't expecting this."

Courtney shrugged.

Dodger exhaled and nodded in resignation. He leaned against a shelf and slid down to the deck. "Might as well get comfortable."

Courtney smiled and sat down next to him, clutching Bobby's journal. She leaned into Dodger and said, "Thanks."

Dodger shrugged. "Hey, don't go gettin' all mushy on me now."

"Wouldn't think of it," Courtney replied.

She didn't read the journal right away. Courtney knew they first had to find a place that was safe, assuming there was such a place on board a busy ship for a couple of stowaways. They waited for half an hour. Plenty of time for the excitement to die down. They might have stayed longer, if the door to the cold storage closet hadn't opened up. A chef stepped in with a large silver bowl, ready to grab some vegetables. When he saw Courtney and Dodger, he froze.

Courtney exclaimed, "Thank goodness! We thought we'd be stuck in here the whole voyage!" She walked past him and gave the surprised chef a peck on the cheek. "Thanks!" she said, and walked out.

The chef was dumbstruck. "Thanks, brother," Dodger said as he walked by. "Don't worry, I ain't gonna kiss ya!" They left the chef standing in the refrigerator, too confused to move.

There was no longer any rush. It was more important to blend in. Courtney and Dodger slowly made their way through the kitchen, the pantry, and the dining room. Once they got back to the passenger area, they noticed that the number of people had thinned considerably. Everyone who had been on board to visit had left. The only people remaining were passengers and crew. People who belonged on the ship.

And them.

They walked casually through Regent Street with its busy shops, headed for the Promenade Deck where they'd first boarded the ship. The sun hit them as soon as they stepped out onto the deck. The first thing Courtney saw was the pier. It was the pier that Saint Dane had driven the cab off of, with them inside. The pier where they first saw the *Queen Mary*. The pier that was now several hundred yards away.

The ship had left New York. Two tugboats were nudging it away from land, into New York Harbor and the Atlantic Ocean. They were on their way to England. They stood at the railing and watched as New York grew smaller.

"What are you thinking?" Dodger asked.

"I'm thinking I want to read a journal."

IBARA

Y̲ou must find Mark.

Courtney, I think I made a huge mistake by coming to Ibara. After seeing what's happening on this territory, the reality of what Saint Dane has accomplished is now clear. Scary clear. Our fears were correct. It isn't about single territories anymore. Saint Dane is tearing down the boundaries of Halla. I don't think I've made things worse by coming here, but I haven't helped much either. The truth is that I should be on First Earth, with you, looking for Mark. You were right. Saint Dane lured me to Ibara and I followed him like a hungry rat sniffing cheese.

Cheese in a trap.

Right now I'm so confused, it's hard to think straight. When we were together on First Earth I told you I thought it was too late to undo what Mark had done. I hope I was wrong. The future of Halla depends on it. That's not an overstatement. Stopping Mark may be the key to stopping Saint Dane.

How could I have been so dumb as to not know that? I guess that's a lame question. I know why. It's my own ego. I keep saying that in order to control Halla, Saint Dane needs to defeat me. I still think that's true, but after matching wits with him for so long, I'm as obsessed with beating him as he is with me. He's gotten into my head, Courtney. It's become a contest between the two of us. That's wrong. What matters is the big picture. I've wanted to bring him down so badly, I've ignored that. That's why I'm on Ibara when I should have stayed on First Earth. While I'm chasing after one single guy, he's busy manipulating all that exists.

Our first instincts were correct. Mark must be stopped. It might be the only way to save Halla. The thing is, it may be too late already. I don't know when First Earth exists, relative to other territories. Yes, it's in the past of Second and Third Earths, but do the rest of the territories exist in the future of First Earth? Or before it? Or do some exist before and some after? I have no idea. Wondering makes my head hurt.

When I left First Earth, I said the most important thing was to save Mark from whatever fate dealt him. Of course I still want my friend, our friend, saved. But given what I've seen on Ibara, I also want him stopped. The only chance we have of defeating Saint Dane, once and for all, is to prevent Mark from introducing Forge technology to First Earth. To understand why, you'll have to read this journal.

Read it fast.

I'm sorry, Courtney. I'm sorry for leaving you alone and being too stupid to realize I should have listened to you. I'm also sorry for laying it out to you like this and throwing such a huge responsibility onto your shoulders. I know you're doing everything you can to find Mark, but I can't tell you strongly enough that it isn't just about saving him. It's about stopping him.

I've already finished this journal. I started it a while ago before I understood what was actually happening here and came back to the beginning to tell you this. Not that you need convincing, but once you read this journal I think you'll understand as well as I do that you, Courtney, you are the last best hope to save Halla.

I hope it isn't too late already.

Siry and I left the rocky ledge that overlooked the colorful fleet of sailing ships and made our way back to the village of Rayne. I needed rest badly. Food, too. When we reached the edge of the village, Siry stopped and stood in front of me.

"Are you with us?" he asked.

"When do we go?" was my answer.

"When everyone is able," he answered. "The wounded Jakills have to recover."

I nodded. He glared at me and cautioned, "If you tell the tribunal of our plans . . ." He let the threat dangle.

"Still don't trust me?" I asked.

He shrugged and walked away.

"One thing," I called after him. "Jakill. What does that mean?"

He shook his head. He wasn't telling. "You're right," he replied. "I don't trust you. Not yet."

Fine. Be that way. The one thing on my mind was sleep. I was so beat, I had trouble lifting my feet and dragging them through the sand. Since my hut had been turned into a makeshift hospital for the Jakills, I wasn't sure if I should go there, but I didn't know where else to go. When I returned, I saw that I didn't have to worry. The injured Jakills were gone. Only Telleo was waiting for me.

"Where are they?" I asked.

"I did what I could for them and helped them to their

homes. They will recover. Are you hungry?"

"I should be polite and say you don't have to go through any trouble, but I'm starving."

"I thought so," Telleo said warmly. "I've prepared some roasted vegetables and broth."

The two of us sat at the wooden table and ate an incredible dinner. Actually it probably wasn't all that great, but I was so hungry I could have eaten the table and thought it was a gourmet treat. By the time my belly was full, I was ready to drift off to sleep for about a month. But that would have been rude.

"Tell me about yourself," I said to Telleo. "You work for the tribunal but you risk your job by helping the Jakills. Isn't that playing the game from both sides?"

"I don't look at it that way," Telleo said. "I love this village and my people. That's all. Siry and his friends are part of the village. I don't discriminate."

"I heard that about you."

Telleo blushed and continued, "I don't understand why Siry is so angry. Does it seem to you like there is something wrong with the way we live?"

"I think it's wrong to keep the truth from people. Don't you ever wonder what else exists out there? Beyond this island?"

"No," Telleo answered quickly. "I can't imagine a better life than this one."

"But that's your choice. I'm not saying I agree with them, but Siry and the Jakills want more choices. They want to know what else this world has to offer."

Telleo shrugged. "I guess I'm selfish. I worry there might be something out there that will change Rayne."

"Or there might be something incredible that will make your lives even better."

"I don't see how."

"Aren't you even a little bit curious?"

"I'm curious about the Flighters," Telleo answered. "It bothers me that they're getting bolder."

"Don't you think it would be smart to find out who they are? Maybe they could be stopped."

"The island security will protect us," she said softly.

Man, she was pretty trusting. "What about the tribunal?" I asked. "Siry says they're keeping secrets from the people."

Telleo looked stung. "I believe the tribunal tells us what we need to know. Why worry about things we can't change?"

"But don't you want to know about your history? Where you came from?"

"Life is about the future, not the past."

"You can learn from the past!"

"Things are wonderful in Rayne," Telleo snapped, getting a little testy. "What could we learn that would improve on perfection?"

"But—"

"Besides," she interrupted, "I trust my father."

Huh? Telleo saw the surprise all over my face.

"You didn't know?" Telleo asked playfully. "I thought you worked fast and had us all figured out."

"Guess not. Who's your father?"

"My full name is Telleo Genj. My father is the chief minister."

Oh man. The next sound we all heard was my jaw hitting the table.

She continued, "I believe he will do what's best for our village."

"Wow," I gasped. My mind raced, trying to calculate what this new twist would mean.

"I know the Jakills don't trust the tribunal," Telleo added.

"Yet they defended them from the Flighters. They care about Rayne. They're just . . . misguided. Once they grow up, they'll appreciate how wonderful we have it here and will stop acting foolishly."

Things had just gotten seriously tricky. I guess they always were and I was just too dumb to realize it. Telleo was cool, but her father was the big cheese. According to Siry, he was the main guy who kept lying to the people. Telleo thought that was a good thing. Siry didn't. Who was right? Don't ask me, I was only passing through. Telleo seemed kind of, I don't know, what's the word? Naive, I guess. She wasn't a dummy or anything, but she had blind faith in everything the authorities told her. She existed in a safe bubble that she didn't want to risk bursting. Who could blame her? She lived in paradise.

On the other hand, it looked like there was more to Ibara than this perfect little island. The village seemed like paradise, but I could see where some might consider it a prison. Making it more confusing, Remudi was on the tribunal, which meant a Traveler agreed with the whole keeping-the-past-a-secret thing. Bottom line? I had no idea who was right. But it wasn't my job to pass judgment. I was there to figure out what Saint Dane was up to, not to interfere. Telleo didn't seem to know about Siry's plan to hijack a ship and leave the island. Fine. I wasn't going to tell her.

"I'd like to show you something," Telleo said. "Would you come with me?"

All I wanted to do was lie down and pass out, but how could I refuse? This girl helped save my life and was taking great care of me. I didn't want to insult her, so I pulled myself to my aching feet, put on my best smile, and declared, "Sure!"

Night had fallen on Rayne. The walkways had come alive with twinkling, golden lights that lined the pathways and sparkled from high in the trees. The effect was magical, like a tropical Christmas. Telleo led me along the path toward the center of the village. In the distance I heard the faint sounds of music.

"Tonight is the beginning of the Ibaran holiday called the 'Festival of Zelin,'" she explained. "It's a time of feasting and fun. It's a perfect time for you to be here. You can see the best of Rayne."

"What's the holiday about?"

"It's all about being thankful for the wonderful island where we live. I think it's just an excuse to have a party."

"Like Ibara Thanksgiving."

"Like what?"

"Never mind."

The closer we got to the center of the village, the louder the music became. Telleo led me to the large thatched canopy where I had seen the musical performance earlier. The place was jammed with people watching a performance. On the raised, circular stage was a band playing loud, lively music that reminded me of the upbeat, fun Irish music from Second Earth. There was lots of percussion and tambourines pounding out the quick rhythm, while several flutes played a lively, fun tune. Telleo grabbed my hand and boldly led me through the crowd until we were nearly at the stage. I found myself in a sea of clapping, smiling people. Drinks were passed around for everyone to share. I was handed a cup and took a sip of what tasted like hyper-buzzed root beer. I wasn't sure if it was alcohol or not, but it wasn't up to me to refuse their hospitality.

I saw familiar faces. I recognized the big security guy who had arrested me and the one who brought me to the tribunal. They didn't look so intimidating now as they laughed and bounced to the music. I looked across the stage to see a small platform built up off the ground, where the three members of the tribunal sat. They weren't rocking like the rest of the crowd, but looked like they were enjoying it just the same. The women clapped to the music while Genj tapped his foot.

There wasn't a single Jakill in the crowd. No big surprise. If they didn't buy into the life here on Rayne, why would they come to party at the Ibara Thanksgiving?

Me? I didn't have any baggage so I was free to enjoy myself. I didn't know if it was the excitement of the crowd, or the frothy drink they were passing around, or the music, but I suddenly felt all sorts of energy. The music was hard to resist. Telleo started dancing. She locked her arm in mine and soon we were spinning to the tune. I had no idea how to dance a traditional Ibaran dance. For that matter, I didn't know any traditional dances on Second Earth, either. But I had rhythm. Pretty soon I was swinging around with Telleo and clapping my hands and locking arms with complete strangers and having a great old time.

The festival was yet another example of how sweet life was in Rayne. The people lived in an idyllic, tropical world on the shores of a warm ocean. Everything they needed was right there for them. They had created a utopian society where everyone played a role in providing for the whole. As I danced among the festive people, I wondered if maybe Siry was wrong. What's that old saying? Ignorance is bliss? The people may have been ignorant about the rest of Ibara, but they were definitely blissful. Maybe that wasn't such a bad thing.

Then I remembered the Flighters.

And the people who mysteriously disappeared.

And the outsiders, who were executed.

And the secrets.

I suddenly didn't feel much like dancing. Telleo must have sensed my change in mood.

"C'mon," she said. "You look exhausted."

I was, in every sense of the word. She took my hand and weaved us back through the throng of revelers.

"I'm sorry," she said. "You need to rest. I just wanted you to see a little about what life is like here."

"I'm glad you did."

Sort of. As we walked back to the hut, I realized how torn I was. Rayne seemed like a pretty cool place. For many of the people, it was perfect. I wanted it to stay perfect for them. Would hijacking a ship to explore the rest of the territory insure that? Or mess it up?

When we got back to the hut, Telleo gave me a warm hug. "Sleep well, Pendragon. I'll bring you some food in the morning."

"Thank you. If there's anything I can do for you . . ."

"Maybe there is. Perhaps tomorrow you can tell me the truth about who you are. That is, if your amnesia isn't still a problem." She gave me a sly smile, as if to say she didn't believe for a second that I had amnesia.

"Good night," I said.

"Good night."

Telleo ran back along the path toward the mountain. I watched her until she disappeared into the palm trees and twinkle lights. I liked Telleo. She was smart and caring and didn't have an ounce of cynicism in her. Maybe she was right. Maybe you shouldn't mess with something that seemed so right. Unfortunately, that led me to another thought. A darker one. Messing with what seemed right was what Saint Dane lived for. Whatever the past of Ibara was, whatever the future had in store, I had no doubt that Saint Dane was going to try and bring it all down. It didn't matter if I agreed with the tribunal or the Jakills, one thing was clear: I had to know what was out there.

I dragged myself into the hut, kicked off my sandals and fell onto a cot, ready to sleep like the dead. I wasn't horizontal for more than thirty seconds before dropping into oblivion.

I can't say how long I was out. Six hours? One hour? Two minutes? All I know was that one second I was closing my eyes, and the next second someone was gently shaking me awake. I wasn't surprised, or scared. My body was too numb for that. My brain wasn't far behind. I had enough trouble trying to focus on who it was that was disturbing my rest.

Looming over me in the dark was a figure. I didn't jump up. I didn't try to defend myself. If this person meant me harm, I'd already be dead. It suddenly hit me that these huts didn't have locks. I didn't move. All my energy went into focusing my thoughts.

"Are you awake?" came a familiar voice.

"Siry?" I croaked. "What the—"

I tried to sit up, but he clamped a hand over my mouth and eased me back down.

"Ready?" he whispered, and took his hand away.

"For what?"

"We've got an hour until dawn. It's time to take our ship."

"Now?" I whispered loudly. "Tonight?"

"You have other plans?" he asked.

"I thought you wanted to wait until all the Jakills were healthy," I stammered.

I heard a squeaky voice from across the hut say, "You didn't think a little bump on the head would slow us down, did ya?"

I looked through my feet to see three more people in the room. The tall blond thief named Loque, the sniffy girl named Twig, and the little rat-eyed guy who now had a bandage around his head. Rat boy stepped forward and banged his bandaged head with the palm of his hand. "Pain keeps me alert."

Freak.

"This was the plan all along, wasn't it?" I asked, reality dawning. "You were always going to take the ship during the festival."

Siry shrugged. "The party is still going strong. It's the perfect time."

"Why didn't you tell me?"

"I didn't trust you," Siry answered. "I still don't. Prove me wrong."

The four Jakills looked down at me. They were ready to go.

So was I.

It was time to steal a ship.

IBARA

We traveled quickly through the predawn silence of Rayne. I could hear the sounds of the all-night party in the distance. Everyone was either still dancing, or asleep. Everyone but the Jakills, that is. And me. I had to shake off the grogginess while trying to keep up with these stealthy rebels as they moved quietly toward their target.

I was having second thoughts. If we failed and were caught, I had no idea what punishment the tribunal would slam on the Jakills. For me it was different. I was an outsider. If outsiders were executed for being outsiders, I didn't want to think about what they'd do to one for trying to hijack one of their cool new sailing ships. Had I made a mistake? Was this the best way to hunt down Saint Dane? I decided it was too late to worry about it.

Everyone seemed to know exactly where they were going. Everybody but me. We moved silently along the shore and into the jungle. The narrow trail wasn't much wider than my shoulders. Thick vegetation clawed at me from either side. If not for the light coming from the sky full of stars, it would have been impossible to see anything. As it was, the only way I could stop from running headlong into the jungle was to keep my eye on the silhouette of the Jakill in front of me.

The trail led us around the rock outcropping where Siry and I had stood the day before to view the colorful fleet of ships. Instead of climbing, we stayed at sea level. After about twenty minutes of dashing through the dark jungle, the silhouette in front of me slowed to a walk. We were approaching the beach. As if on cue, everyone stopped and crouched down. The Jakill in front of me tugged on my shirt and silently motioned for me to move forward on my own. I crouched low and moved quickly to the front of the line.

Waiting for me was Siry. He knelt on the edge of the jungle, scanning the rocky beach with an intensity I hadn't seen in him before. The cocky rebel was gone. There was no fooling around here. He had his game face on. Or maybe he was just scared. Whatever. This was serious. Waves crashed against the volcanic stone, creating a steady white noise that would hide any sound we made.

"We all know how to sail," Siry said softly. "All we need to do is get on board and the ship will be ours."

"What's the plan?" I asked.

Siry motioned for me to follow him out onto the beach. He looked back quickly to the others and motioned for them to wait. He crept ahead, staying close to the edge of the jungle. I followed right behind. We got only a few yards when he stopped and pointed. I looked to see the first of the five long piers about a hundred yards farther up the shore. Tied along our side was a ship with its bow pointed out to sea. In the starlight it looked to be a light yellow color.

"Each ship is guarded by five men," Siry explained. "Three on the pier, two on board. There are sixteen of us, including you. Ten will get in the water and swim to the ship, using blowguns to stay low and breathe."

"Like snorkels."

"Like what?"

"Never mind, keep going."

"The ten swimmers each have cords with hooks, to climb aboard. I'll be with the second group onshore. As soon as I see the swimmers start to climb, we'll move into position near the pier. When I'm sure the swimmers are on board, we'll use the blowguns to knock out the guards on the pier and board the ship. From there we know how to get under way. You don't have to worry about that."

"What *do* I have to worry about?"

"You'll be one of the ten swimmers," he explained. "You can swim, right?"

"What if I said no?"

"We'd leave you here."

"I can swim."

"Once you get on the ship, your job is to take out the two guards on board."

"Take out?"

"It was the weakest part of our plan," Siry explained. "The blowgun darts won't work after they get wet. The only way to get past those guards is to fight them. None of us would be able to handle one of those guards, let alone two. But you—"

Ahhh, now I knew where this was going. They looked at me like some kind of fighting-commando-dude. I didn't.

"I'm no different from you guys," I said quickly.

Siry shot me an incredulous look that said, "Give me a break."

"What would you do if I wasn't here?" I asked.

"You *are* here," Siry said. "You said you wanted to help?

This is it. I don't know where you came from or why you're really here, but maybe this is the way it was meant to be."

I shot Siry a look. "Where did you hear that?"

He shrugged. "It's something my father always said."

How could I argue with that? Though I didn't like being thought of as some kind of professional "muscle." Loor gave me training and tools to defend myself, not to go around "taking out" people. That couldn't be the way it was meant to be. Could it?

Siry continued, "We've got to be quick and quiet. If the other guards hear trouble, they'll come running and people will get hurt."

"We don't want that," I said.

"We *really* don't want that," Siry echoed. "They'll think we're Flighters."

"What does that mean?" I asked.

"They'll kill us."

Oh.

"Understand?" he asked.

I nodded.

He motioned for the others to come forward, then reached into a cloth sack he had strapped to his back. He pulled out one of those short blowgun weapons and a small coil of rope that had a three-pronged hook tied to one end. He held them both out and gave me a dark look. "Don't cross us, Pendragon."

I took them. "Don't worry."

The other Jakills had reached us. They sat crouched along the edge of the jungle. Siry faced them and whispered, "Once we start, there's no going back. We'll be criminals. We may never be able to return to Rayne. If anyone has second thoughts, this is your last chance."

Nobody spoke. Siry smiled.

"There's a huge world out there. It's ours to explore."

Everyone exchanged excited looks. They were ready.

"Be careful," Siry added. "Be smart. Let's go."

There was no cheering, obviously. The Jakills moved quickly and quietly forward, creeping along the edge of the jungle toward the pier. I felt a tug on my arm and saw the blond thief, Loque.

"You're with me," he said, and kept moving.

I gave Siry a quick look. He nodded. I followed Loque. When we got halfway to the pier, Loque motioned toward the water. Instantly he and eight more Jakills split off from the main group. They got on their bellies and crab-walked toward the ocean. I went belly down and followed. The distance from the edge of the jungle to the ocean was about forty yards over rock. I was feeling pretty good. Physically, I mean. The bee stings weren't bothering me anymore, and my strength was back. It's amazing what a little food and sleep will do. It also helped that I was bursting with adrenaline. We got close to the water and dropped down behind low rocks a few yards from the crashing surf. We looked to the ship. There was no movement. No alarm had sounded. So far so good.

"Now what?" I asked Loque.

"Now we swim" was his answer. "Time the waves. Get in quick and move out beyond the break."

Yeah, no kidding. The waves weren't huge, but they were breaking directly on the rocky shore. If we didn't time this right, we'd get thrown right back onto the rocks. Getting bashed would end the mission very quickly. Everyone had their wooden weapons gripped between their teeth and their cords wrapped around their waists. I did the same. They had practiced this. I wished I'd been to a few of those practices. Loque crept closer to the water, scanning the surf. A big set was coming in. Three waves bashed the shore, one after the other.

"Now!" he called out in a strained whisper.

We all ran the last few yards across the rocks and dove into the water. I did a fast crawl to get past the break before the next set came in. It was a jumble of thrashing arms and kicking legs. A couple times I got rapped in the head, but it wasn't the time to stop and complain. A few seconds later we were all floating beyond the break.

With no further instruction, everyone started doing an easy breaststroke toward the ship. We made very little sound. It was more about silence than speed. The breaststroke might not be fast, but it's quiet. As we slowly approached the ship, I wondered how I had gotten involved with this crazy commando mission. Here I was with a bunch of kids who weren't even as old as I was, and who were going to hijack a ship and head off across the sea in search of something they weren't even sure existed. We were about to become outlaws and traitors. Was I nuts? The only thing I could hang on to was that Siry was a Traveler, whether he liked it or not. Whatever was going to play out on Ibara, Siry would have to be part of it. I had to believe that his passion for learning the truth about their history was justified. I just wished we didn't have to go on such an extreme adventure to get there.

When we were about twenty yards from the ship, the Jakills took their weapons out of their teeth and put the ends in their mouths. They did it without a command or signal. Again, they had practiced this. I followed their lead. The wooden tube wasn't the best snorkel in the world, but it allowed us to keep our heads low in the water. That was good, because I caught sight of two people walking on the deck of the ship. The guards. They didn't see us or they'd probably have been pointing and shouting. Instead they looked to be walking casually and not all that alert. Why not? Nobody had ever attacked one of their ships before. Until tonight.

Five of the swimmers broke off and made their way toward the bow of the ship. I shot a questioning look to Loque. He took the snorkel out of his mouth and whispered, "Five on this side, five near the bow on the far side. On my signal swim to the ship and wait. I'll stay here to observe the guards. When the deck is clear, I'll signal to toss the hooks on board. Climb up as quickly as you can. Once you get on board—"

"Yeah, I know. Take out the guards."

"Watch," he said, pointing to the ship. "They walk the same route. From the bow to the stern and back again. All night. Once they leave the bow, I'll signal. You'll have until they reach the stern and turn back to get yourself on board."

I looked to the ship to see exactly what Loque described. Two guards walked toward the bow. They weren't in any hurry. Maybe they were bored. They were going to become unbored very soon. When they reached the bow and started back, Loque gave the command.

"Go," he whispered.

Four of us swam quickly and quietly toward the ship. We reached it in no time and hovered there, treading water. The swell from the waves wasn't too bad, so we were able to hang there without getting thrashed against the hull. Looking up, I guessed the deck was thirty feet above us. It wasn't going to be an easy climb. I followed the others' lead as they gripped their snorkels in their teeth to free their hands and unwrap the cords from around their waists. We spread apart along the hull so we wouldn't catch one another with the hooks when we tossed them. Siry made it sound so easy, but as I bobbed there I wasn't even sure I could throw the hook high enough to catch the deck. Why did I agree to this? What was I thinking?

I kept my back to the hull and watched for Loque's signal. He looked like a dark bubble bobbing on the surface. I hoped I'd be able to recognize his signal when it came. I don't mind admitting that I was getting jittery. We must have floated there for five minutes, waiting. Waiting made me nervous.

Finally I saw a quick movement near the dark bubble. Was that the signal? I looked to either side to see the Jakills throwing their hooks up to the ship. It was time. I grabbed my hook, did my best to wind up, and tossed it. It barely reached halfway up to the deck. It make a lame arc and fell right back toward me. I had to cover my head to avoid getting hit by the falling hook. Pathetic. I tried again. While kicking my legs to get as much of my body out of the water as possible, I held the cord in my left hand while dangling the hook with my right. Like a lasso, I wound up and let it fly. This time the hook hit the hull with a *thunk* and fell back into the water.

A quick look showed me that all three of the other Jakills had gotten their hooks up top and were pulling themselves out of the water. I felt like an idiot, but c'mon! I hadn't practiced this! I was about to try again when I felt the cord being pulled out of my hand. It was Loque. He took the cord, swam back a few feet from the hull, wound up, and let it sail toward the rail. The hook shot straight up and landed on the deck. With a quick tug, Loque imbedded it into the wood. He pulled hard on the cord, making sure it was secure, then handed it to me. I didn't take time to thank him. We were behind schedule.

The other Jakills were already halfway up the side of the ship. Was there still enough time to get up and onto the deck before the guards returned on their next lap? Waiting and wondering wouldn't help things. I grabbed the cord, put my feet against the hull, and started to climb. I saw how the other

Jakills did it, and copied them. With my feet against the side, I sort of walked up while moving hand over hand on the cord. The thin cord had several small knots along its length, so it was easy to grip. Climbing was tough at first, because the water created a suction, but once I muscled my way out of the water, it got easier. While gripping the wooden snorkel in my teeth like some soggy pirate, I inched up toward the deck.

I soon realized I wouldn't have trouble making the climb, and my mind shot ahead to the next challenge, which was all about me. I had to get rid of the guards on deck. How was I supposed to do that? I couldn't just jump them and start wailing away with my wooden snorkel. That would be, like, barbaric. I'm telling you, fighting isn't like what you see on TV. People don't get dropped with one punch and conveniently fall asleep. Hitting somebody hurts. And it could hurt them, too. I couldn't count on knocking them unconscious, so what was I supposed to do? As I climbed the last few feet to the edge of the railing, I decided that the best thing would be to get on deck, pull up the cord, and hope that I could take them on one at a time and tie them up with it. I figured there might even be someplace on board where I could lock them up. I didn't know why Siry thought I could pull this off, because I wasn't sure at all.

The other Jakills clung to their cords, each hanging about a foot below deck level. I wondered why they didn't climb up and over. Maybe they were waiting for me.

They weren't. The one nearest to me held out his hand to signal "Stop!" He pointed above. I could guess what he meant. The guards had returned. The extra time I had taken to climb up had cost us. I figured we'd wait until they got to the bow, turned, and walked past us again. Trouble was, we couldn't see up to the deck, so there was no way to know when it was safe to go.

Loque pulled himself up next to me. While still gripping the cord, he stuck out a finger to me as if to say, "Wait." Cautiously he pulled himself up higher to peer over the rail. It was a risky move. For all he knew, the guards were right there. We watched him slowly rise and peek onto the ship. I can't speak for anybody else, but I held my breath.

I didn't know how long we'd been hanging there, but my arms were getting tired. Tired arms weren't good in a fight. Finally Loque put one hand on the deck and used the other one to motion for me, and only me, to climb up on deck. It was time. There was no chance to think or reconsider or plan out a strategy. The show was about to begin, and I was the first one to step on stage. Hand over hand I climbed the rest of the way and scrambled onto the ship. I hit the deck and rolled back toward the wooden rail, hoping to make myself inconspicuous.

The deck was empty. No guards. No alarms. Nothing to alert anyone that a scabby commando was about to hijack their yellow ship. Though the ship was new, it looked to me like something out of olden times. The deck was made of long strips of wood. There was a wooden cabin structure near the bow that looked about the size of a large shed. Another larger cabin was to the rear. The ship had two heavy masts. I don't know much about sailing ships, but I guess you'd call this thing a square-rigger, because it looked like the sails dropped down from horizontal poles that were positioned about halfway up the masts. A second, smaller horizontal pole was farther up each mast. There was a complicated tangle of lines everywhere. I hoped Siry was right when he said the Jakills knew how to sail this thing, because I sure didn't.

The only sounds came from the roar of the ocean and the groaning ship as it pulled against the ropes that held it to the pier. For a fleeting instant I felt as if I had stepped into another world, and I was on an ancient pirate ship. Stranger still, I was the pirate.

Looking out from the deck, I saw the other nine ships at their piers. They were just as quiet. Just as empty. My confidence grew. I thought maybe the delay I had caused might have made this mission all the easier. It gave the guards the chance to do another lap back to the stern. If Siry and the others attacked with their silent blowguns, maybe all the guards were taken out at once, and my job was over. It was suddenly looking like a piece of cake. I was so confident that I stood up, leaned over the rail, and looked down to the other Jakills.

"All clear," I whispered . . . an instant before I was jumped from behind.

"Ahhhh!" screamed the guard as he grabbed me and threw me to the deck. Where had he come from? He must have heard us climbing aboard and ducked into the wooden cabin near the bow to lie in wait. It was the only place he could have come from so quickly. It didn't matter. The surprise was over. The guy was going Tasmanian on me. The battle for the yellow ship had begun.

I hit the deck on my back and saw I wasn't being attacked by one guard, but two. The second guard was waiting for me, and I obliged him by landing right at his feet. He wound up to kick me. I rolled away. Both guards pounced. They were bigger than I was, but whatever advantage they had in muscle, they lacked in agility. And experience. I realized that right away. They both charged like a couple of bulls. I was able to bounce to my feet and dodge them easily.

They didn't give up. One guy charged again. I ducked him, but got speared by the second guard, who followed right behind. He drove me backward, slamming me into the wooden cabin. At the same time, he reached for his own wooden tube and wound up, ready to drive it into my ribs. He swung the weapon toward me. I blocked the downward thrust with my right arm, then whipped the same arm up to catch him across the cheek. He never saw it coming. I didn't think these guys had ever been in a fight with somebody like me. I had learned from the best and practiced to fight against seasoned warriors. These two tropical guards may have been big and imposing, but they didn't stand a chance. That was the good news.

Bad news was they were about to get help.

A loud horn sounded, tearing through the predawn quiet. Huge spotlights flashed on, bathing the ships in bright, white light. The surprise was really over. This was no longer about taking down a handful of guards. The entire security force that watched these ships would soon be headed our way.

I caught a glimpse of the other swimmers pulling themselves up and over the railing near the bow. I thought they were coming to help me. I thought wrong. They ran to the cabin and jumped inside, headed for I didn't know where. The others spread out along the pier side of the ship and quickly began to cast off the lines. They weren't coming to my rescue; their job was to get this ship under way. The guards were my problem.

It was going to be a race. The Jakills had to get the ship away from the pier and under way before the rest of the security force arrived. All I could do was keep the two guards who were already on the ship occupied, so the Jakills had a chance. I had sent the one guard reeling backward with my backhand punch. The second grabbed me from behind in a bear hug. I bent forward, lifted him up, pushed backward, and drove him into the mast. He barely grunted. I quickly crouched down and shot both my arms forward, which forced him to release his grip. I ducked and swept my leg backward, knocking him down.

The first guard was on me an instant later. He swung. I ducked. He swung again. I dodged. He was getting tired. I had a chance to put this guy away and took it. He swung one last time. I ducked. He overrotated. Perfect. I drilled him in the back of the head with the bottom of my foot. A perfect side kick. He went reeling forward toward the railing. He was stumbling out of control. I could have stopped him. I didn't. Instead, I gave him one last push from behind, and he went tumbling over the side and into the water.

One down. Literally.

I felt the ship rumble. Whatever engines it had were growling to life. I didn't even know this ship *had* engines. But it did, and the Jakills were firing them up.

Shouting came from somewhere on the shore. A few hundred yards away I saw a group of security thugs running along the rocks toward the pier. If they got to us before we shoved off, we'd be done.

The second guard was on me. He'd learned from his mistakes. He didn't charge or throw himself on me. He stood a few yards away, knees bent, fists up, ready to fight. This was trouble. If he was going to come at me with more control, he'd do much better, and there was every possibility I'd be joining his friend in the water. I looked for an advantage, and saw one. My back was to the rail. The Jakill's hooks were still dug into the wooden railing. I turned my back to the guard. I don't think he knew what to make of that, because he hesitated. That was all I needed. I grabbed one of the cords. When I sensed the guard charge, I spun around and lashed it at him like a whip. The wiry cord slashed across the guard's arm. It must have stung, because he yelped in pain. It was probably just as much surprise as pain though. He probably had no idea what hit him. I took the moment to yank the hook out of the wood.

I had a new weapon: a cord with a sharp, nasty three-pronged hook. With the cord in my left hand and the hook dangling from my right, I swung it back and forth, trying to intimidate the guy. His eyes went wide. He didn't want to get impaled. That wouldn't last long. The hook was only valuable as a threat. If he charged, what would I do? Swing it at him? The worst that would happen is it would cut him a little. All I could hope was that he wouldn't realize what a lame weapon this really was. I needed time. The longer I kept him away, the more time the Jakills had to get this boat the hell away from the pier.

I felt the ship lurch. We were moving! Would it be fast enough? My heart leaped. So did the guard. He realized what was happening and knew he had to make his move. He lunged at me. I reared back to throw the hook. Suddenly the guard stopped short. It was as if he froze in his tracks. His mouth hung open. What the heck? A second later he fell to his knees and tumbled face-first onto the deck with a sickening thud. Ouch. He hit and didn't move. I looked up to see that standing behind him was Siry, holding his wooden blowgun to his lips. Sticking out of the back of the guard was a small, green dart.

"Pretty exciting, isn't it?" Siry said, pleased with himself. He was actually having fun. He and the Jakills went looking for adventure. They had found it already.

"Are we going to make it?" I asked.

"We'll know soon enough," he said, sticking his blowgun into his belt. "Help me."

He bent down to pick up the comatose guard. I grabbed his shoulders while Siry grabbed his legs. We struggled to carry him over to the pier side of the ship.

"Lower him over," Siry commanded.

He dropped the guy's legs over the side and I stretched out

as far as I could before letting him go. The sleeping guard fell to the pier and crumpled like a rag doll.

"I hope we didn't hurt him," I said.

"Better than letting him drown," Siry answered.

Rat boy ran up to us and pointed toward shore. "Here they come!" he shouted.

Sure enough, the gang of security thugs had turned onto the pier and were sprinting toward us.

"Speed would be good," I said to Siry.

Siry ran for the ship's wheel. It was an enormous, round wooden wheel that was positioned in front of the rear mast.

"Throttle up!" he screamed.

The ship's engines hummed. I heard it, and felt it in my feet. Slowly, we moved away from the pier. The security thugs screamed and sprinted toward us. It was going to be close. The ship was moving, but painfully slowly. We were seconds from getting away.

"Push off!" Siry commanded.

I looked over the pier side rail to see several sets of hands reach out from portholes just above the water's surface. They each had long, wooden poles that they used to push the ship away from the pier. We didn't need to get far away, just a little farther than jumping distance from the pier. It struck me that Siry had thought of everything, even down to having the Jakills stationed down below to make the final push off.

The security guards sprinted along the pier to the stern of the ship, too late. One made a desperate leap. His hand barely brushed the railing as he tumbled into the water.

We were away. The engines powered up, and in no time we were moving quickly away from the pier and out of harm's way. I couldn't believe it. We'd made it! This group of kids had actually hijacked a ship. I had gotten so caught up in the adventure that I didn't stop to think of how impossible a task it was. Maybe that was a good thing, because as it turned out, it wasn't impossible at all. I looked back to the pier to see the dozen or so security guards standing there, helpless, watching one of their beautiful new ships motoring away.

All the Jakills ran on deck, cheering and hugging. I didn't know how long they had been planning this, but it was definitely a moment of victory.

Loque came up to me and shook my hand.

"You had me worried for a minute," he said.

"Not half as worried as I was," I replied.

"I'm glad you're aboard, Pendragon," he said sincerely.

We were on our way, but to where? Siry guided the ship along the coast, headed toward the mouth of the bay that led to the village of Rayne. Far in the distance, over the ocean, the sun was rising. It was a beautiful sight. It was the beginning of a new chapter in the history of Ibara. It was an awesome moment.

That didn't last long.

Boom! Without thinking, I dropped to the deck. The Jakills didn't. A second later something whistled over our heads. The Jakills stood there, confused.

"Get down!" I screamed. "They're firing at us!"

"'Firing'? What do you mean?" Siry cried. "What was that sound?"

Boom! Another explosion. Nobody moved but me. I covered my head. I heard another sharp whistle as something flew by.

"Get down!" I screamed again.

Siry truly didn't know what was happening. I saw nothing but confusion on the faces of the Jakills. Not fear. Confusion. I realized that they had never heard of weapons that fired missiles, or cannonballs, or whatever it was that was being aimed at us. There was no reason for them to be afraid. That is, until we were hit.

"What is happening?" Loque yelled.

"I don't know!" I screamed back. "But if we get hit, this ship is going down."

"I don't understand," Siry cried.

"They're trying to sink us!" I yelled. "Get away from shore! We've got to get out of range of their weapons."

"No!" Siry yelled. "There are no weapons in Rayne that can do that!"

Boom!

"Then what was that?" I yelled, before covering my head again.

The missile landed close to the ship, kicking up a geyser of water that buffeted us.

Rat boy squealed, "How can they do that?"

"Look," Twig said calmly.

She was pointing out to sea. I got up and joined the others as they ran to the railing to see.

There was another ship. It was a few hundred yards off our port bow and on a collision course.

"What ship is that?" I asked.

"I don't know," Siry answered. "It didn't come from Rayne."

Boom! Another explosion. This time we saw the source. A plume of smoke erupted from the mystery ship. Whatever it was, it had cannons and it was firing at us. Another missile landed a few yards off our bow with a huge splash.

"What is that?" Loque asked in awe.

Siry answered, "I think it's our first look at the world beyond our own."

In all of Siry's planning, he hadn't figured on being attacked by a mystery ship with weapons like none they had ever seen.

And the day was only beginning.

IBARA

We were under attack. The first few volleys of cannon fire from the mystery ship had come dangerously close to hitting our small pirate ship. I didn't know how well our ship was made, but I didn't think it would hold up very long if we started getting nailed by cannon fire. I'm no expert on naval warfare, but as cool as this little ship was, it wasn't an armor-clad battlewagon.

I ran to the bow to try and get a better look at the approaching ship. It was hard to make out because the rising sun was in my face, making the ship more or less a silhouette—like a ghost ship. It was much smaller than the ship we were on, with a low profile and a sharper bow. There were no sails or masts, which meant it was also more modern than our sailing ship.

Boom! Smoke erupted from the attacker's deck. I dropped down and covered up, holding my head tight until I knew if the shot would hit or miss. It missed. Another huge splash of water kicked up. Strangely, it missed even wider than the earlier shots. Either the people firing the weapons had gotten lucky before, or they weren't trying to hit us.

I peeked over the railing as Siry came up next to me. He had an old-fashioned brass telescope that he used to peer at the attacking ship.

"You sure that ship didn't come from Rayne?" I asked.

"I've never seen anything like it." He sounded more curious than frightened. His confidence was back. "It's shooting some kind of projectiles."

Some kind of projectiles. Oh man. I still didn't understand how Ibara worked. On the one hand they had power and lights and running water; on the other hand they had no clue about modern weapons. At least the people of Rayne didn't have a clue. Obviously there was somebody else on Ibara who knew all about them, because they were shooting at us.

Another shot erupted from the cannon. I ducked, but didn't need to. It splashed down even farther in front of us.

"I don't think they're trying to hit us," I concluded.

"Then what are they doing?" a confused Siry asked.

I looked at the shore off to our right. We were moving parallel to the beach, approaching the break that led into the large bay, and Rayne. I think I wrote before, the entrance to the bay was a couple hundred yards wide. The shoreline was rocky beach, then came the opening, then farther on, the rocky beach continued. Between those two rocky spits of land was the gateway to the perfect green bay and the village of Rayne.

Siry frowned.

"What?" I asked.

He raised the telescope and looked to the ship again.

"Flighters," he growled. "It's not about us. They're headed for Rayne."

He handed me the telescope. Our position had changed enough that the attacking ship was no longer in complete shadow. The thing looked military. It was about eighty feet long, with a low flat cabin. At one time it had been gray, but the paint was peeling, and big patches of rust were everywhere. I even saw the faint outline of military-style markings on the bow. I couldn't make it out though, because it was mostly worn off. It looked like one of those old PT boats you'd see in World War II movies. Whatever it was, it was long past its prime. The craft was so full of holes and rust I didn't know how it stayed afloat. There was only one thing about it that didn't look old and rusted: the cannon mounted on its bow. That thing worked just fine.

Five people were on deck. All looked like men, but I couldn't tell for sure. Two were at the cannon, the others were in the stern driving the boat. They all had long hair and raggy-looking clothes. Flighters. When I say the ship we were on was like a pirate ship, I'm talking about the kind of pirate you'd see in the movies. Idealized pirates. Fictional pirates. Disney pirates. The Flighters on this other ship weren't about to sing "Yo-ho-ho and a bottle of rum." No way. They were the real deal. They were a desperate-looking bunch of outlaws on a ship that wasn't the least bit romantic.

"They're trying to scare us off," Siry said, his eyes focused. "They're making a run for the bay."

Several of the other Jakills joined us at the bow.

"What are they doing?" Twig asked nervously.

"They're headed for Rayne," Siry declared.

Loque added, "They could hurt a lot of people with that weapon."

Everyone stood dumbfounded, staring at the ship, which was about a hundred yards away. It was going to pass in front of us. Siry was right. The shots were a warning to keep us back. They were going to attack Rayne.

Siry faced his group of young rebels. He scanned their eyes

as he had earlier, before beginning their mission.

"What do you think?" he asked.

I wasn't sure what he meant. I was the only one. The other Jakills knew exactly what he was talking about.

"Our families are in Rayne," Twig said in a small, shaky voice.

"We don't have a choice," rat boy added.

Siry asked, "Does anyone disagree?"

Nobody reacted. I didn't know what the heck he was talking about, so I couldn't agree or disagree. I probably didn't get a vote anyway.

Loque said, "If we do this, the quest will end before it begins. We may never get another chance to live beyond our shores."

"If we *don't* do this," Siry countered, "we won't be able to live with our*selves*."

Loque nodded. "You're right."

I felt another excited buzz go through the group. What were they talking about?

Siry actually smiled. "We wanted an adventure. We got one." Everyone cheered. Siry ran back to the ship's wheel, barking commands. "Engineers, down below. Raise the sails. We've got a race!"

They all ran off to some predetermined post. I was left alone, feeling stupid. Did I mention how confused I was about everything on Ibara? I had no idea what to do, so I followed Siry and watched as he took his place behind the wheel.

"What are you doing?" I asked.

"We're going to stop the Flighters."

"How? You don't have any weapons. No, you don't even know what weapons are!"

I heard a loud flapping sound as the large main sail was

raised. With a crack it filled with air, and our small ship lurched forward.

"I told you, Pendragon," Siry said with pride. "We've been piloting boats around these waters our whole lives."

"But you don't have any weapons!" I repeated.

Siry smiled slyly and said, "What about the one you're standing on?"

Huh? It took a few seconds for me to get what he meant. When it finally clicked, I wished it hadn't.

"You're going to ram them?" I gasped.

"Our engines aren't powerful," he answered. "But the wind is with us. We can catch that little gray monster and slice her in half."

"What if it shoots back, and this time they try to hit us?"

"Either way we'll sink," he answered. "We can't let the Flighters into that bay."

I wanted to argue. I really did. But he was right. The people of Rayne were sitting ducks. We were the only ones who could stop them. Of course, I wished I wasn't along for the ride on that kamikaze torpedo. All I could do was keep my head down and hope for the best.

Siry and the Jakills kept surprising me. They were a bunch of rebellious kids with no respect for authority and had no problem stealing a ship. But they weren't a bunch of thrill seekers out for a joyride. They really wanted to learn the truth about their world. They felt so strongly about it that they were willing to become exiled outlaws. Now they were throwing their dreams away to protect their village. At best, they'd stop the Flighters but lose the ship and return to Rayne to be arrested. At worst, well, I didn't want to think about that. Either way, their dreams of exploring the rest of Ibara were about to end. There wasn't even a debate. Everybody was in.

As I watched these young sailors expertly guide their ship toward suicide, I realized something important. Whatever happened with this sea battle, whatever became of the Jakills, it was this kind of spirit and curiosity that would guide Ibara through its turning point and into the future. I can't find the words to describe the respect and admiration I had for this small band of curious kids. It wasn't until that moment that I knew for certain I had made the right decision. I was glad to be with the Jakills.

The sails added speed. The distance between our yellow ship and the war ship closed quickly. It helped that the Flighters didn't pick up any speed. As we got closer to their ship, I heard the loud chugging of its engines. From the throaty, belching, misfiring sound of things, the engine of that warship was just as decrepit as its hull. If they were able to pour on the speed and get away from us, they would have. I tried to guesstimate when our paths would cross, and figured we'd collide just before it reached the opening to the bay. The only way they could stop us would be to shoot us out of the water.

Which is exactly what they tried to do.

Boom!

A shot screamed toward us, and sailed so close I felt a breeze as it whistled by. They weren't trying to scare us anymore. We were now a target.

"Speed, my friends," Siry ordered. "Trim!"

Several Jakills sprang to work, pulling on lines, trimming the sails. These guys really knew how to sail. I was nothing more than an interested passenger.

Boom! Another shot. This one nicked one of the horizontal cross bars off the forward mast, splintering the end. They were getting close. It was good that they only had one cannon.

It took time to reload. I figured they'd get off two more shots before we hit them. Of course once we got that close, the second of those two shots would be point blank. Our only hope was that we'd stay afloat long enough to batter them before sinking.

Boom! Another shot tore toward us. This one hit. Square in the bow. The boat shuddered. Were we going down? I ran forward to peer over the bow and survey the damage. The missile had hit us directly on the strong front beam, causing a nasty-looking indent. It was total luck. A foot to either side and it would have torn through the wooden hull. We weren't going to sink. Yet.

We pounded through the waves, getting closer to the ship. We were near enough that I could see the expressions on the faces of the Flighters. They didn't even seem anxious. It didn't matter that a ship twice their size was bearing down, ready to ram them. They went about their business, expressionless. For two of them, that business was to reload the cannon and line up for another shot that would put us at the bottom of the ocean. They worked quickly, carrying what looked like a heavy, silver rocket toward the steel cannon. This wasn't an old-fashioned, front-loading cannon shooting heavy black cannonballs. No, this was a modern weapon.

Siry spun the wheel, putting us onto a final collision course with the marauding ship. It was a race. Would we hit their ship first, or would they fire and sink us? The answer would come in the next several seconds. I ran back and positioned myself near the rear mast. I don't know why I did that. Maybe because it felt solid. Or maybe I wanted something to hide behind if I saw a silver rocket shooting toward my head. We were seconds away from impact. The Flighters scurried around their cannon, desperately preparing to fire the killing shot. It was going to be close. I put my arm around the mast and hugged it. The Flighters finished loading and swung the weapon toward us. We were going to lose the race. The only question left was if our momentum would keep us moving fast enough to damage their ship, or would we be stopped in the water?

"Hang on to something!" Siry warned.

His voice was drowned out by an odd sound. A mechanical sound. It was nothing like I had heard from either of these ships. It was totally alien. Siry was just as confused as I was. The loud sound carried across the water, like some infernal engine was powering to life. The mysterious sound saved us from being shot to bits because the Flighters were surprised as well. They stopped their work to look around in wonder. What was it?

Twig was the first to spot it.

"There!" she shouted, pointing off the starboard bow toward the opening that led into the bay. The water between the two points of land was boiling. White water churned a swirling vortex directly between the two fingers of land. A moment later, something rose up from below. I swear, my first thought was that it was a two-headed sea serpent. I know, that might not be the first thing to jump to most people's minds, but after all I'd been through since I left home, nothing seemed impossible. The creature slowly rose out of the water. Its silver, wet skin reflected the morning light. Everyone stood mesmerized, both Flighters and Jakills. And me.

It was indeed a two-headed beast, but not of the sea-serpent variety. What I saw was impossible, but real. In that moment I realized we were in a very bad place.

"Turn away!" I shouted at Siry. "Now!"

"What?" he shouted back, confused.

"Get us out of here!" I screamed.

He didn't move. We bore down on the Flighter ship, seconds from collision. The Flighters didn't have time to fire their cannon. They were no longer our biggest threat. I jumped next to Siry and screamed in his face, "Get away from their ship *now!*"

Siry was flustered. He didn't know what to do. There wasn't time to explain. I shoved him away, grabbed the wheel and spun it hard to the left. The nose of our ship turned, painfully slowly, to port and away from a collision with the Flighter ship.

"What are you doing?" Siry yelled, and jumped back, fighting me for control of the wheel. I had no choice. I nailed him in the gut with my fist. Siry doubled over, gasping for air. I kept the ship's wheel turned hard to port. We missed the Flighter's ship by only a few feet. As we glided past, it felt like we were close enough to smell them. The grungy Flighters didn't know which way to turn. They were torn between avoiding a collision with us and gaping at the strange, two-headed silver beast that loomed up, blocking their way into the channel that led to Rayne.

Loque ran up to me, frantic. "What are you doing?" he shouted. "We had them!"

Siry's eyes bore into me. "What have you done?"

There was no way they could understand. I was the only one who knew we had to get out of harm's way, so I went for it. Was I right? The answer would come soon enough.

We cleared the Flighters' ship and cruised away as the military boat continued on toward the channel. There was a loud metallic click as the two-headed silver monster finished its ascent. The "heads" of the silver beast were long tubes, wider to the rear and tapered to a narrow, hollow point. Both "heads" turned together. With the metallic sound of turning gears, the hollow tubes lined themselves up on the Flighter's ship.

I was right.

"What kind of beasts are those?" rat boy asked in wonder.

"They aren't beasts," I declared.

As if on cue, both of the long silver tubes unloaded. They were guns. I didn't know what kind of ammunition it fired. The sound wasn't sharp, but more like dull thuds. *Wump, wump, wump, wump.* They fired, point blank, at the Flighters ship. Each time one fired, it recoiled then locked back into position for another shot.

The Flighters didn't stand a chance. The missiles tore into their ship. Or should I say, the missiles tore their ship apart. There were no explosions when they hit. It was more like small laser bombs had ripped through their vessel. Our ship was close enough to be rocked by the impact. Siry jumped for the wheel. This time I let him take over. He knew the truth now. We needed to get out of there. He gripped the large wheel and focused on guiding us out of harm's way.

The Flighters were desperate to escape the attack and dove over the sides of their doomed ship. In seconds the hull was shredded. I had no idea if any were killed, but if there were any of them below deck, there was no way they survived. The guns kept firing with a vengeance. *Thump, thump, thump.* The sounds of tearing, hot metal sounded like fingernails scraping across a blackboard. The silver guns seemed like they were controlled by an unseen hand. As big as they were, they operated simply and smoothly, like a toy. In twenty seconds the Flighters' ship was a memory. All that was left were the bubbles that rose in the water to mark its grave, and a handful of floundering Flighters. I had no doubt they'd make it to shore and be picked up by the security force.

Its mission complete, the guns stopped firing. With a mechanical whir they returned to center position and sank down beneath the water. The whole event, from the time we first heard the whir of the guns to the disappearance of any sign that they had been there, took all of a minute. A single, violent minute.

The Jakills stood staring back at the gateway to Rayne, dumbfounded. All was quiet. The sun continued to rise on a new day. It looked as if nothing had happened.

But nothing was the same.

IBARA

The stunned looks on the faces of the Jakills told the whole story. In those few short minutes they learned about firepower and its violent result.

"It was . . . it was . . . horrible!" Twig cried out.

Loque gasped. "Did anyone know about that weapon?"

Nobody had.

"What about the Flighters' ship?" rat boy whined. "They had a weapon too! We're lucky we're not on the bottom of the ocean right next to them!"

"I'm scared," Twig said.

They fell into an excited babble. Gone were the bold hijackers who were willing to risk their lives to ram the Flighters' ship. Crashing one ship into another made sense to them. Powerful weapons of destruction didn't.

"Stop!" Siry ordered.

Everyone fell silent. Throughout the frantic debate, Siry's eyes had stayed on the horizon. He gripped the ship's large wheel, guiding it as if nothing had happened. It was a good act. I saw the truth. His hands were quivering. When he spoke, he kept his eyes forward. I'm guessing he didn't want to make eye contact or the Jakills would realize he was just as shaken as everybody else.

"What did you expect?" he asked.

"Not that!" rat boy chirped quickly.

"Then wake up!" Siry shot back. "We're out here to discover the truth about our world. Did you really think we'd like everything we found?"

Loque said calmly, "This isn't the rest of the world, Siry. That weapon was here, where we live. Why didn't we know about it?"

"For the same reason we don't know about the rest of the world beyond our island," Siry answered angrily. "The tribunal keeps us ignorant. I don't know what that weapon was or who put it there. That's the whole point. Why don't we know? Why are they keeping secrets?"

The Jakills exchanged nervous looks.

Siry continued. "Nothing has changed except we've had our first taste of life beyond our sheltered little village." He finally looked at the others and continued with passion. "Do we want to learn more? Or was that enough to make us turn around and run back to our lives of peaceful oblivion like frightened children?"

There were tentative looks all around, but nobody raised their hand.

Siry nodded in approval. "Good. Everybody back to their posts. We've got a long sail ahead."

The group dispersed silently but not enthusiastically.

"Take the wheel," Siry ordered Loque.

Loque nodded and took control of the ship. He seemed to be Siry's most trusted friend. I could see why. Loque was a good guy. Siry looked me square in the eye. He seemed shaken.

"Come with me," he ordered, his voice cracking slightly.

The guy was barely holding it together. I knew he'd have questions. I had plenty of my own. He led me toward the bow of the ship and into the wooden cabin. Inside were coiled ropes and poles. It looked like your basic shipboard gear. Nothing unusual. We entered the cabin. Suddenly he turned and sprang at me. I was so surprised, I barely reacted. He grabbed my shirt and pushed me against the wooden wall. Hard.

"Never do that again," he seethed. The guy was really ticked.

"Do what?" was all I could get out.

His eyes were wild with anger. Or fear. "I'm their leader. I don't care who you are, you will not take over like that again."

I realized he was talking about how I took control of the ship's wheel and steered us away from the Flighters' ship.

"Sure, Siry," I said calmly. "Next time we're all about to die and you freeze up, I'll back off so you won't look bad. No problem."

Siry wanted to be angry. I think he wanted to hit me. Instead he shoved me away and walked to the other side of the cabin. The guy looked tortured.

I asked, "This isn't really about me saving the ship, is it?"

Siry pulled his hand through his curly hair. The confident front he put on for the Jakills was gone. "They trust me," he said with a shaky voice. "What have I gotten them into?"

"Want to turn back?"

"No!" he said quickly. "I just want to keep it together."

"You will," I assured him. "You're not alone. You don't have to have all the answers."

"Answers?" he said with an ironic chuckle. "What answers? All I've got are questions. Come see what I found below."

I followed him down a wooden ladder to a lower deck. We climbed down one level and moved aft. The ceiling was low. I had to be careful not to bash my head. We walked along a short corridor with doors on either side. A few feet farther, dead ahead, was a doorway. He motioned for me to enter. I stepped past him into the belly of the ship. The large area took up most of the body of the ship. It was empty, except for long rows of wooden shelves that lined both sides. Each shelf looked about six feet long by two feet across. They were simple with no markings or detail. A quick guesstimate said there were about a hundred. Fifty on either side, two levels each.

"What do you think those are for?" he asked.

"They look like bunks," I answered. "You know, for people to sleep on."

"That's what I think," Siry agreed. "This is no fishing boat. It was built to move people. But who? And to where?"

"I wish I knew" was my honest answer.

Siry looked at me suspiciously. "Who are you, Pendragon? Really? I've trusted you and you still haven't even told me where you're from."

"I thought you didn't want to hear about Travelers and Halla. You think it's all some fantasy your father thought up."

"Can you blame me?"

I couldn't. Siry was scared, and lost. Up until the Flighters' boat showed up, he thought he pretty much had it all wired. That ended as soon as the first shot was fired. He was floundering. It was the first chance I had to try and get through to him.

"First tell me about your father," I said softly. "What was he like?"

Siry paced nervously, running his hand along the wooden

frame of the shelves. It seemed like a load of conflicting emotions were battling for his head space.

"He was a tough guy," he finally began. "People respected him. He started out as one of those security goons, but he was smart and landed on the tribunal."

"If I didn't know better, I'd say you're proud of him."

Siry scoffed. "He was tough with me, too. He wanted me to be, I don't know, perfect. He kept saying that the son of a tribunal member had to set an example. He said I would take his place one day. You know, on the tribunal. I wanted to make him proud."

"So what happened?"

"I found out the tribunal was lying to us. Most people had no idea. But I knew. You didn't have to be a genius to realize something else was out there. All it took was for something to wash up on shore. Knowing there was some greater truth was kind of, I don't know, disturbing. Knowing the tribunal was lying about it made it worse. The people trusted them. They betrayed us."

"And your father was one of them."

Siry nodded.

"So that's when you started the Jakills?"

"I wasn't the only one who felt betrayed. But we were smart enough to keep our ideas to ourselves, not like the people who vanished for asking too many questions. We only shared our thoughts when we were safe from the ears of the tribunal. But it wasn't all about anger. At least, not at first. We had fun, too. Everybody on that island is so, I don't know, behaved. I guess we caused some trouble. It was our way of protesting the lies we had to live with. The tribunal thinks we're a bunch of trouble-making kids. They have no idea that we want to open the eyes of every person on that island. But to do that, we first have to open our own eyes. That's why we're here."

He got right in my face. Some of his swagger was back. "That's my story. Tell me yours."

The time for tact was long gone.

"You're in the middle of a battle that's much bigger than you realize. You're right about one thing though. Your father *did* want you to take his place someday . . . as a Traveler."

Siry scoffed, but it felt like this time it was out of habit. "Yeah, right. Saint Dane, Halla, the future of all existence! My father lied to his people. Why should I believe anything he said?"

"Because it's true," I said flatly. "You said you wanted the truth, that's it. I don't know why your father did what he did, but he was a Traveler. There has to be a good reason."

"And how do you fit in to all this?"

"I've been chosen to be the lead Traveler. Why? I don't know. By who? I don't know that either."

"What *do* you know?"

"I've followed Saint Dane to seven territories. Five times we stopped him. Twice we failed. That's not good enough. I think what's happening on Ibara could be the beginning of the final battle for Halla. He's here, Siry. I don't know where yet, but I guarantee, he's here, and I believe he's going to try and stop you."

"Me?" he asked, surprised. "He doesn't even know me."

"Wrong," I shot back. "You're a Traveler now. He knows all about you. He knows about all of us. I guarantee he also knows the truth about Ibara that you're trying to find. Question is, how is he using that truth to turn this territory upside down and set himself up to win the final battle? That's why I'm here. I'm trying to learn the truth, just like you. The only difference is I'm fighting for Halla, not just this one territory. Whether you believe it or not, you are too."

Siry nodded thoughtfully and sat down on one of the empty bunks. I didn't know if I was getting through to him, or if he thought I was as crazy as I sounded.

"I don't want to be responsible for the future of all existence," he said, sounding tired. "I just think people should be able to choose their own destinies."

"You know what that means?"

"What?"

"It means you've taken your father's place."

Siry almost smiled. Almost. "I hate to admit this," he said, "but we wouldn't have made it this far without your help."

"Does that mean you trust me now?"

He reached under his shirt, where he had a wide blue belt strapped around his waist. He took it off and unfolded it to reveal it was a waterproof pouch. He reached inside the pocket and took out a yellowed piece of paper.

"I found this on the beach a long time ago," he explained. "It was in a tube to keep it dry. The tube was broken. There's some damage."

He treated the document as if it were precious. He gently unfolded the paper and placed it down reverently on one of the wooden shelves.

Before I looked at it, he said, "This is proof the tribunal has been lying. It's what brought the Jakills together and sent us on this adventure."

He stepped aside so I could see the mysterious paper. It was a map. A very old and worn map. It was crude, not like a modern road map with lots of detail. This was more of a hand-drawn antique. There was no telling how old it was. Most of the writing had long ago worn off, but I could still see the detail of land masses.

"What am I looking at?" I asked.

"I know every detail of our island," he explained. "Every cove, every mountain, every stream." He pointed to an outline on the map and declared, "That's it. There's the bay where Rayne is built. There's Tribunal Mountain. It's all there."

I wasn't so much interested in the detail of the island, as I was about the fact that this map showed other land masses. The closest to the island was so large, the borders ran off the edges of the page.

"What's that?" I asked.

"That," Siry declared, "is where we're going. If we're going to find other life, that is the place to start."

There was a peninsula that jutted out from the large landmass. Its tip was the closest piece of land to the island. More interesting was the fact that the peninsula had faded letters on it. It had a name. I couldn't quite make it out, so I took the fragile map and held it up toward a porthole so that light would shine through from behind. The words were faint and not lined up properly, but I could definitely make out the word "Rubity."

"Rubity," Siry said. "That's where we're going."

As I held the paper up to the light, I saw another word, barely visible along one border. The letters weren't evenly spaced and could barely be made out, but there was no mistake. The word was "JAKILL."

"We think it might be the name of the mapmaker," Siry said before I could ask. "That's one mystery solved, right?" he added with a sly smile.

"How long will it take to sail there?" I asked.

"Depends on the wind, but it's not far. A day. Maybe longer."

"That's close," I said, surprised.

"That's why we chose it. But it's also a big risk. If Rubity is populated, there's a good chance we'll find something there we'd rather not."

"What's that?"

"Flighters."

I didn't have much to do on the ship. No, I had nothing to do on the ship, other than to walk around and be impressed by how the Jakills were such good sailors. They expertly trimmed the sails and kept the spider web of lines from tangling and basically sailed the ship like they were born to do it. I took the chance to talk with some of them and learned their major fun growing up was sailing small boats. Some even spent time on the larger fishing vessels or apprenticed under the guidance of experienced sailors. It definitely qualified them to be sailing this minipirate ship.

The trip was cake. The water was calm and the air was warm. In the afternoon when the sun got really hot, we swung off the rails from ropes attached to the mast, plunging into the warm, tropical sea. It was a blast.

I also took the chance to explore the rest of the ship. The engines were small, just as Siry had said. They weren't powerful enough to do much more than maneuver. Loque explained to me that it ran on fuel that was distilled from plants. How cool was that? Organic fuel!

There were several jugs of fresh drinking water on board, but not a lot of food. That was the one part of the plan that the Jakills had to sacrifice. Given the way we had to hijack the ship, there was no way to bring food on board for our voyage. Their hope was that we'd find enough at our destination.

Rubity.

What was Rubity? The concept of there being a whole

world outside the island made sense in theory, but actually seeing a map and learning a name made it real. As excited as I was, I had to think the Jakills were going out of their minds with anticipation. And maybe a little dread.

When night fell, I took the time to begin this journal. I found this paper in a cabin to the stern of the ship that must have been the captain's quarters. It had a single bunk and a table where I could write. There was no artificial light on board, so I sat by a window at the stern and used the bright light from the stars to write by. As I sat there alone, writing by starlight, I felt certain that the closer the ship got to land, the closer I was getting to my next meeting with Saint Dane.

That wasn't the only reason I was feeling anxious. Being with the Jakills and seeing how they'd risked everything to take charge of their lives got me thinking about my own life. I wondered how much longer my quest would go on. How much longer would I have to blindly accept my fate and bounce between territories chasing Saint Dane? Right or wrong, the Jakills had taken control of their own destinies. Was it time I did the same with mine?

I fell asleep that night with those thoughts banging around in my head. I'm surprised I got any sleep at all. I lay down on the bunk in that cabin and tried to push the negative thoughts out of my head. Eventually I nodded off and didn't wake up the entire night. As I slowly came out of dreamland, my stomach gurgled. I hadn't eaten in a while—that was my first thought. My second was that someone was up on deck, screaming.

"Hey! Hey! Everybody!" he shouted. I forced myself to wake up, threw my legs over the side of the bunk, and stood up. It was early. The sky was only beginning to turn from black to deep blue. The sun would soon follow.

"Come on! Everybody on deck!" came the excited voice.

I rubbed my face to get the circulation going and headed out. I made my way along the small corridor to the ladder leading to the top deck. On the way, I ran into Loque and rat boy.

"What's going on?" I asked groggily.

"Don't know," Loque answered.

We all climbed the ladder and headed out on deck. We were met with the sight of several Jakills standing shoulder to shoulder along one railing, gazing out to sea. At first I thought they had seen a whale, or another ship. At least that's what I hoped. I didn't want another run-in with a Flighter warship. I joined the group, gazed off in the same direction, and gasped. I really gasped. The vision in the distance forced it out of me. On the horizon, maybe a few hours' sailing time away, was land. We had reached the shore of the great land mass on Siry's map.

"Closer than I thought," Siry said as he joined us.

"It's beautiful!" Twig said.

"Everything's beautiful from a distance," Siry said.

I couldn't begin to imagine what the Jakills were thinking. Their suspicions were correct. The map was real. There was land beyond their island. What we saw on the horizon was something none of the Jakills had ever seen before. I had, but seeing it here on Ibara, knowing what it meant, made my knees go weak. There before us, on the peninsula marked "Rubity" on the ancient map, was a city. A modern city. The tops of buildings appeared on the horizon first, which meant they were big. Very big. Skyline big. Chicago big. New York big.

"What are those pointy things?" rat boy asked in wonder.

I didn't answer. He would see for himself. The simple island people of Rayne were about to get what they wanted.

They were going to discover the truth about their home.

I, on the other hand, had entirely different expectations. I had absolutely no doubt that somewhere in that mysterious city, Saint Dane was waiting for me.

IBARA

I was struck by the quiet.

It's not often you can say that quiet has such an impact. It didn't seem to bother the Jakills, though. From the moment we saw the city, they were over the moon with excitement. (Assuming that Ibara has a moon, that is.) For years they had spoken in secret whispers about what might lie beyond the shores of their island. They met in the jungle to wonder and plan. They were so driven by their hunger for the truth, they were willing to become outcasts among their own people to find it.

Their long-planned search was about to come to an end in a place called "Rubity."

Those who weren't manning the sails or below tending to the engines were eagerly leaning over the rails as if those few extra inches would get them a better view of this wondrous city. At first there was nothing but enthusiasm. As we sailed closer, their emotions were less obvious. Looking at their faces, I could guess why. I felt it too. Maybe not as strongly as the Jakills, but I felt it. There was still excitement of course, but there was also worry. What if the reality of Ibara turned out to be dismal? That would be bad enough, but it would mean that learning the truth wasn't worth the sacrifices they had made. Nobody spoke. Nobody laughed. Nobody speculated on what it was they were seeing. They all silently kept inside their own heads. One way or another, their lives were about to change. I could only hope that their dreams wouldn't turn into nightmares.

"A pier!" Loque shouted from the bow. "We can tie up there!" He pointed off the starboard bow to what looked like a low structure built out onto the water. It looked like a few other ships were tied up as well. It was as good a place as any for us to aim for. Siry made a slight course adjustment and we glided toward the pier.

For me, the real show was about to begin. I felt as if we were growing closer to Saint Dane. This may sound weird, but the odd quiet of this city made me think of him. Maybe it was because something felt off. The others didn't know what to expect from a city, but I did, and I knew something wasn't right. At first we were too far away to hear anything more specific than a wall of city white noise. We never hit that wall. I listened for random honking car horns, shouts, sirens, music . . . anything! There was nothing but the lonely, hollow sound of wind blowing through the canyons of buildings.

Siry gave the wheel to Loque and took me aside.

"Okay, Traveler," he whispered. "What do you think of this?"

"It's a city," I said. "Think of Rayne, times a few thousand. No biggie."

That seemed to relax Siry. It wouldn't last.

"But something's odd," I added. "It's too quiet. Cities are

cities because they're loaded with people and activity. I don't hear any of that."

Siry listened for a moment, and frowned. "I don't know what I'm listening for."

"Life," I answered. "If you get that many people together in one place, they're going to make noise. Rayne is louder than this."

Siry looked at the buildings that were now growing to the size of skyscrapers. It looked like any city you'd see on Second Earth. Nothing unusual . . . except for the silence. Siry went back to the wheel, saying to Loque, "I'll bring us in."

Loque nodded and called out to the others, "Docking party! With me!"

Five of the Jakills left their vantage points by the rail to join Loque and prepare to tie up the ship at the pier. I wandered back to the bow of our ship and took another look at the looming cityscape. My eye caught something that seemed a little off. We were still pretty far away so I couldn't tell for sure. I had to wait patiently, watching, knowing the closer we got, the more clear it would become.

I glanced down at the water. It was just as green and sparkling as back on the island. Below the surface I was able to make out shapes. At first I thought I was looking at rocks. Or maybe a reef. But as the water grew more shallow, reality became clear. Literally. There were ships down there. Wrecks. A lot of them. They were big, too. It was hard to tell for sure, because I didn't know how deep it was, but some of these sunken ships looked huge. I'm talking ocean-liner huge! We passed over the decks of several wrecks of all sizes. The water was clear enough to see the difference between pleasure boats and others that looked like working boats or freighters. We passed over one monstrous shadow that was definitely an ocean liner. I could tell because toward the tail was the faint blue color of a swimming pool. I got the chills. I was looking down on a graveyard of sunken ships.

I flashed a look back to the buildings. As we grew closer, the truth was slowly emerging. The buildings were no more alive than the ships below the water. I could make out detail. The structures were scarred and pitted. There was more broken glass than intact windows. Some buildings had huge chunks taken out of them. I couldn't tell if the gashes were a result of some kind of attack or simply rotting away. I looked up one wide street between buildings to see that an entire, huge building had crashed and crumbled there. The wide boulevard was totally blocked by the massive hulk of this toppled skyscraper. The ground was mostly covered with rubble. There were massive piles of broken cement and twisted steel. It all had a strange, magical sparkle that was kind of pretty, until I realized the sparkling came from light reflected off tons of shattered glass. There were cars, too. Lots of them. Many were buried, their headlights peeking out as if trying to get a final glimpse of daylight.

The one thing I didn't see was people.

Several Jakills lowered the mainsail. We relied on engine power to continue our slow journey toward the pier. I could now see the ships that were tied up. They looked to be military craft, not unlike the boat that the Flighters used to attack Rayne. These boats looked even worse for wear than the Flighters' junker. Huge patches of rust had eaten through their hulls. I was surprised they were still floating. One was barely above water, with its stern dipped below the surface. It would only be a matter of time before it slipped down and joined the others in the underwater tomb.

Looking at the Jakills, I saw more confusion than concern.

They didn't know what a city was supposed to look like. To them this was normal. Of course the big question was what happened? Why was the city empty? No, not just empty. Abandoned. Was there a war? The thought flashed that maybe there had been some kind of epidemic that wiped out the population, and we were about to be exposed. But whatever happened there, it wasn't recent. This place had been dead for a long time. I had to believe that if there was a nasty biological threat, it would have died off long ago. At least, that's what I told myself.

Siry expertly guided the ship toward the pier. We gently bumped along our starboard side as Loque and the other Jakills jumped over the railing with ropes. There were large cleats that they used to tie us off. As the rest of the Jakills came up from below, Siry gathered the entire group by the bow.

"Pendragon says he's seen places like this before," he announced confidently. "It's called a city."

Rat boy asked, "Where did Pendragon see a city before?"

Everyone looked at me. How was I supposed to answer that?

"I've heard of places like this," I said vaguely. "But I've heard they are busy places that are full of people. This city looks . . . looks—"

"Dead," Loque said soberly.

All eyes turned to the city of rubble.

"Here's the plan," Siry said, sounding businesslike. "We'll send a small party out to explore. The rest should stay here and guard the ship."

"Against what?" rat boy asked. I really had to find out what his name was. Calling somebody "rat boy" wasn't cool.

Siry answered, "There may be Flighters here."

"Who's going?" Twig asked.

"Me, Twig, and Loque," Siry responded.

"I'm going too," I said.

Siry shot me a ticked look, as if I had stepped on his authority again. Too bad. I wasn't about to hang out on that ship. I needed to learn about this city. I didn't want to make this a power struggle, so I quickly said, "If there's only a couple of you going, you might need protection."

How weird was that? I was putting myself out there like some kind of enforcer. Or some kind of . . . Loor. Siry thought about it, then nodded.

"All right, Pendragon will come too." He said this to the group as if it were his idea. I had no problem with that. He saved face and I was going on the scout. Siry addressed the group again. "Do not let anybody aboard. If anything happens to this ship . . ." He let the thought dangle. He didn't need to finish. Nobody wanted to be stranded there. Every Jakill nodded in agreement.

Siry, Loque, Twig, and I prepared for our trip by each taking a wooden blowgun and a pouch with ten blow darts. I wasn't sure if I'd be effective with the blowgun, seeing as I'd never tried it before. I figured the wooden weapon would be better used as a short club. I took the darts just the same, tucking the pouch and the weapon into the waist of my pants.

"We won't be long," Siry announced.

The four of us climbed over the railing and dropped down to the pier. The wood beneath our feet felt like squishy sponge.

"It's rotten!" I called out. "Watch where you walk. You don't want to put your foot through."

We walked gingerly toward shore, mostly with our eyes down, to be sure we weren't stepping on a plank that would splinter and plunge us into the water. Along the way we passed a few more of the military-looking gunboats. Up close these boats looked even worse. Their hulls were rusty. Their decks looked as rotten as the pier. I noticed something that made me a little nervous though. As bad as the boats looked, the large gun that was mounted near each of the bows, the same kind of gun that had fired on us off Rayne, looked pretty clean. It didn't gleam or anything, but it looked to me like it might actually work. I tucked that thought away and kept moving.

We reached the beginning of the pier and stepped onto land. The first thing that caught my eye was a large street sign on the ground that was nearly buried in debris. At one time it was probably bright blue with large white letters. The color had long since faded. The letters had gone gray. But I could read it. There was a large arrow on top, under which it read: FOURTH STREET BRIDGE. I wondered if this was actually English, or my ability as a Traveler translated it for me.

The four of us stood together, silently taking in the remains of what was once a busy metropolis. To say it was a mess is an understatement. The city was in ruins. I was afraid a strong gust of wind might topple one of the huge structures down on top of us. It felt like a giant, fragile, city of cards.

"Let's look around," Siry said, a little less confidently than before.

We walked slowly through the rubble, our sandals crunching the debris. The area near the pier looked like it might have been open space at one time. Maybe it was a park or an area for ships to off-load cargo. Now it was a massive junkyard. Most of the rubble was just that—nondescript rubble. Every so often I'd see something that looked like what it had once been. I saw a suitcase, the skeleton of an umbrella, many bottles of different shapes and colors, even a few shoes. That was creepy. Empty shoes.

Twig took a deep sniff and said, "There's nothing here that grows."

"Really," I agreed. "I think it's been that way a long time."

"How do you know that?" Siry asked.

"Because Twig's right," I answered. "There's nothing organic here. We're not seeing any life, but we're not seeing any death, either."

"What does that mean?" Loque asked.

"There's no bones," I answered glumly. "Everything organic has turned to dust. That doesn't happen overnight."

"What do you think happened?" Loque asked.

"Let's try and find out." I took the lead, making my way through a labyrinth of destruction. I scanned for the remains of an explosion or an earthquake or any other clue as to what might have happened. Nothing jumped out at me. It seemed like the only destructive force that had visited these buildings was time.

"We should go deeper," I said. "Maybe into one of the buildings."

"It all seems so fragile," Loque said thoughtfully

"Anybody want to turn back?" Siry asked.

Nobody did. We walked on.

I lead the group toward the first line of tall buildings and the one street that looked fairly clear. Stepping past the first building was like walking into a canyon. The buildings on either side of us created giant walls that cut much of the light. It was a lot cooler in there because of that. We passed a few cars that were nothing more than skeletons of metal. The interiors had long since dissolved to dust.

Loque asked, "What should we be looking for?" He spoke softly, as if we were walking through a graveyard.

"Signs of life," Siry answered.

We continued on, crossing a few streets, moving farther into the city. The ground level of the buildings looked like it once held shops. My curiosity said to go inside and check one out. My common sense told me it might be suicide. We passed block after desolate block with no clue as to what had happened. Nothing seemed out of the ordinary. The city was simply abandoned. I saw only one thing that didn't quite fit. It was far ahead of us. I couldn't tell exactly how far, because there was a haze of dust in the air that made seeing long distances difficult. It looked like a black wall. Stranger still, the slope of the wall seemed to be at a forty-five degree angle to the street. All the buildings were more or less boxes with vertical or horizontal lines, making this black diagonal slash stand out. I didn't understand why, but the sight of this black wall made me uneasy. I wanted to get there and find out what it was when Siry put on the brakes.

"Stop," he ordered. "We're getting too far away from the ship."

"Just a little farther," I suggested.

"No," Siry said quickly. "There's nothing here for us. We could search for hours and still find nothing."

"What about your quest to discover the truth?" I asked. "We can't turn back now."

"We're not turning back," he bristled. "I'm thinking we came to the wrong place for the wrong reason. There's nobody here. These buildings look ready to collapse. We don't want our quest to begin and end here."

Loque agreed. "The only reason we're here is because it was the closest point on the map. Maybe we should sail up the coast."

It was hard to argue with their logic, but I wanted to keep

going. I kept staring over Siry's shoulder at the distant black wall. What was it?

"I'm hungry," Twig added. "We haven't eaten since yesterday."

"It's true," Loque added. "We need to find food and fresh water."

"I have an idea," Twig said with excitement. "Let's sail back to Ibara, wait till dark, then send a small party to shore to steal supplies."

Siry said, "And what if they start firing that weapon at us?"

"If they wanted to sink us, they would have yesterday," Loque said. "Maybe Twig's idea is a good one. I can swim to shore with a small group. Half of us can steal provisions while the others find a small boat and——"

"Wait," I said abruptly. I had been half listening to their debate, but something Twig said finally sank in. "What did you say, Twig?"

She looked at me uncertainly. "I said maybe we should go home and steal some food."

"No, I mean what did you say exactly?"

The three of them looked at me quizzically. They didn't know where I was going with this. I wasn't so sure either.

"I don't understand," Twig said.

"Where did you say we should sail to?"

"You mean Ibara?"

"Yes!" I exclaimed. "You said we should sail to Ibara."

"What's the problem, Pendragon?" Siry asked.

My pulse started to race. "Twig said we should sail back to Ibara. Why did she say that?"

"To get food," Loque said impatiently.

"No! I mean why didn't she say Rayne?"

The three again exchanged confused looks. Loque answered, "Because Ibara is the name of the island. What's the problem?"

Now my mind was racing along with my pulse. I hoped there was an easy explanation for this.

"You call the island where Rayne is 'Ibara'?" I asked.

"Yes!" Loque answered. "Ibara is the island, Rayne is our village. Didn't you know that?"

Obviously not.

"Then what do you call everywhere else?"

Siry scoffed. Loque stared at me. Twig looked a little scared. To her this was crazy talk. I hoped she was right.

"What are you talking about, Pendragon?" Siry asked.

I felt as if I were about to hyperventilate. "This planet. This world. Whatever. The whole place, not just the island. Is there a name for it?"

Loque laughed, "Of course!"

"Is it Ibara?" I asked hopefully.

"Is this a game?" Loque replied. "Ibara is the name of our island."

"Then what's the name of this planet?" I screamed.

Siry said, "I don't know what game you're playing, but—"

"Humor me!" I shouted. "What's the name of this world? The *whole* world."

Siry answered with one simple, shattering word. "Veelox."

Nothing moved, though it sure seemed as if I'd been swept up into a tornado. It felt like the buildings around us were suddenly spinning. They weren't of course. It was all in my head. That word hammered so hard, I nearly fell over. I could barely breathe.

"Veelox?" I managed to say in a small, pathetic voice. "Siry, the name of this territory is Veelox?"

Twig and Loque looked to each other, holding back nervous, confused giggles. As far as they were concerned, I was insane. At that moment I agreed with them. I felt insane. Siry frowned. I guess he didn't like my reaction.

"Are you all right?" he asked.

I couldn't answer one way or the other. I guess that meant no.

"Rubity," I stammered, thinking out loud. "It's not Rubity. It's Rubic City. This is Rubic City."

"Uh-oh," Loque said.

Yeah. Uh-oh. That's one way of putting it.

"What now?" Siry asked.

I lifted my eyes to Loque. He wasn't giggling anymore. He looked dead serious. Any thought about crazy old Bobby Pendragon spinning out of control and ranting about the name of the planet was gone. He wasn't even looking at me. He was looking past me to something that made him get real serious, real fast.

Holding back his emotion, he said, "We're not alone."

IBARA

It was the first unique sound I'd heard since we'd landed at Rubity. Strike that. Rubic City. We were on Veelox. It was impossible. It was the truth. It made no sense. It didn't matter. At least not just then. We weren't alone. That mattered. The sound was a sharp swish, followed by another and another. I was still too far out of my mind to register what was happening. Reality charged back quickly.

"Ahhhh!" screamed Twig.

The small girl was pulled to the ground and dragged across the debris-strewn street by a group of Flighters. We finally found them. Or maybe I should say they found us. They were on the attack. There were lots of them too. Way too many for us to battle.

"Help!" she screamed in terror.

The *swish* sounds were made by ropes. Lassos. The Flighters were throwing ropes to snare us. They reeled Twig in like a helpless fish. Loque dove for her, sprawling across her body and preventing her from being pulled any farther. I jumped to yank off the rope, but felt the quick tightening of a lasso that snapped around my neck so fast I didn't have time to react. I was jerked forward and pulled to the ground. The rope tightened, choking me. All I could do was grab it and pull back. Hard. The Flighter attached to the other end must not have expected that, because I pulled him off his feet. Idiot. He should have let go. It gave me time to loosen the rope and slip it off.

The Flighters were grouped together, looking like a bunch of zombies, fresh from the grave, complete with rotted clothing. They had the same vacant, emotionless looks as the Flighters I had seen on Rayne. On Ibara. The island. Not the territory. I was on Veelox! They wound up their ropes, ready to try and snare us again. I was ready to charge them, but more kept showing up. They flooded from a building like rampaging rats after ripe garbage. We wouldn't stand a chance in a fight.

Loque freed Twig. Siry knelt by me, bringing his blowgun up to his lips.

"Don't bother," I shouted. "Run."

I didn't have to tell him twice. He helped me to my feet and the four of us took off, back the way we had come. It was a mad sprint to get away from our attackers and back to the ship.

We didn't get far. A handful of Flighters appeared ahead of us, climbing up and over a pile of rubble. We ran right into them. I pulled out the wooden blowgun and held it low, ready to whack the first Flighter who got within whacking range. I expected to get pounced on by a gang, but only one of them came at me. The guy wasn't a fighter, but he was fearless. He charged with no regard for his own safety, swinging his arms wildly, hoping to land a lucky punch. I backed off, easily blocking everything he threw. He drove his head into my chest and pumped his legs, driving me backward like a tackling dummy.

I had no trouble pivoting and using his own energy to throw him over my hip. The Flighters were relentless, but they didn't know how to fight. I looked quickly toward the others and saw both Siry and Loque fighting one Flighter each. That didn't make sense. I saw at least ten of them jump off the pile of rubble. Why were they coming at us one at a time? I sprinted toward Siry and launched myself at his attacker, driving both my feet into his rib age. The Flighter grunted and dropped away.

"Twig!" Siry shouted with such fear it made my heart clutch.

The next few seconds were painful. The Flighters' plan came clear. They weren't as clueless as I'd thought. Siry and Loque and I were attacked by one each because the rest had jumped Twig. They were going to take us out one at a time. Poor Twig was the first target.

"Siry!" she shouted desperately. "Help!"

She was swarmed by several Flighters who dragged her back toward . . . somewhere. I had to make a snap decision. It was one of the toughest things I'd ever done. Siry made a move to help her . . . and I stopped him.

"No!" I shouted. "You can't help her."

"Pendragon!" he protested desperately.

"Look!" I said, pointing beyond the group that was dragging poor Twig away. The mass of Flighters that had first attacked us was growing. There must have been fifty of them headed our way. If we went after Twig, it would be over. For all of us. Siry understood. It didn't make it any less painful, but he understood. I don't think I'll ever forget the look of horror on Twig's face as she was dragged away from us. I could only hope she'd survive the ordeal and we'd get another chance to save her.

"We'll help her, but not now," I said to Siry.

The look on his face was gut-wrenching. This was way more than he bargained for when he set out on a grand adventure with his friends to explore Ibara.

No, to explore Veelox.

"C'mon!" I shouted to get him moving.

Siry reluctantly backed away. We both turned to run. Loque had shaken the Flighter who had attacked him and ran with us. We were down to three. Who would be the next target? Ahead of us to our right, more Flighters poured from another building, cutting off the street and our route back to the ship.

"This way!" Loque shouted, and turned left, headed toward one of the derelict buildings.

It was a dangerous move. There were three of us and dozens of them. If we were clever, and lucky, we might be able to lose them inside one of the empty buildings. If we weren't lucky, the building would collapse on our heads. If we stayed in the street, they'd have us. Jumping into a building was the only move we had. Loque knew it. Siry and I weren't far behind. We followed the blond thief through the first door we came to. Inside was a mess of crushed furniture and broken shelves. It might have been a store at one time. It might have been an office. It might have been a zoo for all I cared. All I wanted was to get through and shake the mass of Flighters. I quickly realized I was with the right guys. They may not have been warriors, but they knew how to dodge the authorities. They had plenty of practice running from the security force in Rayne. To them, running through the twisted labyrinth inside this building was no different than blasting through the dense tropical jungle near their home. I had trouble keeping up with them as they jumped over piles of junk while always looking ahead for the best route.

The Flighters had even more trouble keeping up. There were too many of them. Being only three was definitely an advantage. Loque led us through several rooms of debris. It was almost as if he knew where he was going. Finally he blasted through a doorway that led to a huge, empty atrium. After running through a maze of dark, junky rooms, it was a breathtaking surprise to suddenly land in such a huge space.

It was a giant, glass building. The ceiling and two of the walls were made of colorful stained glass. At one time it might have been some kind of cathedral. The spectacular mosaic pattern was a seascape, complete with schools of fish, coral, whales, and vibrant plant life. The colors were incredibly vivid, made more so because the sun shone through to make them come alive. The whole mosaic was amazingly intact, though there were hundreds of places where sections had fallen out to let unfiltered sun shine in, creating laserlike beams of white light that crisscrossed the entire space. The three of us stood beneath this spectacular glass dome, staring up in awe, trying to catch our breath. It was an awesome sight that I would have appreciated a whole lot more if we hadn't been running for our lives.

"We've got to go back," Siry said, gulping air. "They've got Twig."

"And they'll get us, too," I said. "We'll go back, but on our terms."

"I shouldn't have brought her," Siry cried. "I shouldn't have brought anyone!"

"It was our choice," Loque said. "There were plenty of chances to back out."

"Guys, not the time to second guess," I cautioned. "You can beat yourselves up all you want later. Let's shake those goons first."

Crash!

The sound came from the room we had just run through. The Flighters were smashing their way through. I did a quick scan of the immense atrium, looking for the best escape route.

"We won't make it across this space in time," I concluded. "I say we dig in somewhere and hope they miss us."

There wasn't time to debate. Loque took off again, running along the wall until he found another doorway. He jumped inside. We followed. It was a small room with no light and no exits. If the Flighters found us, we'd be trapped. But there was no turning back, because the Flighters had entered the cathedral.

Siry jumped behind the wreck of something that might have been a cabinet. Or a desk. Loque and I followed, trying to make ourselves invisible. I got down on my belly behind the ancient piece of furniture and found a small opening to peer through. I had a perfect view out the door. No sooner did I settle in, than I saw several Flighters running through the cathedral to the far side. It looked like our plan had worked. They thought we'd kept going. But there were a lot of them. They could have spread out to search the cathedral. We had to be absolutely sure before moving.

It was burning hot in there. Sweat poured down my face. I was about to reach up and wipe my nose, when a shadow crossed the doorway in front of us. I froze. A Flighter crept past silently, on alert. They were searching for us. I didn't even want to breathe, for fear he'd hear me. I didn't put my hand back down either. That's how nervous I was about making the smallest sound. The Flighter barely glanced into the room and kept walking. I kept still. Good thing. Right behind him was another guy who poked his head around the corner and looked directly into the room. Could he see us? Did it matter?

Not if he called a couple of his scurvy pals to come in and turn the place inside out. I mentally prepared myself for that, imagining them entering the room and calculating the best moment to leap up and attack.

The Flighter took a step inside, scanned around, then stepped back out, and kept walking. I figured those guys weren't all that brave on their own, that's why they traveled in such big packs. I didn't dare look to either side to see where Siry and Loque were, for fear I'd make a sound. Another Flighter stalked quietly past the room, glancing in. Then another. I saw several more Flighters in the middle of the cathedral, searching for us. My hopes started to rise. If they hadn't come in this room yet, they might not at all. As the minutes passed, I saw fewer and fewer of the grungy guys walking by the door or out in the atrium. Still, I didn't dare move. For all I knew they were waiting together outside the door for us to stupidly walk into an ambush. Without saying a word we all knew we'd have to wait long enough to make sure they were gone.

Time passed. Five minutes. Ten minutes. I lost track. After not seeing or hearing a Flighter for the longest time, I finally risked turning my head to look at the others. Siry was a few feet from me. He wasn't even looking out the door. He sat with his back to it, his legs curled up. He hugged his knees tightly, staring ahead, unseeing. He looked bad. Not scared, but worse. He looked stunned. I could guess why. His glorious quest had turned into a terrifying odyssey. Twig had been captured. She was probably the must vulnerable of the group. Now she was in the hands of the Flighters. It was anybody's guess as to whether or not she was still alive. Were the Flighters that evil? Would they actually kill someone in cold blood?

I felt someone touch my shoulder and nearly yelped in surprise. I sat up fast and hit my head. It didn't hurt, but the sound seemed as loud as an explosion. Did anyone hear? It was Loque. We sat there, frozen, waiting to see if the Flighters had heard. A few minutes passed. Nobody showed up. It actually gave us more confidence. If nobody heard that loud bang, they were probably gone.

"I'll take a look outside," Loque whispered. "If it's clear, I'll signal, and we can start out."

I nodded. Siry didn't move. Loque gave me a quick smile. "Don't worry, we're going to get out of here and get Twig back."

Siry didn't respond. Loque gave me a worried look and quietly left. He was the perfect person to go. Judging by our earlier stealthy jaunt through the jungle, Loque would be able to make this a quiet scout. I'd probably trip over something and make a huge crash that would bring the Flighters running back.

"You okay?" I whispered to Siry.

He stared ahead, unseeing. "It wasn't supposed to be like this," he said softly.

"I know."

"I'm not leaving this horror city without Twig," he added.

I didn't argue with him. What for? Events would tell us what to do. Hopefully that would include rescuing Twig. As much as I wanted that, I was smart enough to know it wasn't a lock. One thing at a time. I left Siry and snuck to the doorway. Kneeling down, I cautiously peered out to the cathedral. I scanned the whole floor until I saw Loque creeping along the wall to my right. He moved quickly through the piles of junk, making himself nearly invisible as he surveyed the vast space.

Siry joined me, kneeling down and peering out from the other side of the door. We made eye contact. He gave me a nod and a reassuring smile. He looked like a scared little kid, which meant he looked like I did a few years back. Or now.

Loque skirted the immense room, moving closer to the wall that was made entirely of stained glass. The huge mosaic started at the floor and stretched all the way up until it joined with the massive, glass-domed ceiling. It was beautiful. I felt a sudden rush of sadness for the loss of an entire city and its people. This was Veelox. Saint Dane had beaten us here. Were we in the future of that time? Was this what happened to a territory when Saint Dane won? There were so many questions, but they would have to wait until we were safely out of there. Hopefully with Twig.

My eyes traveled over the incredible, huge mosaic of glass. I couldn't say if the artwork was a masterpiece. I'm no judge of that. But the fact that it took up an entire wall that was half the size of a football field made it seem pretty impressive to me.

Loque was halfway along the base of this massive wall. My confidence grew with each step he took. The Flighters were gone. They were looking for us elsewhere. Or maybe they'd lost interest and sank back into whatever rat hole they came from. I didn't care. All that mattered was that we had dodged a pretty huge bullet. But we weren't safe. We still had to find our way back to the ship and decide what to do from there.

Loque stood about eighty yards away from us. He looked so tiny beneath that gigantic wall. He stood up, took one more look around, then waved to us. All was clear. He wanted us to follow. I looked to Siry. He was already getting to his feet. I stood to follow . . . and saw something that made me freeze.

"Wait," I whispered harshly.

Siry stopped. I stood and looked at the giant mosaic. It

may have been a wall, but it was still made of glass. I could see through it. Something was moving outside the building. Something big. It was impossible to tell exactly what it was, because the colored pieces of glass camouflaged things pretty well. It moved slowly from left to right. Whatever it was, it was solid. I didn't see any natural movements. I pointed to it, trying to get Loque to take a look, but he wasn't watching me. I didn't want to chance screaming at him. It might have been nothing, and I didn't want to risk giving ourselves away.

The sun grew brighter. The detail of the strange shadow became clear. The object was taller than Loque. I made out a slender, horizontal streak that seemed to float in the air. It was a silver streak that might have been mounted on something vertical. The horizontal line pivoted, making the sun reflect off its surface. That's all I needed to see. In one horrifying instant, I knew what it was.

"Get away!" I shouted to Loque, running to the center of the cathedral. I no longer cared about getting caught. "Get away from the window!" I waved my arms frantically, trying to get Loque out of there.

Loque motioned with both palms down, as if to say, "Calm down. Be quiet." He even made a "shush" gesture with a finger to his lips.

There was no way I'd calm down or be quiet. Siry ran up beside me and tried to grab my arm to stop me.

"Stop!" he whispered urgently.

I didn't listen. "Run this way! Now!" I screamed at Loque.

Loque glanced around in confusion. He had no idea why I was going off like that. He slowly started walking toward me. Too slowly.

"What's the matter?" he called. "They're gone."

"No, they're not!" I yelled. "They're outside and they've got a—"

Boom! A shot was fired. I'd heard the sound before. It was one of the cannons from the military boat, like the one that fired on our ship. The Flighters weren't gone. They knew we were in that cathedral.

They wanted to make it our tomb.

A split second after the gun fired, the giant stained-glass window exploded into a million brilliant flashes of light. It would have been a spectacular sight, if it hadn't been so horrifying. It was like standing inside an exploding firework skyrocket. Tiny bits of glass whizzed past us. But we weren't the ones in danger. Tons of sharp glass shards rained straight down, directly on Loque.

"No!" shouted Siry. As if that would do any good.

I had the presence of mind to stop running, grab Siry, and pull him back. We weren't totally safe from flying glass. Siry was too stunned to resist. I pulled him away as quickly as I could and shoved him back into the small room where we had been hiding. Once inside, we both turned to look back.

It was a wondrous, magical, horrifying sight. At the sound of the explosion, Loque had stopped in surprise. Or maybe curiosity. It was the worst thing he could have done. He looked back as the glass wall exploded over him. He didn't run. He didn't cower. I think the reality of what was happening didn't hit him, and that was a good thing. Siry and I watched as Loque gazed up in wonder at the spectacular, colorful waterfall of glass . . . that was falling right for him. Seconds later tons of sharp glass hit the blond thief. Siry's best friend. I couldn't watch. I had to bury my eyes in my arm. The sound was enough. It was deafening, like a million shrieking birds. I heard the weight of the fall. It was like thunder, followed by the constant, sharp sounds of tons of glass shattering on the floor. I felt the sting of a thousand tiny shards that dug into my arm as the storm of glass hit us. I should have ducked behind the wall for protection, but I was too stunned to move. I let it hit me. I wanted to feel the burn.

The sound of crashing glass continued for several seconds before settling down. When I felt safe enough to peek up, the first thing I thought was that somebody had turned on a ton of floodlights in the cathedral. They hadn't. With the stained-glass wall gone, the sunlight wasn't filtered anymore. What once had been an immense wall of color, was now a jagged hole of bright white light. At its base was a pile of broken glass that had to be fifteen feet high. I stared at the sparkling mound. I wanted to see Loque walk away from it. I wanted to see him pull himself out of the mess and jog back toward us. He didn't.

Siry ran out of the room, headed for the pile of glass.

"Loque!" he screamed, anguished.

"No, wait!" I shouted.

Siry would not be denied. All I could do was run after him. He sprinted to the pile, desperately scanning for any sign of his friend.

"We can't stay here," I pleaded with him. "Look!"

Through the hole, we now saw the gun clearly. It looked exactly like the cannon that was mounted on the bow of the Flighters' gunboat. Surrounding the gun were Flighters. They knew exactly what they were doing. They couldn't find us, so they decided to bury us. The only one they got was Loque.

Siry gasped. He was looking at something on the floor. My gaze followed his, and I saw something that made my knees get weak. It was a sandal. Loque's sandal. Siry went for the pile of glass, as if ready to dig with his bare hands. I had to stop him or he would have shredded himself.

"We have to go," I yelled. "Now!"

The Flighters were already gingerly poking around the damage. They were headed our way, probably to find proof that we were finished.

Siry was nearly in tears. He had lost two of his trusted Jakills. Loque was his friend. Probably his best friend. The chances of rescuing Twig were remote, but at least it was a possibility. Not so with Loque. I didn't want to think of what shape he was in under that massive, crushing load of glass. I realized that the sandal might be the only recognizable thing left of the blond thief. I had to shake that image, fast.

"Now, Siry." I said softly, but with force.

Siry took a shaky breath, looked up at the oncoming Flighters, then turned and ran back the way we had first entered the cathedral. I was right behind him. I had to force the horrifying memories of the past few minutes out of my head. I'll never forget the images of Twig being dragged away and Loque dying under the waterfall of glass. They'll be with me forever. We couldn't let those memories crush us. We could mourn later. We could try and rescue Twig later. But not if the Flighters got to us first. It was about our survival. I hoped Siry was thinking the same way.

I didn't know which was more important: speed or secrecy. The longer we were in that city, the better the chances the Flighters would find us. Getting back to the ship was crucial, but if we weren't careful, we could easily run right into another bunch of those rats. There was no telling where they were. The city suddenly felt like an old house that was infested with termites. You couldn't see them, but you knew they were there. By the thousands. They could have been watching our every move. Siry and I left the cathedral, running back along the route we had first come through. I hoped the Flighters wouldn't expect that. After dodging through the labyrinth of rooms, I stopped at the doorway out to the street, on the far side of the building. I didn't want to jump right back into another ambush. We crouched down to rest and make a plan.

"I hope they think we're dead," I said, gulping air. "It might give us enough time to get back to the ship and shove off."

Siry's eyes were glassy and vacant, as if he were in shock. "They killed him. They killed my best friend. Why did they have to kill him?"

"I don't know. I don't know anything about them."

"Was it revenge?" Siry continued as if I hadn't said anything. "All we ever did was protect our home from them. They're the ones who attacked. Not us."

I grabbed Siry and gave him a rough shake. He focused on me, surprised.

"Stop!" I seethed. "Keep it together. If we stay here, we're dead too."

"I'm starting not to care," he said quietly.

"What about the other Jakills?" I snapped. "Do you care about them? They'll come looking for us, you know. Unless we get back to warn them, they'll walk right into the same trap we did."

My words hit home. Siry focused, fast.

"We should keep close to the buildings," he said, back in charge. "Less chance of them seeing us."

"No," I said quickly. "These buildings are full of Flighters. If we stay close, they'd be on us before we had a chance to react."

"So what do we do?"

"Run. Fast as we can, right down the middle of the street, as far away from the buildings as possible. That way we can see them coming."

"And what if they see *us* coming?"

"They will. But if we're in the middle of the street, we'll have a few seconds to react."

I could sense the wheels in his head turning, calculating the possibilities. Slowly his head bobbed in agreement, and continued to bob as he got himself psyched up. "One . . . two . . . three . . . GO!" He jumped up and blasted out the doorway.

I was right behind him. Together we sprinted away from the derelict skyscraper, toward the center of the wide street. From there we turned left and kept on running. The large buildings loomed over us as we tore down the center of the street, headed for the ocean. We kept scanning ahead, looking for signs of movement that would say the Flighters had seen us. Every time we passed another pile of rubble, I mentally braced myself for a group of Flighters to leap out and attack.

We were almost to the end of the final block before hitting the wide expanse between the buildings and the pier. My legs burned. I had a stitch in my side. I had trouble getting enough air, but we kept going. Only two days before I had been lying in bed, recovering from a massive bee attack. Now I was sprinting for my life. The run didn't seem to test Siry at all. He didn't even breathe hard. We ran past the final buildings and into the hot sunshine. It was so bright I was nearly blinded. It didn't stop us from running. We were away from the buildings and the dangers they held. My confidence rose. We were going to make it. I was so confident that my thoughts shot ahead to our next move. Getting the ship away from the pier was the most important. Once out to sea, we had to decide on what to do about Twig. I knew that Siry would be all about that, and the other Jakills would surely agree. I wanted to find Twig as well, but there was more in it for me. I needed to learn about

Rubic City, and what had happened to Veelox. I'd yet to find Saint Dane. I felt his presence in everything around me. One way or another, I knew I'd be back in Rubic City.

There were several large mounds of debris between us and the pier. They were so high that they blocked our view of the ship. But we were almost there, so I thought it was okay to ease up. We'd been sprinting for a mile in tropical heat. Once the adrenaline wore off, the fatigue set in.

"Let's slow down," I gasped.

Siry didn't argue. He was finally tired out. The two of us slowed to a jog and then a quick walk. We didn't say anything. We were too busy gulping air. All I could think about was getting onto that ship and getting away before anything else happened.

Siry was the first to see the smoke.

"Look!" he gasped, pointing.

Over the top of the large mound in front of us, in roughly the direction of the pier, was a billowing cloud of black smoke. We stopped to stare for a quick moment, then looked at each other. Rest time was over. We broke into a dead-on sprint. Suddenly we didn't feel so tired. Siry and I dashed toward the last large mound and skirted around it to see the pier . . . and the horror.

Our yellow ship was in flames. Floating offshore were two gunboats with Flighters aboard. We watched in stunned silence as both boats fired their cannons at our doomed ship, point-blank, blasting away at the already burning hull. Another shot was fired that hit the forward mast at its base. I heard a sick, wrenching sound as the mast toppled forward, crashing onto the deck, sending up a shower of sparks. The boat listed to its side. It would only be a matter of minutes before it was on the bottom with all the other wrecks.

"Where are they?" Siry croaked, barely able to get the words out.

I didn't have that answer. The Jakills were nowhere in sight. Had they gotten off before the attack? Or were they consumed by the flames? All I could do was stare at the doomed ship.

"Why would the Flighters do this?" Siry asked. "They're . . . animals."

I had a theory. Or at least an idea. Everything about these Flighters made me believe that somehow, someway, they were being influenced by Saint Dane. I still didn't know why. I didn't know who they were or what they thought they were going to get by targeting the people of Rayne. But I would find out. I had to. It was my job.

"We're trapped," Siry said. "My friends are gone and we're trapped." He looked at me and added, "What are we going to do?"

"We're going to stay safe," I said. "And get answers."

"How?" Siry asked.

"We're going to be Travelers. It's time you accepted that. It's the only hope you have."

IBARA

Our number-one priority was to get to someplace safe. There weren't a lot of choices. Running back into Rubic City was like running into a nest of spiders. Still, we had to chance it. Neither of us was quick to move. That changed when another cannon was fired from one of the gunboats and the ground exploded a few yards from us. Yes, someone had spotted us. It was time to be somewhere else. Without a word Siry and I dodged the mounds of debris and headed back toward the buildings of Rubic City.

Boom! Another pile of dirt blew up to my right, sending a shower of dust and cement bits down on us. I was blinded for a second, but didn't stop running. We were too close to those guns. I kept going while rubbing my eyes and *boom!* The ground erupted behind us. Siry went flying forward and fell on his knees. I scooped him up as I ran. We finally got back to the first block of buildings, just as a cannon shell blew out a wall right next to us. I felt the sharp sting of cement shrapnel on my back, but I was okay. We had made it to safety. Safety? Did I actually write that? We may have been beyond the range of the gunboats, but we were back in the land of Flighters. Frying pan? Fire? You tell me.

"They saw where we entered the city," I said, breathless. "We've got to get as far away from here as possible."

When we reached the first intersection, we turned right and moved away from the line we had been traveling. I had no idea if this would throw anybody off the scent or not, but it seemed like the right thing to do. I wanted to find a place where we could rest and collect our thoughts. We had been doing nothing but react. We had to come up with some kind of a plan. We traveled quickly down a side street, looking for a likely hiding place.

"There!" Siry shouted, pointing.

The door was below ground level. I figured it led into a basement shop. It looked like as good a place to hide as any. I nodded and we ran for it. When we opened the door, we were met by an eerie sound. There was an old-fashioned bell hanging over the door that jingled when the door brushed it. It was supposed to be a pleasant signal to a shop owner that a customer had arrived. Under the circumstances there was nothing pleasant about it.

The store had long counters and display cases, all empty of course. It looked like it might have been a small grocery store. I say that because there were several yellowed signs hanging around that advertised various kinds of gloid. Yeah, gloid. I thought I'd never hear about that stuff again. That was the Jell-O–like food gunk that supposedly had all sorts of nutrition. It was the main food eaten by the people of Veelox. Veelox. My mind was having trouble getting around the concept. Small clues like gloid kept telling me to get over it. I was on Veelox. The big question was, why was Saint Dane here?

We moved through the store into a small back room. There was a door on the far side that opened onto a courtyard. It seemed about as safe a place as we could hope for. If Flighters came in the front way, we could jam out the back. If they came through the back, we could run out the front. If they surrounded us, well, there was no sense in worrying about things we couldn't control. I wanted to catch my breath and my thoughts. I sat on the ground, looking up at the tall buildings that surrounded us. Were Flighters behind any of those windows, watching us? Siry sat in the doorway, his head down. Gone was the cocky, charismatic rebel who wouldn't accept a life of lies. The guy sitting there looked beaten.

"They're gone," he said flatly. "Every one of my friends is dead."

I wasn't so sure he was wrong, but I didn't want to make him feel any worse. "We don't know that," I said, trying to be positive. "The others may have escaped. And Twig may be a prisoner."

"It was a death ship," Siry said. He was sounding more numb than upset. "I asked them to make sure nobody would board. I know that's what they did. Until the end."

"The Jakills are loyal, not dumb. Once the attack started, I'm sure they abandoned ship. Some of them must have."

"It's my fault," he whimpered. "They're dead because of me. And for what?"

"They chose to be here," I insisted. "Don't beat yourself up."

"Why not?"

"Because I need you."

"It's over, Pendragon," he said, defeated.

We were at a crossroads. I was losing Siry. The guilt over

the loss of his friends looked like it might crush him.

"I know you don't buy into the fight against Saint Dane," I said. "I don't blame you. It took me a long time too. But there's something I believe, and I want you to believe it too. No, I *need* you to believe it. I don't know how many of the Jakills died today. Maybe all of them, maybe not. Their deaths were not wasted."

"How can you say that?" he snapped.

"Because you went looking for the truth and found it. Siry, the quest you all began may have saved Veelox from disaster."

Siry didn't know how to react.

"You were right," I continued. "There is more going on here than you were told by the tribunal. I know that for sure now. I know what they've been keeping from you. At least some of it."

He looked at me with total confusion.

"I've been to Veelox before, Siry. I think it was a long time ago. Maybe generations."

"What? Why didn't you tell me?"

"Because I didn't know myself. Some territories are on the same world, but at different times. There are three territories where I come from. What makes a territory a territory isn't just a location. It's about turning points. Saint Dane found ten turning points of Halla. He found moments in history where an event will happen that will determine a territory's future. If events play out the way they should, the territory will continue in peace, the way it was meant to be. Saint Dane has been trying to influence these turning points to go the wrong way and plunge each world into chaos. That's what he wants, Siry. He wants the territories of Halla to crumble, so he can remold them his own way. We've fought over seven territories and lost two. One is Quillan, where your father died. The other is Veelox."

Siry scowled and shook his head. "You were here before, in the past, fought Saint Dane, and lost?"

"Exactly."

"Then if Veelox crumbled, why are we still around?"

"I don't know. The island of Ibara looks like it escaped whatever fate Saint Dane's victory brought to Veelox. Look at this city. The destruction. I think this is what most of Veelox has become. This is the truth that was kept from the people of Ibara."

Siry walked to one of the walls and put his hand against it. The plaster material crumbled. The symbolism wasn't lost on either of us. Veelox had crumbled.

"Let's pretend I believe you," Siry said cautiously. "That means Ibara will fall too. They can't keep the Flighters away forever. If Veelox is truly lost, what's the point?"

"The point is this is a territory," I said. "Remudi was the Traveler. Now you are the Traveler."

He scoffed. I didn't react.

"Each territory has a turning point," I continued. "If I was sent here, that means there is a turning point. Here. It means we might have another chance to save Veelox. You think the Jakills died for nothing? I say they gave us another chance to save this world. If we don't try, if *you* don't try, their lives were truly wasted."

Siry wanted to believe. I saw it in his eyes. But it was a little too much for him to swallow. Okay, maybe a lot too much. I had to convince him. It seemed impossible . . . until I remembered something we had seen earlier.

"I can show you proof that what I'm saying is true. That's what you wanted from the start, right? The truth? If you want to learn the *whole* truth about Veelox, you've got to come with me."

"Where?"

"Have you ever seen a pyramid?" I asked.

Minutes later we were carefully making our way deeper into the city. I knew exactly where to go. When I'd seen it earlier, it hadn't registered. Now I knew. It was the black wall. It had given me an uneasy feeling and now I knew why. Siry and I jogged quickly toward it. We reached the end of one block and stopped, ready to turn the corner.

"If we're going to guide the future of Veelox," I said, "we first have to unravel its past."

We turned the corner. Siry gasped. I would have too, except I knew what to expect. It still gave me a shiver. It was a giant black pyramid. It stood out in its surroundings not only because of its size, but because it didn't look anything like the architecture of the rest of the city. Not even close. I knew there were many more like it all over the territory. These dark monoliths were the cause of the Travelers' loss on Veelox. The incredible technology they contained sent the territory on a path of ruin. No, that's not right. It wasn't the fault of the technology. It was the fault of the people who became slaves to it.

Lifelight.

"What is it?" was all Siry could say.

How was I going to explain this incredible virtual-reality generator to a guy who grew up in a grass hut?

"You should see inside first." I figured it would be easier to explain if he saw it for himself.

The pyramid was so huge that Siry and I had to jog several more blocks before we got to it. I remembered the pyramids having shiny black skins. But that was long ago. Time had done a job on them. The black surface was peeled back now in many places, revealing the framework. The shine was long gone, probably from being exposed to the elements. But for how long? When had I been there before? Decades ago? Centuries? Back then, Rubic City had already begun to decay. The city had been technically still alive, with running water and electricity, but the people had already turned their backs on their homes by leaving reality and entering the fantasy world of Lifelight.

This was the very same Lifelight pyramid I had entered on my first trip to Rubic City. By my own clock that had been only a few years earlier. My memory was still pretty fresh. The base of the pyramid was trashed with the fallen remains of civilization. Mounds of debris were piled several feet up the sides of the structure. Luckily, the revolving-door entrance was clear. It was one of the few bits of good luck we had that day. It was a regular-size revolving door, but it looked like a speck at the base of this massive structure. I gave the door a shove. It didn't budge. Siry joined me, and we both put our shoulders to the door while pushing with our legs. Slowly, painfully, the door let out a screech as the metal gave way. It didn't swing smoothly, but we were able to move it far enough to squeeze ourselves inside.

We were faced with a long corridor. It was the sterilization corridor where long purple lights had killed any microbes that might have hitchhiked their way in on people. The purple lights were now dark, which meant the corridor was too. I couldn't see more than a few feet into the pyramid before daylight gave way to a big, black nothing.

"What do we do?" Siry asked.

"There's another room on the far end of the corridor. Hopefully, there's light in there."

I took his hand. The corridor was narrow enough that,

while holding hands, we could reach the side wall with our free hand. We each kept one hand on the wall while moving slowly forward, shuffling our feet in case something was blocking our way. The corridor was dead black. Something could have been two inches from my nose, and I wouldn't have known it until I walked into it. We had gone only about ten yards when I kicked something. It felt kind of like a pile of hard sticks.

"Kick them aside," I instructed.

Whatever they were, the sticks swept away easily, and we continued on. As we got closer to the end of the corridor, I could make out the doorway on the far end. Light was coming in from somewhere. We were able to move a little quicker and made it into the large ready room of Lifelight. Daylight was seeping in through holes that had been eaten out of the pyramid wall. It wasn't bright, but we could maneuver. The room was as I remembered it. This is where Lifelight jumpers checked in for their jumps. Behind the reception counter I saw something that made me smile. It was a faded oil portrait of a sixteen-year-old guy.

"Who's that?" Siry asked.

"Dr. Zetlin," I answered. "The guy who invented all this."

"What exactly *is* this?"

"I'll show you some things first. It'll be easier to explain then."

Beyond the reception area was a door that I knew would lead to the core—the central control area of the pyramid. The door was halfway open. It was easy to push it the rest of the way. I saw the familiar long corridor with glass walls. Most of the glass was still intact, though several large sections were shattered. Or missing. On either side of the corridor, behind the glass, were the control stations where the phaders worked to monitor the Lifelight jumps. The sight brought back a lot of memories. Not all of them were good.

There was barely enough light to see. We passed a few of the stations and the hundreds of screens that the phaders used to watch the various Lifelight jumps. The screens were dark of course. I wondered how long it had been since the last person had jumped. Siry stared at the technology in wide-eyed wonder. We took a few more steps, then something caught my eye. Ahead of us in one of the control stations, the quality of light was different. Up until then we had been relying on whatever sunlight leaked through the damaged pyramid. The light up ahead seemed warmer. We entered the control station. It looked exactly like the others. Dark, dead, dusty. Except for one thing.

"What is that?" Siry asked.

The control chair was empty. As I remembered, the control panel for each workstation was in the arms of the chair. There was nothing unusual about this one, except that a light was glowing. One single light. It was a small, orange circle that surrounded a silver button. It didn't give off all that much light, but it was enough to create the warm glow that had gotten our attention.

"If that's glowing, there's power," I declared. "Maybe we can figure out how to turn on a couple of lights."

The Lifelight control station was complicated. I could have been flipping switches for a month without finding the light switch. Still, I had to try. I figured the best place to start would be with the button that was glowing. Made sense, right? I leaned over the chair and touched the glowing circle.

A single monitor in front of us flashed white.

"Wha—" Siry shouted in surprise and jumped back. This was a guy who'd never seen a TV.

"It's okay," I said. "It's supposed to do that."

We had power. My first thought was that I could now explain to Siry about Lifelight and Dr. Zetlin and the Reality Bug. I figured that seeing the hardware would make it easier to accept. Or at least understand. Or at least not think I was a total nutburger who dreamed the whole thing up. The screen flickered and fuzzed. I figured if I could turn enough of them on, we'd have light to get around.

I never got the chance.

The screen flashed white, followed by a swirl of colors that formed themselves into an image. The sight actually made me go weak. I had to sit in the phader's control chair or I would have fallen over.

"What's the matter?" Siry asked. "Who is that?"

I couldn't talk, but it didn't matter. The image on-screen was about to say enough for both of us. Just like old times. The screen showed a close-up of a girl I knew very well. She had long blond hair tied back in a tight ponytail, deep blue eyes, and yellow-tinted wire-rimmed glasses. She had on the same dark blue jumpsuit of a phader that she was wearing the last time I saw her. She stared right at us with the same intelligent intensity I remembered so well.

"My name is Aja Killian," she said sharply and precisely. That was Aja. No nonsense about her. "I am the chief phader here in the principal Lifelight pyramid in Rubic City. I am also the Traveler from the territory of Veelox. This is my Journal Number Twelve. It may be the last journal I will get the chance to make. I hope someone, someday, will hear it."

That day had come.

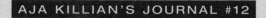

VEELOX

"Hello. Whoever you are. If you're watching this, I'm hoping you already know of the desperate situation we face on Veelox. The virtual reality simulator called Lifelight has proved to be far more tempting a pastime than its inventor, Dr. Zetlin, ever anticipated. People come to these pyramids, slip into their Lifelight jump tubes, enter their own personal fantasies, and choose never to come out. The imaginary worlds that Lifelight creates are too real and too perfect for them to want to leave. It's why I invented the Reality Bug. I tried to make the fantasies less appealing. It failed. My friends Bobby Pendragon and Loor helped avoid a major disaster by destroying the failed bug and saving thousands of lives. It only prolonged the inevitable. Veelox has since died a slow, agonizing death. I'm not sure which would have been worse.

"First to fail was the infrastructure of our cities. Drinking water became scarce because there was nobody to service the pumping and filtration facilities. Roads crumbled. The sewage system wasn't far behind. As pipes burst, raw sewage fought with garbage to claim the streets. The cities slowly went dark as

dwindling power supplies were diverted to keep the Lifelight pyramids functioning. Fresh food was unheard of. Our main sustenance, gloid, became a valuable commodity. Vast stock piles were used to feed the millions of people during their jumps, but the manufacturing of gloid ended. There was nobody to do it. Everyone assumed there would always be someone else to take care of business. There wasn't. Everyone was in Lifelight.

"Most everyone.

"I'm proud to say that many phaders and vedders worked tirelessly to keep Lifelight functioning and the jumpers safe. The hope among all of us was that someday, somehow, enough people would come to their senses and abandon Lifelight. At first we imagined enough people would rejoin reality so that we could revive our world. But time is merciless. The cities decayed beyond repair. Hope then became that enough people would eventually abandon Lifelight so that we could begin anew and create a new society. That day never came. It all happened so impossibly fast. I never appreciated how much effort it takes to keep society functioning, and how quickly it can all come crashing down.

"The inevitable finally happened. The jumpers in Lifelight began to die off. First it was the elderly, then those who already suffered from some sickness. All over the territory, the jump screens went dark. We stopped removing the bodies from the tubes. There weren't enough of us to bury the dead. The Lifelight pyramids became tombs. The deaths actually prolonged the decline. Fewer jumpers meant less energy use, but it was only a matter of time. We soon reached the point of no return.

"Eventually people began leaving Lifelight to discover the horror that their collective neglect had caused. They left their perfect fantasy lives to re-enter a reality that had become a nightmare. Some chose to jump right back into Lifelight to live the rest of their days happily, no matter how short a time that might be.

Many decided to stay away from the jump tubes and rebuild their world. It was an impossible task. It had been too long. The city had become a dangerous place. Wild animals stalked the streets, foraging for food. They first attacked children and the elderly. People went missing. Nighttime was filled with the screams of victims as they were dragged off by savage creatures in search of meat.

"Something had to be done. Desperate measures had to be taken. We knew Veelox was doomed. At least, the Veelox we knew. We couldn't rebuild society, so we chose to create a new one. The remaining phaders and vedders banded together to start a new life.

"The island of Ibara has been chosen as the birthplace of a new civilization. It is a beautiful, tranquil place that was once used as a military base. There hasn't been need for a military force for generations, so the island is now empty. Our plan is to take as many of us as possible and move to Ibara. There we will build a new and simpler society. We are determined never to allow technology to rule our thinking and control our lives. A pact has been made between us all to keep Ibara as a place of harmony and growth. Most important, it will be a place where people interact with other people, not with technology.

"There is a powerful, frightening element here in Rubic City that will try to stop us. We've split into two different groups: those who want to leave and begin anew, and those who want nothing to do with a reorganized society. These are the outlaws, the mercenaries who have ransacked the city for anything they need to survive. They are bound by no laws. There is no police force to stop them. I guess you could call them pirates. Or thieves. Or looters. They feel as if they were born from Lifelight, so they call themselves . . . 'Flighters.' They are a danger to all of us who want to start anew. That's another reason why the island of

Ibara has been chosen as our refuge. There are defenses there. We will be able to keep the Flighters away. It truly is a perfect place to try to salvage a society. Or rather, to create a new one.

"Will we succeed? There's no telling. Maybe creating this idyllic society is nothing more than a desperate dream. Those who are about to leave for Ibara have made a difficult choice. We have decided to give up on the Veelox of old, which means we must abandon Lifelight and the remaining jumpers. Those who remain inside are doomed. The only consolation is that they are already doomed. Our leaving will only make the end come sooner. We are also abandoning an entire world. Rubic City will be left to the wild animals and the Flighters. There isn't much difference. I can't speak for the rest of Veelox. Perhaps other groups are making similar plans. I hope so. If not, it will be up to us to survive long enough so that someday, somehow, we can leave Ibara safely and bring the rest of Veelox back to life. One thing we know for sure, for Veelox to be reborn, it first must die.

"One more thing. I don't know who will be watching this journal, or when. If you are from Veelox, this will serve as a brief explanation of how our world died. If you are a Traveler, I am now speaking to you.

"I too am a Traveler. My responsibility was to protect my territory from Saint Dane. I failed. Miserably. Saint Dane has won. Veelox has fallen into chaos. Now my only hope is to salvage what I can from the remains of a once-great society. Saint Dane has beaten the Travelers on Veelox. He has beaten me. I don't know what his plans are for this territory, and how he intends to use it in his quest to control Halla, but there is one thing I do know: The fight isn't over. I told Pendragon that I wanted another shot at Saint Dane, and I believe that by creating a new world on Ibara, I'm doing just that. Time will tell how successful I am. I hope that Pendragon and the rest of the Travelers are having more

success *against that monster than I had on Veelox. But I promise, I'm not done yet. Veelox is not done yet. Whoever you are,
know that Veelox is not dead. It's alive and living on Ibara. One
day the brave people who are about to make this trip will bring
Veelox back. Maybe it will be their sons and daughters. Or their
grandchildren. However long it takes, they have not given up. As
the Traveler from Veelox, I'm going to do everything I can to help
them.*

*"This is Aja Killian, recording what will probably be my
final journal. I hope that whoever is watching this, is doing so in
better times than the ones we now face."*

IBARA

Aja's image disappeared. I sat staring at the blank, white screen. Everything that she said confirmed my fears. Saint Dane had succeeded in destroying a territory. Was this what he had in mind for Halla? He said Halla needed to be torn down before it could be rebuilt. I didn't see a whole lot of rebuilding going on with Veelox. How long would it be before Quillan was turned to rubble?

"You knew her?" Siry asked.

I nodded.

"So did I," he said softly.

I spun to look at him.

"I didn't *really* know her," he said quickly. "I knew *of* her."

"What the heck does that mean?"

"I've seen the archives of the tribunal. There are ancient letters that outline how Ibara should be built and governed. Aja Killian's name was everywhere. She had a strong voice— one that didn't always take the popular route. She was a rebel in her own way, fighting for the rights of all the people. That's why we took her name."

"I don't get that," I said, totally confused.

"The map. I didn't find it on the beach. I stole it from the tribunal archives. I think she made it. Some letters were worn off, but I was pretty sure what it said."

"Aja Killian," I whispered. "Jakill."

"She's a legend. We wanted to be legends too."

I couldn't help but smile. "Just like Aja. She's not here, but she's still taking charge."

"She was a Traveler?" Siry asked.

"Yeah. We lost the territory, but she never gave up."

"Neither should we," he said with authority.

I liked that. It was the first positive thing he had to say in a while.

"Aja and the people back then gave Veelox a second chance," I said. "That's why Saint Dane is here. He's afraid to lose what he gained. Veelox has another turning point."

Siry nodded. "Seeing what happened to Rubic City . . ." He took a deep breath. It looked like he was holding back tears. "I don't know. Maybe I understand a little of why life is the way it is on Ibara." This was tough for him. He sighed and said, "I wish the others were here to see this. It's the truth we all wanted so badly."

"That island is all that's left of your civilization," I told him. "It's the future of an entire world. I guarantee Saint Dane has his sights on it."

"So how do we stop him?" he asked.

I smiled. Siry was with me. Before I had the chance to say a word, another screen came to life. Then another. And another. One by one, each and every screen in that control cubicle flashed white. The screens in the next cubicle began firing up as well, along with the cubicles across the corridor from us.

"What's happening?" Siry asked in fear.

I had no idea. Soon the whole core was glowing with light. The colored lights on each chair's control panel fired up as well. In seconds the entire core looked as alive as it had the last time I was there, when Lifelight was fully operational.

"Could Aja have done this?" Siry asked.

I didn't have an answer. Someone else did.

"Aja, Aja, Aja!" boomed a familiar voice. It came from every speaker in the core.

Siry covered his ears. He had never heard anything like this before. Unfortunately, I had.

The voice boomed, "That annoying girl has taken quite a bit of credit, considering her miserable failure. Don't you agree, Pendragon?"

Siry shot me a terrified, confused look. I felt bad for him. I really did. I knew what was about to happen. Any last doubts he had about his father's stories were going to be blown away. He had been handed a lot of hard truths in the last few hours. He was about to get another.

"Pendragon?" Siry asked, his voice quivering. "Who is that guy?"

"He's the reason we're here," I answered calmly.

"Look!" he screamed, pointing to a monitor.

On-screen, floating against the white background, was a pair of intense, blue eyes. Evil eyes. Above them red jagged scars appeared. Then the outline of a face. Finally the image snapped clear and he was there. Saint Dane. He was only an image in a monitor, but it was like he could see us. Another of his images appeared on the monitor next to that one. And the next one and the next. Soon Saint Dane's hideous face was staring at us a thousand times over. Siry didn't know which way to turn. Everywhere he looked, he saw the demon Traveler.

"The Convergence is near, Pendragon," his voice boomed from the speakers. "I couldn't care less about this pathetic, primitive society. I've simply chosen Ibara to be my starting point."

"What does he mean?" Siry asked nervously.

I kept my calm and looked around at the multiple monitors. I wasn't sure which one to focus on, though I guessed it didn't matter. Saint Dane would know I was talking to him.

"I don't believe that," I said loudly. "Nothing you do is random. You need Ibara as much as any territory. We've got another chance, and this time we're going to win."

The images of Saint Dane laughed in unison. It chilled me. I couldn't imagine how Siry felt about it.

"I applaud your confidence," he chuckled. "I always have. Your bravura is charming but hardly plausible. Forgive me if I don't feel threatened by someone who until recently didn't know what territory he was on."

"It doesn't matter," I spat back, pacing, staring into his eyes from monitor to monitor. "I know how you operate. You've convinced the Flighters to attack Ibara. But it's a waste of time. Their defenses are too strong. Aja made sure of that. Yeah, a handful of Flighters might get onto the island, but that's not enough to do any real damage. Ibara is strong. The culture there is returning. Your victory here was temporary. We're going to take back Veelox."

I had no idea if any of that was true, but it sounded good. All I really wanted was to goad Saint Dane into tipping his hand and revealing his true plan.

"Pendragon," Saint Dane said with mock patience, "as usual, you know only enough to sound like a fool."

"Then show me how I'm wrong. Dazzle me with your brilliance."

I saw a thousand faces of the demon looking back at me from a thousand monitors. "You've grown full of yourself, " he chuckled. "Your many victories have given you a feeling of . . . invincibility."

"You've won two territories," I shot right back. "The way it's looking now, one of them is coming back to haunt you. It's over. Halla is not going to fall. You've lost. The people of the territories were too strong for you. Things are going to play out the way they were meant to."

"I'm curious," Saint Dane sniffed. "What makes you so certain the way things were meant to be isn't *my* way?"

His words rocked me. I tried not to show it. "I don't believe that," I snarled. "If the Flighters had any chance of conquering Ibara, they would have done it a long time ago. How long has it been since the island was settled? Decades? A century?"

Saint Dane laughed. "Hardly. In Second Earth years, Rubic City has been abandoned for over three centuries."

Yikes. Long time.

"Three hundred years," I repeated. "Ibara was growing stronger the whole time. The Flighters don't stand a chance."

Saint Dane laughed. I hated that, as usual.

"You disappoint me, Pendragon. You should know that time means nothing. It's about decisions, opportunities, and turning points. Ibara is about to reach its turning point, and you still don't have the slightest idea of what it might be."

I didn't say anything. I didn't have to. He knew how clueless I was.

"Enter the pyramid," Saint Dane commanded. "Bring your befuddled young Traveler friend. It's a shame his father will not be here to appreciate what you're about to see. Though I suppose that's my own fault for having killed him."

I shot a look to Siry. His eyes flashed. His spark was back. Saint Dane's words were turning him into a Traveler.

"I'll kill him," Siry hissed through clenched teeth.

"Keep it together," I cautioned. "This is only the beginning."

I could feel Siry's tension. His hatred. Saint Dane had made an enemy. I wasn't sure if that was good, or something that Saint Dane wanted. I wasn't sure of anything except that we needed to learn more. If Saint Dane wanted to show us, that was okay by me.

"Enter the pyramid, Pendragon," Saint Dane's images said. "And step into the future."

"You can't predict the future of Ibara," I said boldly.

"Ibara? I'm referring to the future of Halla," was his cold answer.

IBARA

"Come on," I said to Siry, gently grabbing his arm.

Siry let me lead him, but he felt like a coiled spring. I figured that might be helpful, but not just then. I pulled him out of the workstation and walked along the glass corridor toward the center of the pyramid. Saint Dane's images watched us from thousands of monitors, softly chuckling. It was like being in a surreal fun house where the clown from hell was having a lot more fun than we were.

"We're going into the center of the pyramid," I told Siry. "Where all the jump tubes are. Whatever is inside, it's something Saint Dane wants us to see."

"Why should we do anything he wants?"

"To find out what his plans are. Stay alert. At some point we're going to have to get away. Do as I say and don't hesitate."

Siry nodded. I pushed open the door at the end of the core, and the two of us stepped into the immense center of Lifelight. I'm amazed to say that the space didn't look much different from when I had been there before. Three centuries before. The interior was a huge, cavernous space with multiple balconies built along the sloping walls. The floor had to be the size of two football fields next to one another. The sides were built at a steep angle that eventually came to a point high in the sky—the point of the pyramid. Access to the hundreds of balconies was from a central tube with an elevator that went from the floor all the way to the top of the pyramid. There were hundreds of catwalks that spanned the distance from the tube out to the various levels. I had walked along one of those narrow sky bridges. The memory made my palms sweat. It was the closest I ever came to walking a tightrope.

Each balcony had thousands of rooms that contained the Lifelight jump tubes. From the floor I could look up and see many of the closed doors, just as I remembered. Only this time, no lights were lit outside the doors to indicate a jump was taking place. This was no longer Lifelight. It was a mausoleum. After so many years the jumpers would be nothing more than skeletons. Or dust. The idea that we were looking up at the graves of multiple thousands of people sent a chill up my spine.

I glanced at Siry. He was in awe, though I didn't think he really got the idea of Lifelight or that this had become a place of the dead. It didn't matter. That was ancient history. Looking across the floor, I realized it wasn't the sheer size of the place that stunned Siry. There was something else. Something far more disturbing. Standing maybe twenty yards from us, with his arms folded, was Saint Dane. In the flesh. Or whatever it is he's made out of. Seeing him there, alone, unmoving, made my skin crawl. He was in his normal form, standing well over six feet tall with his all-black suit. The dark suit made his bald head stand out even more starkly. As far away as he was, I could see that he was smiling and staring at us with his cold eyes.

"Welcome back, Pendragon," he called with a sinister

sneer, his voice echoing through the pyramid.

"Where is Twig?" Siry bellowed as he took a threatening step toward him. I quickly held him back.

"Whoa," I cautioned. "That won't help."

"What exactly is a twig?" Saint Dane asked innocently.

"She better not be hurt," Siry shouted, straining against me. I gripped his arm to keep him under control.

Saint Dane shook his head in disappointment. "Haven't you explained to him that there is much more at stake than the life of one of his playmates?"

"Who are you!" Siry screamed in anger.

I gripped him tighter, holding him back.

"Don't you know?" Saint Dane said with glee. "I'm the boogeyman."

"Calm down," I whispered to Siry. "Yelling at him won't help."

Siry backed off. He didn't relax, but he backed off.

"What do you want to show us?" I barked.

Saint Dane strolled casually, glancing up at the balconies. "It's been about Veelox from the beginning, you know," he began. "This is where I've been preparing to stage my conquest of Halla. I guess you could say it's been three hundred years in the making. Once Ibara has been snuffed, the Convergence will begin."

"You haven't told me what the Convergence is," I said casually.

Saint Dane stopped, looked at me, and smiled. "I haven't, have I?"

He didn't then, either. So much for trying to trick him into answering me.

He continued, "To be quite honest, Ibara isn't important. I consider it more of a training exercise."

"Training who?" I asked. "For what?"

"Why, Pendragon!" he exclaimed with mock surprise. "I thought you had so brilliantly put it together."

As if on cue, I sensed movement. Siry tensed. Creeping out of the shadows like rats came the Flighters. Dozens of them. No, more like hundreds. Behind us, several more appeared, forcing us to step closer to Saint Dane. They formed a giant ring around us. Their tattered, rotten clothing now made sense. They were living examples of what had happened to the city itself. Their clothes were falling apart because no new clothing had been manufactured in centuries. They were like rodents, living in squalor. It was no big surprise that Saint Dane was able to organize them into assaulting Ibara. Whatever he promised them would be better than what they had.

"This is beneath you," I said to Saint Dane. "These people are desperate. They'll do whatever you ask. Where's the challenge?"

"It's true," Saint Dane replied. "It wasn't difficult."

"Then what's the point?" I asked. "You always have some grand philosophical reason for targeting a territory and proving how greedy people can be. Or arrogant. Or power hungry. What's the big lesson here? What are you trying to prove? That you can organize a bunch of desperate losers into attacking Ibara? This whole thing seems kind of . . . pathetic."

I was hoping to tick him off. I didn't. He laughed. Again. I've mentioned how much I hate that, right? Only about a hundred times.

"Pendragon, my boy, I had hoped you would one day realize how misguided your efforts have been. I tried, time and again, to demonstrate how the people of the territories are their own worst enemies, but my lessons were never learned.

I will reluctantly admit defeat on that front. You are beyond help. You could have been by my side while the new Halla was created, but I'm afraid that offer is no longer available. All that is left now is to complete what I started."

The ring of Flighters got smaller. They stared at us with dead eyes. Their soulless gazes didn't bother me as much as Saint Dane's words. Something about him had changed. He was as self-assured as ever, but this felt different. It was like he didn't care about me anymore. I've always felt as if he needed to defeat me in order to conquer Halla. His new attitude made me feel as if that didn't matter anymore. Or worse. It felt as if I had already been defeated. I needed to claw myself back into the game.

"You're kidding, right?" I said, scoffing. "This is the future of Halla? You really think this grunge can conquer anything? Sure, they can beat up on a bunch of kids, but you don't seriously think they're going to threaten Ibara? And then what do you plan to do? Take these smelly creeps and march on Second Earth? On Third Earth? Is that your big Convergence?" I laughed. "Go for it! But do me a favor. Make sure I'm around to watch the fun."

Saint Dane continued to smile. I tried to hold mine. It wasn't easy. I knew there had to be more.

"To be sure," he said with a sinister smile. "I most definitely want you there to watch the fun."

The pyramid was suddenly filled with sound. I couldn't tell what it was at first, but it sounded like high-pitched squeaking. It came from everywhere, reverberating off the pyramid walls and bouncing around the cavernous space.

"What is that?" Siry whispered nervously.

My eye caught movement up above. All around us, on every level, the doors leading to the jump tubes opened up.

Every last one of them. I had the fleeting thought that the ghosts of the dead were rising up from their graves. That wasn't the case, unfortunately. I would have liked that a lot better than the truth. People were slowly stepping out of the jump rooms. If every jump room held only one person, there could easily be ten thousand people about to make an appearance.

"Flighters," Siry gasped.

I watched as the people walked slowly and stiffly out the doors, toward the balcony railing that looked down over the center of the pyramid.

Siry was near panic. "We can never fight off that many," he said.

I stared up at the thousands of faces as they walked to the railing and looked down on us. My throat clutched. I knew what I was seeing, but my brain didn't want to accept it. In that one instant Saint Dane's plan became horrifyingly clear. I had underestimated him, again. From what I was seeing, he was absolutely capable of overrunning Ibara. No, worse. I understood why he considered Ibara a training exercise. The tiny island wouldn't stand a chance against this army. My mind was reeling. The possibilities were too horrible to comprehend. This *might* only be the beginning.

Saint Dane chuckled. "Still want to be around to watch, Pendragon?"

His plan for Ibara was becoming clear. His plan for Veelox was becoming clear. His plan to make Veelox his stepping-off point for the destruction of Halla was becoming clear. The truth was all around us, staring down from above.

"Pendragon," Siry said, his voice cracking. "Those aren't Flighters."

They wore the same rotten rags as Flighters, but that's

where the similarity ended. They were much bigger than the Flighters. I could say they looked well fed, but I knew the real reason. I knew these guys. I had fought these guys. On First Earth. At the gate. I had grabbed a handful of clothing and it had disintegrated. Now I realized why. It was all coming together in one, terrifying bundle. On First Earth there were only a few. Here, there were thousands, with no way to know how many more might be right behind.

"They aren't Flighters," I said to Siry. "They're called dados, and Ibara doesn't stand a chance."

IBARA

The ring of Flighters slowly grew tighter around us, while thousands of dados watched from above. As the reality of what we now faced became clear, I was hit with a wave of emotion I'm not sure how to describe, other than to say I felt beaten. Not just on Veelox. Everywhere.

"You're right about the Flighters, Pendragon," Saint Dane said. "They aren't capable of mounting anywhere near the kind of force I need. Though they have been quite helpful. We've been testing the defenses of Ibara for a while now. Their hard work will insure the minimum amount of loss when the fun begins."

Fun. He was about to overrun Halla with a mechanized army. Talk about mixing the territories! Everything else had been prelude. With an army like this, he could wreak havoc on Ibara. And Second Earth. And Third Earth. And every other territory that wouldn't know how to deal with such an invincible foe.

"As I said, it's too late, Pendragon," he chuckled.

"For what?" I asked, not really caring to know.

"For you to join me," he said with mock sympathy. "It wouldn't be the same, now that you know you've been beaten. I wanted you when you thought you still had a chance. Now, well, it would be embarrassing for you to beg. So don't. Unless you feel the need."

"What do we do?" Siry whispered.

"Nothing. It's over."

"It's not," he hissed in anger.

All I wanted was to crawl into one of the Lifelight tubes and make it my home for eternity. Siry grabbed me roughly by the arm.

"Ahhh!" Saint Dane exclaimed with a laugh. "This delusional young Traveler has some fight left. Perhaps you should explain to him how completely hopeless your situation is."

I was in a daze. Instead of trying to come up with our next move, all I could do was imagine an army of dados marching on Washington. Or New York. Or Xhaxhu. I grew more depressed with every passing second . . . while the Flighters closed in.

Siry pulled my arm, forcing me to look at him. His eyes were on fire. He got right in my face and angrily whispered, "We can't give up."

"They're robots, Siry. Mechanical men. They can't die. Even if one did, there'd be a dozen more to take its place."

"We have to warn Ibara," he said, still whispering. "They need to know what's coming. They have the right to try and defend themselves."

"This is way bigger than Ibara."

"Not right now it isn't," Siry shot back. "We can't give up."

I focused on him. Siry had grown up in the last few days. Dealing with death and Armageddon will tend to do that.

Where I had tuned out, he was now thinking clearly. I glanced over his shoulder to see the ring of Flighters tightening up. We were at the center of a large circle that had reached Saint Dane.

"Whispering secrets?" Saint Dane taunted. "Do you actually think you can do anything to stop an army of dados?"

I looked to Siry and saw determination. I looked to Saint Dane and saw arrogance. It was the jolt I needed. The hatred I felt for that guy surged back. We might have been on the verge of defeat, but we were going down swinging.

"Stay close to me," I whispered to Siry.

Before I could talk myself out of it, I bolted toward the center of the pyramid. Siry was right with me. My best hope was that we would catch the Flighters by surprise before they braced themselves to stop us. I blasted toward the smallest one and barreled right through him, shoulder first. With a loud grunt I knocked the vagrant on his butt. We were out of the circle.

Saint Dane's laugh echoed through the pyramid. He was still having fun. Good for him. We'd gotten over the first hurdle. There were plenty more to come. I actually had a plan. It was a desperate one, but that pretty much described our situation. I jammed for the elevator in the center of the pyramid. If we could get inside and close the door, we might be able to get up to another level and lose ourselves. There were all sorts of things wrong with that plan. Dados were everywhere. The elevator might not even be working. Or it might not have been on the ground floor. It was a desperate plan, but at least it was a plan.

The Flighters finally figured they should be doing something and ran after us. They weren't the brightest bunch. We reached the central tube way ahead of them.

"Where are we going?" Siry asked.

"Up!"

The elevator door was open. The car was on the ground. Our luck was holding. We jumped inside and I started hitting buttons. I didn't know how to work this thing, so I figured if I hit them all, the door was bound to close. That was assuming the elevator had power in the first place.

The Flighters were now sprinting for the door.

"We're trapped," Siry said, just as the doors closed in front of us. I heard several loud thuds outside as the Flighters bashed into it. They hammered with their fists, as if that would make it open. It didn't. I saw a lever that I hoped would get us off the ground. I couldn't remember how Aja had run this thing. I feared that if I hit the wrong button, the door would open up again and, "Surprise, you Flighters! Just kidding!" I grabbed the lever and pushed it forward. The elevator lurched. We had power!

"Are we moving?" Siry asked, frightened. He'd never seen an elevator.

"We're going up the central tube," I answered.

"To where?"

"I don't know. I'm thinking we take this thing up as high as it will go, and see what we find."

"Thank you, Pendragon," he said sincerely. "I'm not giving up."

"No, you were right. It would be wrong not to try and warn Ibara. People have the right to choose their own destiny, right?"

Siry gave me a smile and nodded sadly. "There's no hope, is there?"

Things were about as bleak as they'd ever been. At least we were alive and moving. We had to keep trying. It was our job.

"There's always hope," I said. "It's the one thing Saint Dane can't destroy."

"So it's all true," Siry muttered. "Everything my father told me."

I nodded and shrugged.

"Then why was he on the tribunal? If he was concerned about the turning point of Veelox, what did that have to do with the tribunal?"

It was like a ray of light had suddenly cut through the dusty dark. With one simple observation, Siry sparked a thought that made me realize we might not be so done after all.

"Saint Dane wasn't telling us everything," I declared. "This isn't a training exercise. He wants to sway the turning point. That's what he does."

"You say that like it's good news," Siry said, confused.

"It is. It's never about a battle. It's about a decision. A choice. That's what turns the territories. If it were just about winning a war or enemies fighting, Saint Dane would have won every territory. Saint Dane pushes people into making bad decisions, because he's out to prove something."

"Prove what? To who?"

"To who I don't know. If I knew that, I'd unravel this whole thing. But I know what he's trying to prove. He wants to show that the people of Halla are selfish and flawed. He told me that everything he's ever done would never have happened if the people didn't want it to happen."

"Is it true?" Siry asked.

"No!" I replied. "He twists things. He makes people believe they're doing the right thing, when in reality he's pushing them toward destruction. The turning points are critical times in a territory's history. If Remudi was on the tribunal, the turning point must have something to do with Ibara.

That's why Saint Dane wants to attack. It's not about conquering the island. It's about forcing the people into making a bad decision. Then he can say it was all their fault in the first place."

"So what do we do?"

"We have to get back to the tribunal and warn them about the dados. But we've also got to figure out what the turning point is. If we can figure that out, the battle might not even matter."

Siry frowned. "I'm totally confused."

The elevator slowed to a stop. I braced myself, ready to pounce. Or be pounced on. The elevator stopped. A very long moment passed. The doors slid open. I was ready to get hit by a dado. Instead I was hit with blinding light and a fierce wind. The force was so strong it pushed us both back to the rear of the elevator. I fell to my knees, I think by instinct. Siry crept forward and grabbed the edge of the open door. I crawled forward, still squinting against the light, trying to get my eyes to adjust.

"We're on top of the clouds," Siry gasped.

He wasn't far from wrong. The elevator had opened at the uppermost point of the pyramid. Centuries of erosion had eaten huge holes into the steeply slanted walls, which meant we were looking over Rubic City from the highest point possible. To say it was breathtaking is a huge understatement. Laid out before us was the entire city. Beyond that was the ocean. The skyscrapers that seemed so immense from ground level now looked like Lego toys beneath us. I was both awed and saddened. Not many people get the chance to see something like this. Cities are staggeringly huge and complicated creations. Seeing it from so high up gave us that perspective. That sense of awe made it all the more painful to know it was a city of the dead.

There might have been ten feet of floor between the elevator doors and the outside wall. Or what was left of it. The floor itself wasn't in much better shape than the rotten walls. I looked down to see big chunks of floor missing.

"Careful where you step," I cautioned.

I worried that it wouldn't matter how careful we were. The whole floor looked as solid as a piece of dry paper. Neither of us was too quick to leave the elevator, until the doors started closing.

"Get out!" I shouted.

We both hopped out. I held my breath, fearing the floor would collapse under our weight. The elevator doors closed. We heard the sound of the car descending. I had no doubt that it would soon return, loaded with Flighters. Or dados.

"Now what?" Siry asked.

It was looking as if I had led us into a dead end. My escape plan had only delayed the inevitable. We were still prisoners, only with a better view. I walked cautiously across the floor toward the destroyed, slanted wall. The wind blew through the holes, making whistling sounds. I cautiously peeked out of the hole and down the side of the pyramid. The sight made me nearly lose my balance. It was like my inner ear suddenly went all wacky. I pulled myself back in and closed my eyes to fight the vertigo.

"What did you see?" Siry asked.

"It's a long way down," I said, with my eyes still closed. "I think the angle of the wall threw me off a little."

That's when the idea hit me. I took a breath, opened my eyes, and peered back outside. This time I knew what to expect, so I wasn't as rocked. There was no way to judge how high up we were. The wall wasn't straight down, because it was a pyramid. It angled out. Centuries ago the surface was slick and black. Now it was a mess of holes. Some big, some not. Chunks of framework stuck out everywhere. It looked more like a chopped-up field of garbage than the wall of a pyramid.

To me it looked like an escape route.

"We're climbing down the outside," I announced.

"What?" Siry shot back with horror.

"The angle of the wall isn't that steep. There's plenty to grab on to. Unless you've got a better idea, I say we go for it."

Siry joined me at the hole and peered out. He took a long hard look at the surface, then a long hard look at me.

"You're crazy, you know that?"

"Yeah, but in a couple of minutes that elevator is going to hit bottom and Saint Dane is going to get on and bring up some of his pals to take us back. Which way do you want to go down?"

Siry looked sick. I probably did too. I wasn't as confident in this insane plan as I was making it sound. Without waiting for Siry to make a decision, I stuck my foot out of the hole, turned back toward Siry . . . and stepped out onto the face of the pyramid. At first the biggest problem was the wind. I was able to get a foothold on a piece of frame and felt pretty secure. But I was afraid the wind would blow me off. I flattened my belly against the steep wall, trying to create as much friction as possible.

"Don't look down," I called.

"Don't worry."

I carefully started to climb down. It was all about finding secure foot- and handholds. The surface of the pyramid was chewed up, creating several of each. I didn't stop to think about how insane this was. I was hanging against the outside of a building a hundred stories in the air. I wasn't afraid of falling. I was afraid of sliding. One false step and I knew I'd start a slide that would be impossible to stop. It would be just as bad as a fall.

Siry was right behind me. Or right above me. Or . . . something. You get the idea. If he lost his footing, he'd come sliding right down onto me and bye-bye both of us.

"You okay?" I called up.

"I'm still here" was his answer. Good enough.

I always had four choices of where to go next. Between my two hands and two feet, one of them kept finding a lower perch. It was working. We were moving down. I was beginning to think our biggest worry was going to be Saint Dane discovering us creeping down the outside of the building, totally defenseless.

It wasn't. I heard a wrenching *crack* sound.

"Ahhh!" screamed Siry. He lost his grip and started to slide. A moment later he shot right past me. I reached out to grab him. Bad move. The moment I let go with my left hand, I felt myself sliding too. I had to quickly pull my hand back and grab on, or I would have gone down right after him. I watched in horror as Siry picked up speed. Looking down, I realized the idiocy of our plan. Seeing him slide away, and looking beyond him to the ground so far away, brought the vertigo back. The only way I could keep from losing my grip was by closing my eyes and pressing my cheek against the skin of the pyramid. I wanted to pound my fist against it in anger.

I heard a crash and a scream from below. It didn't sound good. Do crashes and screams ever sound good? I took a few deep breaths and looked down to see . . . nothing. Siry was gone. That seemed impossible. No way he would have fallen out of sight so quickly.

"Pendragon?" I heard a dazed voice call.

"Are you all right?" I called back.

"The wall caved in. I'm inside."

He was alive, at least for the moment. I started moving again. Slowly, gradually, I made my way down toward Siry's voice. I had gotten only a few yards when I realized that the surface of the pyramid was becoming unstable. Before I could think of some way to deal with that, the panel beneath me cracked and caved. I fell into the pyramid, tumbling down in a shower of black tiles. I landed next to Siry, who was sitting up, alive but dazed. The two of us stared at each other.

"Let's not do that again," he said.

We were fine. Stunned. A little cut up, but fine. I saw that we were in one of the cubicles that held two jump tubes.

"What are those?" Siry asked.

He pointed to the two round hatches on the wall that covered the tubes. They were closed. I wasn't about to open them. I didn't want to know what was inside. The control lights were dark. The jumps had been over for a long time.

"Jump tubes," I explained. "Where the people entered Lifelight."

"People are in there?" he asked.

"Not anymore." I didn't go into any more details.

I stood up cautiously, making sure my bones were intact. I had a few scrapes, but that was all. Siry got away even easier. We had lived through an impossible stunt, but were still trapped inside a dado-infested pyramid.

I gently pushed the door open. The first thing I saw were two dados marching by. I froze. Had they seen me? No. Or they weren't looking for us. Either way, they didn't stop.

Peering out showed me that we had slid about a quarter of the way down the pyramid. My idea ended up not being that crazy after all. Sort of. Okay, maybe we were nearly killed, but it helped us to get away. At least for a while. We were in the dead center of the long balcony, with jump rooms spread out to either side of us. The balcony was about six feet wide and looked out over the center of the pyramid. The place was alive with dados. They walked slowly and methodically along the balconies that ringed the inside of the pyramid. Many more marched along the catwalks leading to the center tube and the elevator.

"We'll never get past them," Siry sighed.

I glanced around looking for . . . I didn't know what. Anything. Looking back inside the room with the jump tubes, I saw a few pieces of clothing were folded neatly in the corner.

"There's a start," I declared, and jumped back into the room. Lying in the corner neatly folded were a couple pairs of dark pants and some light-colored shirts. There were shoes, too. They looked every bit like the kinds of clothing people wore on Veelox . . . three hundred years before. When I picked them up, they shredded in my hands. The sick thought hit me that these clothes belonged to the two people who were probably still in the jump tubes wearing the green coveralls that all jumpers wore. There wouldn't be anything left of those coveralls. Or the people for that matter. The only thing left of them were the clothes they wore before their jump.

"Put 'em on," I ordered, taking off my own colorful Ibara clothes. "They might think we're Flighters, and we can blend in."

We both quickly changed out of our Ibara clothes and slipped on the ancient clothing of Veelox. We had to be careful, because the fabric crumbled in our hands. But that was good too. The raggier we were, the more we'd look like Flighters. Siry's clothes were too big for him and mine were too small, but that was okay.

"What do you think?" Siry asked, standing up for me to see.

"You're a mess," I said. "Perfect."

The clothes were as uncomfortable as hell. Not just because they felt like sandpaper, but the idea of wearing dead people's clothing was kind of creepy. The only thing we kept of our own clothes were our sandals. The crumbling shoes were no good, and we might have needed to run. Our hair wasn't very ratty-Flighter-looking either. Still, it was the best we could do.

"There's gotta be another way down besides that central elevator," I said.

"Let's find it," Siry answered.

We slipped out of the room and out onto the balcony. Most of the dados had left the balcony and were walking along the catwalks toward the elevator. More interesting were the dados that walked toward either end of the balcony.

"I'll bet that's our way down," I declared.

I stepped forward and looked over the edge. What I saw made my gut clutch, and not just because we were so high up. Far down below, on the floor, the dados were gathering. They streamed out of the elevator and the four corners of the pyramid.

"Look where they're coming from," Siry exclaimed. "There must be a way down at each corner."

He was right. We would find our way down. But that's not what struck me. More and more dados were arriving on the floor and stepping into military-like formation. They were falling in to precise groups of twenty across and forty deep. In between each of these groups, another dado marched, making sure the formation was perfectly correct. The robots stood at attention, as if waiting for orders.

"It's an army," I said quietly. "An organized army. They're getting ready."

"For what?"

"To attack Ibara."

"Pendragon, even if we get out of here, how are we going to get back to Ibara to warn them?"

"That's the easy part," I answered.

Siry gave me a confused look.

"I can get us to Ibara," I said with confidence. "All we have to do is figure out how to get past a swarm of killer bees."

IBARA

It was all about getting back to Ibara.

The people had to know an attack was coming that would be like nothing they'd seen before. Heck, like *nobody* had seen before. Fighting off a handful of grungy Flighters was one thing. Protecting the island from thousands of killer dados was another ball game. I remembered those automatic guns that blew the Flighters' gunboat out of the water. I hoped there were more of those bad boys around Ibara. Fighting the dados with poison blow darts was going to be worse than useless.

Siry and I ran along the balcony until we reached the first corner. Sure enough, there was a doorway that led to a staircase. We quickly charged down. Did I say quickly? It took forever to get down those stairs, because we weren't going straight down. It was a pyramid. The stairs were on a flatter angle than normal stairs. We were moving away from the center of the pyramid as much as we were moving down. On the way, we passed hundreds of dados who were walking slowly, methodically, down the stairs. I was nervous about it at first, thinking they might grab us. They didn't. They must have thought we were Flighters. Or maybe they weren't thinking. They were robots after all. They reminded me of the mindless security goons of Quillan, with their square heads and oversize bodies. Their eyes were just as dead as the dados from Quillan, too. For all I knew, these *were* the dados from Quillan. Saint Dane had gotten these dados from somewhere. From what I'd seen of Veelox, they weren't able to manufacture clothes, let alone sophisticated robots. The walls between the territories were nearly down.

I was too busy running to worry much about the larger implications. I'm guessing it took us about half an hour to finally hit the bottom of the pyramid.

"This is where it gets tricky," I said to Siry, as if everything up to this point hadn't been tricky at all.

As we got closer to ground level, we started seeing Flighters mixed in with the dados. They may have all worn the same raggy clothing, but there was no mistaking the two. The dados were tall and powerful looking with scary-big square heads. The Flighters were much smaller than me, probably a result of centuries of lousy food. Or no food. I don't think any of them had cut their hair. Ever. And they smelled. At least the dados didn't have that foul odor. That would have been gruesome, times many thousand.

Strangely, none of them gave us a second look. I was beginning to think the Flighters didn't have much more brainpower than the robotic dados. If all it took to fool them was a change of clothing, then three hundred years of evolution didn't do much for improving intelligence. Dopes. When we entered the central area of the pyramid, I saw signs that the Flighters had made the Lifelight monolith home. Several slept along the walls. Garbage was everywhere. Smelly, rotten rags were piled up in random areas. It was probably their laundry.

Their *clean* laundry. The smell was pretty rank. There wasn't a whole lot of hygiene going on around there.

"Look," Siry whispered, pointing toward the center of the large area.

It was Saint Dane. He was walking in front of a line of dados with his hands clasped behind his back, like a general inspecting his troops. I'm not sure whether to describe the army of dados as pathetic or frightening. They weren't dressed like an army. There were no uniforms. They all wore threadbare rags, like the Flighters. Many of them wore shredded coveralls that were red, or dark blue, or dark green—the coveralls that had once belonged to the vedders, phaders, and jumpers of Lifelight. They had no weapons, either.

But they were dados. They couldn't be killed. Each one was an exact duplicate of the other. They stood over six feet tall, with broad shoulders and big hands. They looked like muscle guys, though I guess robots don't really have muscles, technically. And those big, square heads made them look like an army of Frankenstein monsters. More intimidating than anything was that there were so many of them. They could throw a thousand dados at Ibara, lose every one, and have thousands more to take their place. They didn't have to be good or experienced or have any great tactical plan. All they had to do was keep coming.

I guess the best word to describe the sight was . . . "overwhelming."

"Why isn't Saint Dane looking for us?" Siry asked.

"He probably thinks we're trapped up in the pyramid. He'd never think we'd be crazy enough to slide down the outside."

Siry added, "I can't believe we were that crazy either."

We ducked down, waiting for Saint Dane to walk far

enough away so he wouldn't catch sight of us. We quickly moved along the wall, headed for the glass corridor of the core, and the exit. We dodged in and out of Flighters who were sleeping or gnawing on bones (I didn't want to know where the bones were from), or watching the spectacle of the dados being assembled. They didn't care about two semiclean Flighters who had no interest in anything other than getting the heck out of there. We made it around the perimeter and back into the core with no problem. Quickly we moved through the glass-walled control rooms of Lifelight. The monitors were still lit. It was amazing that after three hundred years they still had power in the pyramid. I didn't stop to try and figure out why or how.

The last step before leaving the pyramid was a grisly one. Remember I wrote about the sticks we kicked aside in the long corridor on the way in? Now that the lights were on, we saw what they were. Bones. Human bones. Lots of them. I knew they were human because there were a load of skulls, too. Siry froze. He'd never seen anything like that before. Come to think of it, neither had I. The closest I'd ever come was in the quig pen under the Bedoowan castle on Denduron. I've been calling Rubic City a place "of the dead." Until that moment we'd never actually witnessed the physical remains of those who didn't make it. I'd just as soon have gotten out of there without having had that pleasure.

"This is Saint Dane's grand plan for remaking Halla," I said. "Do you need to see any more?"

Siry's eyes were glassy. He gingerly stepped through the scattered bones, trying hard not to disturb them. Moments later we were back out in the warm sunlight of Rubic City.

"I didn't think we'd make it," Siry said.

"We haven't," I cautioned.

"So how do we get back to Ibara?"

"That's the easy part," I said with a smile. "There's a flume in Rubic City. C'mon." I took off running.

This was a no-brainer. The flume could put us back on the island in minutes. I'd never traveled within a territory, but since the flumes always put us where we needed to be when we needed to be there, I was totally confident that we could step into the tunnel in Rubic City and step out on Ibara. Okay, maybe it was more like semiconfident, but we had to try. The more time the people of Rayne had to prepare for the attack, the better. All we had to worry about was getting past the quig-bees. Oh, that. One step at a time.

By my clock it had only been a few years since I'd been to Veelox, so I remembered exactly where to find the manhole that led down to the underground train tunnel and the flume. We jogged quickly along the deserted city. I wasn't even afraid of being jumped by Flighters, because we looked like them now. Idiots. In no time we arrived at the street that held the flume. There was only one problem.

The street was gone. Well, not exactly gone, it was probably still there, only it was buried under the rubble of a collapsed skyscraper. I looked around, thinking—no, hoping—we were on the wrong street. I quickly realized it wouldn't have mattered. The whole block was under a three-story pile of broken stuff.

"Maybe we can dig to it," Siry suggested.

"With what? Our hands?"

We stared at the warlike ruins of what had once been a street lined with pretty brownstone buildings and trees. The flume was a no-go. We both knew what we had to do. Without another word we took off for the pier. It was Plan B time. We had to find a boat to get us back to Ibara. We quickly ran to the block where we had first entered the streets of Rubic City and got a view of the pier. Tied up alongside it was our yellow pirate ship. Though it wasn't yellow anymore. It was a smoking, charred-black wreck that listed hard to the right, with its bow sticking up as if gasping for air. Siry and I stood at the edge of the buildings, staring at the sad remains.

"Do you think any of them are alive?" he asked.

"They could be," I answered with absolutely no confidence.

"We didn't find Twig, either," he added sadly.

"We were lucky to get out ourselves. When this is over, we'll look for them. All of them."

Siry said, "When this is over, Rayne could end up like Rubic City."

We exchanged grim looks. "Let's find a boat."

The rusty gunboats that had attacked our yellow ship were gone. I scanned the harbor, looking for any other usable craft. There was nothing. Zero. Not a ship in sight. Besides the pier with our smoldering ship, two more piers jutted into the harbor. Neither had any boats tied alongside.

"This makes no sense," I said thoughtfully. "If Saint Dane's going to send thousands of dados to attack Ibara, how are they going to get there?"

Siry's eyes widened. He took off his belt with the pouch that contained Aja Killian's ancient map. He unfolded it for both of us to see.

"We're here on this peninsula," he said, pointing to the map. "According to the map, the coast looks pretty rugged on either side."

I scanned the harbor. The water was flat and calm. "Why would they keep their ships anywhere but right here where it's close?" I wondered out loud.

Siry said, "It would take a very big ship to move those dados. Probably more than one. They could tie them right up here to the piers."

The piers. I looked at all three. Something was off. Two looked the exact same, but the one to our far right looked slightly different. It was built higher. Where the other two piers had steel pilings beneath that could be seen when the tide was lower, this pier looked more like a solid structure, with sides that reached down under the water.

"I want to get a closer look at that pier," I said, and started walking.

We moved quickly across a few hundred yards of debris. The closer we got, the more the pier looked like an enclosed structure.

"There could be something in there," I declared. "Inside the pier."

Siry was skeptical. "Like what? It's not tall enough for a ship."

The mystery deepened a few seconds later. Two Flighters appeared from behind a pile of debris at the beginning of the pier. I grabbed Siry and pulled him down behind a pile of twisted steel. The Flighters continued to walk casually along the width of the pier.

"What are they doing?" Siry asked.

"I'll bet they're guarding whatever's inside."

Siry took a cautious peek at the pier. "There really might be something in there."

The only way for us to find out would be to get past the Flighters. I needed a weapon. There was nothing around but piles of rubble . . . and lengths of ancient steel. I grabbed a section of pipe around six feet long and a few inches thick. I tested its strength, felt its weight, then spun it around and snapped it back into fighting position. Perfect.

"Whoa," Siry gasped. "Where did you learn that?"

"Long story," I said.

It was time to put my Loor skills to work. With the pipe clutched at my side, I crept silently forward, dodging between the mounds of wreckage for cover. The Flighters weren't exactly a crack security team. The two were in some kind of argument. Over what, I didn't know or care. The two started shoving each other. It wasn't violent, just heated.

It was about to get very violent. I was about to drop in.

Their attention was so focused on each other that they didn't see me creeping toward them. It was perfect, for about ten seconds. I snuck forward and hid behind the final pile of rubble, looking at twenty yards of open ground between me and my quarry. I couldn't get any closer without being totally exposed. Siry crept up right behind me.

"Once the fight starts," I whispered to Siry. "Run for the pier."

He nodded. His eyes were wide and scared, but he was ready.

There was nothing left for me to do but attack. I leaped out from my cover and sprinted toward the Flighters. I was in the open. All they had to do was turn their heads and they'd see me. Luckily, they were focused on each other. I figured I had a good shot at jumping them before they even saw me.

I was wrong.

I was five yards away. The pipe was pulled back, ready to take these guys out, when one of them saw me. The surprise on his face was almost funny. Almost. This was very serious.

"Ahhh!" he screamed, and turned to protect himself.

I went for the guy who turned. I feinted, as if to swing the pipe one way. When he threw his arms up to protect himself,

I flashed the pipe the other way . . . and totally whiffed. The guy ducked and rolled. He was quicker than I thought. Oops. But it was okay. He didn't jump up to fight. He ran away. I'm serious, he turned and ran. I realized that my back was to the other Flighter, so I spun quickly, ready for his attack. It never came. He was running away too. Both of them sprinted to get the heck away from me. Not exactly dedicated guards. It was the easiest fight I'd had in, well, ever. They were running scared. I figured we had free access to the mysterious warehouse/pier.

I was wrong, again.

One of the Flighters pulled something out of his rotten clothes as he retreated and put it to his mouth. A shrill whistle pierced the air, and my ears. He was sending out an alarm. From one of the buildings a few hundred yards away, doors burst open, and Flighters began pouring out, headed for us. There were so many they reminded me of the quig-spiders on Quillan. We were trapped. The ocean was behind us, the Flighters in front of us. We had to get inside that pier. If there was a ship, there was a slim hope we might be able to get it under way before they reached us. Very slim. We both turned and bolted onto the pier. The floor itself was in way better shape than the pier where we'd first landed. It was cement and solid—a fact that gave me hope there really was something beneath there that they were protecting. That, and the fact that hundreds of Flighters were sprinting closer to keep us away from it.

"How do we get in?" Siry yelled.

I scanned the pier. It was flat. There weren't any doors or ladders or anything that would be the obvious way to get down below. Suddenly I was beginning to fear we were wrong, and this was nothing more than a thicker-than-normal pier. A quick glance back showed me the Flighters were getting closer. I was about to suggest that we run to the end of the pier and dive off. Swimming would be our only way to escape.

"There!" Siry shouted, and ran forward.

He'd spotted a three-foot square in the floor that could be a trapdoor. His fingers played across the surface, desperate to find something to grab on to.

"Got it," he declared.

It was a ring embedded in the surface. He dug his fingers in, lifted the circle up on its hinge, and pulled. The square lifted up. We had our way in, but to what? There wasn't time to be cautious. Without hesitation Siry dropped his legs into the hole. There was a steel ladder that he used to quickly climb down. I was right after him. Before dropping below, I took a look back to see the Flighters were nearly at the pier. It was hopeless. Even if there was a ship down there, there was no way we'd be able to get under way in time. I closed the trapdoor behind me. I know, it wasn't much, but slowing them down for even a second might prove critical. Once the door was slammed, I quickly slid down the ladder, eager to see what was below.

Since I began this adventure, I can't count the number of times I've written about how I'd seen something I hadn't expected. This was one of those times. I think it's safe to say that it came very close to the top of the list on the surprise scale. What I hoped to see was a ship. Preferably one that Siry could figure out how to get moving quickly. I got my wish . . . a few thousand times over. What I saw inside that pier, floating on water, wasn't one ship. Or two or three. I can only guesstimate the number, but I'd say we were looking at a thousand watercraft at least. I say watercraft because these weren't ships. That's what the true surprise was.

They were skimmers. From Cloral. Floating side by side were multiple hundreds of the small, sleek watercraft like the aquaneers of Cloral used to fly over the water. This was how Saint Dane would get his dados to Ibara. Each craft could carry a half dozen of them easily. You remember the skimmers, right? They were like oversize Jet Skis with side pontoons for stability. Their bright white hulls made them look like water rockets. They were fast. They could maneuver tight turns, which meant they could dodge the fire from the guns of Ibara. Even if a few were hit, there would be hundreds more behind it.

Looking at the sea of skimmers bobbing on the water was like seeing the last piece in the puzzle that would bring about the destruction of Ibara. There was only one *good* thing I could say about it. I knew how we were going to get out of there.

Siry was staring out at the small sea of crafts with his mouth open in wonder. There was no time to explain. I could already hear the thundering feet of the Flighters. They were on the pier above our heads, coming our way.

"Let's go!" I ordered, and started sprinting forward along the long, narrow walkway that ran parallel to the skimmers at water level. We had to get to the front of the pack.

"Pendragon?" Siry called while running behind me. "What are these? Where did they come from?"

"Later!" I screamed.

I heard the creak of the trapdoor opening behind us. Flighters began climbing down the ladder. More trapdoors were yanked open over our heads. Flighters poured down from above. It was going to be close.

In seconds we reached the leading edge of the mass of skimmers. I was happy to see that the end of the pier wasn't enclosed. Before us was open ocean. The only thing keeping the bobbing skimmers from floating out were several thick chains draped across the opening.

"Get them down!" I screamed to Siry.

I didn't have to explain. He jumped at the chains and worked to unhook them so we'd have enough space to squeeze out a skimmer. I jumped onto the first skimmer in line. I held my breath. If there was no power, our trip would be over right there. I looked to see the first group of Flighters had landed on the walkway behind us, and they were running forward. I had to stay focused and hope I still knew how to drive a skimmer. One by one I flipped the toggle switches that were lined up on the console. I was rewarded with the high-pitched whining sound of the skimmer coming to life. I wanted to scream, "Yeah!"

Siry was struggling with the chains. If we couldn't get enough of them down, it wouldn't matter how much power the skimmer had. We'd be trapped. I toggled the last two switches. The pontoons, which jutted out on either side of the skimmer like wings, began lowering toward the water with a steady hum. They both needed to be in the water for us to have full propulsion, but these skimmers were so jammed in, it looked like they would hit the skimmer to my right and the walkway to my left, stopping their descent. We were going to have to push the craft into open water so they could fully extend, but the chains still kept us back.

"Help!" Siry called in frustration.

I jumped off the skimmer to help with the snarl of chain. The Flighters were fifty yards back and closing fast.

"Pull!" I ordered. We both grabbed the chain that ran through a loop attached to the side of the pier. It was heavy. It needed all our combined strength. Together we pulled hand over hand, yanking the chain through the loop as quickly as possible. The metal sang as it zipped through the loop. The Flighters started screaming. I didn't know what they were saying, but it definitely sounded angry. They were fired up. If they got to us, there was no telling what they'd do.

With one final yank we pulled the chain out of the loop. It fell into the water. The way was clear. Siry jumped onto the walkway and looked back at the Flighters.

"Hurry!" He shouted and boarded the skimmer.

I leaped back aboard. The engines were whining high. The pontoons were pushing down on the walkway and the next skimmer, straining to go lower, but that wouldn't happen until we moved forward.

"Sit down," I yelled to Siry.

I grabbed the motorcycle-like handlebar controls and twisted the throttle. Slowly, painfully, we moved forward. We wouldn't have full power until the ends of the pontoons dipped into the water.

"C'mon, c'mon!" I coaxed. The skimmer wouldn't listen. We were moving too slowly.

"Pendragon!" Siry called nervously.

I didn't have to look to know what he meant. The Flighters were almost on us. The ends of the pontoons scraped against the walkway and the next skimmer. Only a few more feet. I feared they'd get caught up on something and not be able to get into the water. That would be the end of it.

The first Flighter arrived. He jumped onto the skimmer, headfirst, and tackled Siry. Siry hit the deck at my feet. I turned, grabbed the grungy little guy, and heaved him over the side. More were on the way. I looked right at Siry, who was lying on his back, staring up at me with wide, fearful eyes.

"Hold on," I commanded.

He rolled over and grabbed on to the side of the skimmer.

The two pontoons dipped into the water. I grabbed the handlebars and bent my knees.

"Hobey-ho, let's go," I said, and twisted the throttle.

The next Flighter leaped onto the skimmer just as we launched. He didn't stand a chance. No sooner did his feet touch the deck than he was thrown off balance by the force of the skimmer rocketing forward. His stay on board lasted about a second then he fell over backward, into the water.

"Whoaaaaaa!" Siry yelled as the skimmer flew ahead.

We sailed over the water as smoothly and effortlessly as I remembered skimming over the waters of Cloral. I didn't even look back at the pier and Rubic City. We had jumped the next hurdle. We were on our way back to Ibara.

I'm going to end this journal here, Courtney. I'm finishing it while sitting in the Jakill clearing on Ibara. We made it back, no problem. Okay, maybe there was a little problem. As far as the people of Rayne are concerned, we're outlaws. We had to find a quiet stretch of rocky beach and land the skimmer without being seen. That was fairly easy, because we didn't get back until after dark. I'm guessing this was exactly how the various scouting parties of Flighters traveled from Rubic City to Ibara.

The trip was much quicker than on the pirate ship. Skimmers are fast. Part of me didn't want the people of Rayne to even see the skimmer. I guess I'm still holding by the rules that say territories shouldn't be mixed. The skimmer represents technology these people shouldn't know about. I suppose that's a pretty idiotic concern. Soon they'll be seeing a whole bunch of skimmers. Siry and I have got to figure out a way to get to the tribunal and warn them about what's going to happen. It's the right thing to do, though I have no real hope that the people of Ibara can repel an invasion of dados. Ibara will fall, which means Veelox will fall. Again. There's only one thing that might prevent that.

Find Mark, Courtney. If you can stop him from introducing Forge technology to First Earth, it might change history back to the way it was meant to be. It might stop the dados from being invented. It might stop the invasion. Might.

I've got to figure out what the second turning point of Veelox is. It can't be the attack of the dados. That doesn't fit. There has to be something that was naturally going to happen on Veelox that Saint Dane is trying to influence. If I can learn what the turning point is, there might still be hope. Again, might.

I'll close by saying one more time that I'm sorry, Courtney. I should have stayed on First Earth. My ego brought me to Ibara. To Veelox. I don't believe Saint Dane even cares about me anymore. We escaped from the Lifelight pyramid a little too easily. Am I finished? Is my value as a Traveler gone? Has Saint Dane beaten me? I can't accept that. I've got to keep fighting, no matter how bleak it looks.

Find Mark. Stop him. I believe it's our last and best chance.

END OF JOURNAL #30

◐ FIRST EARTH ◑

The elegant ocean liner *Queen Mary* was escorted safely through New York Harbor by six small tugboats. Its enormous hull dwarfed the feisty little crafts as they pushed and prodded the floating city past the Statue of Liberty, through the Verrazano Narrows, and into the deep trench of the Atlantic Ocean, where they peeled off and bid the grand liner a farewell as it continued under its own power toward England.

Courtney and Dodger didn't see any of that. They had found a quiet little restaurant on a lower deck of the ship that had not yet opened for business. Soon the place would be busy with passengers eager to sample the delights of the renowned kitchens. Until then, it was the perfect place to sit quietly and read Bobby's journal.

Courtney finished first. She left the pages with Dodger and gazed through a round porthole at the ocean. She had never been on an ocean liner and didn't know what to expect. She didn't sense any movement at all, only the steady thrum of the ship's engines. As she looked out on the horizon, she knew what she had to do, but had no clue how to go about it.

"That settles it," Dodger said with finality. "We made the right move. We should be on this ship."

"It's hard to know what to think," Courtney said wistfully. "I'm not sure what's right and wrong anymore. Saint Dane has broken down the barriers between the territories, and it's about to lead to the final destruction of Veelox. But Mark and I interfered with Eelong and it *saved* that territory! Now I'm on a ship from the past, trying to change the future back to what it was in the first place. It's all becoming so incredibly . . . impossible."

"Becoming?" Dodger asked.

He joined Courtney at the porthole. "All I know is what I read in these journals and what you tell me. I can't say if it's okay to monkey with one territory over another. It's all science fiction to me. But I know the difference between right and wrong. Saint Dane is going to take those dado things and hurt a lot of people. That's about as wrong as it gets. If we can stop him by stopping Mark, well, we ain't got a whole lot of choice."

Courtney looked at Dodger. Her eyes were watery. Dodger didn't ask why, and even if he had, Courtney wouldn't have had an answer. The list was too long. "Do you really think we can save Veelox by stopping Mark?"

Dodger chuckled. "I guess it's possible, but you're asking the wrong guy. Besides, what else are we gonna do on this tub? Play shuffleboard?"

Courtney laughed in spite of herself. "This is going to be tough. We're stowaways, but we can't hide. We've got to search the ship."

"Not a problem," Dodger said with confidence. "Hiding is the *worst* thing a stowaway could do. I say we stroll around like we owned the ship. Let people see us. Nobody will know if we've got a cabin or not. You're with the right fella, Courtney. This ship is a floating hotel. I know hotels. We're going to find Mark. The hard part comes after that."

"What do you mean?"

"We've gotta stop him. I can't help you there."

Courtney looked back out at the ocean. The biggest question was still not answered. Why had Mark left Second Earth to change history? Until she learned that, she didn't know how she would convince him to stop.

"We don't have much time," Courtney cautioned.

"Nah, we got six days till we dock, plenty of time."

"But it isn't," Courtney said quickly. "History said that a body from the *Queen Mary* washed up in New Jersey. Maybe it was Mark and maybe it wasn't, but whoever it was, unless you believe a body could float from the middle of the ocean all the way back to New Jersey, the shooting is going to happen while we're still close to the United States."

Dodger whistled in awe. "Hadn't thought of that."

"So on top of everything else, we've got to solve a murder before it happens," Courtney concluded.

"What are we waiting for? Let's get cracking," Dodger announced enthusiastically. "I say we split up. You search the decks. I'll bet Mark is out walking around right now. You don't take a cruise to sit alone in your room."

"You don't know Mark," Courtney cautioned. "He's probably in his cabin eating carrots and reading."

"Carrots?"

"Doesn't matter."

"Yeah, well, that's where I come in," Dodger said confidently. "I'll get hold of the passenger list and find out what cabin he's in."

"How?"

"I told you, I know hotels. Trust me."

Courtney shrugged. Dodger reached out and took off her

floppy hat. "You're a pretty gal. Don't go trying to look like a boy. Dressed like that you're going to stick out like a sore thumb."

Courtney looked down at her woolen pants and sweater. She suddenly wished she had thought ahead enough to have worn one of those creepy dresses she'd seen in the shop windows back in New York.

"I look like one of those immigrants you see in pictures from Ellis Island," Courtney admitted, discouraged.

"Don't worry," Dodger assured her. "I'll scare something up for you."

Courtney nodded. "Where will I find you?"

Dodger thought and said, "I'll meet you on the bow in an hour. Be careful, keep moving. Avoid the crew, but don't be obvious about it. They don't know all the passengers yet."

"Okay, good luck."

"Good hunting." Dodger tipped his cap and ducked out the door.

Courtney was alone again. The task ahead was daunting, but clear. Find Mark. Stop him. Save him, but stop him. She knew she couldn't fail. It was all about his Forge invention. She had to get him to destroy the model. The moment it was gone, she felt sure that history would change, and all would be as it was meant to be. The dados would no longer exist on Veelox, and the war for Ibara would never begin. Bobby would be safe. Mark would be safe. Halla would be safe.

Courtney stuck her hat in her back pocket and tied her hair up to look as presentable as possible. She took off her sweater and untucked her white shirt. She then tied her sweater around her waist, hoping to look like a sporty kind of girl rather than a stowaway. She looked at her reflection in a mirror that took up an entire wall of the restaurant. She turned up her collar to try looking even more stylish. She realized it was hopeless. She was going to stick out like, well, like a stowaway. She knew her best chance of not getting caught by a crew member was not being seen by a crew member. With that impossible challenge in mind, she set out in search of Mark.

Her plan was to stick to the areas with the biggest crowds. She figured the odds of spotting Mark were better there. Just as important, she hoped to blend in. Those hopes evaporated as soon as she stepped onto the Promenade Deck. It was a wide, enclosed deck, with a ceiling and windows to protect against the elements. Though the frenzy of the boarding process had died down, the place was still alive with people. None of them looked anything like Courtney.

There would be no blending in.

The women all wore dresses or neatly tailored suits. The men were in suits and ties. Courtney always imagined a cruise to be a place where people dressed down and wore shorts and ran around having fun. That wasn't the case in 1937. She felt like a little kid at a very grown-up party, which is pretty much exactly what she was. Worse, she had crashed the party. She decided the best thing to do was not worry about anything except finding Mark. She thought that if she skulked around looking guilty, somebody was sure to spot her and turn her in. She covered lots of ground quickly and methodically. She first traversed the entire enclosed Promenade Deck, until she ended up back where she'd started. Along the way she kept peering at the men, getting in their faces, hoping one might be Mark. All she got in return was a bunch of strange looks.

Her next step was to climb up to the Sun Deck, which was named because it had no ceiling and only a handrail along the side. Walking along this deck felt much more like being on a ship. She could feel the sun and the wind and the sea spray. Lifeboats hung high over this deck, which reminded her of the movie *Titanic.* She shook that image out of her head fast. There was enough to worry about without dwelling on ocean disasters.

The late afternoon sun was setting, casting warm light on the water. Courtney wished she could have stopped to enjoy it, like so many of the other passengers who leaned out over the rails. That wasn't going to happen. She was on a mission. She passed a few people she could have sworn were stars she'd seen in ancient movies. What were their names? Clark Gable? Cary Grant? Cary Gable? She saw a chubby guy who looked like an old-time movie comedian, though she wasn't sure if it was Laurel or Hardy. Or neither. She made a mental note of trying not to think of these people as being from the past, because on First Earth they were very much in the present. She saw hundreds of people, but no Mark.

Courtney felt much more at ease on the Sports Deck. Here passengers were playing shuffleboard and tennis. Eager sports-minded passengers were out playing in the dying sunlight. Courtney was happy to see that these players didn't wear dresses and suits. The men wore long pants and sweaters, and the women wore loose skirts. She wanted to hang out on this deck a little more, if only because she didn't stand out so much in the clothes she had on. It was also kind of unique to watch people playing on the deck of a moving ship at the base of the three massive orange-and-black smokestacks. It might actually have been kind of fun, if it weren't keeping her from trying to save all of humanity.

After searching unsuccessfully for nearly an hour, it was time to head toward the bow and her rendezvous with Dodger. She realized with frustration how difficult a task finding Mark was going to be. Finding him would take a huge amount of luck. She hoped that Dodger had been able to find out where his cabin was, because running into Mark by accident seemed impossible.

The ship was way too big. As she walked toward the bow, she tried to think like Mark. Where would he go? What would he do? The obvious answer was that he'd spend most of the time in his cabin, reading. That was Mark. But Mark was curious, too. He'd never been on a ship before. He'd want to know how it worked. He'd explore. What would be one of his first things to do? She didn't think he'd spend the *whole* time reading.

Reading. The realization was as simple as could be. The library. That's where he'd go. Was there a library on this big ship? There had to be. They had everything else. Without the least bit of concern that they'd ask her who she was and if she had paid for the voyage, she marched right up to one of the stewards, who was serving drinks to a couple tucked snugly into deck chairs.

"Excuse me, could you tell me where the library is?" she asked politely.

"Certainly, miss. It's in Regent Street. Take the—"

"Got it, thanks," Courtney said, and jogged off. She didn't even look back to see what she knew would be curious stares at the bold girl in pants. She knew exactly where Regent Street was and how to get there. After being on the *Queen Mary* for only a few hours, she was beginning to know her way around. She quickly ran down several flights of narrow, wooden stairs that brought her back to the Promenade Deck. She entered the Regent Street shopping mall and moved quickly past the fancy shops. All she wanted was the library. She found it on the far end. She burst through the door, startling a woman behind a desk, who Courtney figured was the librarian.

"Oh!" the woman exclaimed.

"Sorry," Courtney apologized. She scanned the small room that was ringed with shelves full of leather-bound books. Plenty of books, no people.

"Can I help you, miss?" the older woman asked pleasantly, having regained her composure.

"No, thanks," Courtney said quickly, then got an idea and approached the desk. "Maybe you can. A friend of mine said he was going to reserve some books and wanted me to pick them up. Could you check for me?"

"Certainly," the woman said with a slight British accent. "What would his name be?"

"Dimond. Mark Dimond."

Courtney knew it was a total stab in the dark, but figured it might lead to some information.

"Mark Dimond?" the woman exclaimed. "Sure enough, you just missed him, dear. He picked up his books not five minutes ago."

Courtney felt as if she'd been hit with a hammer.

"He—He did?" she stuttered. "You're sure his name was Mark Dimond?"

"Sure as can be," she said sweetly, looking through a stack of cards. "I spelled his name incorrectly, and he was quick to point out there was no 'a' in Dimond. Sweet young lad."

Courtney was still reeling. "Dark hair? Bad skin? Glasses?"

"Yes, dear, that's him. Is there a problem?"

"No," Courtney blurted out. "No problem. What's his cabin number?"

The woman held the cards close to her chest. Courtney sensed a sudden air of suspicion. "Forgive me," she said curtly. "I'm not at liberty to give out that information. What did you say your name was?"

"I didn't," Courtney said as she backed toward the door. "Did he say where he was going?"

"Indeed he did. He planned on watching the sunset on the stern with his friend. It's a wonderful sight."

"Thank you," Courtney said. "Thank you very much." She turned for the door, stopped short, and looked back to the librarian. "His friend?"

"Yes. Quite the pretty girl, I must say. That Mr. Dimond must be a catch if he's got two such lovely ladies chasing after him."

Courtney blasted out of the library and hurried for the Promenade Deck. She nearly knocked over a steward as she launched out of Regent Street and sprinted along the wooden deck toward the stern of the ship. She didn't care who gave her a second look. Mark was on the ship. She'd just missed him. Her heart raced, and it wasn't because she was running.

The deck wasn't crowded anymore. Courtney figured everyone was getting settled in and ready for their fancy dinners. That was good. Less people to dodge. She made it to the end of the enclosed portion of the Promenade Deck and ran outside to face a big, orange November sun that was setting over the coast of the United States. The passengers outside were silhouetted against the orange ball, so it was difficult to make out details. She ran to the aft railing of the Promenade Deck and looked to the decks below.

Many people were outside to enjoy the sunset. All eyes were to the west. Nobody was looking back at her. Her frustration grew. It was impossible to make anybody out. She was about to start sprinting along each deck to get a closer look at the people when her eye caught something two decks below. There was a couple standing close to each other. They wore long, dark gray woolen coats to keep the sea chill away. The man wore one of those fedora hats. The woman was a few inches taller than he was. Her hair was dark brown, cut just above her shoulders. It was parted on the side and perfectly combed under a small, gray hat. Though there was a sea breeze, not one hair looked out of place. Her back was to the sun as she spoke to the man, which meant she faced Courtney. Even from where she was, Courtney could tell the woman was pretty. But none of those details mattered as much as the fact that the man clutched two leather books under his arm. The guy might have just come from the library.

He turned to face the woman, and Courtney saw his profile. He wore wire-rimmed glasses. A slight curl of black hair could be seen creeping from under his hat.

Courtney stopped breathing.

"Ma—," she began to yell, but was rudely yanked away from the railing and shoved against an outside wall. She hit the steel hard.

"Ahoy, Chetwynde," came a familiar voice.

Courtney focused on the man who had attacked her. He wore a long dark coat and peered at her from underneath the brim of a gray hat.

"Nothing like a little sea air to get the blood moving, is there?" the guy said, after which he snorted and spit out a loogie onto the deck.

"Mitchell," Courtney gasped.

"Welcome aboard," Andy Mitchell said with a sneer.

Saint Dane was back in play.

◈ FIRST EARTH ◈
(CONTINUED)

"How come you didn't die in that cab?" Mitchell asked obnoxiously.

"Don't give me that," Courtney spat back. "If you wanted to kill me, I'd be dead. You knew we'd get out of there."

Mitchell snickered. "Still sure of yourself, Chetwynde. Right to the end."

He wore the same kind of suit and long coat as many of the passengers, making him look a lot older than seventeen years. His normally long, greasy blond hair was cut short, adding even more years to his look. Of course, Courtney knew he wasn't really seventeen anyway.

Courtney kept her back to the wall, like a trapped animal. She couldn't yell for help. Saint Dane hadn't done anything wrong. The only thing yelling would do was bring the crew down on her.

"I don't know what you did to get Mark to come to First Earth," Courtney said. "But I'm going to stop him from springing Forge on this territory. I got here in time for that."

Mitchell laughed a laugh that turned into a smoker's hack. Courtney cringed.

"In time?" he croaked. "You think you're racing some deadline to stop this territory from learning about Forge? Time is the *last* thing on your side! Where do you think I got that plastic stuff from? Third Earth. That's over three thousand years from now."

"I knew you didn't invent that," Courtney snarled. "The heart of Forge is Mark's computer skeleton, not the plastic skin. All you did was mix technology from different territories. Again."

"Exactly!" Mitchell said. "Tripping through time is a wonderful thing. By Earth years, Lifelight won't be invented for another five centuries after Third Earth. The dados on Quillan were built a century after that and brought to the ruins of Rubic City two hundred years later. Do you really think time is a problem for me? I have all the time in Halla!"

Courtney's mind reeled at the possibilities. The impossibilities.

"C'mon, Chetwynde!" Mitchell scoffed. "Do you really think you've made it here in the nick of time? Why's that so important? You trying to stop the Flighters from destroying Ibara? Is that it? You trying to help Pendragon? That's a joke. That battle ain't gonna happen for thousands of years!"

"No," Courtney said, stalking forward. She was angry enough to think she could bully him the way she used to. Before she knew he was Saint Dane. "It's about Mark, and his invention. It's not about time. It's about tricking the people of the territories into hurting themselves. That's what's important to you. You somehow got Mark to do the wrong thing. I'm going to change that." She got right into Mitchell's face and added with venom, "And you can't stop me."

Andy Mitchell's eyes flashed blue, jolting Courtney back to reality. This wasn't Andy Mitchell, world-class loser. This was Saint Dane, Halla-class demon. She took a few involuntary steps backward and hit the wall.

"Don't forget who you're dealing with," Mitchell snarled. "Andy Mitchell ain't real."

"No, but Mark is," Courtney said, fighting to regain her composure. "And I'm going to save him."

She ran to the railing.

"Mark!" she called out.

But Mark was gone. She looked around quickly, hoping to see the couple strolling away. She was too late. The sun dipped below the horizon. The ship's lights were taking over the job of lighting the decks.

"I'm going to find him," she said as she spun back. "And I'm going to—"

Mitchell was no longer alone. Standing next to him were two ship's officers, both looking very military with their dark blue uniforms.

"I ain't no snitch," Mitchell said to the officers politely. "But she's been running around here bothering a lot of people. I think she might be a stowaway."

There was a frozen moment. The two officers looked at Courtney with grim expressions. Andy Mitchell stood between the two wearing a smug grin. He lifted up his hand and gave her a small, obnoxious wave that only she could see.

"Come with us, miss," said one of the officers as they both took a step toward her. "No trouble now, if you please."

Courtney made a snap decision. She ran. She didn't know where she was going, but she ran. She had to find Mark. She had to find Dodger. Most of all she had to keep from getting taken into custody by the ship's crew, because if that happened, she'd be done. Mark would be done. Halla would be done. She ran down a flight of stairs to the deck below and sprinted back into the structure of the ship. If there was one thing Courtney could do, it was run. She knew that in a flat-out race, she'd beat anybody. It was time for her to kick on the afterburners. She sprinted along the deck, weaving past passengers who strolled casually along. She knew she had an advantage. She might not know the ship, but her pursuers didn't know which way she would go. It was like soccer, she thought. Defense was much tougher than offense because the person with the ball was in charge. Courtney was in charge.

She ran until she hit an inside stairway and took it back up to the Promenade Deck. Her plan was to take as winding a route as possible to try and lose them. She climbed the stairs and took off back toward the stern. Bad move. One of the officers had stayed on that deck and was coming toward her. Oops. He hadn't spotted her yet, so Courtney ducked into the first door she saw.

She found herself in an immense, elegant dining room. The ceiling soared impossibly high overhead, where several rectangular lights cast a warm glow over the room. Polished wooden pillars stood along either side of the space, making the room look as much like an ancient temple as a modern ballroom. On one end of the room was a stage, where a swing orchestra played soft (boring) music. Hundreds of tables were set with fine, white linen and elegant china. People were beginning to arrive for dinner. The men wore tuxedos, the women lavish gowns. Courtney was stunned to think that such an elaborate room could be aboard a floating ship. But there wasn't time to hang out and admire the place. She ran down the center of the room, headed toward the orchestra. To the left of the stage was a swinging door, where she saw waiters entering and exiting. Her plan was to head that way and escape through the kitchen.

The plan changed when one of the ship's officers entered through that door. Courtney made a flash decision. Without breaking stride, she hurdled up onto the stage, past the orchestra leader, and dodged her way through the surprised musicians. None of them missed a note. Courtney found her way backstage and through a narrow corridor. Where to now? At this point she was operating more out of instinct than with any plan. She wanted to lose her pursuers long enough to stop and think about her next move.

The corridor led her through the back side of the busy kitchen, where dozens of chefs prepared the elaborate feast. They paid Courtney no attention as she slid past them and out the far side. She found herself in a service stairwell. It was fifty-fifty. Up or down? She chose down. Lower and lower into the bowels of the ship she went, figuring she'd lose them in the labyrinth of corridors and cabins. She stopped on D Deck, choosing that one to continue her flight.

She knew where she had to go. Dodger would be waiting for her at the bow of the ship. She needed to get there and tell him what had happened. She was a fugitive. It was only a matter of time before her luck ran out. The responsibility of getting to Mark was now on his shoulders. Hopefully, she thought, the crew didn't know there were two stowaways. It was a slight hope, but it was hope.

She continued running forward. She passed through a foyer, hoping to find a corridor where she could open up and sprint. Opening the door on the far side, she got hit with a blast of hot, steamy air. She thought for sure she had found an engine room. Instead she was on a long balcony that looked down on a swimming pool. The sight threw her, since she knew she was so deep in the bowels of the ship. It looked to Courtney like something out of a European estate with its wall carvings and fine tile work. Nobody was swimming, which made it all feel kind of eerie. She wondered why people would take an ocean cruise, only to go swimming in the deep recesses of a ship. There was nothing about 1937 that Courtney understood, or liked very much.

She sprinted along the balcony and left the pool on the far side to find herself in another restaurant. It was nothing like the elegant ballroom off the Promenade Deck. This one had a low ceiling and was crowded with tables and people. It was already filled up for the evening meal. Nobody wore tuxedos or gowns. She figured it was probably for the third-class passengers. She wondered if these people ever got the chance to look at what they were missing up above. Probably not. There'd be a mutiny. She moved quickly through, trying not to attract attention. She left the restaurant on the far end and discovered another stair-well. She figured she had to be nearing the bow so she climbed. And climbed. And climbed up from the depths of the grand ship.

When she finally felt the chill of evening air, she found her-self in what looked like a fancy nightclub. There was a curved bar, where people sat drinking and chatting. It was a festive atmosphere. Many people were listening to a woman singer who stood near a white, grand piano, singing a song Courtney vaguely remembered hearing in an old movie. She realized she had left the lower-class sections of the ship, because everyone was back in tuxedos or gowns. She was scanning the room, looking for her next move, when she realized that one whole wall of the bar was a curved window that looked out over the enormous bow of the ship. She had made it! Almost. She ducked out the door into the chilly night air and followed around a walkway that crossed in front of the curved window.

The forward decks of the ship spread out before her in lay-ers, coming to a point at the bow. The sea was black, but the decks were brightly lit by flood lamps. High above, built into a heavy mast, was the crow's nest, where she knew sailors would be looking out over the ocean for trouble. She hoped they wouldn't also look *down* for trouble, because she had plenty already. Unlike the stern decks, the forward decks weren't pro-tected from the elements by the ship's superstructure. It was chilly. The wind came off the ocean with no obstruction and whistled through the rails. That was good. It meant there wouldn't be many people out, and she'd have a better chance of finding Dodger quickly. She held her hand up to block the flood-light from blinding her. The bow itself looked to be another hundred yards forward from where she stood. She squinted, and saw a figure standing alone, very close to the bow itself. She knew it had to be Dodger.

Courtney wanted to shout for him, but he was too far away and the sea wind was too loud. She would have to go to him. The design of the ship didn't make that easy. She had to climb down stairs to go from the Promenade Deck to the Main Deck, climb down another flight to A Deck, sprint across thirty yards of that deck, and then climb up another set of stairs to get back to the Main Deck level. From there it was another twenty yards to the bow, and Dodger.

She ran, hoping that none of the crew members chasing her would wander into the nightclub and look out the big window to see a tired stowaway scrambling across the decks. It wasn't until she climbed up the final stairs to get back to the Main Deck that Dodger spotted her.

"Hey!" he shouted. "I'm freezing my butt off out here! Where you been?"

"Don't talk. Listen." She grabbed Dodger's arm and pulled him back the way she had come.

"He's here, Courtney," Dodger said. "I found out he's on board."

"I said don't talk. I saw Mark. Saint Dane, too."

"What?" shouted Dodger, stunned.

They kept moving down the stairs to A Deck.

"I tracked Mark through the library. He's on board with a woman."

"Yeah," Dodger agreed. "KEM Limited bought tickets for three people. I got that much, but I couldn't get their cabins."

"Listen to me!" Courtney barked. "They know I'm a stowaway. I've been running from the crew for half an hour."

"Oh," Dodger said flatly. "Not good."

"I don't know if they know about you. Saint Dane might not even know you're here. But they're going to get me sooner or later, so it's up to you. You've got to find Mark. Do you still have his picture?"

Dodger jammed his hand into his coat pocket and pulled out the old photo of Mark and his parents.

"He doesn't look much like that anymore," Courtney said. "His hair is cut short. He's wearing wire-rimmed glasses and a suit that makes him look like he's grown up. But he isn't. He's just . . . Mark."

They made it across A Deck and climbed back up to the Main Deck.

"Saint Dane is in the form of Andy Mitchell," Courtney continued, breathless. "Remember the cab driver who nearly drowned us?"

"Like I could forget?"

"That's him. I don't know who the woman is. I've never seen her before."

"I'm thinking she's some kind of actress," Dodger declared. "You know, a Hollywood-type dame."

"Why?"

"'Cause she's using a made-up name."

"You found her name?"

"I told you, I got three names from the passenger list. Mark Dimond, Andy Mitchell, and a lady. At least, I think it was a lady. I never heard of a name like that."

"What is it?"

Dodger reached for the door that would lead them back into

the enclosed section of the Main Deck. "It's Nevva Winter," he said. "Who ever heard of a crazy name like that?"

Courtney froze.

The door opened before Dodger could grab it. He was pushed behind the open door as two ship's officers stepped out. If Courtney's brain hadn't locked at the sound of that name, she probably would have turned and run. She didn't get the chance. The two officers jumped her and firmly grabbed her arms.

"That's enough gallivanting around for one night, missy," one officer said.

They led her back inside. The door closed behind them. They never saw Dodger.

A few hours later, after being interrogated by the ship's security officer (to whom she said nothing), and officially identified as a stowaway, Courtney found herself alone in a hospital-like room toward the stern of the ship. It was called the "isolation ward." It was where they put people with contagious diseases, to keep them away from the rest of the passengers. There was nothing Courtney liked about that. The room had four white bunk beds with clean sheets, and a sink. It was comfortable enough, and thankfully, there were no other occupants. The metal door closed with a loud *clang* and was locked securely from the outside. A single round window in the door allowed outsiders to check on the occupants of the ward without having to actually breathe the same air. It may have looked like a hospital, but Courtney knew what it really was. A jail cell. She was sentenced to spend the rest of her voyage locked up.

The job of finding Mark and stopping him was officially Dodger's.

● FIRST EARTH ●
(CONTINUED)

Courtney paced the small hospital room, trying to come up with a plan. Any plan. Everything she thought of started with her getting out of that lockup, which was impossible. Time was running out. Mark was in danger. If events followed the history she'd seen on Third Earth, someone was going to shoot him and dump his body overboard. Soon. There was nothing she could do but hope that Dodger would somehow get to him before the killer.

Courtney tried the door handle for the fiftieth time. It was just as locked as the previous forty-nine times. The face of her guard appeared in the round window in the door. He was a friendly enough guy who introduced himself as Sixth Officer Taylor Hantin. It was his job to watch over Courtney and make sure she stayed put, though Courtney didn't think he had to bother. There was no way she was getting out of that steel dungeon. She was about to try the door handle for the fifty-first time, when an idea struck her that was so simple, she kicked herself for not thinking of it before. Now that the crew knew she was on board, there was no longer any need for secrecy. Maybe, she thought, if she couldn't get to Mark, Mark might come to her. She leaped at the door and knocked on the round glass.

"Excuse me!" she called politely.

Sixth Officer Hantin appeared at the window. Courtney thought he was probably in his twenties. He was young to be an officer, but then again he was a *sixth* officer. Not exactly high up in the officer pecking order.

"Yes, miss?" he replied politely.

Courtney was happy she wasn't being treated like a dangerous criminal. The British crew was polite. Or at least, as polite as you can be while locking you into a tin can and watching you with a loaded gun on your hip.

"I know I don't deserve any special consideration, but it's very important that I see one of the passengers," Courtney said. She tried to sound as innocent and helpless as possible.

"I'm afraid that's against regulations, miss," he replied, but with sympathy.

"I know," Courtney pouted. "But I'm in a lot of trouble here, and I've got nobody to turn to except for my friend. He doesn't even know I'm here, but he'd want to."

Every word she spoke was deliberately vague, but the absolute truth.

"I don't know . . ."

Courtney sensed he was weakening.

"Could you at least tell him that I'm here?" she begged.

Sixth Officer Hantin looked at Courtney through the glass window. Courtney tried to look as needy as possible. Finally the officer smiled.

"What's his name?"

"Mark Dimond," Courtney answered quickly. "Thank you so much, Officer. You don't know what a wonderful thing you're doing."

"It's 'Sixth Officer' and let's hope I don't get thrown in the brig the same as you," he said, and walked off.

Courtney punched the air in victory. She absolutely knew that when Mark found out she was on board, he'd come to see her. She realized that getting caught by the crew might have been the best possible thing to have happened. Saint Dane had turned her in, and it was about to backfire on him.

Courtney went from trying to puzzle her way out of the prison, to fretting over what she would say to Mark. There was so much he needed to know. Mark hadn't read any of Bobby's journals from Quillan. He didn't know that the woman he was with, Nevva Winter, was the Traveler from Quillan and a traitor who'd joined Saint Dane. Without Nevva Winter, Quillan would not have fallen. She betrayed her own people, and the Travelers.

Courtney tried to prepare a speech, but didn't know where Mark's head would be. Was he forced into coming to First Earth? Had he been tricked? Or had the unthinkable happened? Had he joined Saint Dane the same as Nevva? She discounted that last option as impossible. No matter what, she knew she had to do two things: stop him from introducing his Forge technology to First Earth, and warn him that somebody on board was going to shoot him. If she could do those two things, dealing with Saint Dane and Nevva Winter would be the least of their problems.

An hour passed. Mark didn't show. Neither did Sixth Officer Hantin. Courtney started to worry. The ship was big, but not *that* big. It wouldn't take Hantin that long to find Mark. Or maybe he'd changed his mind. Or maybe he'd got to Mark and Mark didn't want to see her. Or could the worst thing have happened already? Could Mark already have been shot? All those possibilities raced through Courtney's head, making her pace again. With each passing minute she grew more anxious. She was about to bang on the door again and demand to see a ship's officer, when she heard a squeak.

The door was being unlocked.

Courtney froze. There was a lump in her throat. Her heart raced even faster. She was about to be reunited with Mark. The door opened and Sixth Officer Hantin poked his head in. He spotted Courtney and said, "No funny business now, miss."

Courtney nodded silently. Sixth Officer Hantin stepped back into the corridor, and Courtney heard him say, "You sure you'll be all right?"

There was no answer. The door opened a few inches farther and someone stepped inside.

Nevva Winter.

The fallen Traveler stood there facing Courtney, looking every bit like an older woman from 1937. She wore a beautiful evening gown that sparkled with light cast from the single bulb in Courtney's cell. Over the dress she had on a short fur wrap to guard against the night air. Her hair and makeup were perfect. She looked to Courtney like a glamorous movie star from the golden age of Hollywood.

She also looked like a traitor. Courtney wanted to rip her throat out.

"Do you know who I am?" Nevva asked.

"Where is he?" Courtney asked coldly.

"I'm not a villain, Courtney," Nevva said calmly. "Neither is Saint Dane."

Courtney wasn't sure if she should laugh or scream.

"No, he's a great guy," Courtney said sarcastically. "Sure, he's destroyed a couple of civilizations, but who hasn't?"

"This is a revolution," Nevva said, maintaining her composure. "There are casualties in every revolution. It's unfortunate, but inevitable. The future of all humanity is at stake.

When you think of it that way, no price is too high."

"Do you really believe that?" Courtney asked, her anger rising. "I mean seriously? The guy is a coldblooded killer. No, I take that back. There's nothing cold about it. He *enjoys* it. How could you think whatever it is he has planned for Halla could be justified by the misery he's caused?"

"Because I know what that vision is," Nevva answered.

"Then please, share!" Courtney demanded. "Tell me I'm wrong. Tell me Bobby and the Travelers are wrong. Tell me the thousands—no, millions—of people whose lives he's destroyed are all going to be better off because of his evil. I'd love to hear all that."

Courtney walked closer to Nevva. With each step her anger grew. Nevva didn't move. Courtney was a moment away from taking a swing at her when she saw something that made her stop. Someone else had entered the room. Standing in front of the open door, sheepishly, was Mark Dimond. Courtney saw him and nearly burst into tears. Suddenly Nevva meant nothing.

"Hi, Courtney" was all he said.

Courtney's first thought was that in spite of the incredibly tense situation, Mark didn't stutter. The second thing she realized was that Mark looked grown up. His curly black hair was cut short and, for a change, was combed. The wire-rimmed glasses made him look ten years older than he was. The bizarre image was completed by his tuxedo. He was no longer the nerdy kid from Stony Brook. Mark looked like a man. Courtney could barely breathe, let alone talk.

"I'll leave you two alone," Nevva said, and quietly backed out of the room. Before leaving, she looked at Mark and said, "I'll be right outside."

She left. Mark and Courtney stood facing each other for the first time since the afternoon Bobby's Journal #25 from Quillan had arrived on Second Earth. It was later that night that Mark's parents were killed when their flight disappeared over the Atlantic. It was the beginning of the odyssey that led them to be staring at each other awkwardly in a prison cell on an ocean liner on First Earth. Neither knew what to say. It was Courtney who finally took the leap.

"So, how 'bout them Yankees?" she asked lightly.

Mark chuckled. Courtney did too. The ice had been broken. Sort of.

"What do you think of my stateroom?" Courtney asked with false cheer. "Sweet, huh? You want me to order you something from the kitchen?"

"You shouldn't be here, Courtney," Mark said softly.

Courtney could have sworn his voice was deeper. It was definitely more assured.

"Yes, I should," she said quickly. "It's you who shouldn't be here. But you are."

"You don't know what's happening—"

"Yeah, I do," Courtney snapped. "I know everything." She took a breath, realizing she was getting too emotional. "There's so much I have to tell you, Mark, but I want to hear it from you first. Why did you come here? What happened that night when . . ." She didn't finish her sentence.

Mark finished it for her, saying, "When my parents were killed?"

Courtney nodded. Mark sat down on a wooden chair. Courtney leaned against the bunk. Now that she was about to hear the words she had been waiting to hear for so long, she wasn't so sure she wanted Mark to say them. She feared what she was about to learn.

Mark fidgeted. This was difficult for him. For a moment Courtney thought he was reverting to his old form, the insecure

geek. He wasn't. When he spoke, it was with authority and without a stutter.

"That night Andy Mitchell and I went to clean up his uncle's
florist shop. The sprinkler had broken. It was a mess. If we didn't
salvage all those Christmas flowers, his uncle would lose his
business. That's why we stayed and my parents took the flight to
Florida without us."

"I remember all that," Courtney said.

"Then you know what happened," Mark said solemnly. "Their
plane went down over the Atlantic. Everyone was lost."

Courtney nodded and said, "I'm sorry, Mark."

"I didn't find out about it until nearly midnight," Mark continued. "We'd been working in the store the whole time. The airline
tracked down my cell-phone number. At first I thought it was a
joke. Things like that don't happen in real life, you know? All it
took was one look at CNN to see it was true." Mark hesitated.
The memory was tough to relive. "I tried to call you."

"I know," Courtney choked out. "I'd turned off my phone. I
didn't get the message until the next morning. If only I had—"

"It's okay. There was nothing you could have done. But
somebody showed up who could."

"Who?" Courtney asked, suddenly back on alert.

"Nevva Winter. The Traveler from Quillan. You know that
Saint Dane won Quillan, right?"

"Yeah, I heard something about that," Courtney said dismissively. "Nevva Winter came to Second Earth?"

"She escaped from Quillan before the fall," Mark said. "She
told me that Saint Dane was breaking down the borders between
the territories and Bobby needed my help."

"Oh, did she?" Courtney said sarcastically. "Did our friend
Andy Mitchell hear all this?"

"Yeah," Mark said, hanging his head as if ashamed. "He

shouldn't have, but I wasn't thinking straight. I mean, I'd just heard my parents were killed. Still, I tried to talk to Nevva in private, but she said she needed Andy's help too."

"Yeah, I'll bet she did," Courtney said with even more sarcasm.

"Andy wasn't as surprised as you'd think," Mark continued. "Sure, he was a little freaked, but remember, he'd read Bobby's first journals, so it wasn't totally out of the blue. I admitted to him that we didn't write them after all. I didn't know what else to do. Mitchell knows about the Travelers now. He knows everything."

Courtney realized that Mark still didn't know Andy Mitchell was Saint Dane. She was all sorts of anxious to tell him, but wanted to hear the whole story first.

Mark continued, "Nevva told us that after losing Quillan, Bobby realized the only way to beat Saint Dane was to use his own tactics against him. Any hope of keeping the territories separate was gone, and the demon's next target was Second Earth. It's what we always feared, Courtney. We knew it would happen someday, and that day had finally arrived. But Nevva had a way to stop him."

"I can't wait to hear it," Courtney quipped.

"She said that by changing the past, we could create a new future that Saint Dane wasn't expecting. That's why we came to First Earth."

That was it. Courtney nodded in understanding. It was all about Nevva, just like on Quillan. "Let me understand," Courtney said. "Nevva told you and Mitchell to bring your Forge technology to First Earth and said it would change the course of history so Saint Dane would fail on Second Earth?"

"Yes."

"And you believed her?" Courtney screamed.

"It was more than that."

"I hope so," Courtney shot back. She was getting angrier by the second. "Mark, I love you to death, but I can't believe you'd do something so huge on the word of somebody you didn't even know!"

"There was more," Mark said softly. "Nevva said if we changed the course of events, my parents would survive."

Courtney was about to yell again, but stopped. It was all making sense. Nevva and Saint Dane had fooled Mark into believing he was not only helping to protect Second Earth, but saving his parents as well. Saint Dane knew exactly how to get to Mark. Poor, innocent Mark. Courtney had always feared the demon. Now she hated him. She was going to have to tell Mark the truth. Nothing would bring his parents back. The thought was painful. Mark thought he was doing the right thing. Instead, he gave Saint Dane the tools to bring Halla crashing down.

As horrible as she felt, Courtney also felt a glimmer of hope. Mark was not a villain. He had not put in with Saint Dane. What he had done was for a noble purpose. Mark was still Mark. Better still, he had not yet introduced Forge to the territory. The flume had sent her where she needed to be, when she needed to be there. There was still time to stop him. But to do that, she was going to have to present him with some horrible truths. She knelt down by Mark and took his hands.

"Listen to me, Mark," Courtney began. "I understand why you're doing this. I can't imagine where my head would be if I suddenly lost my parents. I wouldn't be thinking straight either. If somebody threw me a lifeline and said they'd make it all better, man, I'd grab it. This isn't your fault."

"Fault?" Mark said with surprise. "I don't understand."

Courtney took a breath and continued. "You've been lied to. Big-time. Like all good lies, there's just enough truth to make it seem plausible. Yes, the Travelers lost Quillan. Yes, your parents died in that crash. And yes, by bringing Forge technology to First Earth, you can change the future of Second Earth. But that's where the truth takes a very different course than what you were told."

Mark stared right into Courtney's eyes, hanging on her every word.

"I don't know how I'm going to tell you this," she said nervously.

"Just tell me."

"Mark, Andy Mitchell is Saint Dane. He has been ever since we've known him. He worked his way into your life and became your friend so the two of you could create Forge and do exactly what you're doing with it. But it won't save Second Earth, Mark. Forge technology is going to start a chain of events that will lead to the creation of a force that Saint Dane will use to crush Halla. It was his plan from the beginning, Mark. Nevva Winter isn't your friend. She's a Traveler, but she helped Saint Dane win Quillan. I wish I had Bobby's journals here to show you. Nevva Winter is a traitor. The two of them have fooled you into believing that what you're doing is right, but it couldn't be more wrong."

Mark looked at the ground. Courtney couldn't imagine what he was going through. She hated to have to tell him that way.

"Why are you saying all this?" he finally asked.

"Because you have to know. I'm sorry."

"But you're wrong." Mark jumped up and paced to the far side of the room.

"I'm not!" Courtney countered. "I know this is hard to take, but it's the truth. The day after your parents died, I did what you asked me and went to the flume, remember? Something happened while I was there. Mark, I know how Forge is going to change Second Earth. I've seen it. You accelerated the evolution of technology. Things aren't the same. But there's one thing that didn't change."

"What's that?" Mark asked.

Courtney hesitated. She wanted to say it gently, but realized Mark needed convincing, so she didn't pull her punches. "Your parents were still dead, Mark. What you did here on First Earth, what you're *about* to do on First Earth didn't change that. They're gone."

Mark kept staring at the deck.

"That's your proof that Nevva lied to you," Courtney continued. "Your parents will not be saved. They tricked you the way Saint Dane has tricked so many others. They tempted you with the promise of saving Second Earth. Of helping Bobby. Of protecting Halla, and of bringing your parents back from the dead. None of that will happen."

Mark shifted. Courtney thought he was starting to sweat.

"But it's not too late!" she exclaimed encouragingly. "That's why I'm here. Now that you know the truth, you can stop it. You can put Halla back on its natural course. Right here. Right now."

Mark wiped his eyes. Courtney thought he was containing his emotions pretty well, considering what she had just laid on him.

"I don't understand," he said in a very small voice.

"Ask me," Courtney implored. "Anything. I know it all."

Mark looked at her with red eyes. "I don't understand why you're lying to me."

Courtney was rocked. Her mouth hung open. "I—I'm not," she stammered. "Why would you believe Nevva Winter over me?"

"Mark?" came a woman's voice from outside the door.

Courtney recognized the voice, but couldn't place it.

"Come on in," Mark called.

Two people stepped into the ward. When she saw them, Courtney nearly fainted. Her head actually went light. She didn't understand what she was seeing. It made no sense. Her legs buckled and she sat down on the edge of the bunk.

"I was just leaving," Mark told the new visitors.

Courtney looked up at the man and the woman who stood beside Mark. The man wore a tuxedo, the woman was dressed in an evening gown. They looked totally normal, and absolutely impossible.

"We know, Courtney," the woman said kindly, sensing her confusion. "We know everything. Mark explained it all. The Travelers, the territories, and what happened to Bobby Pendragon."

The man added, "We're proud of you, Courtney. We know you've been under a lot of stress with the accident and all. When we get to London, we'll make sure that all the charges are dropped, and we'll pay for your passage. All we want is for you and Mark to finish what you started, and help Bobby stop Saint Dane."

The woman added, "Bobby needs you. Halla needs you. Try to get some rest."

Courtney was speechless. Her brain was doing its best to reject the fact that standing before her were Mr. and Mrs. Dimond. Mark's parents. Alive. On First Earth.

"We'll check on you tomorrow morning," said Mrs. Dimond.

"Good night," Mr. Dimond added.

They left, leaving Mark alone with Courtney. Mark looked at her like a disapproving parent. "Maybe tomorrow you'll explain to me what's really going on."

He left and closed the door behind him. The screeching sound of the lock being thrown echoed through the spartan infirmary. Courtney didn't move. Everything she believed to be true had just been turned inside out. She probably would have sat that way all night, if she hadn't been nudged back to life by a twitching on her finger.

Her ring was activating.

Bobby's next journal was about to arrive.

IBARA

I'm ready to explode.

All I can do is wait. It's killing me. The next few hours will determine the future of Ibara. Of Veelox. Of Halla. It's like waiting for a storm that's slowly creeping closer. You know it's going to hit but there's no way of knowing when. Or where. I want it to hit soon, because I'm ready to hit back. Hard. The last few days I've spent getting ready. Days? Did I say "days"? I have no idea how long it's been since Siry and I came back to Ibara after escaping from Rubic City. Has it been days? Or weeks? I know that makes no sense. After you read this journal, it will.

Courtney, as I'm writing this, I have to believe you haven't found Mark. Or maybe you did, and it didn't make any difference. What's about to happen on Ibara now seems inevitable. I'm ready. I am *so* ready. I can't predict how things are going to go, but if we lose Ibara, it won't be because we didn't try. No way. Right now I'm so charged up, I can't wait for it to begin. I want to make some noise. It's taking all my concentration to sit still and write this journal. It's an important one. Courtney, when I write to you next, assuming I'm able to write to you again, the future of Halla will be determined. Saint Dane will either be finished, or the Convergence will have begun. Either way, I want you to know why I've done what I've done. I'm playing by Saint Dane's rules now. Which means I'm not playing by any rules. I didn't see any other way. Hopefully, when the dust settles, Halla will be safe once and for all.

Until then, it's going to get ugly.

Let me take you back to the night when Siry and I drove the skimmer to Ibara from Rubic City. Like I said, I don't know if that was a few days ago, or a few months ago. Time has lost all meaning for me.

As I wrote, Siry and I landed after dark. We pulled the skimmer into the dense growth just off a quiet, rocky beach and covered it with palm fronds. From there we made our way through the jungle to the Jakill clearing. Seeing the empty clearing in the moonlight was eerie, and sad. This was a place that was full of energy and hope. Now it felt more like a memorial to failed dreams. I could only imagine how Siry felt. His dreams had been crushed. His friends were gone. I had to keep him focused and moving forward. There would be time to grieve later. There was always time to grieve.

We needed to rest. There was some food left around, so we ate what we could. I didn't have much of an appetite. Fear of impending doom will do that. But I ate. Who knew when we'd get another chance? I also finished my previous journal. Again, who knew when I'd get another chance? I'm guessing we sat in the clearing for about three hours. Neither of us slept. The adrenaline was rushing too hard.

"This is dumb," I finally said. "I don't know about you, but I'm too pumped to sleep. We've gotta get to the tribunal and warn them of the attack."

"That won't be easy," Siry said. "We're outlaws. They may lock us up before we get the chance to say a word."

"So how do we get to them?" I asked.

"Telleo," Siry said with confidence. "If anybody can get Genj's ear, it's his daughter."

"Will she do it?"

"I know she will," Siry replied. Siry gave me a grave look. "Pendragon, we have to do everything we can to stop them."

"We will," I said, trying to sound positive.

We made our way back toward the village, guided by moonlight. We ran along narrow jungle paths. I kept my eyes on Siry. If he jumped, I jumped. If he ducked, I ducked. I stumbled and fell only once. When we hit the beach, Siry slowed down and kept to the jungle line. It was a few hours before sunrise. The village was asleep. It was the perfect time for us to get to Telleo. Siry led me past the hut where I had first woken up on Ibara, through the dark village, toward Tribunal Mountain. We finally stopped at a small hut not far from the central meeting area where Telleo and I had danced during the Festival of Zelin. Zelin. Was that some centuries-old version of Zetlin?

Siry gestured at it as if to say, "This is where she lives." He put his finger to his lips in a "shush" gesture, then entered the hut.

The small hut had a few pieces of bamboo furniture and lots of cut flowers. Telleo liked to surround herself with beautiful things. I followed Siry as he moved quickly and stealthily through the first room and into the second. There Telleo lay sleeping on her low bed. She wore the same type of clothes to sleep as she wore during the day. Siry knelt quietly by her bedside. Telleo turned in her sleep. Siry quickly but gently clamped one hand near her mouth and nudged her arm.

"Telleo," he whispered.

Telleo lazily opened her eyes halfway and stared at him in a sleepy haze. Then, as if shot with an electric current, her eyes blew wide open in shock. She sat up, ready to scream. Siry was prepared. He gently held his hand over her mouth.

"It's okay," he whispered soothingly. "It's me and Pendragon."

Telleo recognized him, but didn't relax. At first I thought she was having trouble waking up and shaking off what must have seemed like a nightmare because she kept shaking her head no.

"It's okay," he assured her.

Telleo grabbed Siry's hand and pulled it away from her mouth. She looked terrified. "It's not okay!" she whispered with force.

"It's all right," Siry whispered soothingly. "We need your help."

"You need to get out of here!" she whispered quickly. "They've been watching my hut since you left."

Uh-oh. Telleo's house was under surveillance. That's why she wanted us out, not because we frightened her.

"Go!" she commanded, getting up. "Go back to the jungle before you are—"

"Arrested?" came a bold voice from the doorway to the first room.

Siry and I spun to see several security guards. They were as intimidating as I'd remembered, with their long hair and their heavy clubs strapped to their waists. Or in some cases, held tight in their hands, ready to bean us if we made a move.

Siry thought faster than I did and turned back to Telleo. "Ibara is in danger," he said quickly. "That's why we came back, to warn everyone. We need to speak with the tribunal."

The security force made a move toward us. I didn't fight them. They had us.

"He's serious, Telleo," I said. "We need to speak with your father."

"Stop!" Telleo ordered the security force.

They didn't. They grabbed us roughly, twisting our arms behind our backs.

"I said stop!" Telleo demanded. She pulled one of the goons away from me.

"Please, Telleo," the guy said. "They are thieves and pirates. Let us do our job."

We stood there awkwardly. They wanted to arrest us, but it didn't look like they wanted to go against the daughter of the chief minister, either. Telleo walked right up to me and looked me in the eye. "What kind of danger is Ibara in?"

"The island is going to be attacked," I said. "We think most of the Jakills are dead. If we don't get to your father and warn him, the whole island might end up the same way."

I saw the surprise and horror in her eyes. "Is this true?" she asked Siry.

Siry nodded. "I think they're all dead, Telleo. We found the truth and it's a nightmare. We have to see Genj."

Telleo looked numb. The security goons didn't look much better. Telleo said to them, "I'm not asking you to let them go. I'm asking you to bring them to the tribunal. With me. I'll take responsibility."

The security guys exchanged nervous looks.

"Arrest them," Telleo added. "Do your job. Just let me bring them to the tribunal to tell their story. If they have something to say that will help Ibara, my father should hear it. If they're telling the truth, you don't want to be responsible for keeping it from them."

Several of them looked at the one guy who was holding Siry. My guess was he was the boss.

"All right," he said reluctantly. "But if this is a trick—"

"You're going to wish this were a trick," I said bluntly.

Telleo took charge by boldly walking out the door. The others weren't so sure what to do.

"Hurry!" Telleo shouted from the next room.

Obediently the security goons pushed us out, and we were on our way to Tribunal Mountain. I heard the sounds of birds waking up to start the new day. Sunrise wouldn't be far behind. I worried that along with it would come tens of thousands of dados and complete havoc. When we got to the mountain, Telleo left us alone with the security force in one of the lower-level cavern rooms and went to rouse the tribunal. It was an awkward few minutes. Siry and I sat along one wall, while six security thugs stood across from us with their arms folded, staring. To them we were dirt. They weren't going to like us any better after they heard our story. Too bad for them.

Telleo wasn't gone long. She ran back into the room excited and out of breath. "They'll see you," she announced. "Right now."

"They're here already?" I asked. "Isn't it a little early?"

Telleo's eyes were wide with excitement. "It's an incredible day," she said. "I had no idea!"

"What's going on?" Siry asked.

"Come and see," she said, and hurried off.

We started to follow but were quickly grabbed by the security force. They kept us under control as we followed Telleo. I didn't fight. Truth be told, we deserved this kind of treatment. We *were* thieves and pirates. I was just happy to know we were going to get the chance to talk to the tribunal. We traveled the same route up the stone stairs that I'd taken several days before. The routine was the same. The guards kept us on the far end of the large, cavernlike room until the three members of the tribunal called for us. We had only been in the cavern a few seconds when Genj and the other two women of the tribunal came hurrying across the large space, headed for their seats in the dead center of the room. As he walked, Genj gestured for us to be brought forward. The security guys gave us a shove, and we were on our way. The tribunal sat down and stared at us. They looked anxious, as if we had pulled them away from something important. I wasn't sure if I should talk or wait until I was asked. Telleo stepped forward and kicked things off.

"I know what you think of these boys," she began. "They stole a valuable ship."

Drea, the freckled woman on the tribunal, interjected, "You have no idea just how valuable that ship was."

"I agree," Telleo said. "But whatever you think of their methods, I believe they have discovered something that is vital to the future of Ibara, and today's success."

Today's success? What the heck did that mean? Something big was going on, but what? The tribunal continued to stare at us skeptically. I'm embarrassed to admit that my brain froze. I guess it was because I put myself in their position and imagined what it would be like to hear what I was about to say. I didn't know what to do. Should I just blurt out that an army of deadly robots from another territory was headed to their island on Jet Skis, ready to overrun the place? How could they possibly believe that? It all suddenly seemed so futile.

Luckily, Siry didn't have the same problem. "The ship we stole is on the bottom of the ocean. All my friends are dead."

The tribunal snapped a look at him. He had definitely gotten their attention. The last time we stood there, Siry was belligerent and obnoxious. Now he sounded about as deadly serious as, well, as the situation was.

"All we wanted was to learn the truth about our home and our lives," Siry continued with passion. "I'm sorry to say that we found it. I don't want my friends to have died for nothing. The best thing I can do to honor their memory is to stand here today and tell you that we learned Ibara is in deep trouble."

The members of the tribunal exchanged looks.

"Leave them here," Genj ordered the security team.

"But sir!" the big one protested.

"We'll be fine," Genj assured him. "Keep your men down below. We'll call if we need you."

Once again the security team exchanged nervous looks.

"Go!" Genj ordered.

They backed off quickly, nearly bumping into one another. They left the cavern, though I was sure they were waiting just beyond the entryway. The old man looked between the two of us and took a tired breath.

"So," he asked. "Did you find Rubic City?"

You could have knocked me over. Siry looked as stunned as I felt.

"What is Rubic City?" Telleo asked, as confused as I was, but for different reasons.

Genj stood and paced behind his chair. He looked troubled. He had no idea just how troubled he was about to be.

"You went in search of the truth," Genj said. "A truth that has been kept from the people of Ibara for centuries."

"You admit it?" Siry asked, stunned. "You admit keeping the secrets of our past from your people?"

"It was necessary," Genj replied.

"Necessary?" Siry shouted. "What about all those who

questioned you? The people who disappeared? Was it necessary for them to die?"

"Why do you assume they're dead?" the dark woman, Moman, asked.

"Because they're gone!" Siry snapped. "You can't tell me they're not dead. Or stuck in some dungeon to keep them from causing trouble."

"Would you like to see them?" Drea asked.

Siry froze. He had no comeback for that.

I shot a look at Telleo and asked, "Do you know what's going on?"

"A little, yes," she said. "It's wonderful."

"Wonderful?" Siry blurted out. He was as confused as I was.

Genj said, "This is a day that Remudi worked for as hard and tirelessly as anyone. I could say he dedicated his life to it." He looked to Siry and said, "Would you like to see the greatness your father helped achieve?"

Siry didn't know how to react.

Genj looked to me and added, "Remudi told us of your arrival, Pendragon."

Moman said, "Why do you think we let you free? Do you truly think we believed you suffered from amnesia?"

Oh well, I guess I fooled a grand total of nobody with that ploy.

Drea added, "Remudi said that if he was not here to see this day, a stranger named Pendragon, who wore a silver ring, most certainly would be. He told us to trust this stranger, for he would do all he could to help us."

Genj looked to Siry and said, "And he told us to trust his son. I must admit, I was skeptical. It's why we put the two of you together. The theft of a ship was the last thing I expected."

I took a chance and said, "By stealing that ship, we might have given Ibara a second chance."

"And what of the pilgrimage?" Drea asked. "Those ships are invaluable."

"The what?" Siry asked.

Genj backed away. "Come," he bellowed. "You seek the truth, Siry? It's time you saw it all." He turned and strode across the cavern, followed right behind by Moman and Drea. I wasn't sure what to do, so I looked to Telleo.

"What's going on?" I asked.

"I knew this day was coming," she said. "I had no idea it would be today."

"What's going to happen?" I asked.

"It's the rebirth of Veelox," she said, and gave me a warm hug. She seemed truly ecstatic. "Come on!" She hurried after her father.

Siry shook his head. He had no idea what anybody was talking about. All we could do was follow. We were lead up higher into Tribunal Mountain. We took several winding, rock stairways that brought us into the upper reaches of the peak. After walking through a long tunnel, we emerged into a room with a wide opening that gave us a spectacular view out the back side of the mountain—the side that faced away from the village. The three members of the tribunal stood at this window, looking over a vista that stretched from the dense jungles of Ibara clear down to the ocean. Siry, Telleo, and I joined them to witness a wondrous sight.

Far below in the jungle, a wide trail snaked from somewhere deep on the island. It traveled past the mountain and on toward the sea. The trail ended at the wharf where the ten brightly colored sailing ships were kept. Nine, actually. One was at the bottom of Rubic City's harbor.

Genj announced proudly, "Today is the culmination of a plan that was centuries in the making. The brave people you see below are the pilgrims who will bring our world back to life."

There were dozens of people on the trail below, all dressed in typical, bright Ibara fashion. There were men, women, and children. All walked quickly and orderly toward the wharf and the sailing ships.

Most of the ships had left the wharf and were headed out to sea. Even from where we stood, I could see their decks were loaded with people. Many were still on the docks, boarding the remaining ships. Others scurried around the docks, casting off lines and helping to load freight. Eight of the ships were either out on the ocean already, or starting to push off and raise their sails. It was a spectacular sight to see against the rising sun. I wished to heck I knew what it all meant.

"It's a proud day," Genj said.

It actually looked as if he were crying. The two women of the tribunal were definitely teary. They waved at the people below, bidding them farewell, though they were too far away to see it.

"Where are they going?" Siry asked.

"To the future," Genj said. "Just as Aja Killian planned."

Hearing Aja's name rocked me. I had forgotten that the colony of Ibara was originally her plan . . . conceived three hundred years before.

"Help me out here," I said. "What is happening?"

Without taking his eyes from the ships, Genj said, "You saw Rubic City. Do you know of Lifelight?"

"More than I want to know."

"Then you saw the destruction it caused," Genj explained. "Millions of people died. It was self-inflicted genocide. Aja

Killian was a phader who saw it coming. She banded together with the few who resisted the temptation of Lifelight and created a plan for the future of Veelox."

Siry and I knew of the plan. We had seen Aja's journal. But we didn't know it all.

Genj continued, "They chose this island of Ibara to be their lifeboat. It was at one time a military base used to defend the mainland. Automatic weapons existed to protect it from attack. Forty people left Rubic City to start a new life here. They had a simple philosophy, which was to not let technology define their lives. They didn't want history to repeat itself. That's why we live the way we do, relying minimally on technology. Our culture, our way of life, was carefully planned and chosen by our ancestors. We are all the descendants of the forty."

Drea continued the story saying, "The first part of Aja's plan was to create a settlement. They lived in this mountain at first, since it was already honeycombed with tunnels and rooms. Eventually they built huts that over time became the village of Rayne. Children were born. Families grew. More villages were built across the island. The sad history of Veelox and the origin of Ibara was not passed down to the young. The fear was that the temptation to rediscover Lifelight would be too great. With the passing of each generation, fewer and fewer people knew the true story. Aja's plan allowed for a three-member tribunal that would be voted on by the villagers. Only the tribunals knew the full history, and shared as much of the knowledge as was necessary to carry out the ultimate plan."

"Why?" Siry asked. "Why was it so important to keep the truth a secret?"

Genj snapped a cold look to Siry. "To keep the curious

from doing exactly as you did. The fear was that temptation to leave the island would be too great. Ibara needed to be strong in order to be the seat of a new civilization. Ibara needed its people. All its people."

I said, "So the idea was to create a new population, right here on this island."

"Yes," Genj answered. "The biggest concern was disease. A virus, an infection, any sickness would have been devastating. We needed to keep the island free from all outside contamination, and to do that, we needed to keep our people away from any contact with the rest of Veelox. As you can see, it has been successful, but only because of the secrecy."

I looked down on the ships. The last passengers were boarding the final vessel.

"So what is all this?" I asked.

Moman answered, "The pilgrimage was planned from the beginning. Once the population grew large enough to ensure our survival, we began choosing people from the general population to live in another village on the far side of the island, where they were taught the realities of Veelox. It was an honor to be chosen, for these people would be the pioneers. They would be the first to venture off this island and repopulate the world. They are the pilgrims of Rayne."

Genj added, "Those ships are carrying them off to start colonies throughout the mainland."

Siry asked, "So the people who disappeared became the pilgrims?"

"You're looking at them," Genj answered. "It was Aja Killian's vision from the beginning. It's a shame her life ended in such tragedy."

"What do you mean?" I asked quickly.

Genj answered, "Aja Killian never set foot on Ibara. After creating the plan that would save Veelox, she was assassinated by Flighters only days before the forty sailed for their new home."

I had mixed feelings about all that I heard. I was proud of Aja. She had first tried to save Veelox and beat Saint Dane by creating the Reality Bug. Technology is what endangered Veelox, and she tried to fight back with technology. It failed. So Aja went the opposite way and chose a route that turned its back on technology. Her plan wasn't a quick fix. It was a battle that would be fought over centuries. It was a battle she was on the verge of winning. She wanted another shot at Saint Dane. She got it. Veelox was about to be reborn.

Moman added, "Once the pilgrims are safely away, we will begin the final process, which is to educate the entire island of our heritage. Our population is strong enough now so that people can safely choose for themselves if they wish to stay, or reach out to the rest of our world and join the new colonies. Our mission is nearly complete. Veelox has been saved."

This was it. This was the turning point of Ibara. The second turning point for Veelox. It's why Remudi was on the tribunal. The Traveler from Ibara was working to fulfill the vision of the Traveler from Veelox. It was the way it was meant to be.

"Why today?" I asked.

"The Flighters grow bolder," Genj continued. "The attack two days ago forced our decision. We feared for our ships. They took many years to build. Without them, there would be no pilgrimage." Genj left the window and went right to Siry. "Because of your adventuring, there is one less ship. We decided to go now, before we lost more."

Siry hung his head.

Genj continued. "Your father lived for this day, Siry. Seeing those ships under sail, carrying the hopes for a new Veelox with them, was a sight he would have been proud to witness. I can't say he'd be as proud of you."

Siry looked horrible. I wasn't feeling so hot myself. I helped steal that ship, and I was about to throw a pretty big downer into their glorious day. Pilgrimage or no, there was trouble ahead.

"Maybe we actually helped the pilgrimage," I said.

Genj shot me a look of disdain. "And how could you possibly think that?"

"Because of what we found in Rubic City. There's going to be a war, Genj. Ibara will soon be under attack. I don't know if your defenses are strong enough to repel this army or not, but even if you're able to protect the island, those ships would have been targets. The fact that they're sailing safely away is already a huge victory, even if there are only nine."

Genj looked to the women of the tribunal with dismay. They didn't know what to do with the information. Should they be relieved? Or terrified? My vote would have been for both. The war was coming, but for the first time since I'd seen Rubic City, I felt a ray of hope. Hearing the story of Veelox and Ibara and Aja Killian's brilliant plan made me believe the pilgrimage was the turning point for Ibara. Saint Dane had to know that. Attacking Ibara with his army of dados would have destroyed the pilgrimage and set Veelox back again. No question. But with the launch of the fleet, the impossible had happened.

Saint Dane was too late.

He could attack and lay the entire island to waste, but the hope for Veelox was now out to sea. I almost laughed. Was it possible that Saint Dane would call off the attack once he realized the turning point had passed?

"Did you know about this, Telleo?" Siry asked

"Not everything," she answered. "I knew the time was getting closer for pilgrims to be sent out to explore the rest of the world, but I didn't know the reasons, or the history of Veelox. I still don't."

"Tell us of your involvement, Pendragon," Genj asked. "Who are you really and why has Remudi put his trust in you?"

All eyes turned to me. Gulp. How was I going to explain that? I decided to simply tell them the truth about the army that was amassing in Rubic City. The tribunal had to prepare the island for war. With the passing of the turning point, I could only hope that Saint Dane would back off. But I couldn't guarantee it. I had to convince the tribunal that they would soon be under attack.

Unfortunately, I never got the chance. Our conversation was stopped short by a far-off sound. My heart dropped. Genj was looking right at me when we heard it. I saw the surprise in his eyes. I wanted to hold on to that moment. I didn't want him to see what I feared was happening. This was their moment of triumph, but with that one sound I knew it wouldn't last.

It was the sound of cannon fire.

"No!" cried Moman.

Everyone ran for the opening and gazed out to sea. I walked slowly toward the opening in the rock and saw exactly what I feared. All nine ships were away from their piers and sailing toward open ocean. Most had their sails up or close to it. They were scattered along the coast, headed for different destinations.

Beyond them were four gunboats loaded with Flighters.

The colorful, unarmed ships that carried the hope of a new Veelox were under attack.

Saint Dane wasn't too late.

IBARA

I don't know why I let myself believe, even for a second, that things might work out for the best. When has that ever happened? Ever. Saint Dane was always one step ahead of me. I started this day thinking the biggest threat to the people of Ibara would be the attack of an army of dados. Reality turned out to be much worse. These people were on the verge of a new beginning. They were about to plant the seeds that would, hopefully, grow into a new world. Those are the moments that Saint Dane targets. The moments of victory. The times when hope is at its greatest. That's when he strikes.

This time he struck very hard.

The gunboats swooped in quickly. They were much faster and could outmaneuver the larger, heavier sailing ships. That much I knew because I had been in the middle of just such an attack. I had to think the pilgrim's ships were even more sluggish because they were loaded down with people. They had no defense. Their ships had no guns. They were doomed.

The gunboats first targeted the ships under sail. They fired round after round, point-blank into the hulls of the wooden ships. Even from far away I could hear the sound of the wooden hulls being torn apart. Two ships were on fire and the attack had barely begun. Flames ate up the sails as if they were paper. Terrified people ran up from what must have been carnage below deck. I saw adults grabbing young children and holding tight as they leaped over the side. Some clutched bags for flotation. These ships weren't equipped with modern safety devices like life vests or rafts. The victims were on their own. Many just swam, desperate to get away from the burning ships. That didn't stop the Flighters. They pounded away with their guns, hammering at the ships until they were nothing but floating piles of burning wood.

The automatic defense system of Ibara surfaced from below. The strange, silver guns rose up from beneath the water and unloaded on the gunboats. But the Flighters had learned from their earlier attack. They kept moving, changing direction quickly, doubling back, weaving in and out of the pilgrim's ships. They made it nearly impossible for the guns to hit their marks. Most of the rounds splashed harmlessly into the water.

Worse, the pilgrims made a huge tactical mistake. They moved toward each other. Like circling the wagons in the Old West, they made a desperate attempt to protect themselves. It was the worst thing they could have done. Not only did they make themselves easier targets for the Flighters, they provided cover for the attackers from the guns. The Flighters quickly put the snarl of pilgrim ships between them and the island. Soon the guns were hitting the pilgrims' ships. It was horrifying to see the innocent people getting slammed by the Flighters from one side, and from friendly fire on the other. In no time, each and every pilgrim ship was either on fire, sinking, or already gone. The island's guns stopped firing, having only caused more damage. It didn't look like a single Flighter gunboat was even nicked.

Survivors churned the water. I expected the Flighters to attack them next. They didn't, I'm happy to say. Small fishing boats were already under way, headed to pick them up. The Flighters didn't bother with them, either. It was pretty clear what their mission was. Sink the pilgrim ships. That would end their quest. Murdering them would have been overkill, so to speak. It took all of twenty minutes for the Flighters to put a thundering, fiery end to generations of planning and hope. To Aja's plan. As the last ship dipped beneath the ocean, the Flighters turned and headed back for Rubic City. They had swooped in like avenging hawks, done their job, and left as quickly as they had come.

Battle? Did I call that a battle? There was no battle. It was a slaughter. Watching it unfold from that mountain was worse than horrible. There was nothing any of us could do except watch and cry. Genj and the women of the tribunal were in shock. They may have known about Veelox's past from the writings of their ancestors, but I didn't think they'd ever experienced something as swift and violent as that. There was no telling how many of the pilgrims were killed. The fishing boats were picking up dozens, but I didn't think there was any way they could have all survived. Not the way those ships were blasted into shrapnel. This was a simple, peaceful world . . . that had just been rudely pulled into reality.

Saint Dane told me that defeat is the most devastating when it comes at the moment of victory. That's what happened before on Veelox. It's what happened on Quillan. Seeing the pilgrim ships blown out of the water was like seeing the archives of Mr. Pop being torched on Quillan. It wasn't just about the destruction of items or the loss of life.

It was about the total and complete obliteration of hope.

I went from stunned, to numb, to angry. Saint Dane had won. Again. He found the turning point of the territory and coerced the people to turn it the wrong way. In this case, his allies were the Flighters. They were just as much a part of Veelox as the people of Ibara. The difference was the people of Ibara wanted to rebuild. The Flighters were animals. Saint Dane liked animals. He knew how to manipulate the weak-minded, the opportunists. I wanted to scream. I wanted to get behind the controls of one of those defense guns and shoot something out of the water. I wanted to feel the pulverizing effect on one of those Flighter gunboats.

My anger wasn't just about the poor pilgrims. This was about Ibara. Veelox. Halla. The territory was there for Saint Dane to take. Ibara was the last holdout of civilization. There was no way it could stand up to an attack by the dados. After that, what? Where would Saint Dane go next? Second Earth? Third Earth? I'd never felt the kind of anger I was feeling at that moment. I guess a better word for it was "rage." I wanted a piece of Saint Dane again, right there. I wanted to fight him. I wanted to take him apart.

Nobody said a word. What could they say? For the tribunal the quest was over. It was a mission that had been handed down to them by their ancestors, and it had failed miserably. It was only going to get worse.

I couldn't let that happen. I had been forming a plan since I first saw the dados, but until that moment, I didn't seriously consider it. It was a last-ditch act born of desperation. It was wrong. But looking down on the destruction of the pilgrim fleet, and knowing that the dados were amassing to attack Ibara made something snap in me. Yes, I was angry. Maybe it was about time. Following the proper rules that Uncle Press set out and playing fair and being the good little Traveler wasn't working anymore. Right and wrong didn't matter anymore. It was time to get dirty. It was time to fight back.

"Genj," I said. "You can't let this cripple you. If you do that, Ibara really will be lost."

"We're already lost," he said, dazed. "It will take generations to replace those ships."

"What's out there, Pendragon?" Telleo asked, frightened. "Who is doing this?"

"Someone who wants to crush you," I said. "Remudi knew that. Now he's dead."

"Dead?" Moman repeated, shocked. "How?"

"He died at the hands of the guy who is going to attack this island. I'm here to stop him."

"How?" Siry asked. "The dados—"

"Gather your people together," I ordered Genj. "Bring them to the center of town. Tell them they're going to have to defend Rayne. They saw what happened to the pilgrims. What's coming will be worse. We're going to need every person in this village who can fight."

Genj was shaken. He looked like a confused, old man. "This is . . . is . . . all wrong. So many generations have planned for this day. It just cannot be!"

I took Telleo by the arm and looked her square in the eye. "Get through to him. You've got to be ready when we get back."

"Where are you going?" Telleo asked.

"Don't even ask. It's up to you all to make sure this village is ready to fight."

"How long will you be gone?" Drea asked.

"Not long. Maybe a few hours. We can't afford to be gone any longer than that."

"What's the point, Pendragon?" Siry asked.

"We're going to get help."

Soon after, Siry and I ran through the village, headed for the beach. People were milling around, dazed. Many had witnessed the destruction of the pilgrim fleet. Most had no idea what it all meant. We made one stop. It was back at the tribunal hut where Telleo nursed me to health. There we gathered several small wooden canisters that contained a poison. It was harmless to us, but deadly to its intended target.

Bees.

We left the hut and quickly ran to the beach. It wasn't difficult finding the rocky cave near the shore.

"Why are we here?" Siry asked. "I've been in this cave before. There's nothing here to help us."

I didn't explain. He'd find out soon enough. We entered the cave and moved quickly through the labyrinth of tunnels. Whenever we came to an intersection, I looked at my Traveler ring to show me the way. The gray stone was glowing brighter with every turn. When we were about to enter the large, cathedral-like cavern where I first encountered the quig-bees, I decided not to take any chances. I motioned to Siry. He pulled a stopper out of one of the canisters and tossed it in ahead of us.

"That's enough poison to kill a couple thousand bees," he said.

"You better be right," I said, and poked my head around the corner in time to see a storm of bright yellow lights falling from the ceiling. It was raining quigs. Dead quigs. Thousands of yellow lights soon carpeted the sandy floor.

Siry gasped at the sight. "I've lived here all my life and never saw anything like that."

"Get used to it."

We ran through the cavern, crunching dead quigs under our feet. A few turns later we found the cavern with the rocky pool of water that was the mouth of the flume.

"This is it," I declared.

"This is what? I've been here before. It's just a pool."

I took the poison canisters and placed them along the cavern wall, in case we needed them when we got back. It didn't hurt to be sure, but if my plan worked the way I wanted, we wouldn't be needing them. I stepped up to the pool and looked into the calm, green water. I hadn't yet flumed out of there; I wasn't sure what to do.

"I'll go along with whatever you want, Pendragon. But you have to tell me what this is about."

"You gotta be strong," I said. "You're about to see things you never thought possible. All I can tell you is that your father knew it all. If you have any love or respect for his memory, trust him. Trust me."

"I do trust you."

"Then let's go for a swim,"

I dove headfirst into the pool. Siry was right behind. We didn't bother changing clothes. The time was long past for that, especially with what I had in mind. Was I doing the right thing? I didn't know and didn't care. Not anymore. I wanted to hurt Saint Dane and nothing was going to stop me.

"It's a bottomless pool," Siry said as the two of us treaded water. "There's nothing down there."

"You're wrong," I corrected. "Everything is down there. Everything there ever was or will be." I took a breath and called out, "*Veelox!*"

The water started to swirl. It was like being in a giant Jacuzzi. Lights appeared deep down below.

"Pendragon?" Siry said nervously.

"Relax. It won't hurt a bit."

A moment later we were both sucked down below the surface, and rocketed to the past for what I hoped would be a meeting between me, Siry . . . and a ghost.

IBARA

The two of us sailed side by side through the crystal tunnel across eternity. There wasn't time to bring Siry along slowly and introduce him to the strange wonders of the flume. He was going to have to pick it up as we went along. I suppose I should have worried about how he'd react, but to be honest, that's not where my head was. My focus was on Saint Dane and stopping his dado attack. Siry was along for the ride, and to help where he could. If he slowed me down, I would send him back to Ibara in a heartbeat.

Beyond the crystal walls were more ethereal images from the territories, floating in space. Every time I traveled, there were more. I could barely make out the stars, that's how dense the images had become. Faces tumbled into animals that gave way to marching armies. It was like watching a multilayered movie, where everything was vaguely transparent. It was an ominous sight. A word came to mind that best described it. "Chaos." Or maybe there was another word. "Convergence." Seeing the images swirl around gave me more reason to believe I was doing the right thing. The chaos had to end before it consumed everything.

Siry watched wide-eyed. I didn't know where to begin to explain what it all meant.

"I know" was all I said. "You're going to see some incredible sights and have a thousand questions. I'll answer them all, but not now. You're going to have to trust me."

Siry nodded with his mouth hanging open in awe. If there was anything good that came of this experience, it proved to Siry once and for all that the Travelers were real.

He only asked one question: "My father knew of all this?"

"He was a Traveler," I answered. "This is what we do."

I was afraid Siry might panic. Having your world turned inside out wasn't an easy thing to deal with. Everything he'd seen up to this point may have been incredible, but it was explainable. This . . . wasn't.

"I'm okay, Pendragon," he assured me, as if reading my mind. "Just try to give me a little warning before showing me anything else that might make me go insane, all right?"

I almost chuckled. "Okay. I'll start now. We're traveling back in time to another territory. We're going to Veelox before the final fall."

Siry thought a moment, then said, "I guess I can handle that."

"Good. Can you handle meeting Aja Killian?"

Siry shot me an incredulous look. I wasn't sure if he was going to laugh or cry.

"You're not going to go insane on me, are you?" I asked.

He didn't have time to answer, because the musical notes that always accompanied a flume trip became louder and more frequent, signaling our arrival on Veelox. We landed. The light of the flume drew back. The music drifted away. We were in pitch dark.

"Where are we?" Siry asked.

"In the past. Your past."

A thin sliver of light marked the door leading out of the gate. I pushed it open, and light from the tunnel beyond flooded the rocky cave that held the flume. I stepped out, followed by Siry, and pushed the gray door shut behind us.

"That star marks the gate to the flume," I said, pointing to the star that was etched into the gray wall. I took his hand and held it up. The stone in his Traveler ring was sparkling. I held my hand next to it, showing that my ring glowed as well. "This helps too. The closer you get to a gate, the brighter your ring will sparkle."

"Magic," he gasped.

"I wish it were that easy."

We were in familiar surroundings. For me, anyway. It was a subway tunnel with broken tracks. No trains would be moving through. We started walking.

"How do you know we're in the right time?" Siry asked.

"The flume always puts the Travelers where they need to be, when they need to be there. I don't know if it reads our minds, or if somebody out there is controlling it all like some puppet master. All I know is that, unless I'm totally wrong, we will be on Veelox in the time of Aja Killian."

We reached the metal ladder that led up and out of the tunnel and started to climb. Every time I saw something familiar, it gave me confidence that the flume had done its job. When I reached the top of the ladder, I pushed on the manhole cover. I had a brief thought that if we hadn't landed in the right time, the collapsed skyscraper might already be covering the street. The cover pushed up easily. A few seconds later I was standing on a familiar city street.

Siry climbed up to join me and asked, "Do you know where we are?"

"Yeah. So do you. Rubic City."

Siry looked around in wonder. "No, it isn't. There are trees and signs, and it looks like people actually live here."

"They do. Or they did. This is the past, remember?"

"Where are they?" he asked.

I knew the answer to that, unfortunately. It was time to introduce Siry to Lifelight. We jogged through the empty streets, heading for the pyramid. This was a city that was only beginning its slow spiral into decay. Paper blew along the sidewalks, shops were full of merchandise, and glass windows were still intact. There were smells, too. It made the place feel alive. It would be a long time before the city died completely.

Siry stopped suddenly when he got his first view of the Lifelight pyramid.

"It really is Rubic City," he said softly.

The skin of the pyramid was once again shiny and black. We started jogging toward the entrance. As we got closer, we started seeing people. A few phaders and vedders were hanging around outside, getting a rare glimpse of daylight.

Siry froze in fear.

"It's okay," I assured him. "They're not Flighters."

The Lifelight workers gave us strange looks as we entered the pyramid. Once inside, we moved quickly along the corridor with the purple lights that killed any stray bacteria entering the pyramid. I felt the hair on the back of my neck rise up. It was a comforting feeling. It meant that Lifelight was still functioning. I didn't know for sure exactly when the flume had put us, but it was definitely at a time before the pyramid had failed. Further proof came when we entered the core. Every phader station was operational. All the Lifelight screens were lit. Multiple thousands of jumps were under way. The individual fantasies of every jumper played out on the screens before us. I stole a quick glance at Siry to see his reaction. I think his mind had locked.

"You okay?" I asked.

"I thought you were going to warn me before showing me something that would make me insane."

I heard a familiar, bold voice.

"Tell me it's time," the voice said.

Aja Killian stood in the center of the core corridor, with her hands on her hips and her feet apart, wearing the dark blue coveralls of a phader. She looked every bit as confident as I remembered. Her blond hair was pulled back in a perfect ponytail. She wore the same yellow-tinted, wire-rimmed glasses. The only difference was her eyes. They were as blue and alive as I remembered, but they looked tired. Aja was older, but not just in years.

"Time for what?" I asked.

Aja walked right up to me. "You promised me another shot at that bastard Saint Dane. I want to know if it's time. Nice clothes, by the way," she added sarcastically, checking me out.

"Good to see you, too, Aja."

Aja glanced at Siry. "Who's that?"

Siry didn't move. He must have been in shock. After all, he was in the presence of a legend.

"His name is Siry. He's a Traveler."

"From where?" Aja asked, sizing him up.

"From Ibara."

Aja shot me a stunned look. "Did you say—"

"Yeah. Ibara."

For once the brilliant Aja Killian was speechless.

"There's another turning point on Veelox, Aja," I said. "It's over three hundred years from now, and it's on Ibara. Ever hear of it?"

"You wouldn't be here if you didn't know that answer," she said firmly.

"Here's another answer for you. It's time. You've got your second chance at Saint Dane."

A few hours later the three of us sat in the central core control room of Lifelight. This was Aja's domain. It was the master control area for this particular Lifelight pyramid. Aja had given us a delicious (not) helping of rainbow gloid, the gelatin-like food that was the staple on Veelox. It was exactly as I'd remembered it. Fruity, unfulfilling, but energizing. Siry was reluctant to try it until Aja looked him square in the eye and ordered, "Eat!"

He ate it all like a trained puppy. It was good to be a legend.

I filled Aja in on most of what had happened since I left Veelox. I didn't go into great detail, but told her enough so she understood that the thing Saint Dane called the Convergence was about to happen, and the launching point was going to be Ibara.

I went into a lot more detail describing Ibara. Siry helped me there. He was getting more comfortable with Aja and actually seemed to enjoy sharing tales of his home. It was a home that Aja planned. He wanted her to know how she was (would be) considered a hero for having conceived of it.

Aja liked that.

The flume had brought us back to a time when Aja's plans for Ibara were already formed. She knew that it was only a matter of time before Lifelight would fail. People had already started dying. She hadn't yet chosen the forty colonists, but had selected Ibara as their destination. It was fun telling her how the plan was going to work beautifully. Ibara became an idyllic, flourishing society that didn't rely on technology. The population was renewed. Veelox was on the verge of rebirth.

It wasn't so much fun telling her of the Flighters, and the destruction of the pilgrim ships, and ultimately about the dados that were going to swarm the island. Her plan worked . . . up to a point.

"It's the turning point for Ibara," I concluded. "Saint Dane convinced the Flighters to attack and destroy the pilgrims. The dado invasion won't be far behind. That's why we're here."

Aja paced. She didn't waste time fretting over past problems. She was already looking for solutions.

"It's simple," she declared with confidence. "I'll change the equation. If the people are going to follow my plan, I'll make a better plan. I'll get them to build stronger ships. Or arm them with weapons. Or better, the pilgrimage should begin earlier." She was getting excited. "This is incredible, Pendragon," she said, her eyes wild with enthusiasm. "I know what's going to happen, so I can counter it from the past! I can control the future. "

"No, you can't," I said flatly.

"Why not?" she argued. "We've got the tools; we should use them."

"It won't make a difference. That's the whole point. Halla has become fluid. If we change one thing today, Saint Dane will counter by changing something else tomorrow. He has the overall vision of Halla. It's how he found all the turning points. No matter what we do now, Saint Dane will counter it. If you tell the people to build stronger ships, the Flighters will get stronger weapons. If the pilgrimage begins earlier, the Flighter attack will come earlier. I tried to get Courtney to stop Mark from inventing the dados. It didn't work. Uncle Press always told me things should play out the way they were meant to. That's exactly what Saint Dane is trying to disrupt. He's making sure nothing happens the way it's supposed to, by tearing apart the natural order. Convergence. Chaos. When Halla implodes, he'll rebuild it the way he sees fit."

"So then, why did you come here?" Aja asked.

"I'm going to fight him, Aja." I pointed to Siry and said, "*We're* going to fight him with the people of Ibara. His rules. His war. He said the destruction of Ibara will kick off the Convergence. Fine. That means we have to stop it. Not by skirting it or trying to do something clever by changing history, but by meeting him dead on and beating him with his own tactics."

Aja kept her eyes on me. I was ready for her to argue. "You're not the same person, Pendragon."

"I've grown up."

"That's not it," she said thoughtfully. "I'm sensing, I don't know, anger. Bitterness. Are you letting your emotions cloud your judgment?"

"It's hard not to be angry after seeing what I've seen," I answered honestly.

"I get that," she said. "You know how badly I want to beat Saint Dane. But I haven't lost my ability to operate logically."

"I *am* being logical!" I snapped.

"Then I'll ask you again, why are you here?"

"I need to know everything about Ibara. It was once a military base. I need weapon information. And maps. Anything you have. If we're going to defend the place, I want every advantage there is."

Aja nodded thoughtfully. "There are old plans of the island that describe miles of underground tunnels and give a complete listing of its defenses."

"Perfect!" I shouted. Things were looking up.

"Is that all?"

I wasn't exactly sure how to say what I needed to say. I counted on the fact that she was going to be as logical and unemotional as always, because what I had to tell her was going to hurt.

"I want you to come back with us. We need you. The people of Ibara need you. This is the last stand, Aja. You should be there. It's your second shot at Saint Dane."

I watched her, hoping she would give me a simple, "Sure!" She looked up at the master control panel of Lifelight, turning the idea over in her head.

"I can't," she finally declared. "What would we tell the people? That I'm a ghost from the past? A time traveler? Talk about mixing territories!"

"We won't tell them who you are," I countered. "We'll say we found you in the ruins of Ibara. Yeah, that's it! You'll be a Flighter who changed her ways and wants to helps us beat the dados."

"That's ridiculous!" Aja scoffed.

"I know why he wants you to come," Siry said softly.

"No, you don't," I barked at him.

"Talk to me, Siry," Aja said.

Aja was right. As usual. The plan didn't make sense. I should have known she would see through my flawed thinking. We had to tell her the whole truth. Siry gave me a sheepish look. I shrugged, giving him the okay to go on.

"You're going to be assassinated, Aja," Siry said. "Just before the forty colonists leave for Ibara, you're going to be killed. You'll never set foot on Ibara. I'm sorry."

Aja stared at the wall. I had no idea what was going through her head. How could I? Imagine opening a fortune cookie that said: "You're going to die soon. Enjoy your egg rolls." Talk about a buzz killer. Nobody said anything for a long time. Aja needed to input this information and calculate her choices. That's the way she worked.

Finally Aja looked at me and spoke softly and clearly. "You're right, Pendragon. Saint Dane is all about disrupting the natural order of Halla. I agree that trying to change history would be a mistake. At best it would be futile, at worst a disaster. For that reason I'm having second thoughts about giving you the maps of Ibara. But I can justify it, because the maps exist in the past of Ibara. Who knows? Maybe the tribunal already has them. So I'll give them to you, but I won't go with you. If I'm supposed to die, I should die. Who knows what I'd mess up if I didn't play out history the way it was meant to be."

I fought back tears. I couldn't imagine life without Aja Killian.

"We all have to die, Pendragon," she added. "I want you to go back there and rally those people, the way I know you can, and destroy him. Destroy his robots. Destroy his evil. If you do that, this war might finally be over."

We spent the night in the home of Evangeline, Aja's acolyte. We needed the rest, and there was no rush to get back. I explained to Siry that it wouldn't matter how long we were gone, the flume would put us back on Ibara when we needed to be there. That's why I told Genj and Telleo that we would be gone for only a few hours. He understood, sort of. Heck, I didn't understand myself. But I believed.

When we woke up the next morning, Aja was gone. She'd left a note saying how she didn't want to say good-bye. The next time she heard from us, she wanted it to be all about the great victory on Ibara. In the letter she added a note of caution: "You have fought this war the right way, Pendragon. We all have. We may not always have had success, but we've fought for the right. It is our duty to insure that Halla continues to exist in peace, but we must do it in a way that was meant to be. I know you will make the right decisions. Good luck."

The note was attached to a thick role of paper. The maps of Ibara.

The last line of her note stuck with me. She felt strongly about beating Saint Dane, but also in sticking with our principles and the principles of Halla. I trusted her judgment, but with all due respect, she hadn't been through what I had. I knew that if we wanted to beat Saint Dane, we had to find a new way. Any way. In other words, we had to stop playing fair.

Siry and I went back to the flume feeling rested and full. It still seemed like the calm before the storm, but there was no pressure, because the storm wouldn't arrive until we returned to Ibara. We found the manhole, climbed down, and found the star. In no time we entered the gate and stood inside the mouth of the flume, ready to go.

"How do you feel?" I asked.

"Like I was thrown into the middle of a game that everybody's been playing for a long time, and I don't even know the rules."

I laughed. "That sounds about right."

I held the maps. Siry touched them reverently and asked, "Do you really think there's enough information here to help us stop the dados?"

I glanced into the flume, then back to Siry, debating about how to answer. I decided to tell the truth. "No."

"I didn't think so."

"But it's okay, I never thought the maps would be enough."

"So then why did we come to get them?"

"We're just getting started," I said, and looked into the flume.

Siry stared at me. "We're not going back to Ibara, are we."

"Not yet." I looked into the flume and called out, *"Zadaa!"*

IBARA

I had two goals for our visit to Zadaa. The first was to avoid Loor. I had no doubt that if she learned of my plan to face off in a battle against Saint Dane, she'd want to come back with us. No, she'd *insist* on coming back. No, she wouldn't even discuss it. She'd come back with us.

As much as I would have wanted her to be there for the battle, I didn't think any one person would make a huge difference, no matter how fierce a warrior she was. I was more worried about what was going to happen after the battle. Win, lose, or draw, if anything happened to me, Loor would be the logical choice to take my place as lead Traveler. There were many times I thought she should have been the lead Traveler to begin with, but that wasn't the way it was meant to be, no matter how I felt about it. I wanted to make sure that Loor would be around to fight another day.

The flume deposited us in the large, light brown sandstone cavern that I had been through so many times before. I didn't like most of those memories. Both Loor and Saint Dane were killed there . . . and came back to life. That's when I first began to believe the Travelers weren't normal. Saint Dane said we were illusions. I don't know what that means. I sure don't feel like anything other than a normal guy who was born on Second Earth. But I couldn't deny there was something weird about us. I've actually thought that maybe Loor's dying was the illusion. Maybe we only *thought* it happened. I know, that makes no sense, but it's just as wacky as saying that we're all just figments, right? Whatever the truth is, no way I was taking any chances. Loor had to be kept safe.

The second goal of the trip, the main reason we were there, was to retrieve another tool to help us in the battle.

"Tell me about this territory," Siry said as I led him quickly across the cavern floor.

I gave him a thumbnail account of the war between the Batu and the Rokador, fought over the underground rivers. The poor guy must have been in information overload. He was seeing more of Halla, faster, than any of the Travelers.

We climbed up and out of the flume cavern using the footholds that were dug into the sandstone walls. I briefly thought that a quig-snake might be lurking in the deep shadows, but didn't sweat over it. Saint Dane was done with this territory, which meant the quigs were too. We climbed up through the narrow break in the rock roof, which led to a wooden trapdoor and the entryway to the tunnels that snaked beneath Xhaxhu. Most of the tunnels were destroyed when the underground sea burst. The tunnels leading to the flume weren't touched, I'm happy to say. They looked pretty much the same as they had before the sea gave way.

That was about to change.

I didn't bother closing the wooden trapdoor. I hadn't changed into the Rokador clothes that were stacked near the flume either. I didn't care if we were seen. There was only one thing that mattered—preparing for the battle.

With Siry following close behind, I walked quickly through the maze of twisting, narrow tunnels that I knew would lead to the underground river flowing beneath Xhaxhu. It wasn't long before we made the last turn and stepped into the long cavern where several years before, I had gotten my first look at the rivers of Zadaa.

This river still flowed, fed by the tall waterfall. I wanted to climb out of the underground and see the changes to Xhaxhu brought by the creation of the desert sea. I could imagine Xhaxhu now as a lush, green habitat rather than a dry desert city. It was a huge victory for the Travelers over Saint Dane.

It was history.

When we entered the river cavern, Siry stopped short. I could say he was surprised by the sight of an underground river. Or of a tall, roaring waterfall. He may have been overwhelmed by seeing how such an incredibly beautiful and powerful natural wonder could exist. I could say all those things, but I didn't think they were true. I knew what he was looking at. It was something unlike he'd ever seen before, and probably never would see again. It was the reason we had come to Zadaa. Sitting near the edge of the river was a round, silver, two-seater vehicle.

"What is it?" he asked in awe.

I answered as we inspected the vehicle. "It's called a dygo. The Rokador used them to drill through the earth and create miles of tunnels."

This dygo was one of the smaller models. It was about the size of a golf cart. If you remember, the main cabin was a silver sphere that sat on tractor treads. A circular window wrapped halfway around, so its operators could see outside.

The drilling device was a six-foot-wide hollow funnel that sat in a yoke, and could be positioned at any angle around the sphere. The wide end of the funnel was closest to the operators' cabin, narrowing down to a hollow tip about a foot across. The drill itself was made up of many rings of sharp cutting devices that spun when activated. I'd seen dygos cut through solid rock as if it were cotton candy.

I opened the hatch of the silver sphere and motioned for Siry to enter. The cockpit of a two-seater dygo looked kind of like a small car. It was cramped but comfortable. I sat in the left-hand seat and buckled the seat belt.

"What is that for?" he asked.

"We're going to be moving at different angles. You don't want to tumble out of your seat."

"Oh," he said, sounding sick. He quickly buckled up.

I looked over the familiar controls. In front of me were two joysticks that would control the direction of the sphere. I toggled the starter switch and heard the engine hum to life. I gave a quick reassuring glance to Siry. He smiled nervously.

"Watch this," I said, and started manipulating the joysticks. The round sphere twisted right, then left, then tipped down. I pulled both joysticks, and we rolled back until we were looking skyward.

"Like I said, we're going to be moving at different angles."

"I believe you," Siry said, sounding weak.

I righted the sphere until we were looking at the raging river. This was it. This was the time. We were about to take a step that meant we had truly thrown out the rules. I was operating on Saint Dane's level.

It felt good.

Siry sensed my tension. "I'm just trying to keep up with everything," he said cautiously. "I don't have the right to question anything to do with Travelers, but I have to ask . . . are you sure this is right?"

I didn't want to answer quickly. It was a good question. A huge one. I'd asked it myself a thousand times over.

"The Jakills stole one of the pilgrim ships. Was that right?"

Siry thought for a moment and answered, "No. I think it was wrong."

That shocked me. I thought for sure he would have said that in spite of what happened, they had made the right choice.

He added, "I was going on emotion and anger. We all were. We fired each other up, convincing ourselves that we were doing the right thing. Now they're dead and I'm sitting in a strange machine on the other side of somewhere, about to do it again. You tell me. Was it right to steal that ship?"

"It was," I said with confidence. "If the Jakills hadn't made that trip, we wouldn't be preparing Ibara for the attack."

Siry nodded thoughtfully. "I guess that's true. I just hope we're not doing anything that will make things even worse."

That ticked me off. I was trying to save his home. His people. How could he question me?

"Are you with me or not?" I asked angrily.

"I'm with you, Pendragon," he said. "To the end, whatever that will be."

Discussion over. I twisted the sphere away from the river to face the opposite wall of the cavern—the wall that contained the tunnel that led to the flume. I twisted the handle of one joystick. The drill settled down in front of us. Squeezing the trigger got the drill rings spinning. With a low whine, the sharp cutting device came to life. It was the moment of no return. Once we started digging, there would be no turning back.

I pushed forward. The drill dug into the wall. Siry leaned

back in his seat as if to get away, expecting dirt and rock to hit us. Of course, that didn't happen. The drill cut through easily and we were on our way, forging a new tunnel beneath the sands of Zadaa. We churned through solid rock, occasionally passing through one of the existing tunnels. I kept pushing the machine forward, guessing at the distance we had to travel. After a minute of digging, I angled the dygo downward, and we descended. The only guide I had to know we were headed the right way was my sense of direction, and my Traveler ring. It wasn't long before the gray stone began to twinkle. We were getting closer to the flume. It didn't take long before we blasted through the last wall of rock and drove into the familiar cavern. I stopped to catch my breath. I was sweating. Not from exertion, from nerves.

Siry looked worse than I felt.

"That was interesting," he said with a weak smile.

I spun the sphere around to see the tunnel we had just dug. It wasn't subtle. All across Halla the flumes were hidden in areas that were next to impossible for people to accidentally find. That wasn't the case on Zadaa anymore. People were bound to discover the new tunnel. They were going to see the flume. By breaking through that rock, I had broken down another barrier between the territories. I was definitely playing Saint Dane's game now.

"This machine is a wonder," Siry gasped. "How will it help us beat the dados?"

"It won't. Not directly."

I spun the dygo 180 degrees until we faced the mouth of the flume. I nudged it forward. The treads rolled slowly, until the tunnel to infinity filled our window.

Siry looked at me with confusion. "Then why are we taking it to Ibara?"

"We're not. At least not yet. We've got another stop."

"Where?" Siry asked with wide eyes.

I took a deep breath and called out, *"Denduron!"*

The flume sparkled to life. We drove into the tunnel, and the beginnings of a new Halla.

IBARA

There were two flume gates on Denduron. I had no way of knowing which one we'd be dumped at. One was on top of the snowy mountain that loomed above the Milago village. The other was buried deep below the ground, under tons of rock. Access to that flume had been destroyed when the vein of tak exploded, decimating the glaze mines. Either way, we were prepared. The dygo would either get us down from the mountain or dig us out of the crushed mine tunnels. Getting out of the gate was the least of my worries.

Flying through a flume inside a vehicle was a new experience. If we weren't on such a dire mission, I'd almost say it was fun. I had no control over the flight, so I let go of the joysticks. The power of the flume sent us along. The only view we had was through the narrow window in front of the dygo. Just as well. I didn't want to look out onto the sea of time and space beyond the crystal walls and see any changes that might have happened after what we did on Zadaa.

Since we were sealed inside the dygo, I couldn't hear the musical notes of the flume. They usually gave me the warning that we were nearing the end of a journey. I had to keep my eyes ahead to look for signs of our arrival. I was afraid we'd hit the gate that was buried, and smash against a wall of rock.

I didn't mention that to Siry. He had enough to deal with.

After traveling for several minutes, I decided not to take any chances and fired up the drill bit of the dygo. I figured the drill would chew us through anything. As it turned out, I didn't have to worry. No sooner did the drill start spinning than we were dumped at the mouth of the flume. Bright light flashed in through the narrow window of our digging sphere. Wherever we were, it wasn't under tons of rock.

"Let's get out," I said, and popped the hatch.

It was a familiar sight. We were in the cave on top of the mountain, where I had first set foot on a territory other than my own. Denduron. I immediately thought of Uncle Press. I wondered what he would think about what I was doing. It wasn't a happy thought, so I stopped thinking it.

"Now where are we?" Siry asked. He sounded tired. I didn't think anything would surprise him anymore.

"Denduron is the first territory where the Travelers beat Saint Dane," I explained. "Here, put these on."

There was a pile of leather and fur clothing near the flume. I didn't care about blending into the territory. It wasn't going to matter what we were wearing, if somebody saw us rolling along in a silver dygo. There would be no blending in on Denduron. I was more concerned about the weather. We were wearing lightweight tropical clothing from Ibara. We'd freeze on Denduron. I dumped my Ibara clothes into the dygo and once again strapped on the leathers of Denduron. I noticed a difference right away. The clothes were much better made than when I had been there before. It was the first sign that the Milago had improved their lives after

Saint Dane was defeated. There would be more.

"This area has two tribes," I explained. "The Milago and the Bedoowan. The Milago are farmers. The Bedoowan are more evolved and intellectual. They lived in a slick castle-city where they commanded an army that treated the Milago like slaves. The farmers were forced to mine a precious mineral called glaze, which was the basis for the wealth of the Bedoowan. The mines were treacherous, and the Milago were dying off. They revolted and the Bedoowan were defeated. The Traveler here is named Alder. He's a Bedoowan. He's told me that the two tribes now live in peace. The Bedoowan provide modern expertise, the Milago more practical skills. Bottom line is that Saint Dane was stopped for the first time here.

We finished getting dressed by strapping on leather-soled shoes. I can't believe I'm saying this, but the clothes were almost comfortable. The leather was soft and well crafted. I'm not so sure I would have needed my boxers even if I had them. Which I didn't. We climbed back aboard the dygo. I fired it up and gently nudged the vehicle forward. We rolled through the cave and out into the bright light of Denduron. Our first sight was the vast field of snow where the quig beasts had attacked Uncle Press and me. I'm happy to say there were no quig spines sticking out from the snow. Like on Zadaa, the quigs wouldn't bother us here. The turning point had passed.

The dygo rolled easily across the snow, making deep tracks. Siry was mostly silent, taking in the awesome view of the majestic, snow-capped mountains that surrounded us. It really was a beautiful territory. Rugged, but beautiful. He only made one comment during our descent to the Milago village.

"Am I crazy?" he asked as he looked up at the sky.

"No," I chuckled. "There are three suns."

Siry blinked and sat back in his seat. The guy was dazed. When he set out with the Jakills to learn the truth, he had no idea what he was getting himself into.

As we got lower, the snow gave way to grass. I stopped the dygo, and we got out to survey the scene. We stood high above the valley, looking down on the new Milago village. My last view of this place had shown nothing but devastation. The explosion of the mines destroyed the Bedoowan castle and tore apart the countryside. Much of the Milago village had been destroyed as well. Now there was no sign of destruction. Just the opposite. The Milago huts were rebuilt better than before. They looked larger and sturdier. The dirt paths that wound between them now looked more organized and solid. It looked like they were paved. Beyond the village I saw the vast farmland that fed the population. It looked rich with crops. It looked perfect.

There was something else that made me smile. It was late in the day. The three suns were sinking low on the horizon. Down in the village, street lights winked to life. When I had been there before, the Milago didn't have lights. They didn't have power of any sort. It wasn't until I entered the Bedoowan castle that I realized the territory was more advanced than I originally thought. The Bedoowan had been keeping the Milago in the dark ages. Literally. I was thrilled to see that the Bedoowan were now sharing their knowledge. The Milago village was alive.

"Let's get down before it's too dark," I said.

We climbed back into the dygo and continued our journey. My thoughts went ahead to the next step. It would be the most difficult of all. I didn't want to see Alder, for the same reasons I hadn't wanted to run into Loor. I didn't want him coming back to Ibara. Unfortunately, on Denduron we were going to need his help.

I found a dense stand of pine-looking trees and pulled the dygo beneath them. "We'll walk the rest of the way. Don't want to panic anybody."

We got out of the sphere and covered it up quickly with branches and leaves. It wasn't a very good job of camouflage, but it was the best we could do.

"We need to find the Traveler," I said, and led him down toward the village.

I didn't think anyone would recognize me. It had been a couple of years, and I wasn't the same scared little kid who left there after the destruction of the Bedoowan castle. I was still fairly scared, but I wasn't so little anymore. Siry and I walked through the streets of the busy village without getting any second looks. The community was thriving now. It was no longer the kind of place where everybody knew everybody else. The huts had become houses. The streets were no longer muddy, and lights made the place warm and inviting. It was nothing like the village I had left in ruins. Except for one thing. Along one street was an open square that, at first, looked like a park. A low, black fence surrounded a grassy clearing, where I could easily imagine people stopping for a picnic. But it wasn't a park. It was a memorial. In the center of the square was a wide ring of stones that I recognized as the entrance to one of the old glaze mines. It was on this stone platform where Saint Dane conducted his sadistic Transfer ceremony, where a miner was chosen and weighed against the day's haul of glaze. If the glaze didn't weigh as much as the miner, the miner was tossed to his death inside the mine shaft. It seemed this stone structure was left there as a memorial, and a reminder.

We asked a villager where we might find the camp of the Bedoowan knights. I figured that was as good a place as any to look for Alder. The villager directed us to the bluffs over-looking the ocean, where the Bedoowan castle once stood. I knew the way. We made it through the village and across a grassy field, then we saw the glow of lights up ahead. I explained to Siry that before the battle, the grassy bluff went straight out to the ocean. From on top you'd never know that a massive castle was built into the cliff below. When the mines were destroyed the immense castle fell into the sea, taking much of the land above with it.

As we walked closer, we saw that the lights were coming from the destroyed foundation of the castle-city. It had become the compound of the Bedoowan knights. A set of ancient stone steps led down to a large, open area that I recognized as the ruins of the arena where we battled the quig beasts. The memory gave me a chill. I never thought I'd see this place again.

Siry and I stood on the edge of the ruins, looking down on what looked like some kind of game. Several knights were gathered around a circle, watching two other knights wrestle. It wasn't an angry competition. The knights cheered and cajoled the two combatants. It looked like a bunch of guys having fun. It was an odd feeling. When I was there before, they were the bad guys. Not anymore.

"Care to place a wager?" came a voice from behind us.

I didn't have to turn around to know who it was.

"Only if you were the one fighting," I said. "I only bet on a sure thing."

I was suddenly swept up in a bear hug. If I didn't know better I'd think he was trying to crush me. Nothing could be further from the truth.

"Hello, Pendragon," Alder said warmly.

"Man, I am glad to see you," I replied.

Alder let go and backed off. I'd forgotten what a big guy

he was. Though I'd grown a few inches, he still towered over me. His brown hair had grown longer and nearly touched his shoulders. He wore light leathers, similar to ours, rather than the heavy, black leather armor of a Bedoowan knight. He must have been off duty. As I've written before, Alder was a trained knight, but his aggressive side only came out in battle. He was actually a gentle guy who always had a smile.

But not just then. Alder's expression was dark. "I wish I could say the same. I saw the machine, Pendragon. Many of us did. I do not know how to explain that to my people. Why would you bring such a thing from another territory?"

"To save Halla" was my answer.

He was upset. I understood. I had to explain myself. After introducing Siry, the three of us sat on the rim of the old arena, and I brought Alder up to speed. I didn't hold anything back. He listened to everything I had to say. It was for Siry's benefit too. My plan for battling Saint Dane on Ibara went against everything we knew to be right, but it was the only way. When I finally told Alder why we had come to Denduron, I felt as if I'd hit him in the gut. He didn't say anything for a long while. He sat looking down at his comrades, who were laughing and having a great time. I felt bad. If we hadn't been there, Alder probably would have been down there with them. That wasn't the way it was meant to be. He was a Traveler.

He finally took a tired breath and said, "By doing what you ask, we could harm the future of Denduron as well. Have you thought of that?"

"I have. But this isn't just about Veelox, Alder. It's about Halla. If Saint Dane overruns Ibara, you may soon be facing an army of dados right here."

"What you are asking is dangerous," Alder said gravely. "We cannot do it alone."

"Can you get help?" I asked.

"People remember you, Pendragon. They remember how you helped save the Milago from the tyranny of the Bedoowan. The only person they revere more is Press. But he is not here, is he?"

Again I got the feeling that Uncle Press would not have approved of what we were doing. But as Alder said, he wasn't there. It was my show now.

"I can get people to help you," he said. "There is only one condition."

"Name it."

"You must take me to Ibara."

"No way," I shouted, and jumped up. "I won't risk your life. Not again. Twice was twice too many."

"Pendragon," Alder said calmly. "This is not a negotiation. My place is with you, battling Saint Dane. Why would you refuse that, unless you question what it is you are doing?"

"Of course I question what I'm doing," I shouted back. "I'm trying to figure it out as I go along. If something happens to me, to us, what will happen to the Travelers? It's why I didn't contact Loor. If three of us don't make it through this battle, and with Gunny and Spader trapped on Eelong, that would only leave Patrick, Loor, Aja, and Elli from Quillan. They would need you, Alder. We can't risk it."

"If this battle is as important as you say," Alder said calmly, "it would not matter how many Travelers were left. The war would be over."

"Agreed, but I don't want you to be part of this."

"Why?" Alder asked. "What is the real reason? Is it because you fear I will be hurt? Or because you have doubts about what you are doing?"

"I don't have doubts," I said adamantly.

"Then my position is not negotiable," Alder said with finality.

I was stuck. I tried desperately to think of another reason for him to stay home, but came up blank.

"I kind of like the idea of him coming along," Siry added.

"Fine," I finally blurted out. "You're in. I'm against it, but you're in."

Alder said, "Or maybe you could say that you are happy I will be there to help."

"Yeah, that too."

I realized I was sounding pretty ungrateful. Alder was putting himself on the line for me again. He was a good friend and Traveler. I shouldn't have been so angry.

"I'm sorry, Alder," I said, softening. "I'm glad you're going to help us. I just don't want anything to happen to you."

Alder stood and put a hand on my shoulder, saying, "From what you tell me, the best way to make sure nothing happens to any of us is to beat Saint Dane on Ibara."

It was getting late. We needed rest. Alder found us comfortable beds in the knights' quarters in the castle ruins. It kind of creeped me out to be back in that castle, considering I was the one who blew it up in the first place. Sleeping was tough. The task ahead was going to be difficult and dangerous. I'm not talking about the battle with Saint Dane. I'm talking about the task on Denduron.

Alder got up early the next morning to make preparations. By the time Siry and I woke up and got something to eat, Alder had already gathered a group of twenty volunteers from the Milago village. We met them in the clearing between the village and the castle ruins. I recognized some of the men. The biggest difference from when I was there before was that they looked healthy now. Back then, all the men had the same gray look of death, from working in the mines and breathing the poisonous fumes that were emitted when glaze was torn from the rock. Now they looked strong and well fed. I felt bad for what I was about to ask them to do.

Leading these volunteers was a man I remembered well. It was Rellin, the chief miner and leader of the revolution against the Bedoowan. He was now the leader of the Milago. He was as powerful and confident a leader as I remembered. The one thing missing was the anger he once held. He was now at peace with his world. I hoped I wasn't going to disrupt that too much.

"You've grown up, Pendragon," he said while giving me a warm hug.

"I can't believe what I see here," I said to the man. "It's a whole new village."

"It is, in great part thanks to you and Press. I was sorry to hear of his passing."

I nodded in appreciation.

"In his memory, and because of the part you played in creating a new world for us, we are willing to do what you ask," Rellin said. "There will be danger. Do you understand that?"

"Yes, I do," I said. "I wouldn't be asking for help if it weren't so incredibly important."

"And what makes it so?" he asked.

I knew I'd have to answer that question at some point. I couldn't tell Rellin the whole truth, of course. But he deserved to know some form of it.

"There is a village a long way from here that needs my help. Like the Milago, they are in danger of being destroyed by a powerful, evil force. I am trying my best to help them."

"You are quite the adventurer, Pendragon," Rellin said. "It

is a noble but dangerous calling to become involved in such conflicts."

He pretty much nailed that one square on the freakin' head.

"Yes, but it's the right thing to do," I said.

"Then for you and your noble calling, I will send my men back down into the mines in search of tak."

"Thank you," I said sincerely.

These were brave guys. I wished I could tell them how they would be mining the tak to protect their own future as well.

Rellin said, "You understand the veins of tak were buried deep below the ground. It will take much effort to uncover them."

"Not as much as you think," I declared.

I led Rellin and the miners to the dygo. Siry walked alongside me.

"What's so special about tak?" he whispered.

"It's a natural substance they discovered while mining for glaze. It's a soft, red dirt you can roll into balls, like clay."

"What is it, poison?"

"It's an incredibly powerful explosive. A tiny dot could blow one of those huts off the face of Denduron. The miners were going to use it against the Bedoowan, but it would have changed the evolution of the society. With tak, the Milago would have become warriors. After defeating the Bedoowan, Rellin was going to try and conquer other areas of Denduron. This peaceful village would have become a city of warriors. They never got the chance. After the explosion the tak mines were buried too deep for them to get to."

"Except with a dygo," Siry said.

"Exactly. I want to blow Saint Dane back to wherever it

was he came from. With a weapon like tak, we've got a chance against his army. Without it . . ." I didn't finish the sentence.

Siry said, "But once we dig a tunnel, won't the Milago be able to keep mining it?"

"No, this is a different place," I said quickly. "They aren't at war anymore."

Siry looked troubled. "I just hope we don't blow the people of Denduron back to where they came from too."

"We won't," I snapped.

Siry didn't say another word.

Rellin and the twenty miners were in absolute awe of the dygo. No big surprise. I gave them a story about how it came from a city on the far side of the mountains. I knew they had plenty of questions, but I didn't give them the chance to ask. Siry and I boarded the sphere and rolled toward the castle. There was no way of knowing where a vein of tak might be located. I stopped the machine at a remote spot that wouldn't interfere with the normal routine of the village. As the miners watched in awe, I engaged the drill and dipped it toward the ground. With a push on the foot pedals, the drill bit into the ground. We were under way.

Digging the mine was simple. Finding tak wasn't. My plan was to dig several shallow tunnels and have the miners inspect them for tak. If we came up empty, we'd dig a new tunnel. And another and another until we found what we came for. It was a laborious process. We spent several days on Denduron with no luck. We found small deposits of glaze, but the miners didn't dare dig it out. They had seen enough of the blue gem to last a few hundred lifetimes.

While we dug, other miners constructed crates for us to transport the explosive. The crates were critical. Tak dissolved when mixed with water. Since our entry to Ibara was through a pool of water, the crates needed to be watertight. The miners also built a large, flat sled we could use to drag the tak up and over the mountain. Of course, they didn't know we were only going halfway.

I was really touched by how hard everyone worked. More and more volunteers joined when they heard who they were working for. Some even volunteered to come with us and help in the fight, but there was no way I could accept that. Eventually there were enough miners to split into shifts, so there was always someone working during the daylight hours. I felt sure that if there was tak to be found, we would find it.

It was great being with Alder. He gave Siry pointers on fighting. He demonstrated the art of using the long, wooden stave that he and Loor were such experts with. Siry was an eager student, but there was no way to turn him into a fighter in such a short time. It was more for fun, which was almost as important. It had been a long time since we had done anything that was even close to fun.

Watching those two spar with the long staves gave me an idea. After digging a new mine shaft with the dygo, I drove the vehicle back up the mountain to the flume. I didn't tell the others I was going, because I wasn't planning on being gone long. I parked outside the cave, entered, and stepped into the flume.

"*Quillan*," I announced, and was quickly pulled toward a territory that held nothing but dark memories for me.

I arrived at the gate and quickly changed into the gray, nondescript clothing near the flume. I didn't run into any of the mechanical spider-quigs. No surprise there. This territory was done. I left the vast warehouse that held the gate to the flume, and climbed up to the incredible gaming arcade that had been my first taste of Quillan. I'm sorry to say that the arcade was rocking. The Quillan games were back, and busier than ever. It hurt to watch.

On the street nothing had changed. I didn't know how much time had passed by Quillan standards, but the territory looked the same as when I had first seen it. The city streets were jammed with people moving like lifeless zombies. The huge screens on the buildings above showed the same geometric patterns, broken up by the occasional announcement given by a nameless reporter. It killed me. Blok had won. Saint Dane had won. I had failed miserably on Quillan.

My destination was the abandoned underground mall where I spent time with the members of the small resistance that called themselves "revivers." I knew the route well. I found the building that was built over the forgotten mall, descended through ancient stairways, walked through a twisting series of corridors, and finally came to the break in the cement wall that was the entrance the revivers had created.

I never saw a reviver. Or Elli, the Traveler. It didn't matter. I wasn't there to learn about Quillan. I came for weapons. I found them in a long-forgotten store deep within the mall. It hurts me to say that no revivers were there to guard them. It was another sign that the revival had failed. They no longer needed their weapons.

But I did. I found a stack of the six-foot-long, black metal rods. Dado killers. I didn't know what they were made out of, or why they worked. All I knew was that when you impaled a dado with one of those rods, it neutralized its power source. The result? Dead dado.

I stood looking at the pile of weapons, wondering why I had bothered to come. We were about to fight a war against thousands of dados. If it came down to using those rods, the war would be lost. Still, using weapons like those was all I knew. Seeing Alder instructing Siry made me realize that. I guess you could say that having them was a confidence builder. I needed all the confidence I could get. I grabbed a dozen of the lightweight weapons and headed back for the flume.

I knew getting them back to the flume would be risky. If a security dado spotted me, I'd be done. I camouflaged the rods as best I could with a rotten old blanket that had been tossed aside by a reviver. With luck, people would think I was carrying lengths of wood. Or brooms. Or skis. (Yeah, right.) Or anything besides dado-killing weapons. When I got to the surface, I kept close to the buildings, trying to be invisible. At one point I saw two security dados marching toward me. My stomach fell. It suddenly felt like a very stupid idea to have gone to Quillan. I had risked the entire battle just to give myself an ounce of comfort. I held my breath.

The dados walked right past me.

My trip back to Denduron was uneventful. I changed back into my leather clothing at the gate and jumped into the flume. In the cave on Denduron I placed the pile of weapons at the side of the flume, got right back into the dygo, and made my way down the mountain. In all, I was gone for only a few hours. Nobody knew I had left. Not even Alder and Siry. I had taken a big risk going to Quillan, but I was glad I did it.

I didn't know how to measure time exactly on Denduron. If I were to guess, I'd say we were on that territory for about three weeks. I was beginning to think it was going to be for nothing. If the tak was deeper than the shallow tunnels we had been digging, it meant we had to create a much more complex mining operation to get the miners down deep. It would also mean spending lots of time down there, and I didn't want to risk poisoning these hard-working guys. After weeks of coming up empty, I started to face the possibility that we would have to battle the dados without tak . . .

When we saw the first telltale streak of red. The miners gathered to inspect the possible find. Rellin dug out a piece of the red dirt with his fingers and rolled it into a small ball. He walked back to the mouth of the tunnel, and with everyone watching, he flung it at a rock ledge. *Boom!* The rock disintegrated, creating a small avalanche of stones. It was so loud, my ears rang. When the air cleared, Rellin turned to me and smiled. I in turn looked to Siry.

"That," I said, "is tak."

Siry looked stunned. "Maybe we really do have a chance."

The process of mining the mineral was even more dangerous. If hit the wrong way, it could explode. The miners took their time, which was fine with me. They only had the crude tools they hadn't used since the days of mining glaze. The vein turned out to be the mother lode. They dug cautiously, filling rough bags with the mineral and hauling it out of the tunnel. It took several days, but every wooden crate was eventually filled. We could have filled more, but I wasn't sure how much the dygo would be able to pull. The crates were then sealed with wax to make them watertight.

Finally the job was complete. The dygo was fitted with heavy ropes that were attached to the sled and the crates were loaded aboard.

"You sure this won't blow up on the way up the mountain?" Siry asked.

"No" was my honest answer. "I don't know what'll happen when we go through the flume, either."

"I didn't need to hear that," Siry said soberly.

After many thank-yous and good-byes, we were ready to

go. I told Rellin that he and his men had done an important thing that would hopefully ensure peace to Siry's home for a long time to come.

"I do not doubt you, Pendragon," Rellin said. "Tak helped bring peace to the Milago. I trust it will be as useful again."

Alder, Siry, and I climbed into the dygo. It wasn't built for three people, and we had to avoid one another's elbows and knees. Siry was the smallest of the three, so he sat in the middle, wedged between the two seats. We were all happy that it wasn't a very long trip . . . for a lot of reasons.

"Slowly," Alder cautioned. "Avoid the bumps."

Yeah, no kidding. I engaged the dygo. With only a slight strain from the weight of the tak, we moved forward. The trip was nerve-racking. We were hauling enough explosives to level the entire mountain. One rough jostle and we'd be vapor. I wondered how protected we were inside the steel sphere of the dygo. That thing was built to withstand some pretty intense pressure. I guess I don't have to say that I hoped we wouldn't find out.

I picked a path that seemed to be the one with the fewest bumps. Every time the dygo bounced, I slowed down even more, so the tak wouldn't be knocked around. We were all sweating so much, it got pretty steamy and rank inside. We had to stop a couple of times to open the hatch and air the sphere out.

We all felt a little better when we reached the snow. Rolling across packed snow was much smoother than grass and rocks. Finally the terrain leveled out, and I saw the mouth of the gate. It had been a grueling journey, but we'd made it.

"How do we do this?" Alder asked. "Do we drive right into the flume and out the other side in Ibara?"

"No," I answered. "We'll have to make several trips. I'll go with the dygo first and clear out the gate area. You guys stack the crates near the flume and wait for me."

We unhooked the sled, and I drove the sphere into the cave. I rolled right into the flume and called out, *"Ibara!"*

Moments later I was swept up and away. I had to trust that the flume would continue to send me where I needed to be, when I needed to be there. If it started messing with me now, well, I didn't want to think about that. There was nothing I could do about it, so I focused on the task ahead. It was a moving job, nothing more. Okay, a *dangerous* moving job, but still a moving job.

When the dygo reached Ibara, I engaged the drill. The moment the sphere bobbed to the water's surface I started digging. I blasted up and out of the stone pool that was the mouth of the flume, destroying a section of the circle and spewing water all over the floor of the cavern. I didn't stop to worry about it and kept moving across the wet sand. The next step was to bore a new tunnel through the rocky wall of the cavern. We needed to get thirty heavy containers of tak out of there. Dragging them through the winding labyrinth of tunnels would take weeks. We didn't have weeks. The time for being secretive was over. I drilled straight through the rock, and didn't stop until I saw sunlight on the beach of Ibara.

Spinning the dygo around, I saw that I had created a tunnel that led straight back to the flume. It was a hundred yards long. No twists, no turns, no subtlety. If anybody wandered by, they'd find the flume. I didn't care. After the battle, there was no telling what this area was going to look like anyway. All bets were off. I rolled back through the tunnel to the shattered pool, got out of the dygo, and stepped up to the edge of the flume.

"Denduron!" I shouted, and dove in headfirst. As I traveled

along, I closed my eyes. I didn't want to see the images of Halla staring back at me. In no time I was back in Denduron, where Alder and Siry were waiting. I shouldn't have worried. The flume did its job. The crates were stacked high, ready for transport.

Alder held one of the metal weapons I'd brought from Quillan. "What is this?"

I took it from him, spun it expertly, and jabbed at Siry. "Dado killers. From Quillan."

"How did they get here?" Siry asked.

"I went there a few days ago. Is that a problem?"

Alder said, "Not if mixing the territories is no longer a concern."

I dropped the weapon on the pile with the others. "It isn't. Not anymore. We're playing by Saint Dane's rules now, remember? It wasn't my choice."

Alder gave me a grave look. He touched one of the crates of tak. "I remember. But you should remember that we always have a choice."

"And we made it," I snapped at him. "We'll take one crate each and travel to Ibara. Taking more would be too awkward, and we don't want to go dropping these things. After we've moved them all, I'll come back for the weapons."

Alder nodded. Siry shrugged. I went first. I grabbed a heavy crate and backed into the flume. *"Ibara!"* I called, and was on my way.

The tricky part came on the other side. The crate floated, but it was difficult pushing it up and out of the break in the stone circle I'd made with the dygo. The crate was heavy, and it was hard getting enough leverage to lift it out while treading water. But I did it, and placed it a safe distance from the flume.

The others arrived shortly after. I helped them take their crates out of the water and placed them near the first. After that the three of us dove into the water with a shout of *"Denduron!"* and started back the other way.

It was a tiring, grueling, boring process. None of us let down our guard though. There was always the possibility of a slip and a drop and a boom. It took us a couple of hours, but all went well. When we were done, thirty crates of tak were stacked up on the territory of Ibara.

Alder, Siry, and I sat on the edge of the flume to get a much-needed rest. It wouldn't last. It couldn't last.

"We're back on the clock," I announced.

"What does that mean?" Siry asked.

"It means we're on Ibara time again. There's an invasion coming, remember?"

I'll end this journal here, Courtney. I'm getting too antsy to write any more. I'll tell you about our preparations in my next journal. Assuming there is a next journal. Alder is here with us, and I'm glad. He's already proved to be an incredible help, and knowing he'll be by my side during the battle gives me confidence that we actually have a chance. How good a chance? I don't know. At least I can say that we've done all that we can.

I'm scared and I'm excited. Now that we can look back on all that's happened, it's pretty clear that Saint Dane's plan has been leading to this all along. He thinks Ibara is going to be the first domino to fall in the toppling of Halla. I say he's got a very big surprise coming. I wish I could see his face when we blow his army to oblivion. Even if we lose, I'm going to make sure we take as many of those dados with us as possible. I'm playing by his rules now. He's

mixed the territories to try and crush Halla. I've mixed the
territories to try and stop him.

Only one of us will prove to be right.

And so we go.

END OF JOURNAL #31

● FIRST EARTH ●

Courtney crumpled the pages of Bobby's journal and tossed them against the wall. She was frightened and angry. Angry at herself. She had let Bobby down. Because of her failure, the final boundaries between territories were about to come crashing down . . . on Bobby's head.

Making it all the more dire was the fact that the more she learned about the situation with Mark, the less she understood. How could his parents be alive? She left Second Earth *after* history was altered. She knew how the changes that Mark made on First Earth would affect Second Earth. They did *not* include his parents being saved from dying in that plane crash.

Yet, they were alive and well.

Courtney thought that maybe one of the Dimonds might have been Saint Dane in disguise. Then who was the other person? Saint Dane could do a lot of things. He couldn't split himself in two. Since Nevva Winter was with Mark's parents, Courtney figured that unless another Traveler with shape-shifting abilities had suddenly entered the story, those people really were Mr. and Mrs. Dimond. She hated herself for being upset that Mark's parents were alive, but it made no sense to her.

Worse. Courtney knew that Bobby and the Travelers often had to make horrible choices for the greater good. She couldn't think of a single time when any of them had to make a choice as difficult as the one Mark had faced. He had to decide whether or not the people he loved the most should live or die. He chose to save them, and Nevva Winter delivered on her promise. By going to First Earth, Mark saved his parents. Courtney didn't think there was any way to convince Mark that he had been tricked. He would introduce Forge to First Earth, starting a chain reaction that would lead to the creation of the dados, the fall of Ibara . . . and his own murder.

Courtney decided she didn't like ocean voyages.

There was a knock on the door, followed quickly by the screech of the lock opening. Sixth Officer Hantin poked his head in.

"Time for a little supper, miss," he said warmly.

"I'm not hungry."

"Now, now," the ship's officer cajoled. "Don't want you to become a patient in this hospital ward, do we?"

He was followed quickly by a steward wearing a white coat, pushing a rolling table that was draped with a white tablecloth. Silver domes covered plates of food that Courtney had no intention of eating. She rolled over in her bunk.

The steward cleared his throat and said, "Come now, miss. Me thinks you're gonna be liking this, I do!"

Courtney had heard that strange accent before. She looked up in time to see the steward stand straight up, wink at her, then spin and swing a punch at Sixth Officer Hantin. He landed a haymaker that was so unexpected, it sent Hantin sprawling back against the bulkhead. Hantin tried to push off, but the steward nailed him with another punch that straightened him up. He hung there for a second, then crashed down onto the rolling table, unconscious, sending food and plates flying everywhere.

"Now I *know* I'm going to be sacked from the hotel," Dodger said as he shook his aching hand.

Courtney stared at the little guy with her mouth open in shock.

"Don't look so surprised," he said, insulted. "I was a Golden Gloves champ three years running."

Courtney jumped off the bunk and threw her arms around him. "I can't believe you found me!"

"I told you, this is nothing more than a floating hotel." He pushed away from Courtney and went to work. First he cleaned up the overturned cart. "Word of a stowaway travels fast. I know how to listen. Alls I did was pinch this outfit from the linens, grab a tray like I owned the place, and brought it right here. Easy-peasy."

"Yeah, right. You are awesome."

"Agreed. Now, we've got to be crafty. Once they figure out you're gone they'll be looking for a scruffy tomboy, not a beautiful young society lady."

"Know any?"

Dodger reached under the cart and pulled out a sparkling white evening gown and matching shoes.

"I do now," he said with a smile.

Courtney's eyes lit up as she grabbed the dress. "Where did you get this?"

"Went shopping on Regent Street," Dodger answered casually.

"You stole it."

"Nah." He pulled a piece of paper out of his pocket. "This was charged to a Mr. and Mrs. Anthony Galvao, suite twelve-twelve, cabin class. They won't see their bill until we dock. That should be interesting."

Courtney laughed, jumped behind the bunks, and started pulling off her clothes. As she changed, Dodger went through Hantin's pockets. He pulled out keys, a pair of handcuffs, and finally his pistol. He dragged Hantin to one of the bunks and hoisted him in. He handcuffed him to the rail, and pulled the blanket up to cover his face.

"Anybody peeks in, this is you, sleeping like a baby."

"What happens when he wakes up?"

"He could scream his head off and nobody'll hear. We're fine until somebody comes to relieve him."

Courtney stepped from behind the bunk. The dress fit perfectly. It was slim and silky, with short sleeves that showed off her muscular arms. Dodger whistled.

"Wowee. I knew there was a girl hiding in there somewhere."

"I'll take your word for it," Courtney said with a scowl, though she liked the compliment. "What about you? I don't think the stewards hang out with the passengers."

"Right you are," Dodger exclaimed.

He unbuttoned his white steward jacket and pulled it off to reveal he was wearing a tuxedo. It was perfect, right down to the shiny black shoes and slick tie. Dodger brushed his hair back and held his hands out for Courtney to appreciate him. "Not too shabby, huh?"

"Courtesy of the Galvaos?"

"They're a very generous pair," Dodger replied. "Let's get out of here. I found out what suite Mark is in and—"

"He was here, Dodger."

Dodger froze. "Uh . . . what?"

"He came here, to this cell. With Nevva Winter. I know her, Dodger. She's a Traveler. And she's a traitor. She helped Saint Dane win Quillan. It was Nevva Winter that got to Mark on Second Earth and told him that if he changed history he could save his parents from dying in that plane crash."

Dodger blinked and scowled, taking a second to let the wave of information sink in.

"Wow," he gasped. "It was simple as that? She flat-out lied and he bought it?"

"Not so simple. Mark's parents were here too. They're alive."

"But—"

"Yeah, I know," Courtney interrupted. "I don't get it either. Nevva delivered. It's hard to blame Mark for doing what he did."

"Even if it meant giving Saint Dane an army to conquer Halla?"

"I don't think she mentioned that part," Courtney answered sarcastically. "Mark didn't know Andy Mitchell is Saint Dane. I told him but he didn't believe me."

Dodger scratched his head and whistled in wonder. "So Mark is still a good guy."

"Yes, but we're going to have a hard time convincing him to destroy Forge."

Dodger frowned. "Yeah, I'll say."

"I can do it," Courtney said with certainty. "Mark is my friend. My best friend. If we can get him alone, away from the others, I'll convince him."

She went for the door. Dodger followed right behind. He took one last look to make sure everything seemed in order, then closed the heavy door and used Hantin's key to lock it. "Snug as a bug," he declared.

The two walked quickly forward down a long passageway. Courtney did her best to tie her hair up, trying to make it look like it was actually an intentional hairdo.

"Where's his cabin?" Courtney asked.

"Not cabin, suite. Those people from England spent a pretty penny to bring him over. They must know how valuable his gizmo is."

"Okay, where's his suite?" Courtney asked, getting impatient.

"Main Deck forward. But he's not there."

"How do you know that?"

"Because there was a dinner reservation for five, the Dimond party, in the cabin-class dining room," Dodger said proudly.

"You're amazing."

"Yes, yes I am."

The two moved quickly through the ship, up from the depths to the Promenade Deck and the same elegant restaurant that Courtney had sprinted through earlier. They forced themselves to calm down and walk slowly, pretending to belong. They got a few second glances, but Courtney was sure it was as much because her hair was a mess as anything. The two strolled casually, arm in arm, through the wide-open doors of the dining room.

Music from the big band filled the elegant room, which was now busy with diners. Inside the double doors was a sitting area with a huge fireplace and comfy chairs for passengers to sit in while waiting for their tables. To the right was a velvet rope leading up to a podium where a stiff-looking host with a slim mustache greeted passengers and showed them to their seats. Courtney and Dodger made a point to avoid that guy. They strolled past him into the sitting area. From there they had a view into the large dining room. Peering through a potted palm plant, Courtney and Dodger scanned for their quarry.

"There," Courtney said, pointing.

Halfway across the room, toward the stage, was a table for five with Mark, Andy, Nevva, and the Dimonds. Nevva and Andy were laughing and having a good old time. Mark and the Dimonds seemed more reserved. Mark twiddled his spoon, not interested in the food in front of him.

"May I help you two?" came a stern voice from behind.

Courtney and Dodger turned slowly to face the sour-looking host who loomed over them.

"No, thank you," Dodger said. "Just looking for some friends."

"Do you have reservations?" the host asked as if he already knew they didn't.

"No, we won't be dining here tonight," Courtney answered.

The host gave them a skeptical look. Dodger went on the offensive. He stood up straight and snapped, "Is there some problem we can help you with?"

The host backed off.

"Forgive me," he said apologetically with a deep bow. "If there is anything I might do for you, please do not hesitate."

"We won't," Dodger said coldly.

The host slinked off, chastised.

"That was great," Courtney giggled.

"Hey, we're paying customers. He can't treat us like we don't belong."

"Except we didn't pay and we don't belong."

"Details."

"So now what do we do?"

"No problem, I got this covered."

Courtney gave him a doubtful look.

"What?" Dodger said, offended. "Have I ever let you down?"

"I barely know you."

"But what you know, you like. Admit it," he cajoled.

"Dodger! This isn't a game."

"Sure it is, and I know how to play," he said confidently. "Keep an eye on them. When you get the chance, pull Mark outta there."

"What? How?"

Dodger smiled. "Trust me. Bring him to the stern. I'll meet you there."

"Where are you going?" Courtney asked.

Dodger put a finger to his lips. "Shhh, trade secrets. Just be ready."

He took Courtney's hand and gave it an elegant kiss. He then winked and backed away, headed toward the host. Courtney watched as he whispered a moment in the guy's ear and cagily slipped him something that could have been money for a tip. He cuffed the host on the arm as if they were old friends, and left the restaurant. What was going on? The host left his post and walked casually through the dining room, headed for the band. There was a dance floor between the dining tables and the stage, where several people moved to slow music. The host approached the bandleader and whispered something to him. The bandleader nodded and the host left.

What had Dodger done?

It was time for Courtney to start doing her part. She had to get close to Mark's table without being seen. She slipped through the potted palms, nearly falling over a table where an elderly couple sat.

"Oops, sorry," she said as she caught a bottle of wine that nearly fell to the floor.

"You!" the elderly woman exclaimed in anger. It was the same woman she and Dodger ran into, literally, when they first boarded the ship. The woman looked around for someone she could call to deal with Courtney.

"Sorry, ma'am, my fault," Courtney said as she carefully placed the bottle of wine back on the table. "This wine is on me. Charge it to my room. Twelve-twelve. Galvao."

"Why, uh, thank you," the elderly man exclaimed.

The woman just looked sour. She gave Courtney an annoyed look and went back to eating her soup. Courtney got away from her and moved closer to Mark's table, always trying to stay shielded by other diners. She got as close as one of the wide, wooden columns that was only a few yards from Mark. She stood with her back to it, waiting for . . . what?

The answer came quickly. A young steward hurried through the dining room holding a silver tray with a note on top. He went right to Mark's table, where Courtney heard him say, "This came in on the wireless for Mister Mitchell. From London. Apparently there is some urgency."

"Thanks," Courtney heard Andy say. Her skin crawled, knowing it was Saint Dane.

Andy read the note and scowled. "Shoot," he exclaimed angrily.

"What's the trouble?" Nevva asked.

"It's from KEM," Andy shot back. "I gotta wire them back. Now. C'mon, Nevva."

Courtney heard him push his chair back.

"Excuse us, please," Nevva said politely.

"Is there a problem?" Mr. Dimond asked.

"Nothin' I can't handle," Andy growled.

Andy and Nevva left the table and walked by the column where Courtney was hiding. They passed right by her on either side, inches away. Courtney held her breath. If they turned around, they'd see her. Courtney wanted to kick herself for getting so close. She watched as the two hurried away through the crowd without looking back. Courtney started breathing again. Now what? Was this her chance? Should she confront all three Dimonds? She liked Mr. and Mrs. Dimond. Maybe they'd listen to her. Or maybe they'd call the authorities, and she'd land back in the brig. She figured she had to take the chance. She was about to round the pillar when the band stopped playing and the bandleader stepped up to the microphone.

"We have a special request," he announced. "A spotlight dance for a happy couple who we understand are celebrating a very special occasion. Let's bring up Mr. and Mrs. Dimond. Where are you folks?"

The audience applauded and looked around, searching for the mystery couple. Courtney smiled. She knew that Mr. Dimond would be mortified. He wasn't a very good dancer. She also knew that Mrs. Dimond would drag him onto the floor anyway. She loved to dance. Courtney also knew that Dodger was a very crafty guy.

The room went dark. A spotlight kicked on and scanned the diners until settling on the Dimonds. The crowd continued to applaud as Mrs. Dimond dragged Mr. Dimond up to the dance floor. All eyes were on the Dimonds. Courtney slowly peered around the pillar to see Mark sitting alone, his chin in his hand, drumming his spoon absently on the table.

"Ten minutes," she said as she walked toward him. "That's all I'm asking for."

Mark jumped as if there were an electric charge in his seat.

"C-Courtney? How d-did you—"

"You're stuttering. That means my Mark is still in there. Please come with me."

"I c-can't," Mark said, looking sheepish.

"Yes, you can, Mark," Courtney implored. "You have to."

"Please, Courtney," Mark begged. "You can't ask me to do anything that might hurt them."

They both looked up at his parents, who danced alone in the spotlight. Courtney thought they looked radiant and happy.

"Hurting them is the last thing I want to do. But you have to know what's going on. There's a lot at stake here. You of all people should know that. Or did you forget everything that's happened over the past three years?"

Mark's glance darted nervously from his parents to Courtney.

"We don't have a lot of time," Courtney said. "Bobby is about to go to war, and you're the only one who can stop it."

Mark's eyes focused. Courtney knew that look. She'd seen it many times as they read Bobby's journals together and puzzled over the realities of time and space. She'd seen it as they were about to step into the flume, when they saw Black Water for the first time, and when the flume was created before their eyes in the basement of the Sherwood house. She knew she hadn't lost him.

"You gotta get back in the game, Mark."

Mark glanced at his parents. A sad smile crossed his face. He took a breath, tossed his spoon on the table, and stood up to face her.

"Hobey-ho," he said.

◉ FIRST EARTH ◉
(CONTINUED)

They moved quickly through the ship, avoiding crowds, taking routes that kept them away from curious eyes. Courtney knew they didn't have much time. She figured that when everyone returned to the table to discover Mark was gone, they'd probably give him a few minutes, assuming he went to the bathroom or something. That would be it. Saint Dane and Nevva would know something was wrong. Soon they'd have the whole ship looking for Mark. They'd discover Courtney had escaped. It was all going to fall apart very quickly. Courtney figured she had a small window to save Halla, and Mark.

They broke outside on A Deck and ran to the stern of the ship. The deck was empty. Nobody would bother them. At least not for a while. They hit the rail and stopped. Courtney looked down to the frothing ocean that was being churned up in the wake of the massive ship. It was a long way down. She turned to Mark, and for that one moment, she saw the little boy she had known for so long.

"I miss you, Courtney," Mark said.

The two hugged. Courtney squeezed her friend tight, allowing herself to think for that one moment that everything was going to be okay.

"You're freezing," Mark said, and took off his tuxedo jacket. He wrapped it around Courtney's shoulders.

"Thanks."

"A lot's happened," Mark said sadly.

"You have no idea," Courtney replied. "I've got to make sure you do. Mark, I understand what you told me. I understand why you did what you did."

"You say that like it's already done," Mark said. "We haven't gotten to England yet."

"That's why I'm here," Courtney said. "That's why the flume sent me back to before you brought Forge to that KEM company."

"You know about it?" Mark asked, surprised.

Courtney wanted to laugh. Did she know about it? She knew more than she ever wanted to know.

"There is so much to tell you," she said quickly. "But we don't have time. They're probably hunting for us right now. I've wrestled over a million different ways of how to get you to understand what really happened. Or what's about to happen. What I finally realized is that none of it matters, except for one single fact. It's the most important thing I can get you to believe, because everything else follows from it."

"What is it?" Mark asked.

"What I told you before is the truth. Andy Mitchell is Saint Dane. From the day we met him in kindergarten. This story didn't begin when Bobby left home. Saint Dane has been setting us up our whole lives. Setting *you* up. He got you to fear him. Then he seduced you by suddenly revealing he was a genius. Then he got you to trust him when he helped you rescue me after the accident in the mountains. It was all planned, Mark. You know what he's done on other territories. You know how he works his way into people's confidence to get them to make mistakes. That's what he's been doing on Second Earth. He's been working us. You have to believe me, Mark."

Mark didn't take his eyes off Courtney. She tried to read his mind. She hoped he was moving in fast forward through everything that got them to this point, looking at it from a new perspective. Mark was brilliant. He may feel used, he may feel betrayed, he may even feel like an idiot, but she felt sure he would understand and accept what happened. There was no other explanation.

"You're wrong," Mark finally said.

"But—"

"There's only one fact that matters to me. If events played out the way they were supposed to, my parents would be dead."

"But they are!" Courtney shouted. "I mean, I don't know what I mean, but I saw Second Earth after the past was changed. After *you* changed it. Your parents still went down with that plane."

"Then why are they here, right now, dancing in a spotlight?"

Courtney faltered. She didn't have an answer.

"Courtney!" Dodger called as he jogged up to them.

Mark stiffened.

"It's okay," she said. "This is Dodger. He's Gunny's acolyte."

Dodger stuck out his hand and shook Mark's.

"Pleased to meet you, chum," Dodger said amiably. "You're a tough one to get hold of. But now everything's fine. Right?"

Mark and Courtney both looked down to the deck.

Dodger frowned. "You told him about Saint Dane, right?"

"He still doesn't believe me."

"What proof do you have, Courtney?" Mark asked.

"You can read Bobby's journals," Courtney said weakly.

"That's not enough," Mark barked. "I have my parents. Here.

Alive. You're asking me to destroy Forge, right? That's like saying you want me to kill my parents."

"I know, it's hard," Courtney said.

"Hard?" Mark shouted. "That doesn't come close to describing it."

"Mark, something isn't right!" Courtney countered. "By introducing Forge to First Earth, you're going to set off a chain of events that leads to the creation of a technology Saint Dane is using to topple Halla. That's a fact. You don't know. You haven't read the journals."

"Maybe the journals are wrong," Mark countered. "You're saying how Saint Dane was able to fool us our entire lives, and fool me into starting Armageddon, maybe he was smart enough to monkey with those journals. Did you think of that?"

"No," Courtney said, shaking her head furiously. "You know that can't be right."

"But your version isn't true!" Mark barked. "My parents are proof. All you have are words on a page. I have living proof."

"But I was there!" Courtney cried, tears of frustration welling up. "I saw how Second Earth was changed."

"I'm sorry, Courtney," Mark said. "I think Saint Dane must have a hand in this somewhere, but it looks like you are the one he's been working. Like he did at that Stansfield Academy. I'm going to deliver Forge to that company in England. They are going to do with it whatever they will and begin a series of events that will save the lives of my parents. I don't know what Saint Dane did to you, but your version of events is not the way it was meant to be. We'll figure this all out once we get to London."

Mark touched Courtney on the shoulder warmly and began to walk away.

"Stay right there, Mark," Dodger said.

Mark looked up in surprise to see Dodger standing in his

way, holding the pistol he had taken from Sixth Officer Hantin.

"Dodger? What are you doing?" Courtney exclaimed, stunned.

"This is our last chance, Courtney," Dodger said. "Once he leaves, we're both going to get pinched by the crew and spend the rest of this trip in the brig. It's now or never."

"Put that away!" Courtney ordered.

Dodger didn't waver. Mark backed toward the rail nervously.

"He doesn't believe you!" Dodger complained. "You know what's going to happen if he leaves. Is that what you want?"

"No!" Courtney exclaimed. She turned to Mark with tears. "Please. Mark. I'm telling you the truth. I can't explain why your parents are alive, but if you don't destroy Forge, you could be destroying Halla."

"I believe you believe that, Courtney," Mark said. "I don't."

"Please don't make me do this," Dodger begged. His voice was nearly as shaky as Courtney's. His gun hand wasn't too steady either.

"I'm going to deliver Forge," Mark said, his voice growing more confident. "And I am going to save my parents."

He took a bold step toward Dodger. Dodger wavered. Courtney grabbed the gun out of Dodger's hand and held it on Mark.

"Stop!" Courtney commanded, crying. Her hand was shaking, but the gun stayed on Mark.

"C-Courtney?" Mark stammered as if his brain wouldn't accept what his eyes were seeing.

"There's more I haven't told you," Courtney said through the tears. "Bobby and I went to Third Earth. We looked back through history. Everything I said was true, Mark. Even this. Your body washed up on shore with a bullet in it. The computers didn't know who the killer was, but I think that mystery has been solved. It looks like it was . . . me."

"N-No," Mark stuttered. "I don't believe you'll shoot me."

"I love you, Mark," Courtney said, sobbing. "But I can't let you do this. I can't let you change history."

Mark stood frozen. Courtney cocked the pistol. Mark backed into the rail. There was nowhere to go.

"I love you too, Courtney," Mark said softly. "I guess this is the way it was really meant to be."

Courtney raised the pistol, squinting through her tears. Mark tensed up. He closed his eyes. Courtney took aim. She tightened her finger on the trigger. Nobody moved. The moment stayed frozen for an eternity. Courtney blinked, took a step to her right, and tossed the pistol overboard. It fell into the dark ocean, lost in the swirl of the ship's wake. Mark let out a breath he had been holding for a long time. Courtney ran to him and hugged him. Both let out the rush of emotions through their tears.

"Courtney!" Dodger shouted. "What are you doing?"

"I think I'm changing history," she answered. "Mark was killed on this ship. Now he's safe. Maybe I just bought us some more time to make things right." She looked at Mark and added, "I'm sorry."

"I am too," he said. "But I'm not going to change my mind."

"About what?" came a woman's voice.

Mr. and Mrs. Dimond approached the group, arm in arm.

"Is everything okay?" Mr. Dimond asked.

"Everything's fine," Mark said, though it didn't sound to anybody as if he meant it.

Mr. Dimond said, "We're still trying to understand all this, Courtney. We want to help you, and help Bobby. What can we do?"

Courtney looked at Mark. Mark looked away. She looked at Dodger, who gave her a helpless shrug. "It's your show."

The Dimonds huddled close to each other, waiting for Courtney to speak. Courtney had gotten to know the Dimonds once she and Mark had become acolytes. She thought they were terrific. The idea that she would want them to die, no matter how right history said that would be, was painful to Courtney. She wanted everything to be better and for the Dimonds to live their lives the way they were meant to. As she stood on the back of that ship, feeling hopelessly lost, a thought came to her.

"Maybe you *can* help," she said. "Maybe you're the only ones who can help."

"Anything," Mrs. Dimond said.

"You said Mark told you everything? About Halla and Saint Dane and the Travelers, right?"

"We're still in shock," Mrs. Dimond said.

"How much did you tell *him*? I mean about what happened with the flight to Florida?"

The Dimonds looked at each other with confusion.

"There isn't much to tell," Mr. Dimond said. "We didn't get on the plane. If we had, we wouldn't be here, right?"

"Yeah, but *why* didn't you get on the plane?" Courtney asked, her mind racing. "Mark thinks that by coming to First Earth he set in motion a series of events that saved your lives. I want to know what that was. What stopped you from getting on that plane?"

Mr. Dimond shrugged. "It was Nevva Winter. She caught us just as we were about to board. I thought Mark knew."

Courtney shot a look to Mark.

Mark slowly shook his head and said softly, "I didn't know that."

Courtney closed her eyes and smiled. It was such a feeling of relief that she wanted to fall to her knees and cry.

"Is it that important?" Mr. Dimond asked.

"It's everything," Courtney said. "Mark, that's your proof. Nevva knew what was going to happen and stopped your parents from boarding. She's from another territory. Nothing you're going to do here will have any effect on her. Or on that plane. It's still going to crash. Your parents are alive because Saint Dane saved them, in order to convince you to do exactly what you're doing."

Mark leaned back against the railing, staring at the deck but seeing nothing. Courtney desperately hoped that things would finally start to click into place.

"Mark," Courtney said boldly. "You can put things right, and your parents don't have to die. Please. Help Bobby."

Mark shot a pained look to Courtney and asked a simple, poignant question. "What have I done?"

"Nothing," Courtney said quickly. "Not yet, anyway."

Mark left the rail and pushed past the others, heading forward.

"Where are you going?" Mr. Dimond asked.

Without stopping, Mark said, "To destroy Forge."

◎ FIRST EARTH ◎

(CONTINUED)

"There they are!" shouted Andy Mitchell from above.

He was at the railing of the Promenade Deck, looking down on the Main Deck, where Mark had just left the others. With him were Nevva and two ship's officers.

"Go!" Courtney shouted.

Mark started running. Courtney and Dodger took off after him.

"Slow them down," Courtney ordered the Dimonds.

Mark disappeared inside the ship's structure, followed right behind by Courtney and Dodger. Andy led the officers down the outside stairs in pursuit, only to run into the Dimonds, who blocked his way at the bottom of the stairs.

"Hi, Andy," Mr. Dimond said jovially.

"Get out of the way!" Andy ordered.

The Dimonds held their ground. "I think you've got some explaining to do," Mrs. Dimond scolded.

Andy gave her a cold look that nearly knocked her off her feet. For a brief moment his eyes flashed blue with anger. Mrs.

Dimond gasped. Andy reared back as if to hit someone, but the ship's officer arrived behind him.

"Here now," the officer commanded. "No need for that. They're on a ship. They can't hide for long."

Andy spun to the officer, ready to lash at him. He saw Nevva standing on top of the stairs behind the officers and motioned for her to go back the other way. Andy pushed past the officer, headed back up the stairs.

Mrs. Dimond looked to her husband and said, "Can life get any stranger?"

Mark sprinted down the passageway of the Main Deck. He didn't double back or take a route that was hard to follow. It was all about speed. Courtney and Dodger were right behind him. They no longer cared about being seen. Spending the rest of the voyage locked up no longer mattered. It had come down to this. A race. They had to get back to Mark's suite before anyone else. Before Andy or Nevva. It was the final leg of their mission.

They had to destroy Forge.

Up ahead of them, a group of elegantly dressed passengers strolled out of the dining room, laughing and singing.

"Get out of the way!" Mark screamed.

He didn't wait for them to obey. He ran straight at them. Men dove away, women scattered. Courtney would have laughed if she weren't about to hit them herself. Just as the passengers gathered their wits, Courtney arrived at full speed.

"Get out of the way!" she yelled as the surprised passengers flung themselves to the walls. Courtney and Dodger flew past with no apologies.

Mark sprinted down a long passageway that was lined with elegant, white doors. He slowed down enough to focus on the door numbers, which allowed Courtney and Dodger to catch up.

"Is this it?" Courtney yelled. "Is this where your suite is?"

"Yeah," Mark answered, gulping air while digging in his pocket for keys.

"Fast is our friend," Courtney cautioned.

"Going as fast as I can," Mark snapped back.

He stopped at a door and worked to get the key in the lock.

"Mark, stop!" came a screaming voice from behind them. Andy Mitchell appeared at the far end of the passageway.

"Gotta hurry, chum," Dodger implored.

Mark fumbled with the key.

"I'm too f-freaking nervous!" Mark shouted. "There!"

He twisted the key and threw the door open. All three jumped inside. Dodger closed the door behind them and locked it. Mark dove for the small wooden dresser and yanked the top drawer open, digging through socks.

Dodger turned around and whistled. "Wow, nice digs." He plopped himself down on a couch and put his arms behind his head. "Might as well enjoy it, seeing as we'll be spending the rest of the trip in irons."

Courtney stood behind Mark, watching nervously. "Tell me it's still there," she begged.

"Got it!" Mark announced.

He held up the innocuous little device that was about to change history. Courtney remembered it all too well. To her it looked like a small ball of Silly Putty. Inside was a complex skeleton that was controlled by an advanced computer of Mark's design that changed shape in response to voice commands. The plastic skin Saint Dane had stolen from Third Earth. The computer technology was all Mark's. He called it "Forge." It was the brainchild of the Dimond Alpha Digital Organization. It was a little ball of clay. It was the grandfather of the dados.

"Kill it," Courtney commanded.

Mark held his invention up and stared at it like a loving parent.

Dodger jumped up and put his ear to the door.

"They're coming," he said calmly. "Now would be good."

"I'm sorry, Courtney," Mark said softly. "I didn't mean for any of this to happen."

"We'll have all the time in Halla to talk about it later. Do it!"

The anguish on Mark's face was obvious. He dropped the high-tech ball onto the deck, closed his eyes, and stamped his foot down. Courtney heard the satisfying crack and crumble, as Forge was crushed into history. At the exact instant Mark's foot destroyed Forge . . .

Courtney's ring came to life. She held it up for the others to see.

"Does this mean things have changed back?" Mark asked.

"I think we're about to find out," Courtney answered.

She took the ring off and placed it on the deck.

Dodger kept his ear to the door. "I don't hear them coming anymore. Do you think they know?"

"I guarantee they know," Courtney replied.

Mark twisted his foot into the carpet, making sure every last bit was pulverized. He scooped up the remains and tossed them out the porthole. Forge was no more.

The ring grew as light flashed through the room. Dodger joined the other two and watched the show. Moments later the ring returned to normal. Next to it was a rolled parchment.

"That didn't take long," Courtney said nervously.

"Time flies when you're flying through time," Dodger said.

Courtney picked up the pages and clutched them to her chest. "I guess we'll read this in the brig. I'm proud of you, Mark."

She leaned over and gave him a kiss on the cheek. Mark stared at the floor.

"You did the right thing, chum," Dodger said. "Sorry for, you know, nearly shooting you before. I didn't want to."

Mark didn't react. He kept staring at the floor.

"Are you okay?" Courtney asked.

"I don't know," Mark answered. "I won't know until I find out if my parents are still alive."

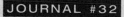

IBARA

This is my last journal.

I know I've written words like that before, but it was always out of fear that something might prevent me from writing. That's not the case here. Nothing is going to happen to me. Not anymore. I made sure of that. As I write this journal, I feel safe for the first time since I left home to become a Traveler. It wasn't easy getting to this place. In fact, it was a nightmare. But it's over now. Sort of. I'm going to have to relive it in these pages. Part of me wants to skip writing it all down, because it's too painful. That wouldn't be fair. Not to you, Courtney. Not to the other Travelers. Not to Uncle Press. I have to finish what I started, just as I did here on Ibara. After looking back on all that's happened since I wrote my last journal, there is one thing I can say with absolute certainty. The battle for Halla is over. How that happened will be related to you here, in my final journal. I hope I can find the right words to paint the picture as it happened. As I saw it. As it was meant to be.

When we returned to the island of Ibara with the tak, we

dressed Alder in local clothes and hurried out of the newly dug tunnel, headed for Tribunal Mountain. Not a single quig-bee bothered us. The poison must have killed them all. When we reached the village, the people were milling around nervously. Many cried. Others consoled them. There was an air of foreboding.

"It's like we never left," Siry said to me in wonder.

"I told you. The flume puts us where we need to be, when we need to be there. It looks like the Flighters attacked the pilgrims only a few hours ago."

"Amazing," Siry whispered in awe.

I didn't think it was amazing at all. The amazing thing was that I didn't question it. As we hurried through the village, I saw that Alder was taking it all in. Analyzing our chances. He didn't have anything good to say.

"Where is the army?" he asked.

"There is no army" was my sober answer.

"Then who will fight the dados?"

"You're looking at them," I answered.

"These people are not prepared for war," he declared. "They are not trained. How do you plan to fight off an army of machines with fishermen?"

"Now you see why we need the tak" was my answer.

As we got closer to the mountain, I saw that Genj had done what I'd asked. A crowd had formed at the mountain's base. The security force was rounding up every person in the village who was willing and able to fight. Seeing this crowd of frightened villagers made me realize just how right Alder was. These people had no chance of defending their island.

The tribunal was waiting for us in their cavern room. Telleo was there too. The security guys waved us right in. Man, things had changed. We were no longer outlaws.

"This is Alder," I announced. "He is a warrior. He can help us."

When Genj saw us, he frowned. "You went for help and returned with a single man?"

Genj looked skeptical. So did Moman and Drea. Telleo didn't look so thrilled either. That was okay. They didn't know Alder.

"There's no way to know how long we have," I said. "We need to form our defense now."

"I don't understand," Moman said. "The Flighters have already attacked. The pilgrim ships are destroyed. Why would they attack again?"

"It's not the Flighters we have to worry about," I explained. "There is an army gathered on Rubic City that is going to invade Ibara. They are worse than Flighters. They're machines."

Genj and the others stared at me as if I were from Neptune. Or wherever it was crazy people came from on Veelox.

"I've seen it," Siry added. "They're going to come here on small ships. Thousands of them."

Genj asked, "And who is this person who controls the army? The man who killed Remudi?"

"He's the leader of the Flighters," I answered. It was only a small lie. He *was* leading the Flighters. Of course, he had bigger plans than that, but I didn't want to go there just then. Or ever. The tribunal exchanged looks. They still needed convincing.

"Look," I said sharply. "Either let us help you, or everything you've worked for, everything your ancestors worked to build, everything Aja Killian envisioned for Ibara is going to be destroyed. The choice is yours."

That stung them.

"I believe Pendragon," Telleo said. "The Flighters have destroyed our future. Why do we doubt they'll stop there?"

"We aren't warriors," Genj declared.

"I know," I said. "We've got to be smart . . . and lucky."

It was time to prepare for the defense of Ibara. My idea of bringing tak was to use it as a weapon against the dados. My thoughts didn't go much beyond that. Having Alder around suddenly seemed like a brilliant idea. He knew tactics. He was part of an army. Okay, it was an army of knights, but it was still an army. We spread out the maps of Ibara that Aja had given me on the tribunal's table and huddled around.

"Where did you get these?" Genj asked in surprise.

"Rubic City" was my simple answer. I didn't mention that it was Rubic City a few hundred years before, and that they were handed to me by Aja Killian. That would have made his brain melt.

Scanning the map, I immediately recognized the large bay where Rayne was constructed. Alder leaned in close, surveying the details of the island.

"There is only one place on the island where a large invasion can land," Alder concluded. "Here in the bay."

"That's why Rayne was built here," Genj explained. "It is the only workable port. The rest of the island is ringed by rocky cliffs and treacherous beaches."

"Then we know where to put our defenses," Alder said. He pointed to several red squares that were positioned in the water just outside the bay. "And what are these?"

Moman answered, "They are the guns the military installed generations ago. They are positioned to defend the entrance to the bay."

Alder looked to me. He wasn't familiar with guns.

"They fire automatically?" I asked.

"No," Genj answered. "They are controlled and maintained by our security force from here in the mountain."

"We'll need to see how they work," I said.

Genj shook his head. He didn't like something. "This is difficult for us. From the time Ibara was settled, the tribunals have kept the military workings of this island a secret from the population. The guns have rarely been used, and then only at night for training."

"Genj," I said, trying to sound patient. "Do you seriously believe, after what happened to the pilgrims, that there is a single person left in Rayne who doesn't know about those guns?"

Genj looked to Moman and Drea with anguish. I felt for them. They had dedicated their lives to following the guidelines set by Aja Killian centuries before. They were now learning that it no longer mattered. Their mission had changed from one of hope, to one of desperation.

"Continue," he finally said to me.

"What is this thing?" I pointed to a thick, dark line that ran directly beneath the village, parallel to the beach.

"A tunnel," Genj answered. "The military used it to store weapons."

"Is anything left down there?" I asked hopefully. "Any weapons I mean?"

"No," Genj answered. "They were destroyed when the military abandoned the island."

"What other weapons do you have?" Alder asked.

Siry answered. "Blowguns. With poison tips."

Alder and I exchanged dark looks. "Not a lot of good they'll do against machines," I said.

Genj added, "We also have bows that fire arrows longer distances. Would they help?"

Alder actually perked up after hearing that. "They will," he declared.

I knew what he was thinking. Arrows could deliver tak.

"We must not waste time," Alder concluded. "I have a plan."

The plan was one part genius, one part clever, and eight parts desperation. The only real hope we had of defending the island was to pick off the dados as they landed. Our only advantage was that we could hide our defenses. The dados had to come at us. We would be waiting.

The first thing we did was address the people of Rayne in the large, outdoor theater. The place was jammed with anxious, frightened people. They had all seen the pilgrim ships being attacked. It didn't take much to convince them that another attack was imminent. Genj did the talking, telling the people they weren't the last of a dying world, they were the first of a *new* world. He gave them both hope and fear—hope for a new beginning and fear that they wouldn't get the chance unless they defended the island. He was good. I had new respect for the guy. He wanted to do what was right for his people. I could argue that the people of Ibara should never have been kept in the dark for so long, but that wasn't Genj's fault. He was only following the instructions handed down for generations. Instructions that came from Aja. How weird was that?

Genj introduced Alder and me to the crowd. He told them how we had come from across the sea with the know-how to defend Ibara. Genj told them to follow our orders as if we were on the tribunal ourselves.

He put the trust of the people and the future of Ibara square into our hands.

Many things needed to be done quickly. Alder gave Telleo

the task of organizing all those who couldn't fight. That meant the children and the elderly. Several people were assigned to take them away from the village to a secure spot in a village across the island. While that exodus was under way, Siry led a group of thirty people to the rocky caves by the shore to transport the tak into the village.

He asked me, "What do I tell them about the dygo?"

"Tell them it's something we brought to Ibara from far away. It'll freak them out and give us total credibility." I added, "And make sure nobody drops anything. The last sound they'll hear is a very big boom."

With that sobering thought in mind, Siry took off with his team.

Alder and I got a crash course in the guns of Ibara from a security dude. The firing room was built into the mountain, with a view high over the bay. From there, every gun position could be seen. There was a single chair that swiveled left and right. In front of the chair was a control panel, and a joystick with a trigger. Each of the ten weapons were controlled from that one spot. It was explained to us by the security guy that from the first day Ibara was settled, there was always one person manning the guns in case of an attack. It wasn't until recently that they were needed.

Before leaving the room I looked out the rocky opening in the direction of Rubic City. The sea was empty. We still had time.

Once Siry and his team brought the tak to the mountain, they began the delicate task of fixing small bits of the explosive to the tips of arrows. Thousands of arrows were brought from storage deep within the mountain, along with several hundred bows. Siry took charge, organizing the men and women into assembly lines to efficiently turn out explosive arrows. He was a natural leader. He cajoled, ordered, threatened, and begged the people to ensure maximum output. They ended up creating an arsenal of thousands of arrows. Unfortunately there were many thousands of dados.

Alder's plan called for archers to be positioned in four lines, parallel to the shore. The first line would begin near the water and others would continue on back toward the mountain. The archers would pick the dados off as they landed. Of course, there was no way they could get them all. As the dados grew closer, the lines would retreat and join the others to the rear, where they would continue to shoot. The goal was to take out as many as possible before they reached Tribunal Mountain.

Our final stand would be made from the mountain. It was the best defensive position to take. The archers would gradually move farther and farther back, until they all ended up inside the mountain. With luck, enough of the dados would have been taken out so we could successfully defend the mountain. If not, the mountain would become our tomb.

While Siry supervised the arrow making, Alder and I were taken into the tunnels beneath the village. The entrance was in Tribunal Mountain. We descended ancient stone stairs to find a long, narrow passageway that looked like a mine tunnel cut through solid rock. My sense of direction told me that it led toward the beach. We jogged the length of it, passing a few smaller cross-tunnels that weren't even on the map. We finally hit the end of this first tunnel and an intersection where we had to turn either right or left. This was the large tunnel from the map. It stretched into darkness on either side of us for as far as I could see, parallel to the beach. There were ancient ladders propped up toward the ceiling every ten feet or so. Alder climbed one and peered into a cutout in the rock.

"I see the water," he announced. "These are defensive positions. We will position our third line down here. The dados will not know where the attack is coming from."

When Alder jumped down he actually had a smile on his face. "We may have a chance after all, Pendragon."

I looked up and down the dark tunnel. An idea was forming.

"What are you thinking?" Alder asked.

"This tunnel is our secret weapon. The trick is to figure out how best to use it."

It was getting late in the day. The sun dipped down over the mountain, casting long shadows over Rayne. Alder thought the chances of the dados attacking at night were pretty slim. It took a little pressure off. Very little. When the sun came up the next day, it would be over the water. That meant it would be in our eyes.

Alder said, "If they are smart, they will attack at dawn when the sun is at its lowest point."

"You mean when we'd be blind," I said.

Alder nodded. Great. We had to prepare as if dawn would bring the dados. Dawn of the Dados. Sounds like a bad horror movie. Maybe it was.

Telleo returned after dark to report that the children and the older folks were safe on the far side of the island. Safe? Did I say "safe"? For how long? It wasn't something I wanted to think about.

The last event of the night was to bring our makeshift army back to the gathering place to pass along final orders. This wasn't a real army. There were no officers or sergeants or any true organization. Besides Alder, none of us had any experience with waging a war. We were making it up as we went along.

I left it to Siry to organize his people. He divided them into groups. Those who felt confident with the bows and arrows were moved to one side. My quick count said there were around a hundred potential archers. Another group was chosen for their speed. They would be the messengers who would relay orders from the mountain command post to the lines of archers. The final group would be the utility players. They would go where they were needed, whether it be to move ammunition around, help the wounded, or in the worst case, take the bows and tak arrows from those who fell, to be used elsewhere.

It was going to be a war and it was going to be ugly.

Alder explained his strategy to the group, showing them on the map where each line should be when the invasion began. He told them they should stay in their positions as long as possible and wait for the order to move back before retreating. The final move would be into the mountain, where they would continue their defense for as long as possible.

As long as possible. Who knew how long that would be? What had Saint Dane told the dados to do? How would this end? Would there be a chance for surrender? Or was their mission to wipe out the entire population? I didn't want to go there, but it was a very real possibility.

While Alder spoke, I sat behind him, looking into the faces of the people of Ibara. There were about two hundred who stayed to fight. Nobody said a word. They listened intently. Every last one of them looked scared. They were listening for anything that might give them a little assurance that they actually had a chance. They had seen what happened to the pilgrims. They may not have understood their enemy, but they knew what they were capable of. Out of the nine hundred pilgrims who left on ships that morning, only half had survived the attack.

Up until that moment, the only thing on my mind was beating Saint Dane. Like I've said, the battle for Ibara was likely to be the first battle for all of Halla. But staring into those frightened faces made me realize that it was also their battle. These weren't pawns to be used for some grander conflict. They were innocent people who had lived peaceful, productive lives. This was their home. They'd done nothing to bring on the horror that was about to descend on them. The future of all existence now rested on their shoulders. It wasn't fair. Saint Dane has said how the people of the territories always brought on their own misfortune. What had these people done wrong? Their sole mission was to survive and try to revive a dying culture. What had they done to deserve this? The answer was nothing, and it made me hate Saint Dane all the more. I wanted to win this battle for all the reasons I've said, but after spending time with these people and feeling their fear, I wanted to win for them, too.

When Alder was finished, he asked if I wanted to say something to the people. It was a tough thing. What could I say that would make them understand how important the fight was going to be? Or to give them hope that there was a chance they wouldn't be slaughtered? I stood on the stage, alone, looking out on their frightened faces. The tribunal sat to the side of the stage, trying to look confident. I knew they were just as scared as everyone else, including me. Telleo sat next to her father. She gave me a smile and a nod of support. I wanted to say something to make them feel better, but what? Most of them didn't know about the world beyond their shore. How could I begin to explain Halla? They had no idea that they were about to play a pivotal role in the future of all that ever existed, or would exist. What could I possibly tell these people that would give them confidence? They all stared at me, looking for answers. Or inspiration. Or something.

"This battle isn't our entire future," I finally said. "This isn't the end. It's only a moment in time. No matter what happens, there will always be a future. It's up to us to make it a better one. I believe we can do that. Never, ever give up hope, because that's exactly what they want. No matter how this battle turns out, if we continue to believe there is hope for a better future, we will have won."

That's all I said. I left the stage feeling as if I had failed. The first person I saw when I stepped down was Siry. He had tears in his eyes.

"What's the matter?" I asked.

"Of all the things you've told me, those are the words I will remember."

I felt a hand on my shoulder. It was Telleo.

"Destiny brought you here for us, Pendragon," she said. "You are our future."

She leaned forward, kissed me on the cheek, and hugged me close. I hugged back. For that one moment, I let myself believe that everything was going to be okay.

Alder and I returned to the community hut that I had made my home. That's where I finished my last journal and sent it to you. There was no way I could sleep. What would the morning bring? How would this play out? Was this going to be the beginning of the end? Or the greatest victory of all time? No, of all *times*.

For so many years we've lived by Uncle Press's mandate that the territories should never be mixed. Each territory is supposed to live out its own destiny without interference. That's the way it was meant to be. But Saint Dane changed that and forced me to make a difficult choice. Is there a price that is too high to pay for victory? Should we have let the klee of

Eelong kill off the gars? Should I have left Quillan without entering the Grand X? Saying things should happen the way they were meant to be doesn't mean that things will always turn out for the best. We shouldn't interfere with the natural order of the territories, but neither should Saint Dane. Because of his devious influence things have not played out the way they were supposed to. Anywhere. Will two wrongs make a right? I don't know. The only thing I can say for sure is that it's too late to turn back now.

As I finished that last journal, I still held out hope that you had gotten to Mark, Courtney. I imagined the sun rising with no dados on the horizon. I imagined waiting for a battle that was not to happen, because the dados had ceased to exist. It actually made me more anxious. I couldn't let myself think that way. I had to prepare as if the battle were inevitable. I had to put my game face on. Lying at my feet was one of the black dado weapons from Quillan. I wanted to use it. I wanted the sun to rise.

I wanted to fight.

IBARA

Alder and I left early the next morning for Tribunal Mountain. We walked through Rayne in the dark. With an hour to go before sunrise, the archers were already taking up their positions. For all I knew, they'd been there all night. The first line was at the edge of the beach. The next line was inside the village itself, using huts for protection. The third line was underground, peering out from the tunnel beneath the sand. The fourth and final line was behind that, halfway to the mountain. We made brief eye contact with some of the archers. I saw fear, but confidence. They weren't soldiers, but they were ready to fight a war. No words were exchanged, only slight nods of acknowledgment.

The command post was set up inside the firing room that controlled the underwater guns. From there we had a clear view of the bay, the ocean beyond it, and the village below. The battle would play out beneath us. We had the best seats in the house.

The three members of the tribunal were already there, along with Siry and the big guy who arrested me when I first got to Ibara. This guy was our first line of defense. He sat in the gunner's chair. Also there were three young guys who were runners, to pass along commands to the archers.

I approached the gunner and asked straight out, "How good are you?"

The big guy swiveled his chair toward me and boldly said, "The best there is."

The guy had total confidence. That made a grand total of exactly one of us.

The map of Ibara hung on the rock wall. Lines were drawn to show where the archers were placed. I stood staring at it, wondering how it would all play out. I could envision the battle, what I couldn't see was the end game. Of course, I hoped we'd obliterate the dados before they did any real damage, but that didn't seem likely. I didn't want to be a pessimist, but the numbers weren't on our side.

As if reading my thoughts, Genj approached and said, "If this goes badly, will they accept surrender?"

"I don't know. We'll have to figure that out when the time comes."

"*If* the time comes," Siry corrected.

He was feeling confident too. Now there were exactly two of us.

"Where's Telleo?" I asked.

Genj answered, "I sent her to be in charge of the villagers who are in hiding."

Drea asked, "Is there a chance this might not happen at all?"

"We can hope" was the best answer I could give.

I left the map and went to the wide window that was cut into the rock. The sky was beginning to lighten. Soon we would be able to make out detail on the ocean and learn if anything was out there. Alder joined me. We both looked out onto the black sea.

"I do not know if what we are doing is right," he said. "But I do not believe we had a choice."

I nodded, grateful for the support.

The inky sky slowly turned blue, followed by a thin line of light that appeared on the horizon. Sunlight was minutes away. We all stood at the window, focused intently on the glowing band.

"I don't see anything," Siry said hopefully. "Shouldn't we see them by now?"

I didn't answer. I didn't know.

"This is good news," Moman proclaimed hopefully. "Perhaps the sinking of the pilgrim ships was all they wanted."

I had my own hopes. I hoped that you had found Mark, and there was no longer any such thing as dados.

"You may be right about the pilgrims," Drea added. "They may have felt threatened by our attempt to move off the island and only wanted to make sure we'd stay here and—"

"There," Alder announced sharply. "Something is out there."

It was next to impossible to see anything. The water was still black.

"I don't see anything," Siry said.

We had to wait a few painful minutes for the sun to throw more light over the horizon. When the first direct rays spilled onto the ocean, it all came clear. Drea gasped. Considering what we were looking at, it was a pretty mild reaction.

Genj said softly, "What manner of evil could have created such a thing?"

I knew the answer, but didn't think he wanted to hear it. What we saw on the ocean that morning was indeed evil.

There's no better word to describe it. At that moment I knew how those German soldiers must have felt on the beach in France during World War II when they woke up one morning to see the entire Allied fleet on the horizon.

Out on the open ocean, beyond the break in the beach that led into the bay, were thousands of skimmers. I'll repeat that. Thousands. They moved slowly, in tight formation, headed directly for us. The first line had about fifty craft. Followed by another. And another and another. Too many to count. It looked as if each skimmer held three passengers. The rising sun made them look like ghostly silhouettes. They were angels of death. The waiting and wondering was over.

We were about to be invaded.

"They have weapons," Alder announced.

From as far away as we were, we could see that one dado on each craft held a golden rifle. They looked like weapons from Quillan. The gunner stood next to me, staring in wide-eyed wonder.

"You say you're the best," I said to him. "Prove it."

The gunner stiffened with resolve and jumped for his chair. The controls were simple. In front of him was a panel with a series of toggle switches. The chair was high enough for him to look down onto his weapons in the sea below. A series of mirrors were embedded in the stone beneath this window, each giving him the view of a particular gun.

"What kind of ammunition does it fire?" I asked.

"Small projectiles, propelled by water pressure."

Oh. That didn't exactly sound like a devastating weapon of mass destruction, but it was a little late to be picky.

"How many shots do you have?"

His answer was a frown that meant "not enough."

The lines of skimmers tightened up as they drew closer to

the opening of the bay. That was good. It made for a smaller target.

"Raise the guns!" Genj ordered, his anxiety growing. "Fire!"

"They aren't in range," the gunner replied, concentrating. "Don't worry. When they get closer, I'll give them a special welcome."

I saw a black flash swoop through the sky, flying past the mountain, headed out to sea. It looked like an oversize black bird. I'd never seen anything like it on Ibara, but I'd seen it before.

"Saint Dane," I whispered to Alder.

Alder added, "It appears he will be viewing his war from above."

"Yeah, let's give him a good show."

My palms were sweating. Out of habit I picked up the black dado-killing wand. It served absolutely no purpose other than to give me something to hold on to. I kept squeezing it while watching the dados approach. More and more lines kept appearing. It looked as if there were an endless number.

"Little closer," the gunner coaxed. His hand gripped the joystick. "Little closer."

The dados tightened further. The first line was fifty yards from entering the bay. They were in range. All was silent. That wouldn't last.

"Welcome to Ibara," the gunner said, and reached for the control panel, quickly flipping a line of switches.

One by one the guns of Ibara rose up out of the water. Before this I'd only seen one set of guns. Now ten silver dual cannons came out of the depths and locked into position, forming a protective half circle in front of the bay. The dado armada was sailing right into their sights. The battle for Ibara was about to begin. The gunner's right hand was on the joystick to aim and fire. His left hand was on the control panel to alternate between guns.

"Now, now!" Genj ordered.

The gunner let loose. With his chair swiveling quickly to line himself up with the series of gun sights, he unleashed a torrent of missiles. *Thump, thump, thump, thump.* Instantly dados exploded before our eyes. It would have been a gruesome sight if they had been people. But they were machines. It was like shooting a dishwasher. A deadly dishwasher, but still, a dishwasher. I dug every second of it.

The gunner spun back and forth quickly, lining up his sights, using his left hand to alternate between the ten dual guns, blasting the dados into eternity. It was a beautiful thing. He was good. Then again, there were so many dados, he could have fired with his eyes closed and nailed one every time. Since the drivers of each skimmer stood to the front of their crafts, they were always the first hit. Once they were either knocked off their feet or blasted to bits, the skimmer would lie dead in the water while the other dados scrambled to take control. It caused a massive jam up. The skimmers piled into one another. The chain reaction kept growing until it was chaos on water. S eet.

war w ll be over before it starts," the gunner shouted
k pt firing.

fish in a barrel" sprang to mind. The
shot meant one dead dado. Sometimes
d with floating dado parts.

pped her hands, exclaiming,
s!"

. He watched the carnage with a

scowl. I knew he was thinking the same thing I was. The gunner was doing better than we could have hoped. He was destroying hundreds upon hundreds of dados. Unfortunately, there were thousands upon thousands of dados. We were only in the first quarter.

I grabbed one of the runners and shouted, "Get down to the first line of archers. Tell them to hold their fire until the dados step onto the beach."

He nodded and ran off.

"What do you mean?" Drea asked in dismay. "It doesn't look like they'll get beyond the opening to the bay, let alone the beach."

"They'll turn back," Genj said with confidence. "Now that they see how well we're defended, they'll cut their losses."

"They won't," I said flatly.

"How can you know that?" Moman asked.

"They already knew about the guns," I answered. "Why do you think they sent so many? They're machines. They don't care how many are destroyed. They'll just keep coming until our ammunition runs out."

The gunner continued his onslaught. The water was a debris field of destruction. Skimmers flew along with no drivers, smashing into other skimmers. The dados in the water couldn't swim. If a missile didn't kill them, the water did. Hundreds thrashed wildly before sinking. Many were hit by speeding skimmers, or from the next line of dados. It was a slaughter.

"I'm nearly done," the gunner called out.

"Keep firing!" Genj ordered.

The gunner didn't miss a beat. He kept swivel spinning, changing his guns, destroying dados. I re he was using fewer and fewer of the guns. Soon, h firing between only four. Then three and two and finally one. With a last destructive burst, the guns fell silent.

"That's it," the gunner said, exhausted. He was covered with sweat and breathing hard.

Down below there was a logjam at the entrance to the bay. The dados from the rear couldn't push past.

"This obstruction will not last long," Alder observed.

He was right. Several skimmers left the rear ranks and zoomed around to either side of the bottleneck of dead skimmers and dados. Methodically they pushed the debris out of the way.

"They know what they're doing," Siry said. "They expected this."

I didn't know how many dados the gunner had gotten. Three hundred? Five hundred? Maybe a thousand? Who cared when there were thousands more out there with only a hundred yards of wreckage between them and the bay.

The tribunal realized that their brief moment of triumph was already a memory.

"It's up to the archers," Siry said.

There was nothing we could do but wait, and worry. It was like being in the eye of a hurricane. It was a false calm. The storm would start again soon enough. Down below I saw the first line of archers tensing up. They knew what was coming. It was going to come down to numbers. If the tak-charged arrows could knock out enough dados, it might end the invasion. Looking out at the multiple lines of dados in skimmers, waiting for their pathway to clear, I didn't like our chances.

"I'm no use up here," the gunner said. "I'm going down to join my line."

"You were incredible," I told him.

"I'm proud of you," Genj added. "We all are."

The gunner nodded in thanks, and was gone.

The dados waited patiently on their skimmers for the path to be cleared. Those not clearing the debris had re-formed into tight groups that looked exactly wide enough to pass through the opening into the bay. They knew what they were doing all right. Still, there was no way they could know what waited for them in Rayne. They knew about the guns. They didn't know about tak.

"This is it," I declared.

The entrance to the bay was clear. The skimmers fired up and moved forward. The eye of the hurricane was on its way out.

"Wait," I whispered. I wanted the first line of archers to do just that. My fear was that they'd start shooting too soon and the dados would scatter. We needed to draw as many as we could into the trap and maximize the destructive power of the tak arrows.

The dados were in no hurry. They moved slowly and in perfect formation into the bay. They looked more like conquering heroes, who had arrived to capture their spoils, than an invading army ready for battle.

"They think the battle is over," Siry said hopefully. "They have no idea they're about to hit a firestorm."

The armada grew closer to the beach. I hoped the runner had gotten to the line with my message to wait. It had to be terrifying to be down there, watching the enemy get closer. But they had to be patient. The longer their nerves held out, the more dados would go down.

"They are doing it," Alder declared. "They are waiting. We may have a chance."

The first line of dados hit the beach. They didn't jump off their skimmers and dive into the sand to protect themselves.

Just the opposite. They all looked to one another as if making sure they had arrived safely, then casually got off their skimmers and began to walk toward the village. There was no tension. No fear. No battle readiness whatsoever. The dados with guns didn't even take aim. They held them casually, pointing at the sky.

It was perfect.

"Now," I growled, hoping somebody would be bold and fire the first arrow.

Nobody did. More dados landed on the beach and followed the others toward Rayne.

"Why aren't they shooting?" Genj cried. "Something is wrong."

"Either that," I said, "or those guys have more guts than we gave them credit for."

The dados kept coming. More and more landed and amassed on the beach. Soon there would be multiple hundreds, and it would be too late for the arrows to have any effect. Just as I was beginning to think our plan had failed . . .

The first dado exploded. I mean, exploded. It happened so suddenly, we all jumped in surprise. The arrow was totally silent. The first sign that anything had happened was that a dado in the middle of the first line found himself in pieces all over the beach. The others stopped and looked around in confusion. Or at least in as much confusion as a robot can show. They had no idea what happened. Seconds later a dozen more dados exploded in white hot flashes, raining parts onto the sand.

Alder said, "They do not understand what is happening." I heard excitement in his voice. I felt it myself. Was it possible? Did we stand a chance?

The archers fired steadily. The explosions were deafening.

One after the other, dados were blasted to bits. Smoke filled the beach. I worried that it would hurt the aim of the archers, but it didn't matter. There were so many dados, even if an arrow missed one, and then another, it would eventually hit something.

Finally the dados took cover. They dove to the ground and crawled forward in the sand. It didn't matter. That didn't stop the archers. They continued to fire, blasting them into shrapnel. Flying bits of burning dado did as much damage to the other dados as the arrows themselves. More dados arrived on the beach, stepping into the metal grinder. They fell by the dozens. Dados from the rear had to step over their fallen buddies to move forward, only to be blasted into oblivion themselves. The whole scene took on a surreal quality, like time was slowing down. I'd never seen anything like it before and hoped I never would again.

Things were going very well . . . until the dados began fighting back.

The dados with weapons stopped advancing. They took cover behind the wreckage of the first to fall, and started firing. I heard the familiar *fum, fum, fum* of their guns. These were definitely weapons from Quillan. On Quillan these weapons fired a burst of energy that incapacitated whoever got shot. Here on Ibara it looked like the weapons packed more punch. Trees exploded. Sand blew into the air.

Archers died.

I saw three different archers fall. I only knew they were dead because the runners who went to examine them would take their bows and arrows. That was their mission. Take the weapons from those who could no longer use them. The battle had become all too real.

The explosions slowed, because the archers were being

more cautious. Being shot at will do that. Still, the archers kept taking out dados. The beach was chaos, but their line was holding. The dados who were still on the water were having trouble getting to shore. There were too many skimmers in their way. And dado parts. It looked like a macabre junkyard. But they kept coming. And coming. The bay was filled with skimmers. Many more waited out in the ocean for their turn to enter. The dados weren't done. Not even close. They crawled, inch by inch up the beach, moving closer to the first line of archers.

My biggest fear was that we would run out of arrows.

"We're going to have to pull back the first line," Alder declared.

"Do it now," I said. "They've got to be running low on arrows. Get them back."

We sent off another runner to deliver that message. The second line hadn't fired a single arrow. Moving the first line back would mean an infusion of fresh ammo, and archers. It took several minutes for the runner to reach the forward line. He gave the message to the archer directly in the center, who signaled those to his side. Word passed quickly and the archers started moving back.

It was a bad move. As soon as they started to move, so did the dados. It was as if they knew they had a window, and they took it. They unleashed a barrage of fire at the archers, hitting several. A few archers made it back to the second line, but the dados kept coming. They fired mercilessly. Huts were blasted and set on fire. Trees toppled. The second line of archers could barely get off any arrows. By the time they were able to start firing, dozens of archers lay dead or wounded, and the leading edge of the village was on fire.

The tone of the battle had changed. The archers were now playing defense.

"It is a nightmare," Genj muttered.

Alder grabbed the last runner and screamed, "Get them behind the third line."

The runner took off instantly.

"We need the protection of the tunnel," Alder declared. "The battle will be won or lost by the third line."

Smoke rose over the village. Fires burned. Bodies were everywhere. I felt as if I were looking at the future of Halla. Was this what Saint Dane had in store for the other territories? Was he going to march on the Milago village? On the barge city of Magorran? We fought dados in the subway on First Earth. Was Saint Dane already smuggling them to Earth?

The runner made it to the second line safely and passed the word to retreat. This time the archers moved back more cautiously, shooting arrows as they retreated. I was getting used to the sound of the explosions. Or maybe I was just numb. At least the explosions meant more dados were done. It was the *fum* from the Quillan weapons that made my skin crawl. That meant archers were in their sights.

The retreat went well. As soon as the first and second lines got behind the line of underground archers, a storm of arrows flew. There were so many explosions together that I thought my eardrums had popped. The village lit up again and again. I saw pieces of dado flying everywhere. It was the most intense barrage since the water guns had opened fire out on the ocean. The underground archers were protected and didn't let up. The dados didn't know where to shoot. The archers unloaded on them.

You know what the grand finale is like at a fireworks display? That's the best way I can describe what was happening in the village. The explosions came on top of one another. Over and over, relentlessly pounding the dados. There was so much smoke I couldn't see the water anymore. Still the explosions kept coming.

I glanced at the tribunal. They watched the display, stone faced, with tears in their eyes.

Genj shook his head sadly. "How could life have gone so wrong?"

I knew why. The answer was flying somewhere over the smoke, looking down on the carnage. I began to imagine that each of the explosions was like a shot fired directly at Saint Dane. I hoped it hurt.

As quickly as it began, the barrage stopped. I hoped they weren't out of arrows. At that moment there was nothing to see but smoke. The archers may have decided to let the smoke clear to survey what they'd done. Of course, the dados would be doing the same thing.

"That is the most we can throw at them," Alder said. "When the smoke clears, we will know if it was enough."

I stepped away from the window. I needed a break. I could only imagine how the brave archers down below felt. I walked to the map on the wall. I realized that even if the dados were turned back, Rayne would be changed. A good third of the village would be in ruins. I looked at the drawing of the tunnel that ran beneath the village. If we won, it would be because of that tunnel.

"The smoke is clearing," Drea announced.

I hurried back to the window to see that the slight, onshore tropical breeze was blowing the smoke off the battlefield.

"The invaders can't have survived that," Genj said. "Can they?"

"We'll know soon enough," I replied.

The smoke cleared. What we saw was both horrifying . . .

and beautiful. From the tunnel to the shore, nothing moved. Nothing. That area of the village was destroyed, but it was a small price to pay, because the dados that had landed were done. It was a vast junkyard of mechanical body parts. I could barely make out any sand beneath the jumble of wreckage.

"Is it possible?" Moman asked. "Is it over?"

I didn't want to let myself believe it, but the plan had actually worked. The tak had worked. The dados had been turned back. Saint Dane's army had been stopped in its tracks. I was already thinking ahead to what his next move might be, when Alder grabbed my arm.

"What?" I asked, surprised.

He pointed out to the bay. I looked, and my knees buckled.

"That was only the first wave," he said soberly.

Another armada of dados on skimmers was passing through the opening, headed for the beach.

"The battle is just beginning," I said.

IBARA

Genj panicked.

"Get my people out of there!" he screamed. "Pull them back. We'll throw ourselves on their mercy. They won't slaughter us! Not if we surrender. I'll speak to their leader. I'll reason with him. His terms may be harsh, but we will survive. We must survive. I will contact him and—"

"Genj!" I interrupted. "He wants to destroy Ibara. Nothing you can say will change that."

"But what choice do we have?" the man said, red faced. "This is suicide!"

He might have been right, but I wasn't ready to give up. Not yet, anyway. I walked back to the map and stared at it. An idea had been forming for a while. It would be an act of desperation. I hoped it wouldn't come to that, but somehow I knew it would. It always did.

"We cannot hold back another attack, Pendragon," Alder said calmly.

I ran to the window to see the progress of the next wave of dados. They had entered the bay and were moving slowly, cautiously. They had learned from their mistakes. That was okay by me. We needed all the time we could get.

"There's a chance," I said quickly. "But we have to commit now or there won't be enough time."

"Whatever it is, let's do it!" Siry announced with confidence. "We've been through too much to give up now."

"What do you suggest, Pendragon," Alder asked.

"Siry, how many crates of tak are left?"

"Three," he answered quickly. "They're at the base of the mountain."

I faced the group and said, "You're right, Genj. Leaving the archers out there is suicide. Alder, get everyone back. Take twenty or so archers and set up on the fourth line of defense." I pointed to the line we had drawn that was halfway between the mountain and the beach. "Get everyone else into the mountain. Everyone. The battle is over for them. Send runners down and evacuate the tunnel."

"Pendragon," Alder said worriedly. "We cannot hold back a fresh invasion for long with only twenty archers."

"You won't have to. Let the dados land, and come forward. But stop them here." I stabbed my finger on the map ahead of where the underground tunnel was located. "You don't have to put on a massive defense. Just keep them from advancing beyond this point. The more dados that join them from the rear, the better."

Alder stared at the map, trying to understand my thinking. A second later I saw the light go on. He smiled and said, "It might work."

"What might work?" Siry asked, frustrated. "What am I missing?"

"We're gonna let 'em come," I answered. "Pack 'em in. The more the merrier. The last sound they'll hear is a very big boom."

Siry's eyes went wide when he figured it out. "We're going to blow up the rest of the tak down in the tunnel," he gasped.

"Right under their robot butts," I confirmed.

Genj and the ladies exchanged concerned looks. "It sounds dangerous," Drea said.

"*Sounds* dangerous?" I laughed. "It's insane!" I looked to Siry and Alder. "If you're with me, say so now, because we don't have much time."

Siry quickly shouted, "Are you kidding? Let's do it."

"I will find the runners," Alder said, and started for the door.

I hurried after him and stopped him just as he was about to leave. "You can't be anywhere near the trap when I spring it, but I have no way of letting you know when it's going to go."

"Do not worry, Pendragon. I will make sure we keep our distance. But how will you explode the tak?"

I shrugged, "Haven't gotten that far yet."

Alder gave me a quick hug and said, "I know I have said this before, but I am proud that you are the lead Traveler."

"And I'm glad you talked me into letting you come here. Go!"

Alder took off running. I went back to the tribunal. "You'll be safe up here. Everyone in the mountain should be safe. If this fails, get out. Take everyone that's left and get out. Go to the far side of the island. Find the others and leave. Take fishing boats. Take anything that floats, but get away. Whatever happens do *not* let Saint Dane get to you. You people are now the pilgrims of Rayne."

Genj nodded. He got it. The poor guy looked pale. Drea and Moman didn't look so hot either.

"Thank you," Genj said.

"I'm counting on you to survive," I told him. "The future of Veelox is yours."

"And yours," he added.

I grabbed my black dado rod, put it through the back of my shirt to free my hands, and headed for the door. Siry was right behind me. Timing would be everything. We had to be ready when the dados marched into the trap. We ran down the stone steps to the base of the mountain. The large ground-level cavern was being used as a makeshift battlefield hospital. Bodies of wounded archers were being carried in and placed on the floor. I was actually happy to hear them groaning. It meant they were still alive. Several runners tended to the wounded, bringing them water or bandaging up wounded limbs. One woman was working exceptionally hard.

"Telleo!" I called out. "I thought you were on the far side of the island."

"I'm more valuable here. This is insane, Pendragon. Is the battle over?"

"It will be soon. We're going to end it."

"Will you surrender?"

"Nah. We're setting up a little welcome gift for our guests. Should be a real blast. That's a joke."

She didn't laugh. Neither did Siry.

"Be careful," she said, and went back to helping the wounded.

Careful? That was an even better joke. The two of us ran to the far corner of the cavern, where a runner guarded the last three crates of explosives. We each lifted one of the heavy, square crates and lugged it toward the stairs that led to the tunnels below. The word to evacuate had already been given. We had to push our way past the stream of archers that climbed up and out. Their eyes were wide and frightened.

They were all too happy to get out of that tunnel. They looked shell shocked. Or tak shocked.

Between lugging the heavy crates and fighting against the stream of retreating archers, it was slow going. A couple of times I got jostled and nearly dropped the crate. That would have been messy. Finally the archers thinned out, and Siry and I had a clear path.

"How will we know when to set off the tak?" he asked as we shuffled along.

"We should hear the battle sounds above us. As soon as that starts, we'll know the dados have arrived."

"And how do we set off the explosion?"

I didn't answer him. I didn't think he'd want to hear what I had in mind.

"Pendragon?" Siry insisted. He *did* want to know.

"It's easy to explode tak," I answered. "The trick is to be somewhere else when it goes off."

"So?"

"So I won't be. Somewhere else, I mean."

"What!" Siry exclaimed. He stopped short and put his crate down.

I put my own crate down. "There's no way you're going to understand this, because I don't either. Saint Dane told me the Travelers are illusions. The more I see, the more I think he wasn't lying."

Siry's response was to stare at me dumbly. No big surprise.

"I've killed Saint Dane and he didn't die," I said. "He killed Loor and somehow she came back from the dead."

"But my father is dead. And what about all the others who died?"

"I don't think they're gone. At least not entirely."

"That makes no sense," Siry cried. "Where are they?"

"I don't know," I answered. "There's so much about Halla we don't know. Who created the flumes? What power controls them? How can Saint Dane do the things he does? He's a Traveler. We're Travelers. We may be more like him than we know. I don't think Travelers can die, at least not the way we think of it."

"That's just crazy," he shouted.

"I know, but I think it's true. Uncle Press promised me I'd see him again. I believe him. Maybe that time has come."

Siry shook his head. He didn't want to accept what I was saying.

"Trust me, I don't want to do this," I added. "But I think it's the only way to save Ibara. And Veelox. And Halla."

"Let me do it," Siry said with conviction. "This is my territory. It's my fault all this happened anyway."

"It's not!" I exclaimed. "If not for you and the Jakills, Ibara never would have had a chance. Once this battle is over, the people are going to need you. You've got to help rebuild Ibara and Veelox. Beating Saint Dane and the dados is only the beginning. You and Genj and the others will be the new pilgrims."

"What will the Travelers do without you?" he cried.

"I don't think they *will* be without me. The same way that I've felt Uncle Press was with me these past years, I think I'll still be with them, and with you. Believe me, if there was any other way, I'd—"

"Wait," Siry said. He was staring at something on the ground. "Maybe there *is* another way."

I looked to where he was staring. Lying there was a bow that one of the archers dropped as he fled from the tunnel.

"Maybe you're right about everything," he said thoughtfully. "Maybe we're illusions. Maybe we can't die. But you don't know for sure. You *can't* know. I say we put off finding out."

I understood what he meant. There *was* another way.

"Go back," I said quickly. "Get the arrows. I'll place the tak."

Siry didn't hesitate. He turned and ran back toward the mountain. That's when we heard the first explosion from above. The final battle had begun. Siry stopped and looked back at me, saying, "You will wait for me, right?'

"Hurry."

He was off, sprinting back the way we had come. I meant every word I said to him. I was prepared to find out the truth about the Travelers. Was I totally sure that I would somehow live on? No. But I was ready to take the risk. In some ways that felt like giving up. It was a drastic act of desperation to beat Saint Dane. If there was a way to beat him without going that far, I wanted to take it. Siry might have found that way.

I picked up one of the crates and hurried along the tunnel. I wished I could have taken them both, but it would have been too heavy, and I didn't want to risk dropping one. It was another fifty yards before I reached the intersection that was under the kill zone. A few more explosions went off above. Sand rained down on me from the concussions. Though the battle had begun, the explosions were few and far between. Alder was being smart. He didn't want them to know it was a trap. The full assault hadn't begun. The dados hadn't arrived in force. We still had time.

I placed the first crate of tak on the ground at the intersection of the tunnel that lead to the mountain and the tunnel that ran parallel to the shore. Before going back for the second, I pulled the dado weapon from the back of my shirt. I wouldn't need it anymore. I could run faster without it. I dropped it on the ground next to the crate and sprinted back for the next load. More explosions sounded from above. Things were getting hotter. Siry had to hurry. I got to the second crate, picked it up, and hurried back to the intersection. When I arrived, I decided to place the second crate on top of the first. Raising the height would help our plan. It was done. The trap was set. I was about to turn and run back for the bow, when I realized something was wrong.

The dado weapon was gone. I looked around quickly. Was I crazy? I knew I'd put it down right by the crate just a minute before. Did it roll away? I heard a scraping sound come from the tunnel off to my left. I crouched down on full alert and gazed into the darkness. The tunnel was empty except for the ladders that led up to the lookout points.

"Hello?" I called. "Are you all right?" I figured it was one of the archers who was hurt and got left behind. I had to get him out of there fast. Leaving him there would be a death sentence. I heard shuffling footsteps. Somebody was definitely there.

"Hey, you've got to get out of here," I called. "There's going to be a—"

The words caught in my throat when I saw who it was. Or I should say *what* it was. Walking stiffly from out of the darkness was a dado. I figured it must have somehow dug its way into the tunnel from above. It was one of the surviving dados from the first wave of the invasion. It moved strangely, as if its circuits were scrambled. It held my dado weapon, leaning on it like a crutch for support. I didn't know what to do. The machine was acting all wacky, as if it were on its last legs. I relaxed, thinking it would take a couple more steps and then . . . lights out.

I was wrong. Without warning, the dado attacked. It

swung the rod at me. I ducked and felt the sharp breeze as it whistled by, barely missing my head. Its next shot didn't miss. It whipped the metal rod back and cuffed me across the forehead, sending me reeling. I hit the far wall of the tunnel hard. Before I could get my feet under me, the dado came at me, holding the rod out like a spear. It was going to stab me. I threw myself backward. The tip of the rod dug into the wall where my body had been a second before.

I grabbed the rod with both hands and drove myself backward, bending my legs and digging in my heels. The dado didn't expect that. It held on to the rod and came with me. The two of us staggered together, until I lost my balance and fell back, pulling the dado along. We both crashed to the ground next to the crates of tak. If we had landed on them, well, the fight would have ended with a bang. The dado and I were jumbled together in a heap, clutching the weapon. Neither had control.

The dado's movements were jerky and rough. There was definitely something haywire with its system that must have affected its thinking, too, because it made a fatal mistake. It let go of the rod with one hand to punch me in the head. It clocked me pretty good. Man, I saw stars. But I didn't let go of the rod. I knew it was the one thing that would save me. I somehow kept my wits, and as the dado cocked back to hit me again, I twisted the rod out of its grasp. It swung again. This time I drove my legs and sprang out of the way. The dado hit nothing but air, and I was on my feet. I had the weapon. The dado followed through with the punch and landed on its back. I stood over it with the rod. The fight was over. Grasping the weapon firmly, I drove it into the dado's chest. Instantly the lights went out. The dado lay lifeless with the weapon pointing straight up. I staggered back, still dizzy from taking so many shots. Still, I wasn't so dizzy that it kept me from hearing a mechanical, wheezing sound behind me.

I spun quickly to see another dado approach. This one looked even worse than the last. It walked on stiff legs, as if its knee joints were fused, and its head twitched sharply, as if it were trying to focus but couldn't. One of its arms was blown off. This thing would have been no threat . . . except that it held a weapon. In its one good hand it grasped one of the golden rifles I figured was Quillan. Slowly, painfully, it lifted the weapon toward me. I was too far away to attack.

I dove for the dead dado, and the rod. I yanked it out of the dead machine, reared back, and heaved it like a spear. The weapon sailed across the tunnel and found its mark. I nailed the second dado right in the stomach. It never got the gun to shooting level. It was dead on its feet, literally. The dado hung there for a moment, then crumpled into a heap. Done.

Several more explosions sounded above. The battle was intensifying. Part of me wanted to end it right there and set off the tak, but it might have been too soon. And Siry might have been on his way back.

And the second dead dado had a gun!

I ran to the machine and pulled the rifle from its dead grasp. It was perfect. I had no doubt that this gun would ignite the tak, and from a decent distance away, too. Without waiting another second I ran back through the tunnel toward the mountain, stopping when I reached the abandoned bow. Looking ahead, there was no sign of Siry. More explosions went off. The time was growing near. Was it too soon? I turned back to face the end of the tunnel, and the tak. I saw the two crates far in the distance. It was incredible to think of the power those two small crates contained. How intense would the explosion be? How much damage would it do? I knew it would obliterate whatever dados were overhead. My fear was what it might do to the good guys. To Alder. To Rayne.

The explosions above grew more furious. Was it time? Should I wait? There was no way I could know for sure, and I was too nervous to wait any longer. It was time for the big boom. I raised the rifle and put the tak crates in my sight. My plan was to fire, drop the gun, and run like hell. If the tak didn't go off, I'd come back and do it again. And again, until ignition. I'd never fired one of those guns, but I knew how to fire rifles at home. I was good. I could shoot. Confidence was high. I took one last deep breath and lined up the bottom crate. Things were about to change forever.

I pulled the trigger.

Click. Nothing happened. I pulled it again. And again. The weapon was no good. Either it was out of ammunition or it was damaged from the battle.

"Oh . . . so . . . close," came a voice from behind me.

My stomach dropped. I felt dizzy. How could it be?

"Like I've always said," the voice said. "Defeat is the worst when it comes at the very moment you think you've won."

I turned slowly to face him. Saint Dane stood in the center of the tunnel, staring at me with his demon blue eyes.

"And you really did think you'd won, didn't you?" he asked with glee.

IBARA

"This moment is particularly satisfying, Pendragon," Saint Dane sneered with his superior attitude. "I knew you'd eventually come down from your righteous pedestal and get yourself . . . how should I say it? . . . dirty. You've finally realized the only way to save Halla is to make it one. It's what I've been saying all along. The true glory of Halla will come with unity. Only then can the ultimate victory be achieved."

"Victory?" I asked. "Victory over what? You talk about saving Halla and breaking down walls between territories, but . . . why? What's the point?"

"Surely you must have some idea by now," the demon asked, amused.

Explosions rumbled above. This wasn't the time to be interrogating Saint Dane, but he was saying things I hadn't heard before.

"You said you were trying to prove the people of the territories weren't capable of guiding their own destiny. Who are you trying to prove it to?"

"You're getting warmer," he teased.

My mind raced. I was closer to the truth than ever before, and it scared the hell out of me. More than the tak arrows exploding above.

"What happens after the Convergence?" I demanded. "If you have your way and the territories fall under your influence, what then? Is that it? Is that the whole point? You become the king of all territories?"

He chuckled. "Something like that."

"Then who's the king now?" I asked flat-out.

Saint Dane took a step closer to me. I could feel the chill coming off him. I didn't move. "And now you finally see the truth," he hissed.

"I don't see anything. What truth?"

His eyes were locked on mine. When he spoke, it was with a seething intensity that I had never seen from him. "There is a new order coming, Pendragon. Halla is only the beginning."

I nearly fainted. Could that be true? There was something greater than Halla? How could that be? I did all that I could to keep my voice from cracking and said, "I'm going to stop you. Right here, right now."

Saint Dane sneered. "There are a few thousand dados above us who might take issue with that."

"This isn't about armies," I said with total confidence. "Or weapons. It's about right and wrong. No matter how you twist it, your way is wrong."

Explosions pounded above. The tunnel shuddered.

"No," Saint Dane said. "It is about armies and weapons. And fear. And strength. Fear is my greatest weapon. Halla will be my strength. That is the way it was meant to be, because it is the way I will make it."

There was only one thing to do. I turned and ran. Not away from Saint Dane. I ran toward the tak. I had to detonate it. I didn't get far. The demon tackled me from behind. After all the battles. All the mysteries and miseries. The territories lost and those that were saved. The deaths and the resurrections. It had come down to this. A fight between Saint Dane and me. I scrambled to get loose, but he held me tightly in his cold hands.

"Time is not your friend, Pendragon," he hissed. "They cannot hold the dados back much longer."

I drove my elbow into his nose. He screamed in pain. Man, it felt good. I wanted him to hurt. He reeled back. I broke loose. I only got a few steps before he grabbed me again, and threw me against the wall. He was fast. Inhumanly fast. I hit so hard that I broke stones loose from the tunnel. They fell on my head and rolled at my feet.

The tunnel rumbled under the explosions that were now coming quickly. I had to get to the tak. Alder wouldn't be able to keep the dados pinned for long. I picked up a stone and faked throwing it at Saint Dane. He threw his hands up in defense, and I attacked. I launched myself at him feetfirst, my body parallel to the ground. Both feet hit him square in the chest, knocking him back into the side of the tunnel. He grunted, but bounced off the wall and came right at me. I didn't expect that. He was just so fast. He grabbed me in a bear hug and wrestled me to the ground. He was strong, too. I couldn't break loose. In seconds I was on my back with Saint Dane sitting on my chest. His knees pinned my arms. I tried to kick, but had no leverage. I was trapped.

The guy's eyes were on fire. He was out of control. From somewhere he pulled out a three-clawed tang knife. I only glimpsed it for a second before he brought it down and held it to my neck. He stared down at me, breathing hard, a touch of spittle dripping from his mouth. The red scars on his bald head pulsed with blood . . . or whatever it was that ran through his veins.

"Are you so misguided that you are ready to die for your beliefs?" he spat.

I fought to get away, but he pressed harder. The pressure from the knife was choking me.

"You've lost, Pendragon," he hissed with more than a touch of insanity. "You no longer matter."

I was going to die. I wasn't afraid. I really wasn't. I believed what I'd told Siry. And I believed what Saint Dane had told me. Travelers were illusions, and in some twisted way, I wanted to know what that meant.

"Ahhhhh!" came a wild scream.

Saint Dane was knocked off me as if he'd been hit by a speeding car. He flew over my head and rolled on the ground, along with the driving force that slammed into him. . . .

Siry.

"Hurry!" he screamed at me as he wrestled with the demon Traveler.

Siry had no idea how to fight. It didn't matter. He was unstoppable. Saint Dane tried to pull away from him, but Siry tied him up long enough for me to stand and see something resting on top of the abandoned bow. Siry had brought back three tak arrows.

Explosions shook the tunnel. It was time. I ran for the bow. Saint Dane wouldn't be held back for long. I'd be lucky to get off one shot. It had to count. I grabbed one of the arrows with my right hand and the bow with the other. I hadn't shot a bow and arrow in a long time, but I didn't think it would matter. That was the thing about tak, you didn't have to hit the bull's-eyes. Close was close enough.

Moving quickly but carefully, I stood up straight, my left

shoulder facing down the tunnel. I nocked the arrow onto the string. I had to stay focused. There would only be one chance. A fumble now would be disastrous.

Saint Dane finally pulled away from Siry. He twisted toward me, still on his back. I could feel his rage. He would be up and on me in seconds. With my left arm out straight, I lifted the bow and pulled the string back until I felt the feathery tail tickling my cheek.

Saint Dane struggled to get to his feet.

"Pendragon!" Siry shouted.

"Stay down," I commanded calmly.

I was ready. In a second Saint Dane would be in the way. I had to let it fly. The instant before I released it, Saint Dane's head snapped back and he fell forward, hitting the ground face-first. Siry had tackled him from behind.

"Shoot!" Siry screamed.

"This is the end," I said, and let it fly.

An instant later Saint Dane melted into smoke and blew past me. Siry and I were alone, fifty yards from Armageddon.

"Run!" I screamed, and did just that.

I dropped the bow and took off. Siry was right behind me. We sprinted for our lives. The first sound I heard was a short, crisp hiss. I'd heard that sound before. The tak was igniting. A second later . . .

The world erupted behind us. The tunnel lit up with the fire from the explosion. I felt the heat and then heard the blast. It was unbearable. A quick glance back showed a fireball coming up the tunnel behind us. The floor shook, making it hard to run. I thought we'd be cooked, but we hit one of the smaller cross-tunnels and dove out of the way as the force of the blast shot past us. The monstrous wave of fire blew by, its heat scorching my face. I thought my clothes would ignite. We had dodged the fire, but the force of the explosion was tearing the tunnel apart. Rocks and sand fell around us. It was like being underground in the middle of an earthquake. The main tunnel was an inferno. We had to run deeper into the cross-tunnel.

"There's gotta be another way out," I said, pushing Siry forward.

The ground shook, throwing us off balance. The ancient tunnel couldn't handle it. Rocks pummeled us. We held our arms over our heads as we ran. Behind us the tunnel collapsed. If there wasn't another way out ahead of us, we would be buried.

We were buried.

The tunnel ahead of us collapsed too.

"Under there!" I yelled, and pushed Siry beneath a section of fallen roof. Or floor. Or something. It was a long, thick piece of rock that had fallen leaving a small opening beneath. It looked strong enough to protect us from anything falling from above, so long as the rock itself didn't give way and crush us. Siry and I squeezed into the space under the collapsed section and huddled together, waiting for the end. A world of rock and sand rained down on us. I could barely breathe. My lungs felt like they were filling with dust. Siry and I held each other close. We would either survive, or be crushed. Together.

Thirty seconds. That's my guess as to how long the entire event took from the time the tak ignited, to the moment when the rumble died down. It was a thirty-second lifetime. But we were both still breathing. Barely. There wasn't much air. Neither of us moved for the longest time, for fear of bumping something that might trigger a collapse.

"Is it over?" Siry asked meekly.

I peered out between my two crossed arms. There was a whole lot of nothing to see. Slowly, cautiously, I poked my head out from beneath the rock slab. The air was filled with dust and dirt, making it impossible to see anything . . . except dust and dirt. I lifted my shirt and held it over my mouth to try and keep some of the debris from going into my lungs. Slowly, painfully, the air began to clear. After a few agonizing minutes I got my first look at what we had to deal with.

I laughed.

"What?" Siry asked.

The tunnel had collapsed on either side of us. It turned out to be a good thing. I saw a faint shaft of sunlight peeking through the carnage. As the dust settled completely, I saw a sliver of blue sky.

"We can climb out!" I cried.

I reached back, took Siry's outstretched hand, and pulled him from our temporary shelter. We scrambled up a steep pitch of rocks that soon gave way to sand. In no time we were on the surface, staring at Tribunal Mountain. Intact.

"Look!" Siry said, pointing above us.

On the rocky ledges of the mountain were people. The people of Rayne. They were alive. They had survived the blast. They crowded together, silently looking out over their village . . . and their future.

IBARA

8iry and I climbed out of the ruins of the tunnel and made our way back toward Tribunal Mountain. A cloud of smoke and sand hung over the village behind us, making it impossible to see what damage the tak bomb had done. One thing I saw right away was that the ground wasn't the same. The force of the explosion really did act like an earthquake. The shock waves were probably carried along by the tunnel. Whatever. The result was that we couldn't find the path back to the mountain, because there was no path. At least, it didn't look much like a path anymore.

"Pendragon!" came a welcome shout.

It was Alder. Alive. He ran to us from out of the swirling dust. It was the most beautiful sight I could have asked for. His big smile beamed through the smoke. When he got to us, we all hugged.

The brave knight from Denduron pulled back and asked, "Hey, did you hear that?"

Siry and I stared at him blankly.

"It was a joke," Alder said quickly. "You are not the only one with a sense of humor, Pendragon."

Alder had made a joke. A dumb joke, but a joke.

"Wow," I laughed. "I guess it's official. Halla is never going to be the same."

He gave me a friendly cuff on the shoulder.

"What about the dados?" Siry asked.

"It was difficult holding them back," Alder answered, his joking finished. "There were more of them in the second wave. Many more. We couldn't have kept them back much longer."

"I want to see," I said.

Alder led us over chunks of debris that had been pushed up from underground. It seemed most of the rocky tunnel was now on the surface. Still, there was so much dust and debris in the air, I couldn't see more than a few feet ahead of us.

"The archers were heroic," Alder said as we picked our way through. "I have fought beside warriors who had more skill, but none as brave. Even as the number of dados grew, they did not flinch. I ran between positions, showing them where to direct their arrows to best keep the dados off balance. I could not be everywhere. They quickly learned on their own."

"So what happened when the tak exploded?" Siry asked.

"I told them that when they felt the ground rumble, that was the sign. When it came, they did not hesitate. They dropped their weapons and ran back. The ground felt as if it were growing under our feet. It threw us forward like a wave, but I do not believe there were any serious injuries. We were lucky."

"And the dados?" I asked.

He led us to a huge mound of sand and rock that hadn't been there earlier. The three of us climbed to the top to get a better view of the battlefield. Or what was left of it.

The smoke hung like a spooky haze over all we could see.

When the tropical breeze thinned it enough to make out detail, my mind wouldn't accept what I was seeing. I thought there must be some mistake.

"It's gone," Siry gasped in awe.

The village of Rayne no longer existed. In its place was a mess of destroyed huts and fallen trees. Directly in front of us was a huge blast crater.

"They were directly over the tak," Alder said. "Thousands of them. Many more pushed up from the rear. I believe they no longer exist. I do not know the word for it."

"Vaporized," I said.

"Yes," Alder agreed. "Those who were not vaporized were blown into small bits. Perhaps some escaped back to the sea, but there could not have been many."

Siry looked at me, and spoke as if in a daze. "Is it possible? Did we destroy an entire army?"

"That is exactly what we did," Alder declared. "Ibara is safe."

I stepped away from them and looked over the remains of the village. Yes, we had won. Against incredible odds. I should have felt like celebrating. I didn't. I was relieved, sure, but I wasn't in the mood for throwing any high fives. The battle was over. Saint Dane was defeated. But at what cost? Rayne was destroyed. It would take generations to bring it back. Just as important, the second turning point of Veelox had gone the wrong way. As dramatic as the dado battle was, it was not the turning point. The turning point had been when the Flighters destroyed the pilgrim ships. The rest of Veelox could not be rebuilt for a good long time. To me it felt like a case of winning the battle, but losing the war.

Most troubling of all was knowing what I had to do to win this battle. I had lowered myself to Saint Dane's level by using technology and elements from other territories. Was it all worth it? Was Ibara a win or a loss? As I stood there looking at the destruction, I wasn't so sure.

I heard the sound of a sharp *caw!* overhead. Looking up, I saw a large black bird sailing over the village, as if inspecting the damage. I knew who it was. He had lost his army, but he would fight again. What would his next evil plan be? And the next? And the one after that? Was this war going to continue until he finally found the way to bring about the Convergence that would put Halla under his control? And after that, what? What did he mean by Halla being "the beginning"? What else was out there? It all felt so incredibly hopeless.

As I stood on that mound, surveying the results of a questionable victory, I realized that the battle wasn't over. There was more to do on Ibara.

"We've got to get back to the mountain now," I said to Alder and Siry.

"Why?" Siry asked. "It's over!"

"No, it isn't."

"What are you saying, Pendragon?" Alder asked.

I looked my friend dead in the eye and said, "We're going after Saint Dane."

The three of us ran as quickly as possible through the rubble of Rayne, headed for Tribunal Mountain. We worked our way through the scores of wounded archers to find the last remaining crate of tak. While Alder carried it outside, I instructed Siry to get the remaining dado weapons. Finally, I took a bow from one of the wounded archers, along with two of his arrows.

"What is your plan, Pendragon?" Alder asked me.

"First we get to the flume."

When Siry returned with the weapons, we set out for the

beach. Moving through the remains of the village was depressing. So many years of work had been destroyed in seconds. By me. I wasn't proud of myself. We took turns carrying the crate of tak, because it was awkward and heavy. When we got to the beach I was surprised to see that the rocky cliffs that contained the flume were still intact. The power of the explosion hadn't touched them. The dygo was parked at the mouth of the newly drilled tunnel, right where we'd left it.

I took a moment to look out onto the ocean. The blue-green waters were as calm as ever. It was hard to imagine that not long ago an armada of dados had come across it. It actually gave me hope that at some point, Ibara could be returned to its original beauty. Hopefully the same could be said for the rest of Veelox. It was that hope that convinced me I was about to do the right thing.

"First we're going to return these things to their own territories," I said. "Siry, can you drive the dygo?"

"Absolutely!"

"Bring it back to Zadaa. Alder, you bring these weapons back to Quillan. Leave them at the gate. Same thing with the dygo. Leave it at the gate and get out."

"Does the tak stay?" Siry asked. "Is that how we're going to get Saint Dane?"

"Yeah," I said. "The tak stays."

"Why is this so important, Pendragon?" Alder asked.

"It was bad enough that we brought this here in the first place," I answered. "I want it gone now. All of it."

"What about the dados? And the skimmers?" Siry asked. "We're not going to send all the skimmers back, are we? And it'll take forever to clean up the dado parts."

"We didn't bring those," I answered quickly. "I want whatever we brought gone."

Alder and Siry exchanged looks. They thought I was crazy. They weren't far off.

"All right," Alder said. "If that is what you feel is right."

Siry went for the dygo. He was psyched to take it for a spin. As he was about to board, I called, "Siry!"

He looked back at me.

"Your father would have been proud of you."

Siry gave me the kind of warm smile I didn't think he had in him. He entered the dygo and in no time got it rolling through the tunnel, headed for the flume. Alder and I walked behind him with the tak and the Quillan weapons. Alder kept glancing at me. Something was bothering him. I wasn't surprised. Alder was a smart guy.

"What are you thinking, Pendragon? You have been strangely quiet since the battle."

"Just trying to get my head around all that's happened."

Siry stopped the dygo short of the break I had drilled through the circular pool that was the mouth of the flume. He held open the hatch and said, "Anybody want to come? This should be fun."

He suddenly seemed like a normal fifteen-year-old kid.

"Enjoy the ride," I called out.

He closed the hatch, then opened it back up again and shouted out, *"Zadaa!"* He looked at me and added, "See? I'm learning. I'll be right back."

The flume came to life. The water swirled. I waited until the musical notes were at their loudest, then motioned for him to drive forward. Siry hit the throttle. The dygo rolled up and into the stone circle of water. It leaned forward and seemed to fall into the flume. A moment later it was gone.

"Your turn," I said to Alder.

The knight picked up the remaining weapons. "What is next?" he asked.

"Like I said, we're going after Saint Dane."

Alder nodded but his heart wasn't in it. He knew something was wrong. "You know I will always be there for you."

I nodded in thanks, though I swear I almost cried.

"Quillan!" he called out, and the flume came back to life.

I hugged him. "I don't know what to say."

"Say you will think twice before doing something you may regret."

I didn't answer that. Alder looked into my eyes. He was searching for some clue as to what I was thinking. I looked away. It killed me. Alder stepped up to the edge of the pool.

"Good-bye, my friend," he said. The sparkling light filled the cavern, and he was gone.

I didn't know how much time I had before they would be back, so I moved quickly. I ran for the crate of tak and lugged it into the cavern. I placed the heavy explosives gently in the sand, directly against the stone ring of the flume. Without wasting a second, I scooped up the bow and the tak arrows and sprinted out of the tunnel. When I reached the mouth, I turned back and dropped to one knee.

"Caw!" came the familiar cry from overhead. Looking up, I saw the dark bird circling high above me.

"It's just you and me now," I said to myself. Or to him. I looked at my Traveler ring. It was still sparkling. I picked up the arrow, nocked it onto the string, and aimed into the tunnel. I closed my left eye, looking down the length of the arrow shaft until I saw the flume.

"Good-bye, guys," I whispered. "Good luck."

I let the arrow fly and dove to the sand. The shaft whistled as it flew into the dark tunnel. There was a small explosion, then a hiss, followed by an eruption. I jumped up and ran toward the ocean, ahead of the fireball that blasted out of the tunnel. The concussion knocked me to the sand. I hit hard, feeling the heat on my back. I lay there, afraid to move. Bits of rock rained down on me. I covered my head in case something bigger than gravel was coming my way. The sound of the immense blast echoed away. I waited. The gravel stopped falling. I cautiously looked up to see what was left of the rocky cliff.

There wasn't much. What had been a tall, steep cliff face, was now rubble. The tunnel was gone, buried under tons of rock. I looked at my ring. The sparkle was gone. It was once again gray stone. It was the proof I needed.

I had destroyed the flume on Ibara.

Saint Dane was not going to leave this territory.

Neither was I.

IBARA

I'm writing this journal from a small room somewhere deep within Tribunal Mountain. It has become my home. I hope what happened hasn't shocked you, Courtney. It's been a while since I destroyed the flume, so I've had time to think about it. Now that the emotion and excitement have died down, I still believe I did the right thing.

I've given everything I have in the battle against Saint Dane. I've made lots of mistakes, but I'm only human. At least, I think I'm human. Actually, I don't think I'm human at all, but you know what I mean. Since the loss on Quillan, I haven't been the same. Quillan took a lot out of me. From the beginning I always felt as if there would be an end to this quest. Especially since we seemed to be beating Saint Dane on most territories. Quillan changed things for me. I began to feel as if this battle would be endless. Who says that every territory has only one turning point? What's stopping Saint Dane from returning to any of them to try and turn things his way? On Ibara he convinced the Flighters to attack the pilgrims of Rayne, which was classic Saint Dane. But what about the dados? There was no turning point involved there. It was flat-out war. What's to stop him from doing the same kind of thing on another territory? He could assemble another dado army on Quillan or march down Stony Brook Avenue.

That's why I took such a drastic step. The flume here on Ibara is history. Saint Dane is trapped. If that's what it took to end this war, it was worth it. I haven't seen any sign of him since I blew up the flume. But I will. I'm sure of it.

Of course, destroying the flume means that I'm trapped here with him. This is hard to admit, especially to you, but I think that's a good thing too. Truth is, I'm done, Courtney. I feel as if I've lost sight of the values that Uncle Press said were so important. Seeing the wreckage of Rayne was hard. Sure, we stopped the dado army, but we might have taken the heart from this territory in the process. I was out of control. My obsession with beating Saint Dane was all I cared about, when I should have been worried about the welfare of a territory. Saint Dane manipulates people to bring about their own ruin. I'm afraid the person he manipulated on Ibara was me. I made the choices. I changed the destiny of Ibara by mixing territories.

Neither of us can do that anymore.

Instead of fighting an endless battle to prevent chaos, I want to be positive. I want to look forward. I want to build something. I see that chance here on Ibara. The village was destroyed. Many people were killed. Rebuilding will take decades. I want to be a part of it. And the Flighters are still out there. That conflict hasn't gone away. The defenses here are now weak. If the Flighters decide to attack, the people of Rayne may not be able to stop them. That's another reason that I'm happy to stay here. I want to protect these people better than I did before. They've even asked me to be on the tribunal. Can you believe that? I wonder if they'll give me a title? My mandate will be to carry out the vision of Aja Killian. Maybe that was always the way it was meant to be.

Telleo has become my good friend. She reminds me a lot of you, Courtney. She's strong. She has opinions. She doesn't take grief from me. That's probably why I like her. We spend hours at night talking about the past of Veelox and the future of Ibara. I don't think I'll tell her about the Travelers. It has no importance here. Not anymore. Especially since I am no longer a Traveler.

I miss Siry. In many ways I think he should be here with me, with his people. He would want to help them build their new lives. It's exactly what the Jakills set out to do. But I didn't want to trap two Travelers. My hope is that he will stay with Alder, or join with Loor. Together maybe they can learn the real truth about Travelers, and their own lives. They deserve to know that. We all do.

I don't know if you will ever meet Siry, but if you do, please tell him something for me. Days after the dado war, I was sitting alone on the beach, staring at the sea beyond the bay, thinking of nothing for a change. It felt good. On the horizon I saw a dot. It was a skimmer, moving fast, headed for the opening to the bay. My first instinct was that it was a group of dados or Flighters, and I was about to rally the security force. As the skimmer drew close, I saw that it wasn't a dado at all. Four people were on board. I thought I was seeing ghosts.

Flying over the water were four of the Jakills. One of them was rat boy, whose name I still don't know. There was another guy and two girls. The girl driving the skimmer was Twig. They had been hiding in Rubic City and finally managed to steal one of the few skimmers that the dados didn't use to attack Rayne. All I could do was stand there in the sand and laugh. I took it as a sign that there was real hope for the future of Ibara.

Of all the difficult things I've described in these journals, what I am now about to write is the hardest. But it's reality. I don't think I will ever see you again, Courtney. Or Mark. You are my best friends. You will always be my best friends. My biggest regret over what I've done is that I won't know if Mark is all right. I think that will haunt me for the rest of my life. But I take comfort in the fact that by doing what I've done, I have saved Halla. Saint Dane said some disturbing things. The idea that Halla was only the beginning for some even grander plan of evil was too much for me to accept. It was the final straw in making my decision. Saint Dane is done.

So is Bobby Pendragon.

I will still write to you every so often, to let you know how things are going here. I hope you don't mind. It's the only way I can think to hold on to a little bit of my old life. I think of you and Mark every day. I remember the fun we had, before all this started. I never want to forget that, even though remembering makes me sad. But I'm not alone here. I have Telleo, and her father. It's time to start a new life, and help these people find their own.

I don't know if this is the way it was meant to be, but it's the way it's going to be.

I miss you both. I love you both.

Remember me.

END OF JOURNAL #32

● FIRST EARTH ●

Courtney had to read the last journal from Bobby Pendragon alone in her "cell," back in the isolation ward of the *Queen Mary*. Dodger was alone in his own "cell" across the passageway. Until she was released and reunited with Mark and Dodger, she would have to deal with the news on her own. She felt as if the term "isolation ward" could not have fit her situation any better.

She didn't cry over the loss of her friend. She wasn't elated over the saving of another territory. She didn't take solace in the fact that Saint Dane may have been defeated forever. She felt numb. Empty. Being Courtney, her mind naturally raced ahead to the next challenge. What would the next impossible hurdle of their mission be? The strange reality was, there were no more hurdles. There was nothing more to do. Yes, there were questions. Why hadn't the dados ceased to exist once Mark destroyed Forge? If Saint Dane was trapped on Veelox, what did that mean for Andy Mitchell? Was he gone? Or maybe it didn't make a difference, because First Earth existed in another time from Veelox. Or maybe Andy was stuck here, because if he traveled anywhere else it would create a time paradox. Or maybe . . . or maybe . . .

Courtney tried to stop thinking. There were no answers. None that mattered, anyway. There was only the empty feeling of knowing Bobby was gone from her life forever, and their mission was over. She felt as if she should be thrilled, because it meant Halla was saved. Her home on Second Earth was saved. But she wasn't thrilled. She felt overwhelmingly sad.

She spent the next three days in that cell. Alone. With no contact from anyone she knew. It was torture. The room was comfortable enough and they fed her well, but she was going out of her mind because of the isolation. Her only view of the outside world was through a single porthole. Not that there was much to see except ocean, but it kept her from going totally out of her mind.

On the fourth day there was a knock on the door at the usual breakfast time. When the door opened, instead of a steward wheeling in her morning meal, Mark Dimond stepped into the room.

"Congratulations," he declared. "You're officially free and a paying passenger. Want to play shuffleboard?"

Courtney threw her arms around him. Finally she cried. It all came out. All the emotion she had bottled up for the last few days. Mark held her and tried to soothe her.

"It's okay," he said. "It's over now."

"You have no idea how true that is," Courtney sniffed through her tears.

Mark let her cry.

Later that morning Mark and Courtney sat in Mark's suite, where a few days before Mark had destroyed his invention. It was the act they all thought would change history, but it didn't. Mark and his parents had arranged to pay for Courtney and Dodger's passage. Mr. Dimond was a lawyer. He was very convincing in getting the stowaway charges dropped against both of them. Mr. and Mrs. Dimond left the two alone. They knew Mark and Courtney had a lot to say to each other. Even Dodger respectfully stayed away.

Courtney did most of the talking. She brought Mark up to speed on what had happened on Quillan. She told Mark about the dados, explaining how Saint Dane had brought the advanced plastic skin from Third Earth. Andy Mitchell wasn't a genius after all. He was a thief. That was the nicest thing Courtney had to say about him. He was Saint Dane. Courtney led Mark into the future of his invention, describing how it changed technology on Second Earth, and evolved into the humanlike dados of Third Earth . . . that looked like Mark. She told him how that technology was brought to Quillan, where dados became servants and soldiers. Finally she said how Saint Dane created an army of dados that was to be his engine to destroy Ibara, and the rest of Halla.

"Still," she said thoughtfully, "I don't know why that didn't all change when you destroyed Forge."

"I know why," Mark said, dropping his head. "After you and Dodger were arrested again, I wired the KEM corporation to say the deal was off. The whole reason for going to England was to deliver the prototype, and sign contracts to officially create the Dimond Alpha Digital Organization."

Mark laughed ironically. "I came up with that name. I thought it sounded important. Some joke, huh?"

"What did they say?" Courtney asked.

"They wired back to say it was too late. Turned out the signing of papers was only a formality. My father explained it to me. We already accepted money from them. Heck, they paid for this voyage. Even without a signed contract, when you accept money, it's as good as a done deal. They had been going forward assuming we had a deal."

"But how? Without the prototype, how could they go forward?" Courtney asked.

"Remember the science competition? Our presentation wasn't just the Forge prototype. We created detailed plans to explain how it all worked. Andy was in charge of those plans and—"

"And he sent them to KEM."

Mark nodded.

"So you're telling me a science project presentation is what nearly caused the downfall of Halla?"

"It was slick, too. Full color. Nice fonts."

"That's not funny," Courtney said with a frown.

"I know."

"So we never had a chance of stopping you. The flume didn't put us where we needed to be, when we needed to be there."

"Or maybe there was another reason you had to be here that we don't know about."

"Yeah, like to murder you!" Courtney shouted. "At least we stopped that."

"Yeah, I'm glad about that one."

The two fell silent, remembering that horrible almost-moment.

"They're gone, by the way," Mark said.

"Who's gone?"

"Andy and Nevva. It's not like they're turning the ship inside out looking for them, but I know they're gone."

"Maybe that's a good thing," Courtney offered. "Maybe it means Saint Dane really is trapped on Ibara."

Mark stood up and paced. "I feel so stupid," he said, his voice rising. "It was all about me. All along. I nearly caused the downfall of Halla."

"You can't look at it that way. You didn't create an army, you invented a toy. An incredible toy. Everything else was Saint Dane."

"But I should have seen through it. I believed everything he told me, because he told me everything I wanted to hear."

"Exactly," Courtney exclaimed. "You aren't the first. Let's hope you're the last."

Courtney couldn't stand being cooped up anymore. She and Mark went out onto the Sun Deck for some much needed fresh air. It was the first moment that Courtney could enjoy being on that ship without looking over her shoulder to see if somebody was chasing her. It was time to heal. Having Mark back and safe was a great feeling, even though she knew things would never be the same as before. Mark had changed. He'd grown up. He was no longer a nerdy little boy. They had both changed. They'd been through too much to be the same people they'd always been before. For Courtney it felt right, but sad. They had lost out on their last few moments of childhood.

Their stroll took them to the bow of the ship. The two stood together at the rail, looking ahead.

"Do you think it's really over?" Mark asked. "I mean, are we safe?"

"I guess it's possible," Courtney answered. "But how can things truly be right if we never see Bobby again?"

"I miss him so much," Mark said.

Courtney nodded and leaned in to him.

"How did I know I'd find you two here?" came a voice from behind. Dodger strutted up to them, flashing a big smile. "Here's an interesting little tidbit you two should know about. When I thanked Mr. Dimond for helping us out of the slammer, I told him I thought he was brilliant for getting me off with no assault charges against that officer."

"He's good," Mark said.

"Yeah, well he's not that good," Dodger replied. "He didn't know what the heck I was talking about. He said there were no assault charges. I figured the guy I clocked was letting me off easy, so I went looking for Sixth Officer Hantin to apologize. Guess what? There *is* no Sixth Officer Hantin. This ship doesn't even *have* a sixth officer. What do you make of that?"

Courtney rolled the events around in her head. "It was his gun," she exclaimed. "History said you were shot, Mark. We got the gun from that phantom officer! Do you think—"

"Yeah, I do," Mark gasped. "It was Saint Dane."

"He wanted you dead and he wanted me to kill you."

Dodger added, "I guess things didn't turn out the way he planned."

Mark asked, "So does that mean there was more to his plan than we thought?"

Nobody had an answer. They all silently looked forward at the gray line that was forming on the horizon. They were steaming toward England.

❖ VEELOX ❖

High above the ancient city of Rubic, a lone figure stood at
the very pinnacle of a Lifelight pyramid, surveying the decay
below, his dark suit snapping in the wind. It was the loftiest point
in the city. Only the other pyramids, far in the distance, reached
as high. It was an impossible perch. The only way to get there
was to fly.

A large black raven sailed urgently through the clouds. It
swooped down to the pyramid and landed next to the lone figure.
The figure didn't move or acknowledge the new arrival. After a
brief transformation, two figures stood together above the city.

"Are you pleased?" the new arrival asked.

Saint Dane showed no expression. "There were a few surprises. No matter. The end result is the same. Pendragon is no
longer a factor."

"Forgive me for questioning," the visitor said. "Can we be
truly certain of that?"

Saint Dane took a tired breath. "He and his kind have drawn
strength from the belief they have been battling my evil for the

greater good of Halla. Now he understands there is no clear definition of evil. He has caused destruction and suffering. He has manipulated the people of the territories as much as I. It took many battles for him to learn. Now he knows he is no different from me. That realization has crushed his desire to go on. He is finished."

"Will it be enough to keep him away?"

Saint Dane gave his visitor an icy stare. "You question me?"

The visitor shuddered, but tried not to show weakness. "Of course not. I've never questioned your intent. But he is strong."

The scars on Saint Dane's head blazed in anger. "Not strong enough, or he would not have been manipulated so easily."

"Do you think he understands what he has done?"

"If not, he will soon," Saint Dane answered. "I told him long ago that Denduron would be the first domino to fall. By unearthing the tak, he assured that. Pendragon himself created our victory. I look forward to the moment when he realizes that."

"And you're certain it will crush his spirit?"

Saint Dane looked down at his visitor with a fatherly gaze. He reached out and stroked the visitor's black hair. "So many questions."

He quickly and violently grabbed a handful of hair and yanked it, making the visitor cry in pain. "Concern yourself with your own task," he spat angrily. "Make him love Ibara. Make him want nothing more than to live there and help create his version of a perfect world. Who knows? Perhaps he will fall in love. By then it will be too late for him to strike back."

He pushed the visitor away. He was back in control, his anger gone. "I look forward to the moment when he learns the true nature of our conflict and how futile his mission was from the beginning. We will stand together, he and I. One in victory, one in shame. Only then can I truly own the power of Halla." He cracked a self-assured smile. "How sweet the moment of revelation will be, when he learns that he handed it to me."

The visitor nodded, afraid to make eye contact with the demon.

"Forgive me, Nevva," Saint Dane said softly. "I am the victim of my own passion."

Nevva Winter wiped back a tear and replied, "It's why I believe in you. That passion is what will ensure your ultimate triumph."

"Our triumph," Saint Dane corrected.

Nevva added, "But please, don't call me Nevva on this territory."

Saint Dane chuckled. "I appreciate the way you so fully immerse yourself in your roles."

"I too am passionate about our quest," Nevva replied.

"And for that you will be rewarded. Once the power of Halla is mine, we can truly begin. Together." Saint Dane took a step away from Nevva Winter and began to transform.

"Until then, good-bye . . . Telleo."

The black cloud that was Saint Dane molded into the form of a raven. The bird launched from its perch, swooping down over the crumbled buildings of Rubic City before disappearing into the clouds . . .

And entering the Convergence.

To Be Continued

Bobby Pendragon learned early on that every territory of Halla has a Traveler. Like Bobby, these Travelers lived for years—some even for decades—before learning of their true destinies. What was life like for Bobby's fellow Travelers before they joined him in the fight to save every time and place that has ever existed? What led up to their becoming the guardians of Halla? The answers are coming!

PENDRAGON
BEFORE THE WAR

The Travelers Book One, *Book Two*, and *Book Three* will be available wherever books are sold in January, February, and March 2009.

But you don't have to wait until January—all you have to do is turn the page for a sneak peek at Spader's story!

"I think that's everything and everyone," the man on the Crasker loading dock called up. "You're ready to go."

The two-day trip to Crasker had been uneventful. They had arrived on schedule and the shipment of thermal regulators and ballast equalizers had been waiting for them. Three engineers who had designed experimental devices they planned to test on the underwater farms on Grallion had also come aboard with their equipment.

Crasker was interesting, but not really Spader's style. A habitat devoted to manufacturing, Crasker didn't have the beautiful farms and open spaces he loved on Grallion.

Or maybe it was seeing the Watsu name blazoned across so many of the buildings. Per's family manufactured many of the ships used throughout Cloral, and Crasker was one of the biggest habitats dedicated to building them. Even the cruiser they were on was a Watsu. The vessel followed the same basic design of the other ships its size: cargo holds below, living quarters in the middle, the upper deck, and then the pilot's tower. It was a fairly small vessel, carrying ten crewmembers who split day and night shifts. Happily, Per and

Spader, as the juniors aboard, were put on different shifts and they barely saw each other.

Once the ship had cleared the habitat, Clayton, Spader's shift supervisor, joined him at the rail. "Ready for some more drills?" Clayton asked.

"Always!" Spader replied.

"We'll do some more watersled work," Clayton said.

"I'll fetch one," Spader said, turning to head to the equipment storage below.

"Not so fast." Clayton tossed Spader a globe. "You're going to access a sled from the water."

Spader put on the globe. "I can do that?"

"You're going to try," Clayton replied, putting on an airglobe so they'd be able to communicate while Spader was underwater. "Put on a harness too."

Harnesses were stretchy cords that kept workers attached to the ship. Some were clipped onto rings on the hull; others, like the one Spader was going to wear, were attached to a winch on deck manned by senior staff. This way a trainee in trouble could be hoisted back onto the ship.

Spader hated wearing the harness—it made him feel like a wee baby just learning to be water safe—but he knew they were required for drills while the boat was underway. He put his arms through the openings and buckled the harness belt around his waist.

"All set," Spader announced.

"This is a timed drill," Clayton explained. "In an emergency you may not have a globe with you, so it's important to work quickly. If you fell overboard, for example."

"You mean like this?" Spader slid across the deck flailing his arms. With a loud "Whooooo-ah!" he somersaulted over the rail and splashed into the water.

When he resurfaced, he saw Clayton laughing above him. "Yeah, something like that," Clayton said.

The ship was moving at a good clip and the harness was dragging Spader with it. He swam to the hull and clutched the grips that were spaced in intervals along the sides. He placed his feet in the lower grips and leaned out, relishing the invigorating feel of the breeze and the spray. He had spent many hours riding "ships-sides" on his father's runs.

"Steady on?" Clayton asked.

"Like the ship and I are molded from the same piece!" Spader replied. "So what do I do?"

"The storage units in the holds can also be opened from the water. So you'll need to find the hatches that correspond with those units."

"All right," Spader said.

"Pop the hatch open and get out the sled. Keep in mind, you could need to do this without a harness, an airglobe, and while the ship is moving."

"Is that all?" Spader quipped.

"I'll be here with the lines," Clayton said. He glanced at his watch. "And the timer! Go!"

Spader scooted along the hull using the hand and foot grips. He had to push against the force of the water rushing over him, but he made it pretty quickly. Now he just had to figure out how to open the hatch and pull out the sled without falling off the side of the ship, or letting in too much water.

He gazed toward the horizon. A wave was approaching. If he timed it just right . . .

Hang on . . . Hang on . . . The swell of the wave raised the ship, taking Spader with it. At the top of the crest he quickly popped open the latch and yanked out a watersled and shut the hatch. As the boat slammed back down the backside of the wave, Spader kicked away from the ship on the watersled.

"Well done!" Clayton cheered. "Fastest time I've ever seen."

"Easy-o," Spader said.

"Now for repair drills," Clayton said.

"Slack me," Spader said. "And I'll be back in a flash."

Clayton released the entire length of the harness so that Spader could maneuver. Spader had run the same drills en route to Crasker so he knew what to do.

He submerged the sled and zipped to each of the intake valves under the ship that he'd inspect if he were checking for damage or maintenance. He quickly returned to his starting point and resurfaced.

Strange . . . The light had changed. Clayton stood at the rail staring up at the sky. It had grown dark and ominous.

"Come in," Clayton said. "Now."

"Should I put back the sled first?" Spader asked, guiding the sled alongside the hull. "Or carry it on board?"

Clayton's answer was drowned out by a sudden torrential downpour. A huge wave knocked Spader off the sled—and about ten wickams away from the ship. Only the harness kept him from being swept farther out.

It was hard to see with the rain pouring down, but he could just about make out Clayton struggling with the winch. He thought he could feel the harness pulling him, but it might have been the violent chop of the storm.

Another wave crashed down, but this time Spader was lucky. The undertow brought him back in line with the ship.

"Hang on!" Clayton called above the howling storm.

"Doin' my best, mate!" Spader shouted back. The high winds and waves buffeted him around badly, wearing him down. His muscles burned as he fought the heavy, roiling water to get to the ladder.

There it was. Spader kicked hard and stretched as far as he could to grab a rung. Yes! He pulled himself halfway out of the water but was instantly swept off by another wave. It slammed him into the side of the boat. His body went limp and he slipped underwater.

"I'll try to lift you. Forget about the ladder!" Clayton hollered.

Spader felt himself being pulled out of the water. *Wham!* He slammed back into the side of the boat again.

"Too much slack!" Spader cried. "The ropes are getting tangled."

Wham! He hit the side of the ship again.

Could he keep fighting the storm to make it back on board? Or was he going to be pounded senseless first?

Spader spun himself a few times, then faced the hull. This shortened the harness straps, giving them a lot less play and allowing him to control it better.

"Let me try something," Spader told Clayton. He slipped underwater. He needed to stay out of the raging wind. If he could just keep hold of the grips, he might be able to get to the ladder and try climbing again with less slack. He pulled himself along the side of the boat until he was at the ladder.

He rode out another wave, clinging to the hull. The moment it began to recede he clambered up the ladder. Clayton grabbed his shoulder straps and helped him up and over the rail and onto the deck.

"You all right?" Clayton asked.

"In one piece," Spader said.

"Man overboard!" someone cried.

"Get out the rescue lines," Clayton instructed Spader, who quickly unbuckled his harness.

"On it!" Spader raced to one of the units where the lines were kept. Someone stood there struggling with the latches.

"Here to help," Spader said.

The worker turned around. "I can do it," Per Watsu snarled.

Spader took a step back. "Yeah? Then why are the lines still in there, instead of out here where they can do some good?"

"I said, I've got it." Per turned his back on Spader and went back to trying to get the hold open.

Spader shoved Per aside. "I can do it faster."

"Spader. Get below, now."

Spader turned to find Clayton glaring at him.

"But—" Spader protested.

"You're more harmful than helpful up here. If you two can't work together, you're useless."

Spader's cheeks burned with humiliation. He hated being called out like this. And it killed him that Clayton seemed to think he was the one to blame.

"To the engineering level," Clayton snapped. "Now."

Spader hurried down two levels, his blood boiling. He had done it again. Let Per Watsu get to him.

It was a busy scene on this level too. Water filled the area knee-high, and two crewmembers worked to bring the water pressure back in line.

"What can I do?" Spader asked the nearest crewmember. Maybe no one would realize he had been sent down below as a reprimand. At least for now.

"Help Jofels with the connector tubes!" the crewmember replied. "The regulators couldn't handle the sudden influx of water!"

Spader joined Jofels, who was pounding a large pipe back into place in the ceiling. By the time they got the pipe back together, Spader noticed that the deck wasn't bucking like a crazed spinney fish anymore.

"I think the storm is losing power," Jofels said. "We're good here, Spader, so go check back in with Clayton."

Rain still came down in sheets, but the wind had calmed and so had the waves. Still, visibility was nil, and Spader's muscles ached from the pounding they'd taken while he was batted around by the waves. He hoped this battle with the elements would be over soon. But he hurried over to Clayton, eager to prove himself.

"Jofels sent me up," Spader said, wanting to be clear that he wasn't disobeying Clayton's instructions.

"Check levels on the upper equalizers," Clayton instructed. "See how close we are to getting back online."

Like all ships on Cloral, the vessel was powered by carefully calibrated water pressure. "Got it." Spader hurried to the nearest gauge. It was off, but was clearly dropping back to a normal level. They didn't want the pressure to drop too quickly or it could cause an implosion. But the reading wasn't in the danger area. He made his way carefully across the slippery deck to the next gauge.

A thick fog made it impossible to see much farther than a few feet. Spader wondered how far off course they were, and if there was any serious damage.

Clayton came up beside him. "Well, we're not in danger of capsizing or sinking anymore. But until we've reached full equalization, we're not going to be moving."

"Makes sense."

"Go up to the pilot's tower. With some of the systems still off-line and this fog, they'll need help navigating."

Spader climbed up the ladder to reach the pilot's tower

where the navigation systems were. "I'm your extra eyes," he told the pilot and the navigator. He placed himself in the forward windows and stared out into the gloom.

"The engineers called up and said the lights should be working any minute now. That will help," the pilot said.

As promised, the lights at the bow of the ship came on.

Spader blinked. "Where did that come from?"

Not too far off starboard was another vessel, barely visible in the fog.

"It looks disabled," the navigator said. "See how it's drifting?"

"Probably damaged in the storm," the pilot commented.

"It looks as if it's heading straight toward us!" Spader said.

"They might not be able to steer properly," the navigator said. "It's up to us to keep out of the way."

"Until we do a thorough check, we can't rely on the navigational systems," the pilot said. "Spader, call out instructions based on what you're seeing, while we monitor the instruments as backup. We should be able to get safely past."

There didn't seem to be any signs of life on the disabled vessel. All lights were out and it just floated steadily toward them. Suddenly there was a loud boom—and the window to the pilothouse shattered. Glass and water spewed everywhere.

The pilot keeled over and landed on the floor beside Spader.

Dead.

"Take cover!" Spader shouted to the navigator. "Raiders go for the pilot's crew first!"

He hit the deck as another blast ripped through the pilot's tower. He rolled quickly across the wet floor just as the navigator thudded down beside him. A quick glance told him the navigator was also dead.

He peered over the instrument board. The raider ship was much smaller than the vessel he was on. That should mean fewer raiders than crewmembers. Would the crew be able to fend them off?

Only if we have enough weapons. Spader tried to remember from his orientation. Most dangers they faced traveling between habitats were natural—like the storm they had just weathered. Raider attacks were actually pretty rare.

"Stand down!" a voice boomed over the loudspeaker. It sounded like Clayton. "We have a larger crew and weapons to match. And we aren't carrying anything of value."

Spader's held his breath. Would the bluff be enough?

"We'll see about that!" a voice challenged from the raider vessel. "Our ship was damaged in the storm. Why should we bother repairing it when you've got a perfectly good one for us to take!"

"Our ship was damaged as well," Clayton said.

Spader knew Clayton must have been stalling for time while the crew either got the ship underway or found a way to attack the raiders. Then he realized—the only way to get the ship moving was from the pilot's tower. His crew didn't know both the pilot and the navigator were dead.

A nasty laugh came over the raiders' system. "You proved it's perfectly sea-worthy when you maneuvered out of our way."

It's a trap, Spader thought. *And we fell right into it.*

Usually the raiders kept everyone under guard while they off-loaded whatever cargo they wanted. This time they wanted the ship itself—and they wouldn't want any passengers along. That meant everyone on board would either escape or die.

Spader knew which category he wanted to be in.

Another boom rocked the boat. *The raiders must have water canons,* Spader realized. *Only water missiles could do such serious damage.*

The speakers crackled and Spader heard a crash as something toppled onto the deck.

He crawled to the instrument panel. The raiders probably figured they had taken out the pilot and navigator since the ship wasn't moving. They didn't know that there was one more person still in the tower—and Spader intended to keep it that way.

He pushed the sounds of splashes and the exchange of water bullets, screams, and shouts out of his mind. He had to stay focused. He didn't know the panel well enough to work it blind from the floor, so he pulled himself up into a crouch, keeping his head low.

He peered over the control board. Several skimmers and a life raft bobbed on the water, making good speed. One of the jobs of the acquaneers was to ensure the safety of the passengers. Spader figured the personnel from Crasker were in the raft with acquaneers on the skimmers guiding them. The rest of the crew would defend the ship.

It was up to him to get them out of there.

The magic continues
with more fantasies
from Aladdin Paperbacks

The Dragon Chronicles
by Susan Fletcher

Flight of the Dragon Kyn
0-689-81515-8

Dragon's Milk
0-689-71623-0

Sign of the Dove
0-689-82449-1

Silverwing
Kenneth Oppel
1-4169-4998-4

*Mrs. Frisby and the
Rats of NIMH*
Robert C. O'Brien
A Newbery Medal Winner
0-689-71068-2

The Chronus Chronicles
The Shadow Thieves
Anne Ursu
1-4169-0588-X

May Bird and the Ever After
Jodi Lynn Anderson
1-4169-0607-X

May Bird Among the Stars
Jodi Lynn Anderson
1-4169-0608-8

The Gideon Trilogy
The Time Travelers
Linda Buckley-Archer
1-4169-1526-5

Aladdin Paperbacks
Simon & Schuster Children's Publishing
www.SimonSaysKids.com

DON'T MISS THIS UnFOOGETTABLE ADVENTURE!

Fourteen-year-old Leven Thumps is in for the journey of a lifetime
when he learns about a secret gateway that bridges two worlds:
the real world and Foo. A place created at the beginning of time in
the folds of the mind, Foo makes it possible for mankind to dream
and hope, aspire and imagine . . . and it's up to Leven to save it.